TRISTAN'S FOLLY

TRISTAN'S FOLLY

MARCUS LEE

BOOK 2
THE GIFTED AND THE CURSED

Copyright © 2020 by Marcus Lee

All rights reserved. The rights of Marcus Lee to be identified as the author of this Work has been asserted by him in accordance with sections 77 and 78 of the Copyright, Design and Patents Act 1988.

This is a work of fiction. Names, characters, places, and incidents either are the product of the author's imagination or are used fictitiously. Any resemblance to actual persons, living or dead, events, or locales is entirely coincidental.

No part of this publication may be reproduced, stored in retrieval systems, copied in any form or by any means, electronic, mechanical, photocopying, recording or otherwise transmitted without written permission from the publisher except for the use of quotations in a book review.

ISBN: 9798698105718

For more information visit: www.marcusleebooks.com

First paperback edition October 2020
First ebook edition October 2020

Book design by Jacqueline Abromeit

M&M
♥

BY THE SAME AUTHOR

THE GIFTED AND THE CURSED TRILOGY

***

KINGS AND DAEMONS

TRISTAN'S FOLLY

THE END OF DREAMS

ACKNOWLEDGEMENTS

Many deserve to be thanked for their incredible support during the writing of this trilogy or simply for gifting me with their friendship and love for which I'll be eternally grateful.

Sadly, these pages are not long enough to list you all, but the following deserve special mention.

Jarrod F - a brother in arms
Jonathan B - darker than the night
Leon F - the brightest sun
Cami C - a guiding light
Lawrence W - the rock of ages
Alain D - a fallen star
Suz B - eternal friend
Amanda F - so close yet far

Chapter I

Taran held Maya's hand as they walked along the track, rutted by the passing of many wagons, toward the mighty Freestates fortress. It sat astride the eastern end of the pass through the Forelorn mountains and was soon to be their home, their sanctuary.

Their steps matched one another's perfectly, and while no word passed between them; their thoughts were shared by Taran's gift, and were full of light, hope and love.

His gift of knowing, of reading, the thoughts of others, had recently evolved into sharing his thoughts too. Now, it was serving to bring them even closer, as they each felt inside the love the other's love in an almost spiritual way.

It was only as they drew closer to the rear gates, that the group began to fully appreciate the size of the fortress.

The keep appeared to grow from the mountainside itself, the snow-capped peaks of which were lost in the clouds above. Yet that only served to add to its feeling of size. The rear wall of the fortress on the Freestates side was not that large, whereas the one beyond the keep was so high that it blotted out everything on the other side.

Rakan whistled. 'I've only heard of this but never seen it myself. Supposedly the Freestates almost ran out of gold when they first built it all those years ago. However, it will have been money well spent if they've gathered the forces to defend it. If so, Daleth is going to find himself getting a bloody nose.'

Yet as they drew much closer, they started to see signs of disrepair. Large cracks webbed across the wall, blocks of stone were misaligned, and gaps peppered the mortar. They paused briefly to let a wagon pass then followed it through the gate and looked around as men came forward to unload its cargo.

To the north of the courtyard where they stood were the steps leading up to the keep entrance. Maya pointed, and everyone turned to see a man in red robes halfway down, while a few steps above him was stood a man in shining, bejewelled armour.

'That's Astren in the red,' Maya confirmed.

'And that can only be Tristan in the fancy armour,' observed Rakan.

Kalas nodded. 'The wealth of the kings of the Freestates was legendary even in my day. Those other two with him look to be his generals or bodyguards. Let's go meet them,' he said, as they turned toward the steps.

'Astren,' Maya called, and the man opened his arms in welcome.

The gates behind them closed, pushed shut by guards and Rakan looked around. 'They have a lot of guards stationed here considering this is the rear of the fortress. Those archers would be better placed on the west walls.'

'Let's hope they have as many on every wall,' Kalas replied, as they crossed the courtyard and reached the bottom of the steps.

Maya stepped forward to embrace Astren, and Taran breathed a sigh of relief.

'Welcome to my fortress,' said a voice, and they looked to see Tristan step down with a small, green-skinned man on one side and a large dark one on the other. 'I've heard much about you, Maya. Astren swears you've a gift that will be invaluable to us all and I admit I'm impatient to see it. Then I'll know whether Astren spoke the truth, or if he'll blush as red as his robes if it's proven he misled me. So, show me this gift and save his embarrassment and my disappointment.'

Maya smiled, then knelt before him.

'No need for that,' Tristan said, and stepped forward intending to raise Maya to her feet. But he quickly stopped and moved back, as the two men with him also shied away, for Maya was glowing.

The ground of the courtyard was hard-packed earth and rock, and yet as Maya placed her hands against the sparse soil, long-dormant seeds sprang to life. As everyone watched, a circle of green grass started to form around Maya. It quickly spread to the steps of the keep where vines began to sprout, crawling up from the ground, finding hold between the giant blocks of stone. Then, moments later, everything burst into a rainbow of colour.

The whole courtyard had fallen utterly silent and not a single eye blinked as this spectacle unfolded. Finally, Maya stood, arms open to encompass what she'd done.

'I wouldn't have believed it without seeing it,' whispered Tristan. 'It's true, you've a gift from the very gods themselves.'

He stepped past Maya to the rest of the group, his eyes still wide. 'Welcome lady,' he greeted Yana. 'Please go with Drizt, the captain of my archers. He'll find you lodgings suitable for one of noble birth that I hear you are.'

Yana curtsied and put a hand to her heart in gratitude.

Tristan turned to Kalas, gripping his wrist. 'Welcome, warrior. We're in sore need of experienced men. Go with Trom here, and he'll show you to the barracks and discuss how you can assist us.'

He moved to Rakan and repeated the welcome.

Finally, Tristan approached Taran and gripped his wrist. 'Go with Trom, young man, for we need the strength of your youth more than you know.'

Maya's heart beat happily; they'd actually made it, and she moved toward Taran to hold his other hand.

As she reached out, Taran suddenly pulled Tristan hard, then spun him, his arm going tight around Tristan's throat. In the other hand was his dagger, and he held its edge against Tristan's neck, drawing blood.

'Taran, NO!' cried Maya in disbelief.

But even as the words left Maya's mouth, Taran's voice echoed in her head, and from the look on Rakan, Kalas, and Yana's face, they heard the same as well.

'They plan to kill us!'

In moments, the sound of a hundred swords scraping free of scabbards filled the courtyard, yet only one voice was heard.

'If anyone takes a single step towards us, I'll cut his bastard's throat from ear to ear,' Taran shouted, and he stepped back between Rakan and Kalas, whose swords were in their hands. Yana and Maya swiftly joined them.

Their feelings of hope were dashed instantly, to be replaced by despair.

They'd escaped one king intent on killing them, only to find another!

Daleth was in a monumentally good mood as he sat astride the saddle of his great, black warhorse. He was a day ahead of the army vanguard, Alano at his side, while three dozen of his bodyguard rode nearby.

As they moved east, the land itself fed him more, as being further from Kingshold, the erstwhile capital, it hadn't entirely given up its life. He felt younger again, full of boundless energy.

Even the march taking longer than anticipated due to unseasonal rain hadn't dampened his frame of mind. If anything, it allowed the army to replenish its water supplies. Dehydration was always a threat to a soldier's health during a march, and to transport sufficient water was nigh on impossible.

The wagons also carried enough food supplies to last six months, and this was supplemented by fresh meat brought in by hunters.

Even if he and his commanders believed the siege would be over within a week if not sooner, he had ensured there were enough provisions for the entire campaign ahead.

He doubted Tristan or the other greedy lords of the Freestates would have the stomach to do what was needed to slow his invading army down. To scorch the very earth as they retreated, burning the land to ashes to deny his forces sustenance, yet even the slightest possibility of this happening had been accounted for. So behind him, the kingdom had been plundered of resources before beginning this campaign and his great army was moving slowly, ladened, but well provided for.

Yet, however slowly this vast horde moved, the vanguard was now only seven days from the pass. Then, with several more days for the whole army to arrive, his invasion of the Freestates would be underway by the new moon.

He gazed up at the enormous mountains before him, to where their peaks disappeared into the clouds.

'Do you think the gods live up there?' Daleth joked, turning to Alano.

The daemon slowly shook its head, eyes glowing red even in the middle of the day.

'I know; I know there are no gods. I was just trying to make conversation,' sighed Daleth in frustration. 'Can't you even let the old Alano out just a little? He would at least pretend to find my conversation entertaining at times.'

Again the daemon shook his head, saying nothing.

'What does this shaking of the head mean. Answer me, dammit!' demanded Daleth, his good humour evaporating.

'You joke about there being no gods, but ask yourself this, my king,' and the way Alano said those words made Daleth lean forward. 'If there are daemons and we come from the nine hells, then what makes you so certain there are no gods?'

Daleth thought briefly on Alano's words, and then his mouth dropped open in disbelief. 'Truly, there are gods? No mocking answer now, daemon. Tell me, truthfully!'

Alano's red eyes stared back. 'I've already said more than I should. We, who aren't of this world, are bound by certain rules of non-divulgence. Isn't it puzzling though, that the magic users of old, found ways to bring daemons to this world and ignored seeking the help of the gods? What does that say about the minds of the wisest men, that they sought one, but not the other? A final thing I suggest you think about, my king, is to ask yourself this. Why are some humans gifted beyond their brethren? Now I can say no more on this matter.'

Daleth pressed further, but Alano remained silent.

He rode for the rest of the morning, mulling over the daemon's words. His gift had been bestowed upon him by the gods, so truly he was blessed and destined for greatness. He'd never doubted his right to rule, yet now it felt a divine right.

'I am gifted by the gods,' he said softly in wonder under his breath.

Alano cast a sidelong glance at him, and quietly replied so that his words were all but carried away on the breeze.

'Gifted beyond most you are, but cursed in equal measure as well.'

Kalas' eyes flickered around, assessing the situation, reading in an instant that the rear gates were closed and too far away. Dozens of the famed Eyre archers had bows fully drawn, arrows tracking their every step. The longer they remained in the open, the more likely this would come to a bloody and final end. He didn't like the conclusion he came to, but it would bring them quickly to safety, at least for now, and that was all that mattered. 'Into the keep!' he ordered, and the six of them edged cautiously toward the steps.

Taran kept his dagger firmly against Tristan's throat, ensuring the king had no chance to escape, but the two captains blocked their way.

'Tell them to move,' growled Taran, and relaxed his hold just enough for the king to issue the order.

Trom and Drizt reluctantly moved aside, eyes glaring, looking for an opportunity to strike, but they found none that wouldn't send Tristan straight to the next world.

'Astren, how could you?' demanded Maya, disappointment thick in her voice as they moved past.

Astren's hands pressed together as he pleaded with her. 'You're making a dreadful mistake. We're offering you sanctuary, and you offer violence. What by all the gods are you doing? Stop now, before it's too late!'

'What are *we* doing?' shouted Taran, his face red. 'Your king's orders for Drizt and Trom here, are to take us to the barracks to be butchered out of sight. Maya was to be spared and told that we'd been sent to the capital as an explanation of our absence.'

The group paused for a moment as they backed up the steps.

'That's not true,' Tristan managed to gasp. 'Why would you think that? We were offering you the hand of friendship!'

'Ask yourself this, King Tristan. How do I know that you organised this without Astren's knowledge? How do I know that Drizt is thinking of using a poisoned dagger to try and kill me even as we speak - and that he'll be dead before it even leaves his hand if he tries.' He stared into Drizt's eyes and saw his words hit home.

'You think Maya's the gifted one, and the truth is, she's gifted beyond anyone I know. However, I've a gift too, of reading minds, of knowing people's thoughts and intentions. So, tell me I'm wrong,' challenged Taran. 'Tell me that Drizt and Trom haven't convinced you that the danger of us being spies, assassins, or just untrustworthy deserters, was too great a risk to take. Tell me there aren't a dozen men deep in the fortress with daggers waiting for the each of us?'

Astren looked at Drizt and Trom, then at his king, seeing the truth on their faces before Tristan nodded weakly. 'I didn't know, Maya. Truly I didn't know. Please believe me!' Astren cried.

Maya looked unconvinced.

Astren was aghast. 'Tristan, how could you? I promised them safety. I told Maya to bring them here. How could you do this? By all the gods,' cried Astren. 'This is so wrong. We're supposed to be on the side of righteousness. Daleth is supposed to be the evil monster, not you!'

'The time for talking is over,' interrupted Kalas. 'We need to find a way out of this situation that keeps your king's head on his shoulders, and us alive too. Time to move inside.'

'Let me come with you?' asked Astren.

Kalas looked to Taran and Maya, who both nodded.

'So be it,' Kalas replied, and they continued up the steps to the entrance of the keep. Neither Drizt nor Trom made a move to follow, merely standing there in disbelief at what they'd witnessed.

The group backed inside, into the cool shadows, eyes wary, looking at the mass of men staring at them from behind bared swords and drawn bows.

'Where are the damned gates?' asked Rakan, as he went to close them. 'Oh forget it. Let's get to the top of this damned place. That way, we only need to worry about defending downwards while we decide what to do.'

Decision made, they hastily made their way up the winding steps, swords at the ready.

As they reached the second landing, they came face to face with nearly thirty armed soldiers, and both parties came to an awkward stop.

'Save me,' Tristan managed to gasp before Taran squeezed his arm harder around the king's throat.

Several of the soldiers laughed, but it was tinged with mockery. 'We aren't here to save you. We're here to end you,' called a giant corporal from the middle of the group, and they surged forward.

Kalas and Rakan, who were at the front of the group, didn't hesitate. The only way was upward. At their heels were the steps down which was the courtyard full of hundreds of waiting men.

Taran thrust Tristan hard into the wall, next to where Astren now cowered. 'Watch them,' he shouted at Yana, then ran to join the fight pulling his sword from its scabbard. He reached Rakan's side just in time. The landing was broad, and the soldiers were about to encircle his father as Taran attacked.

He swung his sword, the blade biting through the chainmail links of his opponent's raised arm in a gory spray. As his victim spun around, screaming, he thrust with his dagger into the man's neck, silencing the cries.

Taran focussed on holding his side of the landing with Rakan. While the two of them held, it allowed Kalas to deal death without worrying about the rest of them. Yet they were hard-pressed, and with so many assailants, it was nigh on impossible to use his gift. He blocked a thrust from one, while only just managing to parry a swinging sword with his dagger, then ducked a thrown hand axe.

He managed to kill two assailants in quick succession, but the next man was the huge corporal who'd called out earlier. Taran had to cross his sword and dagger to parry an enormous overhand strike that would have clove him in two. The moment both Taran's weapons were briefly engaged, the corporal launched himself forward, using his vast weight to bring Taran to the floor. Instead of trying to push him away, Taran wrapped his sword arm around the back of the man's thick neck, pulling him even closer. He bit the soldier's nose, ripping half of it away. As the man pulled upward, screaming, Taran drove his dagger through the soldier's ear, into the brain, killing him instantly.

He wriggled frantically, pushing the suffocating weight away, to find two soldiers standing above him. He swung with his sword, severing one man's leg just above the ankle, but knew he was unable to stop the second soldier's thrust. He tensed in anticipation of a blow that never landed.

The man toppled backwards, an arrow protruding from his forehead, and Taran scrambled to his feet. Maya, who'd now strung her bow, shot from behind him, the arrows whistling past his shoulder punching several more approaching men from their feet. He quickly pushed forward again into the thinning and now scared enemy.

Rakan had managed to kill a half dozen, his screams and bloodlust keeping those still opposite him hesitant. Then Kalas hit like a storm, flinging the last dozen aside in a whirlwind of blows.

Suddenly the ringing tones of steel on steel were replaced by heavy breathing from the living and moaning from the man with the severed foot.

Rakan knelt above him. 'Why?' he growled, his hand gripping the man's shirt, pulling him into a sitting position.

'Elender promised us that the Witch-King ...' the man managed to gasp, but then his eyes rolled back, and Rakan let the now limp body fall back in disgust.

Taran looked around at the carnage and noticed Maya had her bow drawn, aimed down the steps. As Taran ran to her side, he heard the pounding of boots and men shouting.

'Quickly,' Kalas called, pointing up the next flight of steps.

Rakan ran up ahead, to ensure there were no more surprises as Yana pushed Astren and Tristan along, their wide eyes fixed upon the dead bodies.

'It seems we might well have saved your lives,' Yana hissed, 'when you were looking to take ours!'

They ran up two more flights to find Rakan waiting, the bodies of an archer and spearman crumpled against the wall.

'They were already dead, probably killed by our friends downstairs,' he offered, and pointed along a richly appointed corridor to a chamber at the end.

They ran, the sounds of pursuit loud in their ears and slammed the heavy door behind them, dropping a locking bar into place.

Taran looked around. They'd escaped, but now they were also trapped.

Drizt and Trom stood looking at the closed door at the far end of the corridor behind which the fugitives sheltered. At their feet lay the corpses of two sentries, one from the Eyre, the other from the desert.

'I need to know whether King Tristan is still alive,' Drizt shouted.

Moments later, the thick door at the other end was briefly opened to show Tristan standing with a sword to his throat before being slammed shut again.

Muffled noises came from below as the garrison soldiers removed the dead bodies.

'The dead downstairs weren't those we had waiting in the barracks to greet our visitors,' Drizt mused. 'and what were they doing so high in the keep. Only our men were allowed up unless escorted.'

Trom knelt down, examining the wounds on the bodies. 'One man did this,' he said, 'a dagger from close in. These sentries would have heard the fighting from downstairs and drawn their weapons, but they're still scabbarded. The bodies are almost cold too. They weren't killed by the fugitives.'

'What a mess,' groaned Drizt. 'It would seem those dead soldiers killed our men, which would lead me to believe they weren't trying to kill just the newcomers, but rather Tristan. We always knew there was a risk of there being more bad apples here. I think we might just have found the whole rotting barrel.'

They turned, walking back down the steps. Thirty of Trom's spearmen stood, shields locked, facing an angry mob. About fifty garrison soldiers, having removed the bodies of their dead comrades, were shouting angrily. They demanded to be let through to mete out justice at the point of a sword.

Trom rarely spoke loudly, but he drew breath and bellowed so loud that everyone stopped, shocked by the noise.

The spearmen parted ranks, allowing him and Drizt through to stand side by side. They faced the group who now looked uncertain with the two senior captains of the fortress confronting them.

'I understand your confusion and anger,' Drizt started, his hands raised placatingly. 'There's much more here than meets the eye. The people upstairs are not our enemy.'

'Not our enemy? They've killed our friends and captured the King!' screamed a soldier, coming to stand in front of the diminutive Drizt, venting his anger at the smaller man. 'You stinking, green piece of Eyre filth …'

Whatever he was going to say next never left his lips. Drizt's left hand snapped out fast, and his fist crashed squarely against the man's jaw.

Trom stepped forward and grabbed the man's tunic, holding the unconscious man upright, then stepped forward, pushing him into the arms of the shocked crowd.

'If ANY of you disrespect my heritage, or forget my rank again,' hissed Drizt, 'you'll find yourself in the nine hells alongside those you thought were your friends. They killed two of our men upstairs,' he explained, to the confused looks. 'You know of Elender's betrayal. Well, it appears it went deeper than just him. Now, who amongst you is honest?'

'I am,' said a bearded soldier. 'My name is Valance, and I do not lie.' He stood tall, a proud look on his face.

'Well, Valance. I want you to search the barrack room of your dead comrades thoroughly,' commanded Drizt. 'Only you. Then I want you to meet me in the courtyard within the hour to tell me and everyone else what you've found that seems unusual.

'Now, the rest of you MOVE. Get outside and don't do anything that will incur my wrath!'

The muttering group turned around, carrying their unconscious friend with them, Trom and Drizt following.

'By the gods,' muttered Drizt, as they returned to the courtyard, 'there's something terribly wrong with that picture.'

The front of the keep, covered in vines, flowers, grass across the courtyard, had looked like a temple, now it had bleeding bodies of thirty dead men laid out before it.

Drizt nodded to several of his archers who came running over. 'I want you to get those bodies out of here and buried. The longer they're lying there in front of everyone, the more hatred is going to fester.'

'My men will ensure yours aren't interfered with,' Trom rumbled and turned to give orders to some nearby spearmen.

The archer's nodded, running off, and shortly dozens of them were carrying the bodies out of the rear gate while Trom's spearmen lined up in an unbroken wall of spear and shield.

'What next?' Trom asked.

'We wait, and hope that man Valance finds something convincing to back up our claim.'

'And if he doesn't?' prompted Trom.

'Then a lot more bodies will be buried today,' muttered Drizt, 'and King Tristan might be one of them!'

'I'm sorry,' apologised Kalas, 'I led us into the keep, there's no escaping from here.'

It had only taken minutes to realise there was no other exit to the chamber that didn't involve scaling the sheer sides of the mountain abutting the balcony.

Maya laid her hand on his arm. 'If the fault rests on anyone's shoulders, it is mine. I convinced you all to come here, to fight Daleth.'

'No,' Rakan said gruffly. 'No blame attaches to any of us, and it serves no purpose talking this way. We need to decide what to do.'

'I don't think we can escape,' Taran stated. 'There seemed to be only one way up or down this keep, and we have hundreds, perhaps thousands of soldiers waiting to kill us if we try. Even with a dagger to Tristan's throat, I don't think we'd get out of here alive.'

'Agreed,' Kalas nodded. 'We'd die against such numbers, especially with the Eyre archers amongst them. Even attempting it would destroy everything we hoped for. We came here hoping to stand alongside these people to fight Daleth. If Tristan dies, or we die, all of that comes undone. Daleth will win.'

'Then we need to find a way to end this without further bloodshed,' Maya said.

'Tristan knows we saved his life. He heard what that corporal said. He could vouch that we weren't trying to kill him,' suggested Yana looking across at Tristan huddled in a corner alongside Astren.

'Good point,' Kalas acknowledged. 'The problem is we can't just walk out of here to tell everyone. We'll have to wait and see what Tristan's captains decide to do next. 'If they attack, we kill the king. He started this with his stupid plan.'

'I don't agree,' Maya said, eyes fierce.

But no one added their voice to hers.

'So now we wait,' Taran said.

Everyone nodded, and the only sound in the room was that of Rakan sharpening his dagger on a whetstone he'd pulled from his belt.

'Sixty gold coins, just sixty,' Drizt shouted. 'That was the value they placed on your lives. They weren't just betraying the king, but all of you too. They weren't your friends, they were a hidden enemy. Their actions would've meant not just your deaths, but that of your families and thousands of others.

'Those men and women who took Tristan hostage, did so to save their own lives, but they haven't harmed him. In fact,' Drizt scuffed his boots in the dust, a little embarrassed, 'it was my mistake that led to this happening. But one good thing came from this. Valance here found the gold, and those turncoats in our midst are in the ground where they belong.

'Now, as it's my mistake that saw your king taken hostage, I'll be the one to decide how to put it right.'

'And what if you can't reason with them lot whose holding him,' called a soldier.

'Then if they don't answer to reason, they'll answer to our swords and arrows. So, let's pray the gods intervene and don't allow it to come to that. Now, back to your duties, but standby for orders.'

The garrison soldiers slowly began to disperse, grumbling.

'The thing is,' muttered Drizt under his breath, to Trom standing alongside him, 'I fear the outcome wouldn't be too one-sided if it comes to a fight. Those fugitives are something else. They killed thirty-odd men without loss between them … what a slaughter.

'Not forgetting that Taran is a reader of minds. Such a gift to know someone's thoughts.'

Trom looked thoughtfully at Drizt. 'For a quick man, you're pretty slow,' he rumbled. 'Imagine finding out a friend is not a friend, a lover is just after your money, or having the sadness in someone's heart added to your own.'

Drizt smiled wryly at the insight. 'Still, his gift saved their lives, so it's not all that bad, eh?'

'I can't argue with that,' Trom replied. 'So, if they don't reason, do we really kill them all? They'll slaughter Tristan if we try, especially as that lad appears to know what we're going to do before we do it.'

Drizt shook his head. 'That's a good point. What Astren said also hit hard. We're supposed to be the good ones. If we hadn't planned to kill them, we might be sitting down drinking some good wine together by now, assuming those turncoats were dead.'

'I like good wine,' rumbled Trom. 'I think I'd prefer drinking with them than killing them. They're certainly not assassins, or Tristan would be dead already. So I think they're good people, or if not, at least not what we feared them to be.'

'So, what's the plan then?' asked Drizt. 'Believe me, I never thought to be asking a slow, desert tribesman what to do next.'

Trom chuckled. 'You already came up with the plan. We go drink wine with them.'

'Really?' Drizt laughed. 'That's the best plan I ever devised without realising it. Right, let's go to my quarters. I've helped myself to some of Tristan's finest wine these last days, and now I can't think of a better time to share it.'

They turned and walked up the steps into the keep.

Trom paused. 'It's a good thing we don't have gates,' he boomed. 'Imagine being locked out of our own keep; it would've been most embarrassing,' and they entered the depths to find Dritz's wine.

Chapter II

Tristan sat on the cold, stone floor in the corner of the main chamber where Sancen had met his death days before. There was a dark stain where the tribesman's blood had pooled, and which no amount of scrubbing had been able to remove completely. There was every chance his own blood might soon darken the stain, he thought.

He hadn't been restrained, for which he felt grateful, but his mood was dark, and he still shook from the butchery he'd witnessed. The fact that Taran and the others hadn't bothered to bind him made him feel insignificant, and it wasn't a feeling he was used to.

Astren sat with him, silent, the accusatory look saying more than words, irking him even more.

Across the chamber, the others stood, casting occasional looks in his direction, discussing his fate and no doubt their next move, yet however hard he tried, he couldn't hear them.

'Is this where it ends?' whispered Tristan. 'Not at the hands of Daleth, but at the hands of …' yet, he couldn't find the right word.

'Someone who might have been a friend or ally had you not followed through with your stupid plan,' Astren finished for him.

Tristan felt his face flush as he suppressed his anger, keeping his voice low. 'Drizt's argument was sound. They were deserters, traitors, or spies at best, and assassins at worse, and none of those sounded worth the risk. If I could take back my decision, I would, and not just because I think they're wondering about whether to cut my throat. Why didn't you tell me the young man had a gift too? Didn't you think it worth mentioning?'

Astren shrugged his shoulders. 'I'd no idea. In many ways, I'm glad I didn't know, for I've no idea how this would have ended otherwise, but I'm pretty sure it would have been worse.'

'Worse! How could it be worse?' hissed Tristan. 'I'm a prisoner in my own keep.'

'You could be dead in your own keep, and that could still happen unless we offer them a way out of this,' replied Astren.

A loud knocking on the door interrupted everyone's conversation, and the sound of voices was replaced by the metallic whisper of swords being drawn.

Yana came across, holding a wickedly curved dagger, to stand over Tristan and Astren. 'I'm sorry,' she said sweetly, 'but if this is an attempt to rescue you, I'm going to have to kill you. I'll make it quick, not because I'm kind, but because we can't risk you living, and us dying, can we?' She laughed, but her eyes were cold.

Tristan gulped hard, and Astren felt his stomach flip.

Kalas peered through a small crack in the heavy door. 'It's Tristan's two captains,' he growled, gripping the hilt of his sword.

'Shall I kill them now?' Yana asked loudly.

Tristan almost lost control of his bladder.

'Hold on a moment,' instructed Kalas, raising his hand, 'there's no one else with them, although they seem to be carrying ... ' and then he relaxed and began unbolting the door.

'What are you doing?' demanded Rakan angrily.

Kalas sounded thoughtful. 'I'm intrigued. They've brought some wine by the looks of it, and I for one am dying of thirst. Let's hear what they have to say. If it's poisoned, then Maya can save us.'

Tristan turned to Astren in shock. 'What's this about?' he whispered. 'They're coming here to have a drink, not to save me?'

Astren contemplated silently for a moment. 'I've a feeling this was their only way to save you, for the best way to defeat an enemy without bloodshed is to make him your friend. I think we can both breathe easier now, but best we stay quiet and see.'

Taran ordered both Drizt and Trom to stay outside the chamber as he read their thoughts. In both, he saw regret and a sincere hope that they could somehow rescue the situation they found themselves in. He laughed softly, surprising everyone, for Drizt's thoughts revealed that he'd stolen the wine from Tristan.

'Do you have any weapons on you?' Taran asked.

Drizt and Trom shook their heads, looking pensive at the barely concealed anger on Rakan's face.

Taran perceived no deceit, but he still asked Rakan to search them.

Rakan was thorough and not at all gentle, but it wasn't long before he stood back, nodding his head.

Kalas motioned Drizt and Trom in before barring the door behind them.

Taran turned to Maya. 'What do you think?' he asked. 'Is this a time for spilling blood or getting drunk and spilling wine?'

Maya laughed, and it seemed to dispel some of the darkness in the room. She loved the way Taran played with words. 'I think we should definitely encourage Kalas to get drunk and spill wine as opposed to spilling blood and drinking that instead,' she joked.

Kalas' eyes opened wide as Rakan snorted in amusement.

'Was that a little too soon?' asked Maya, covering her mouth with her hand.

Now Kalas' laughter rang out, much to the confusion of some in the room.

'Let me guess,' said Rakan, turning to Kalas. 'You prefer a good red?'

More laughter echoed, and the atmosphere relaxed.

Only Yana seemed a little disappointed at having to let Tristan up from his corner to join the discussions starting at the table.

The chamber was painted with the subtle brushstrokes of the setting sun's amber glow when the now civil discussion came to a natural halt.

Tristan remained reserved, chilled even, Taran noted, although there was no doubt the king was happy to be alive. The door had been unbarred some time before, and food had been brought in by Trom's men to help soak up the wine, proving that trust had been established.

Cloth and bowls of water were provided, to wash the blood away that covered them all. During the early discussions that had been fraught and at times bordering hostile, Maya had pushed for reconciliation, reminding everyone of their common goals. If they could overcome such a bloody start, then they'd be the stronger for it. It had taken some time, but anger and resentment were finally washed away too.

With this in mind, Taran chose his words carefully.

'When I look around at you all,' he began, 'I now see comrades where once there were enemies. Rakan over there,' and he raised his goblet, 'thought to kill me when first he laid eyes on me. Now he's the father I never had.'

Rakan raised his own goblet, the warmth of his smile extending to his eyes at Taran openly bestowing this title on him.

Taran continued. 'When first I met Maya, I was taking her to certain death, and yet now I'd give my very life to save hers, and I know she would do the same for me.'

Maya leaned in to kiss him softly on the cheek.

'Kalas over there, well, he wanted to kill Rakan, Maya, and I, and also came close to killing Yana. Instead, he now intends to fulfil his oath to kill Daleth as you now all know.'

Taran considered his next words. 'Then we have King Tristan, Drizt and Trom,' and he raised his goblet again. 'You wanted to put an end to our lives rather unexpectedly.' He paused, suddenly unsure how to continue, but Maya squeezed his hand, and her soft voice held everyone's attention as much as Taran's strong one.

'What my Taran is trying to say,' Maya went on, 'is that we've all, at the most important of times, somehow managed to put aside the sword. To take a life is easy, but to give life; therein lies a true power that few in this world possess.'

Taran smiled, hearing Maya repeating the words he'd spoken many days before.

'As new friends, we must learn to trust one another, fight for one another, bleed for one another, and if necessary die for one another.' Maya's voice rose at the end, and her eyes challenged anyone to disagree. With none forthcoming, she went around the room embracing everyone, and hesitantly the others mirrored her move.

Tristan cleared his throat loudly, and the room quietened down. 'You've already heard my thanks for saving my life and my apologies, and any king, especially me, rarely ever makes those. Thankfully, we're no longer enemies, and while friendship is important, a king does not have friends; he has only enemies or subjects.'

The room quietened, the hard-won warmth evaporating a little.

'I speak now as king, not as a friend. We needed this reconciliation, to avoid a bloody ending for us all, and for that, I'm grateful. However, while we made peace this day, soon, another will bring war. Daleth is an enemy who'll never become a friend or ally.

'I've learned a lot about you in these last hours and acknowledge your desire to help face his invasion as well as find sanctuary. However, as we've heard from Trom's men throughout the day, despite you saving my life, many of the garrison soldiers are still angered by your actions. I need to ensure you're accepted, as otherwise, we'll face dissent from within the ranks.'

'I also intend to make amends for what transpired as an apology at this stage is not enough.'

'An apology *is* enough,' Maya offered.

Tristan shook his head. 'In other circumstances, yes, but you desire to stay. I cannot have you fighting alongside us as deserters and renegades; otherwise, the men here will forever view you with distrust. I also need to know that while in my kingdom, you'll obey my commands without question!

'I see one way forward. I'll have Astren draft documents accepting you as Freestates citizens subject to your swearing allegiance. The men can then join the Freestates army with the pay associated to the rank bestowed. We don't have women in our military, yet be assured your appointments will be commensurate with your skills,' he said, nodding to Maya, 'and to your previous rank,' he added, looking at Yana.

Taran quickly opened his mind to Rakan, Maya, Kalas, and Yana. 'There's no duplicity, and what he suggests makes sense.'

'If we become citizens, then the Freestates could be our new home,' Maya thought. 'This is what I hoped for.'

The others agreed, so one by one, they gave their assent to Tristan.

'Now we come to my final demand,' said Tristan, looking gravely at Taran. 'Tell me. Can you control this reading of minds? Do you read all of our thoughts as we sit here?'

Taran met Tristan's gaze. 'It's a conscious decision to delve into a mind, and I know from where your concern arises. Even without looking into yours,' he added quickly, as a frown appeared on Tristan's brow. 'I never use my gift to intrude on a friends' thoughts, nor in general with other people, unless a need arises. It might be hard to appreciate, but it's not such a pleasant gift to use as you may think.'

Tristan looked thoughtful. 'Astren has sworn an oath not to use his gift in certain ways when around me, and now I would place a similar restriction on you. You must swear an oath not to read my thoughts from hereon, on pain of death.'

Rakan hammered his fist down on the table, but Taran looked his father in the eye and shook his head subtly. 'I've no problem making that oath,' he replied. 'I wouldn't break an oath when given to a friend, let alone a king.'

Tristan nodded. 'Well spoken! Now, Drizt, Trom and I will go address the garrison soldiers to ensure no further misunderstandings happen. They'll be told that any assault on you will be met with a sentence of death.

'A difficult day lies ahead of us on the morrow. We'll meet around sunrise. Drizt will summon you when I'm ready.

'Astren, keep our new allies well away from the barracks, have them sleep near you, just in case.'

Tristan got up, and everyone stood with him. 'Until the morrow,' he said, indicating the door.

As Taran, Maya, and the others followed Astren down the steps, it was finally with a renewed sense of hope.

The next morning came too soon for Taran. The keep's huge gong was being bashed with a rare ferocity by one of the resident garrison soldiers to signal the beginning of the new day and to rouse everyone from their sleep.

He lay on a musty old camp bed that last night had been hurriedly fitted with several blankets to make it useable. Maya was nestled into his shoulder; her hair, as usual, tickling his nose. Her body felt so warm and inviting that he just wanted to ignore the sound, roll over and lose himself in her, yet he knew they'd be called on shortly, and this room wasn't exactly the most private either.

The night candles flickered, burning low. Reluctantly Taran disentangled himself, for, with no windows and this deep inside the mountain, the blackness would be absolute. His feet recoiled from the cold stone floor before he steeled himself, and hurried across the room to light another candle, before reaching for his clothes.

The others were in separate rooms adjoining the passageway that led to Maya and Taran's at the end. It seemed space was not an issue, for the warren of rooms, stores and barracks excavated deep into the mountainside had been intended to support thousands more than they currently contained.

Maya's eyes opened slightly. 'Is it really time to rise?' she groaned sleepily, knowing the answer already as the gong continued to be struck. 'Surely it can't be sunrise, it's far too dark to be sunrise.'

Taran sighed. 'It's time,' he said sadly, 'and believe you me, if I could come back to bed, I would in an instant.'

Maya smiled mischievously and pulled the blanket back a little, exposing her long, bare leg. 'Are you absolutely sure it's time to rise right now?' and she reached out to take Taran's hand. 'Let's just find a little more time for each other,' she whispered huskily in his ear, as she pulled him down and draped the blanket back over him. Her lips found his and the noise of the gong faded away, and for a short while, the only sound they could hear was the fast beat of their hearts.

A loud knocking on their wooden door brought them back to reality.

'Drizt just dropped by to summon us,' Rakan called out. 'So, can the two of you stop saying good morning to one another and join us at the keep entrance as soon as you can.'

Taran and Maya could hear him chuckling as his footsteps became fainter.

They quickly dressed before hurrying down the dimly lit corridors, following markers on the walls. Soon they came to the large chamber they'd passed through the night before, to see soldiers breaking fast, and hurriedly grabbed some of the available food.

'Did you see some of the cold stares we got?' asked Maya.

Taran just nodded.

The sunlight was weak as they stepped outside. Rakan, Kalas and Yana were there already. Yana had picked some blooms from the vines adorning the keep and had woven some into her hair. She was trying to put some in Kalas' as well, and they laughed as he resisted her attempts at embellishing his appearance.

'Just in time,' Rakan noted, as Tristan appeared from the keep with Drizt and Trom beside him.

'Follow me,' commanded Tristan, moving past them. 'Let's show you the fortress and then afterwards we have something in mind before the midday sun passes.'

The rest of the morning saw the group inspect the entirety of the defences. While some soldiers greeted them cordially, others said nothing, looks of resentment on their faces.

'My men and Drizt's have no problems with you,' offered Trom, 'but the garrison soldiers feel shame. Their pride is hurt, by the traitors in their midst, and by how easily you killed them. It will take time for it to mend.'

Kalas and Rakan, both being long term military men, asked a constant stream of questions, most of which went unanswered. While they were locked in conversation with Drizt and Trom, Taran took the opportunity to walk alongside Maya, who was quietly talking with Yana.

Yana glanced at Taran briefly as he came alongside, then moved ahead, giving them a little space.

'I thought you'd prefer walking with the men, talking war,' Maya teased, trying to lighten the mood.

Taran shrugged his shoulders. 'Rakan taught me a lot, and I feel capable as a soldier. Yet, when I listen to Kalas, I realise there's a lot more to this than being good with a sword. He's talking about everything, from supplies to spare weapons, and how many soldiers are expected to die each day. It goes on and on, and I've a feeling it isn't just my head that's spinning. Rakan seems to have a good grasp, but it's obvious Drizt, Trom, and Tristan don't know the most of it, although they know a little more than me.'

Maya squeezed his hand. 'I, for one, am glad you're not so familiar with the ways of war. I doubt I'd have fallen for you otherwise.' As she said this, she went up on tiptoes and kissed him briefly before they caught up with the others.

They finally reached the curtain wall having inspected the condition of every corner of the fortress, from the towers to the broken catapults. Now, at last, they stood at the base of this mighty, first line of defence that loomed above them.

'Here's what should be our greatest strength, but is instead our greatest weakness,' Drizt advised, as he led them to the dark tunnel under the gatehouse. 'No matter how tall the wall, the fact there are no gates is a problem we've been unable to overcome.'

As they walked within the cool shadows, soldiers brought in small rocks, piling them against the walls.

'We've sent for mortar and lime,' Drizt continued, 'yet the main problem is we don't have the tools or time to hew large enough blocks to fill this passage properly. These rocks are too small, and neither do we have the skill or equipment to dislodge and transport any of the existing blocks from other areas of the fortress.'

'The gates from the other walls?' suggested Rakan.

Trom's voice boomed in the tunnel. 'They don't fit, and even if they did, we still have a wall without gates, not forgetting the keep as well.'

They stood there for a while talking about whether the tunnel could be filled sufficiently - when Maya stepped forward.

'You don't need gates, just for the tunnel to be filled?' she asked.

Drizt nodded. 'Indeed. I'm quite sure trade won't be resumed any time soon,' and he laughed a little at his own joke.

Maya looked at the desert soldiers standing guard in the pass just outside the walls and turned to Trom. 'Tell me. What wood are your spears made from?'

'Ironwood,' Trom replied proudly.

'Ironwood,' Maya repeated. 'Am I right in thinking it's incredibly hard and doesn't catch fire?'

Trom nodded.

'Then I can block this tunnel for you. Would you like it blocked now or later?' she asked.

Rakan brought his palm up, lightly slapping his own forehead. 'Of course, she can block it. It's so obvious. Why didn't I think of that?'

A short while later, the polished wooden ends of the desert tribesmen's spears had been laboriously worked into the packed ground throughout the tunnel with only a small space between them.

Maya knelt at the tunnel entrance as everyone except Taran slowly backed away. She took his hand in hers and the other she placed on the ground, focussing her thoughts on the spears.

The very ground seemed to shift as Maya let her gift flow. Where they crouched was rocky, so it didn't erupt with grass like the main courtyard, yet the spears themselves began to vibrate, split, reform and grow. Each one sprouted roots that pushed into the bedrock, causing it to crack, and then pushed upward to the top of the tunnel. Before everyone's wide eyes, each spear grew into a slim trunk until there was barely a gap between them at all.

Dust drifted down from the tunnel roof, as the strange, leafless trees, reached their full growth, pushing against it.

Maya stood, her arm snaking around Taran's waist and turned to see the others smiling.

'If only we had another fifteen thousand spears we might have been able to block the entire pass,' mused Kalas.

Trom glared, worried that Kalas might ask for more of the treasured weapons, but the other spears his men carried wouldn't have been enough.

'Incredible,' exclaimed Tristan. 'Even though we saw something similar yesterday, that gift is beyond priceless.'

'What about the catapults?' pondered Rakan. 'As we saw, they need new beams.'

Maya nodded. 'I can help with that and more.'

They walked back toward the keep, positivity surrounding them. Yet, as they reached the main courtyard, there waiting, stood a dozen of Drizt and Trom's men with all manner of weapons around.

'What's this?' growled Rakan.

Drizt raised his hands placatingly. 'Fret not, my new friend, there's no betrayal here. Rather it's something the men of the garrison asked for last night. They wanted a chance to prove their skills against yours. However, we felt it best to minimise the chances of further bad blood. So, instead, these are our finest Eyre and desert fighters. We'd like to see how you men fare in a practice bout or two if you care to entertain us.'

Yana stepped forward, glaring frostily. 'It's not just the men who can fight!'

Maya added her voice. 'Yana has skill with her swords, whereas I've more skill with a bow.'

'I wouldn't underestimate them,' Taran said with pride. 'Maya is an amazing hunter. I haven't seen her like.'

Maya's cheeks flushed at the praise.

'We'll see,' acknowledged Drizt.

Tristan relaxed on the keep steps, while the garrison soldiers lined the wall tops, calling out encouragement to the mercenary champions. They were keen to see the strange new arrivals humbled and taught a lesson.

'I'll go first,' Kalas decided, stripping off his weapons. He bent down to pick up two practice swords which he swung smoothly, testing their balance.

'So be it,' Drizt agreed. 'Which one of my men would you like to fight? You get to choose, but be wary, even if we're renowned for our archery, most underestimate our skill with a sword to their peril. Likewise, Trom's brothers in arms are spearmen without peer.'

Kalas grinned. 'Thanks for the warning. I'll fight them all.'

Trom roared with laughter. 'You're a bit slow,' he said without malice. 'You can fight them all, of course. But which one first? It would be unfair if you fought the twelve of them at once.'

Kalas continued limbering up. 'You don't seem to understand,' he replied. 'It would be unfair, but not on me. Now enough chat, let me show you gentlemen the art of war.'

He stepped forward to meet his opponents before pausing briefly. 'Kalas is coming!' he yelled, and the roar of the watching crowd rose to match his own.

Maya rolled her shoulders, loosening them, stretching her arms. The sun was now sitting atop the third wall and seemed reluctant to drop further, perhaps wishing to witness this final test.

It was almost time.

Earlier, following his shouted challenge, Kalas had finished his combat against the twelve opponents in a breath-taking display. It was over before his opponents could barely register his attack. He'd spun and twirled, blades flicking out, deflecting then striking, his body twisting from blows that never came close, leaving the previously roaring crowd in shocked silence.

His heavy practice weapons had floored every opponent, and he'd gone to each one, raising them to their feet, ensuring they were uninjured before the crowd found its voice and shouted their approval.

Rakan had fought next. Those facing him were fearful, expecting the same, and he'd taken advantage of their trepidation. He'd fought them in pairs and defeated them all.

Taran had followed, and her heart had beaten rapidly despite it being a practice bout. His opponents were fresh, having replaced their defeated comrades. They were determined to regain some honour for their brothers and were determined to beat their young opponent as a way of doing so.

Yet her worries were unfounded for he fared even better than had Rakan. While not as smooth as Kalas, he'd read every move before it was made and floored all his opponents speedily and efficiently.

Yana hadn't fared so well, losing her bouts, yet still, she'd fought with determination and the crowd while happy that she'd been defeated, weren't unkind in their remarks.

Now, Maya looked around, not focussing, but still taking in everything around her. She wanted to *feel* the space she was in. A subtle breeze wafted her hair, the dust danced then sat down again, and heat rose from the ground.

She stood in the centre of the courtyard, the buzz of the watching troops' conversation showed their growing disinterest.

Compared to the flashing swordplay, target shooting wasn't that exciting.

Taran, Rakan, and Kalas were watching intently with Tristan alongside. Trom stood talking to Yana, mesmerised by her good looks.

Drizt approached, offering the quiver of arrows that she'd left in her room. She took it, and in this instance, settled it over her shoulder, so the flights rose above her right ear.

Surprisingly, he offered his own bow, keeping hers, smiling. There was something in his look that made Maya realise that this was a subtle part of his test. Every bow was different, and it took a while to familiarise to the tension of a new draw. She could have asked for her own, but instead nodded her thanks.

Taking the weapon, she hefted it, assessing its balance and weight, admiring the strange, polished, green sheen. It wasn't a hunting bow, rather this was a powerful, warrior's weapon, able to shoot an arrow that could pierce armour.

She tested the draw, pulling the string smoothly to her cheek, and saw Drizt's eyes open slightly. She smiled to herself. This had been a test of her strength.

Drizt raised his voice, catching the attention of the crowd. 'This is our final test of the day, so enjoy the display.'

A table had been turned on one end in front of the rear gates about forty paces away. Upon the wood, Eyre archers had daubed a small circle using the green dye that stained the feathers of their arrows.

Drizt stepped to one side, making a small bow and theatrical gesture with his hand.

Maya pulled a face at him, chose an arrow, drew, sighted, and smoothly released as she exhaled. The arrow thunked into the table, quivering, a full handspan above the mark.

The crowd laughed, and the beginnings of a small, disappointed smile appeared at the edges of Drizt's lips.

Maya felt her cheeks flush. The bow was even more powerful than she'd realised. Now, however, she understood its strength.

Without waiting to be invited, she sent three more arrows after the first, each one hitting near the centre of the target. This time some of the crowd clapped, and Drizt nodded in approval.

She adjusted the quiver strap, so the arrows now rested behind her left ear and took the bow in her other hand.

'Really?' asked Drizt, and his smile grew wider and wider as Maya's next three shots followed the others. 'Now, *that* is quite impressive,' he admitted.

Drizt whistled through his teeth, and one of his archers ran forward, holding some wooden plates from the eating hall.

The crowd which had been mostly disinterested until now began to cheer enthusiastically as Maya hit plate after plate that was thrown high into the air, splitting them one after another.

Drizt laughed. 'I should have known a thrown plate is easier to hit than a bird in flight. Yet, what about three plates?'

Maya nodded, and drew three arrows from her quiver, nocking one while the others loosely dangled from her draw hand.

Drizt raised his arm, three fingers extended, and this time the crowd hushed in expectation. 'There's a scorpion on your boot,' Drizt pointed, eyes wide.

As she looked down, distracted, the Eyre archer tossed the three plates swiftly into the air. She didn't hesitate.

The three arrows left her bow smacking into the first two before they even reached the zenith of their flight and the third as it plummeted back down. Splinters flew, and the crowd roared.

'I could hit four,' Maya offered.

Drizt shook his head in amazement. 'I'll assume you taught yourself that shooting technique,' he shouted above the noise. 'I haven't seen anyone outside of the Eyre ever attempt it. Incredible! Unless we want to be eating off the table tops, we'll save the rest of the plates for another day I think.'

Maya went to return the bow, but Drizt shyly shook his head.

'The greatest honour an Eyre archer can bestow upon someone is the gifting of their bow. You have a skill that would make an Eyre archer even greener with jealousy, and thus you deserve mine. Don't worry,' he added with a wink, seeing Maya ready to refuse, 'I have a spare.'

Maya bowed, humbled and honoured by such an incredible gift. 'How many could you have hit?' she asked as they walked toward Taran and the appreciative crowd.

Drizt laughed. 'Let's just say you need to practice a fair bit more before you get close. Now, this is your moment, let's enjoy it.'

Taran came forward, sweeping her into his arms, and the crowd chanted her name.

Chapter III

'From all I've been told and from what I've seen today, we can hold a week, maybe a few more days if we're fortunate,' Kalas said, his face grim.

A deathly silence filled the chamber. It was in stark contrast to the first hour where praise had flowed along with wine as toast after toast was drunk. The exhibition bouts had shown everyone how impressive the martial skills of the newcomers were and had gone a long way to having them accepted.

Now, however, following Astren's report wherein he'd outlined in great detail the forces arranged against them, everyone had sobered. It was as if they'd been drinking water, not wine. The description of Daleth's siege engines had crushed all hopes of success, laying bare the reality of their predicament.

'Are you sure?' Tristan demanded, still in denial. 'We have three walls even if they could be in better repair. Drizt and Trom knew of the siege engines a week ago. Neither gave such dire predictions!'

'I can assure you I'm right.' Kalas confirmed. 'According to Astren, they're twice the size of our catapults. We'll be outranged, and they'll be able to destroy the walls unopposed. Once the walls come down, it will be one hundred thousand men against whatever we have left.

'I can't believe it,' whispered Maya, 'We came here seeking hope, not damnation.'

Kalas leaned forward to answer Maya, but he spoke to everyone. 'There's still some hope, I can assure you. Never underestimate the fickle nature of the gods of war.

'Now, for us to realise our hopes, we need to accomplish two things. One is to delay Daleth's army for as long as possible while inflicting heavy casualties. The other is to have an alliance army of desert tribesmen and Eyre, ready and large enough to defeat Daleth's horde when it breaks through.'

'Why don't we pray for the gods themselves to strike Daleth down while we're looking for miracles,' Drizt joked.

Trom slapped him on the back, laughing along.

Tristan glowered at them both. 'This isn't funny. We already know we can't delay them and the riders we sent won't reach the Eyre for another week and the desert tribes for nearly two months. The Freestates will be a smouldering ruin before they even get the request for help.'

Taran stood up. 'Then it's up to all of us to find a solution. If we don't, then it won't just be the Freestates that goes up in flames. However bad the odds, I won't be running anymore.'

'Nor I,' stated Maya firmly. Rakan and Yana echoed her comment.

'My spearmen are too slow to run away,' rumbled Trom.

Drizt shook his head. 'You're all crazy,' he winked. 'But the greatest test of an archer's skill isn't hunting game. If Tristan hadn't paid us to fight, we'd have paid him to let us come. My people have been the target of Daleth's troops for decades. Now it's time for us to return the favour.'

'Then we're all still committed to this cause, whatever our reasons,' Kalas stated firmly. 'Now we have a week to find a solution to our problems.'

Tristan stood, drawing attention back to him. 'It's reassuring to hear of everyone's commitment, even if things are worse than I'd feared. It's been a long day, and we all need to rest.

'Drizt, Trom, Astren; we still have much to discuss. The rest of you may leave.'

As Taran, Maya, Kalas, Rakan and Yana walked tiredly out of the doorway, Tristan called after them.

'We meet again on the morrow.'

He could act cordially if that's what it took to get what he needed. His throat was bruised and painful as he took a sip of watered wine.

The indignity and fear he'd experienced would be neither forgotten, nor forgiven.

Astren stared angrily at the stars, wondering which one of the gods hated him. Everyone else was heading to sleep, to rest, but he was still expected to drain his strength to confirm what they already knew.

The meeting had finally brought the stark reality of approaching defeat to Astren. Whatever the brave words, death was coming.

But he'd already expected to die here anyway.

Everyone believed his gift was limited to spirit talk and travel, yet there was more. Sometimes he could see what was to be. He kept this a secret as the premonitions foretold unavoidable happenings of ill omen and only affected him.

At first, he'd sought to change what might happen when he began to recognise these visions for what they were. Yet try as he might, there seemed to be no escaping what the fates had decreed. So, whenever he experienced a dream of foretelling, he was filled with trepidation.

Fortunately, they'd only occurred half a dozen times since he'd recognised them for what they were, but each had shown an event that would change his life.

When young, following weeks of dreams of his parents fading from sight as he reached for them, they'd been slaughtered before his eyes. To this day it haunted him that perhaps had he said something, his parents would have survived that night.

His previous dismissal from Tristan's court years before had been preceded by dreams in which he'd fallen down the steps of the Royal Palace.

Others came true over the years, yet all paled in comparison to the dream he now experienced.

It had started back in Freemantle. He'd awaken, covered in sweat, having witnessed his death at the hands of a faceless evil within a darkened room, dozens of faces leering at him, watching his misery before he passed.

Initially, he'd hoped the constant scouting of Daleth's kingdom and the knowledge of the coming invasion had caused the dreams, but after several days, there was no denying what they were.

He'd made plans to leave Freemantle before the fortress fell, reassured his escape would see him removed from the Witch-King's clutches for years to come.

Tristan ordering him to the fortress had put paid to this plan.

Now his death at Daleth's hands seemed inescapable.

Astren brought his mind back to the present and soared higher above the battlements, then cautiously headed west over the shell of the enemy fortress. He continued until he saw the mass of Daleth's army, thousands of fires blinking in the distance. As expected, Daleth's army was a mere seven days' march away at most.

He turned around, having confirmed what they already knew, but paused. The premonition weighed heavily on him, the inevitability making him feel nauseous even in spirit form. Suddenly, a rare, brave thought entered his mind. Perhaps he could defy the fates and choose the end of his own story instead.

His mind made up, he flew toward the enemy encampment, finding, then hovering above the large tent of the Witch-King himself. Even though it was night-time, the camp was a bustle of activity.

He steeled himself, then drifted down into the tent to see Daleth eating heartily, sitting on a camp chair with a goblet of wine in his hand and a platter of food by his side. In front of Daleth was a table on which was placed a martial board, covered in wooden pieces depicting cavalry, infantry, castles, and artillery. Seated opposite was a soldier, competing with the king in this game of strategy.

Astren couldn't believe he felt so cold when the physical senses were mostly denied in spirit form. His fleeting courage wavered for a moment as the enormity of what he was about to do hit him.

He moved to Daleth's side, his resolve firming, and projected his form, allowing it to shine in the semi-darkness of the tent. The soldier fell backwards off his chair, scrabbling for the sword at his waist, and Astren felt a moment's power at scaring a hardened warrior.

Daleth laughed, deep and loud and turned to look at him, raising his goblet in salute. 'Welcome, brave little spy,' he said, dismissing the soldier with a wave of his hand who sheathed his sword before stalking outside. 'Have you come to discuss terms for your surrender. I'll offer clemency to you and all the soldiers within if that's the case. Why don't you sit?' offered Daleth smoothly, setting the recently vacated chair upright once more. 'I know it offers no rest in your current form, yet it's how civilised men should speak.'

Daleth raised an eyebrow as Astren hesitated. 'Fear not, your bravery will be rewarded. My men will not kill you in spirit form this night. On this, you have my word. There's nothing you can gain from your spying now.'

Astren sat down. 'Would you truly offer clemency to us all if we surrendered?' he asked, disarmed by Daleth's friendly disposition.

'No!' Daleth answered candidly. 'I am the death of nations, not some pathetic, forgiving priest. Now, in exchange for my gift of safety this night, tell me. Does that weak fool Tristan still rule in Freemantle and how many men hold the fortress awaiting our arrival?'

Astren thought for a moment before responding. 'Tristan still rules, despite an attempt on his life by one of your agents. Now, he and twenty-five thousand men are waiting for you with reinforcements on the way. We shan't bend the knee to you, nor will we allow you passage into our lands.'

This time, Daleth's demeanour was anything but friendly. 'I believe you're lying to me, little spy.' He leaned forward, eyes darkening. 'It's unwise to speak to me with such blatant deceit. Yet I shall offer you a bargain in recognition of your loyalty and bravery, both of which I admire.

'I planned to have you tortured to death in the most horrible of ways had you fallen into my hands. Yet, by answering that one, simple, question honestly, I will grant you clemency when the time comes, and neither me nor mine will bring ill upon you.'

Astren's astral heart beat so fast in his chest, he was sure it would burst. Had the gods, recognising his bravery, offered him this way to avoid his fate? It wouldn't matter if Daleth knew how many faced him, he'd find out soon enough anyway.

'How do I know you'll keep your word?' asked Astren.

Victory shone in Daleth's eyes. 'Would you believe that I never break my word? I know you consider me evil, and perhaps I am, but a man, however dark, should always stand by his word.'

The Witch-King clapped his hands, and a dozen Rangers in spirit form drifted through the sides of the tent to surround Astren, astral swords ready to plunge into his body. Then as quickly as they appeared, they left.

Astren shivered in fear.

'There, you have your proof. I promised you'd live this night. Now, answer me!'

Astren bowed his head. 'We have only fifteen hundred men to defend the fortress.' Shame flowed through him as he spoke the words.

Daleth looked closely at Astren. 'Go now. Know your life is spared.'

Astren stood and bowed, and rose out of the tent, past the hovering Rangers, whose cold eyes and mocking stares flayed his courage. He fled into the sky, a chill in his very soul at his betrayal, however small.

He flew back to the fortress as fast as he could, through the corridors to his body, completing the merge with his physical self. When he opened his eyes and sat up in bed, he shook like a leaf in the wind.

Rising, he took his night candle and used it to light more and more until his room shone with light. His heart settled a little, and to distract himself, he focussed on the many small tapestries that hung from the walls.

He'd chosen this room, for unlike any others it had been decorated. They were faded, old remnants from when the keep was first built and garrisoned by thousands of troops. They were so dusty, and he raised his hand, brushing away some of the debris from the fabric of one, and as he did so, it crumbled, falling to the floor. Astren stepped back, his heart beating furiously again.

Slowly he went around the room, pulling the tapestries down one by one, a strange mixture of both fear and euphoria running through his veins.

He sat on his bed, staring in disbelief, looking at the paintings hung upon the walls that had been covered by the decorative cloths. The faces of Freestates' kings long dead stared down at him with lifeless, mocking eyes.

His premonition had been true. Daleth's choice of words about a torturous death, and now the paintings ... this was where he would have died! But now, having made the bargain with Daleth, he'd cheated the fates.

Tears ran down his face, but they were tears of joy.

Tristan squinted into the rising sun as he sipped from a goblet of cold water. The top floor of the keep gave unparalleled views from east to west, yet it wasn't always to his comfort.

Following the meeting, Drizt and Trom had offered him counsel on how best to employ the new arrivals' skills. The fugitives possessed some unparalleled abilities, and he was desperate to exploit them, as long as he could control them. To this end, Astren had finished drafting the contracts of citizenship.

Now, as he swept his eyes across the expectant faces of everyone in the room, he recited the words he'd been practising into the night.

'I told you I'd make amends for my previous misjudgement, but as you know, in the Freestates everything comes at a price.

'So, as I said before, what I'm offering is on the condition that you put your blood mark on the documents Astren has prepared, and swear an oath of fealty to me,' Tristan stated.

'Maya and Yana. I offer you the title of Ladies of the Royal Court with accommodation in the royal palace, and an annual salary as befits your status.' Yana beamed, whereas Maya shook her head. Tristan ignored her apparent disinterest and continued. 'However, you'll first assist in defending the fortress, and specifically with the treating of the wounded.'

Yana huffed. 'I'm no nurse …' she began.

Before she could continue, Tristan cut her off, his voice raised. 'You're whatever I say you are if you wish to stay on the right side of this fortress' walls! I'm not sure Daleth would give you such a generous offer.'

Yana's objections subsided.

'I'll help those in need, but I'll fight by Taran's side first and foremost,' Maya said bluntly, looking steadily into Tristan's eyes.

Tristan sighed, smiling slightly. 'Of course, I expected nothing else.

'Now, Kalas. You've been the subject of much discussion. We've witnessed your skills with a blade, and your knowledge of warfare could only have come from a position of rank. So, while it's hard to believe the entirety of your story, your experience is undeniable. Drizt and Trom have recommended that you receive a position of senior rank because your knowledge far outstrips theirs. It's rare to have such honest advisors, rarer still for me to agree with them. That leads me to offer you the rank of Lord Commander, making you the highest ranked soldier in my kingdom.'

A brief silence settled over the room as the enormity of what had been bestowed was taken in. Then Rakan and Taran were clapping Kalas' shoulders in congratulation as everyone else looked on, voicing approval.

Kalas bowed his head subtly. 'I accept.'

Tristan carried on. 'You answer only to me. Drizt and Trom will serve under you, so I expect you to take control with immediate effect. You know the poisoned chalice I've handed you. Our success or failure rests on your shoulders.'

Tristan turned to Rakan. 'You previously held the rank of captain so it would be poor recompense if that were not upheld. Consequently, you'll hold the same seniority as Drizt and Trom.'

Rakan nodded.

Lastly, he turned to Taran. 'It seems you were a corporal and the least experienced in terms of strategic expertise. However, your gift and skill with a blade makes you a fearsome warrior. I admit to being unsure as to what to do with you, but ...'

Kalas cleared his throat, interrupting, and everyone looked to him. 'As lord commander of your forces, I'll make this decision. Taran is to be my second, promoted to the rank of commander.'

Silent disbelief greeted this declaration to be broken by Taran himself.

'I'm sorry, that's not a good idea,' Taran declared. 'I'm honoured, but I don't have any experience in command. I'm also much younger than many in the garrison. I've a feeling they won't enjoy taking orders from me despite my ability to beat them all with a sword.'

Tristan, Drizt, and Trom voiced disapproval of Kalas' suggestion, and the calm of the room was destroyed by raised voices. Only Rakan, Maya and Yana kept quiet.

'Enough!' shouted Kalas, and even Tristan was shocked into silence by the command in his voice. 'None of you, it seems, has the vision to see Taran's absolute importance in the days to come. It isn't about his age, experience, his skill with a sword, nor about whether the men will respect him. It's all about how many lives he will save, how much quicker we'll be able to react to a breach, how swiftly we can get orders to the men.'

Silence greeted his announcement, the faces looking back at him remained unconvinced.

'All of you, follow me,' Kalas instructed, walking out onto the balcony from which Elender had met his fate. As they all filed out, Kalas pointed downward over the edge toward a group of soldiers milling around chatting in the morning sun.

'Men!' shouted Kalas, but they couldn't hear him. 'Men, get to the walls. The enemy are coming!' but again, the wind and distance took his words away. He turned to Taran. 'Commander, can you tell them they have less than ten heartbeats to get to the top of the wall, or their pay will be halved, but the first to get there receives double pay next coin day.'

As everyone watched, the soldiers below scrambled toward the nearest steps, pushing and pulling one another to ensure they reached the battlements first. A young soldier with blond hair won the race and raised his hands in triumph before lowering them, looking around in puzzlement. The others joined him shortly after, equally bemused.

Kalas turned back to Tristan. 'You see, Taran needs authority over everyone in this fortress, and they need to respond to his orders in a heartbeat. He can reach into their minds to tell them to seal a breach, to help a comrade, to attend their king, or simply to win a race.

'Despite my thoughts yesterday, I intend to find a way to frustrate Daleth's expectations of an easy victory. We will hold this piece of rock and bleed Daleth and his horde. By the time they wear us down, we better have raised another army ready to face him and beat him, for I don't want such sacrifice to be for nothing. I need Taran in that position of rank, to have a chance of making this happen.'

Kalas looked at Drizt and Trom, his eyes fierce, challenging.

Drizt flashed a disarming smile. 'Who do I salute first?' he asked, and this easy acceptance defrosted the tense mood.

Tristan grimaced. 'Even if I don't entirely agree, I can hardly counter my lord commander's first order. So be it. I believe, Taran, you're now the youngest commander the Freestates has ever had.' He turned to Kalas, 'Then again, if your tale is true, then I think you're likely the oldest.

'Now,' Tristan continued, indicating the parchments back in the chamber, 'make your blood mark on the parchments and swear the oath. Once you do so, then you're bound in service to me and are officially nobles or soldiers of the Freestates, subject to my will.'

Tristan breathed a quiet sigh of relief once everyone had done so and fixed a smile upon his face.

Looking at Kalas and Taran, he grimaced. 'Elender seemed to like spending my money on uniforms and armour, so it might be we can get you outfitted in something more appropriate to your new rank.'

Kalas shook his head. 'My armour stays as it is, but Taran needs something suitable.'

'I'll have it attended to,' Tristan assured Taran. 'Now, I've much to think on, and breakfast to eat,' and he gestured toward the door.

Tristan waited for everyone to leave and the voices to fade down the hallway before he slumped into a comfortable chair and helped himself to some watered wine, smiling in satisfaction.

He enjoyed this game of kings and had played this round exceptionally well. He now had a committed lord commander, sworn to service and could extricate himself from the fortress. It couldn't be held, but the main thing was he wouldn't be here when it fell. Kalas was a gift from the gods who'd do everything it took to fulfil his oath and defeat Daleth and would fight to his last breath while doing so.

Using people and manipulating them, along with creating wealth, were his greatest skills. The two went hand in hand. Gold was of course more valuable than anything else, but then he thought of Maya and the realisation that this was no longer true shocked him to his core.

Would the gods of greed agree with him or curse him for such blasphemy? Only time would tell.

Chapter IV

Hundreds of men gasped for breath, sweat streaming down their bodies, limbs shaking with fatigue.

Rakan felt like laying on the ground and allowing them to do the same, but he stood straight, pretending to be unfazed while his body screamed silently for an end to the torture.

As he allowed the men to have a short respite, he wondered how Taran was getting on under the guidance of Kalas. After a morning of the different units working together, they'd taken the spearmen and archers to train separately by the keep.

Rakan gazed at the garrison soldiers with a stern eye. Their sword skills, while universally solid, weren't good enough, and needed to improve. So, they, and everyone else would be training relentlessly for the next few days.

Each wall was nominally divided into three sections; the wall above the gate, then the ramparts north and south. The entire morning had seen the garrison soldiers sparring relentlessly atop their assigned section, with brief rotations to recover below. Others, assigned as stretcher-bearers, were running backwards and forwards burdened by rocks and buckets of water.

He led by example, and all the while shouted commands and threw in random events to throw everyone off balance.

'Withdraw to wall two,' he bellowed, shaking everyone from their all too brief respite.

'I've had enough,' a large, swarthy sergeant, shouted back, 'no more for me today,' and he stood, hands upon hips, staring at Rakan, angry, defiance in his eyes.

Shocked silence greeted this declaration, and everyone stopped to see what would happen next.

Rakan smiled grimly to himself. He'd seen the sullen look the man and a small group of his friends had been casting his direction all morning. The challenge to his authority had taken longer than expected but had now arrived.

This had to be dealt with quickly. In days past, he'd have killed the sergeant without a second thought, spilling his guts. He sighed. Trying to be a better man wasn't easy.

He unbuckled his swordbelt, letting it drop to the ground.

'There'll be times,' he shouted, 'when unforeseen events will challenge us. How we deal with such adversity shows the measure of the men we are. Now, gather round and see!'

'You're no man, just a filthy foreigner who has somehow bribed his way to a captain's rank,' taunted the sergeant, stepping forward, emboldened by Rakan's lack of weapons.

'A filthy foreigner,' Rakan repeated, nodding his head. 'I want to make it clear that whatever happens next, no punishment will be brought against this man,' he stated, looking around.

'Now,' he yelled, pointing at the sergeant, 'soon it will be your duty to kill every filthy foreigner who comes over that wall. So, why don't you get a head start by trying to kill me!'

The sergeant looked for support, and seeing a few encouraging nods from his small group of friends, edged forward, hands balled into fists.

'What's wrong with you,' taunted Rakan, 'use your sword!'

The sergeant drew his weapon, swinging it back and forth, confidence growing on his face.

'I might be a filthy foreigner to some of you, Rakan shouted at the hushed crowd, as he backed away from the glittering blade, 'but be grateful I'm not your enemy!'

The sword flashed for his face, but he swayed first left, then right as the lunge was repeated, then spun away, the sergeant following.

'An enemy would not waste their time teaching you a lesson,' he mocked, ducking under a whistling cut, stepping forward to sink his fist into the sergeant's side, before twisting away.

'He wouldn't show you the error of your ways!' Rakan jabbed twice, splitting his opponent's lip as the man's sword bit into the ground where he'd just been standing.

'Nor will he go easy on you when you grow tired.' This time he spun the sergeant from his feet with a crushing blow to the chin.

He stooped down, picking up the fallen sword and stood above the dazed man, whose panicked eyes struggled to focus.

'But whatever you do, believe me, when I say, your enemy will show NO MERCY!' Rakan screamed, and hammered the sword down.

He stepped away, leaving the blade quivering in the ground, a hair's breadth from the sergeant's throat who lay in a widening puddle of urine.

'The next time anyone, and I mean anyone, questions my command, you'll be surrounded by a pool of blood, not piss!' Rakan growled, settling his sword belt back around his waist. He hauled the dazed sergeant upright. 'Now, withdraw to wall two!'

The men responded instantly, streaming back over the wooden bridges above the fire trench, through the gateway. Some peeled off to help close the gates while the others ran up the steps to the walls where rocks had been placed to throw over.

Suddenly he laughed, realising for the first time since being cast out from the Nightstalkers, that he no longer cared. He was home.

'Back to the first wall,' he yelled.

The men frantically converged on the opening gates, the bare steel in this crazy madman's hand adding a sinister emphasis to the command.

'We need to eat,' complained one of the stragglers fearfully.

The next moment Rakan had stretcher-bearers lugging rocks to the fortress to exchange for food. He ordered the men up to the battlements, letting them eat in rotation as they came off the wall.

The punishing training routine continued throughout the day. To keep things competitive, he split the men into smaller groups, to race and wrestle, to duel and box.

It wasn't until late evening that Kalas, Taran, and Maya, led the archers and spearmen to where Rakan and his men sat in the shadow of the curtain wall.

Rakan watched as Kalas climbed the stone steps to stand above the gatehouse, standing resplendent in his silver armour, highlighted against the red sky behind.

Everyone else waited expectantly, eyes half-open, clothes stained with sweat. They wanted to hear their lord commander's speech that would send them to the food hall before they found their beds.

With the mountainside and walls funnelling Kalas' words, they carried loudly to everyone with little effort.

'Men, I feel your exhaustion; I feel your pain. As I stand before you, I'm proud of the effort you've displayed, whether under my watchful eye or commander Taran's.' Kalas shouted. 'You deserve a good meal, and you need sleep.' He paused as the grateful mutterings of the soldiers rose up, waiting till they subsided before he continued. 'But know this, the enemy may decide not to let you sleep, or eat. You need to know, if that is asked of you, then you're ready to answer the call.'

A horrified silence followed this announcement.

Kalas looked to Taran and nodded.

Taran rose to his feet. 'Prepare to defend the wall,' he yelled. 'Archers to volley position, spearmen defend the archers, swordsmen to the wall. Stretcher-bearers, bring torches to help us fight throughout the night.'

'Move!' screamed Rakan, drawing his sword, running to whack some of the slower soldiers painfully with the flat of the blade. 'You can sleep when you're dead,' and his limitless energy helped combat the lethargy that had taken hold.

The last few days had seen morale within the fortress transform, thought Tristan, as he looked down from the balcony at the activity below.

In the afternoon, wagons, filled with supplies; iron ingots, wood, and spare weapons had arrived. More importantly, men and women skilled in the art of healing came too, reassuring the soldiers that their lives mattered.

Yet it was Maya's presence that had the most influence, and his eyes followed her closely as she walked with Taran by her side.

The men of the fortress had, at last, embraced these new arrivals. Now, they gazed upon her with something approaching awe. Since arriving, her gift manifested itself everywhere she spent time. Vibrant moss erupted between blocks of stone, sprouting small flowers while vines appeared almost out of nowhere with fresh blooms appearing between sunrise and sunset. What many had seen as a cemetery, was being turned into a temple of breath-taking beauty.

She also captivated the soldiers with her stories of living under the rule of the Witch-King. Her tales of how the land and people across the border were dying, stripped of life by Daleth's dark gift were the most powerful. The men now understood that death was coming whether by the blade or the cold hand of hunger should Daleth prevail. It gave them more resolve to know they were fighting a righteous cause.

Tristan laughed to himself, for a believer would always fight harder, and Maya strengthened the defence as much as anyone by making believers of them all.

Then there was the way that Kalas, Taran, and Rakan were working alongside Trom and Drizt to get the men ready for battle. The garrison soldiers were beginning to believe in themselves as their skills were honed.

The promotion of Taran, which he'd initially thought ill-advised, was turning out to be one of genius.

The soldiers, whether of the Freestates, Desert or Eyre, after harbouring some initial reservations, now accepted and supported his promotion. They admired his martial skills, and he was showing a natural flair for leadership. They also recognised how his gift could help them fight more cohesively, and now showed him genuine respect.

To see units react and move, reinforcements hurry to perceived breaches, archers reposition to provide covering fire for a withdrawal almost instantly, was something to behold.

But it still wouldn't be enough, and it would all be for nothing unless someone came up with the solution to the enemy siege engines that could bring the walls down in days.

This now left him thinking about his departure. Who to bring with him and who to leave behind as sacrifice for the greater good. He took a sip of exquisite wine. Yes, there was no way he'd leave that behind.

If only they could get news about the forming of the alliance. That would be the ideal reason to leave early. Who else could but the King of the Freestates could lead the other kingdoms in this cause? No one could ever accuse him of cowardice in the face of the enemy if he had that excuse.

There was much to consider, and he sat pondering while the sun made its well-travelled journey across the sky. His mind made up he sent for Astren, for the seer's talents would be invaluable in days to come.

'Your fighting area is but four steps wide,' shouted Kalas, 'and there's no room for fancy footwork. More importantly, every wasted moment it takes to kill your opponent brings another over the wall to his side.

'This is not about duelling. This is about killing, and this is about murder. You need to be brutal, for only then will you have a chance to live.'

He moved to stand between two long lines of spears laid parallel on the ground. 'Come at me!' he commanded the two soldiers who stood waiting. The crowd watched, expecting to see a repeat of Kalas' dazzling sword skills that they'd all witnessed several days before.

As they stepped forward cautiously, practice weapons pointing from behind shields, Kalas suddenly charged, driving forward and upward, shield-bashing them backwards. As they tumbled to the ground, he stepped back.

'They're both dead,' he shouted, 'and I haven't even used my sword. They've just fallen off the back of the wall, and their brains are splashed on the ground. Your shield is a weapon, your head is a weapon, your elbows and feet are weapons and so are your teeth.

Kalas indicated for two different men to face him. They stepped forward cautiously, shields raised, peering over the reinforced rims, waiting for the shield bash.

Suddenly a whistling noise preceded two arrows that thunked into the side of the cuirasses that both men wore.

'What the hells,' one of the men shouted as the arrows fell to the floor. He picked it up, looking at the heavy bulb of wax wrapped around the end that had replaced the point.

Kalas waved at Drizt and Maya in thanks. 'Let's not forget that we'll have the Eyre archers watching our backs as well. If you're in trouble, they'll see it, and do their best to help you out. But first and foremost rely on yourselves and the soldier next to you. Keep your shields up at all times, as the enemy arrows won't be so kind.

'Now, everyone to work. I want you all to practice shield bashing each other off your feet, one garrison soldier with one of Trom's men where possible.'

Trom's men laughed at the look of trepidation on the faces of their opponents. All the desert spearmen, were, on the whole, larger than the garrison soldiers. They weren't so skilled with the sword but relished any kind of physical competition. After years of constant warfare in the dunes of the desert they called home, they were as tough as could be.

Kalas turned to Rakan and Taran who'd be watching along with everyone else. 'You two should join in wherever you can. Do you need any additional pointers?'

Rakan huffed. 'This isn't new to me. In fact, I reckon as I'm a little bigger, I might be able to teach you a thing or two!'

Kalas smiled, showing his teeth. 'I do believe I've been challenged. So, come, let's see. Who's better, one of Daleth's finest, or a relic from the Ember Kingdom?'

Taran stood back, laughing, but also studying them both.

Rakan was indeed bulkier, heavily muscled, with legs thick from years of marching and training. He epitomised brute force, and his swarthy skin, black hair, dark stubble and ferocious look made him look sinister.

Kalas was strong too, not an ounce of fat on him; leaner, relying on speed. He was fairer, green-eyed, light-skinned, a comely face, and of course, was shining in silver armour; a virtuous hero.

It was light against dark, and yet both these men were of good heart and nature, at least now. Now that one was without his amulet, and the other without his daemon.

This would be an interesting test, Taran thought, as the shouts of battling men echoed off the mountainside. Kalas was the deadliest of all swordsmen. But this wasn't about swords.

Rakan laughed in sheer joy as he lifted his shield, Kalas did the same.

Taran scraped some lines in the dust with the toe of his boot to replicate the width of the wall top, and stood back, raising his hand. After a moment to let the tension rise, he brought it chopping down.

Rakan edged forward, his weight over his front foot, his shoulder pushed up to the shield, legs loaded, ready to drive upwards.

Kalas, on the other hand, surprised Taran, for he was not doing the same, even though he'd shown this technique and power when defeating the two soldiers earlier.

Rakan's attack was telegraphed subtly by the shift of his feet as he ensured they had firm purchase. He drove forward, his shield smashing into Kalas' in a ringing blow that would throw the leaner man off his feet ... but it never happened.

Kalas, instead of meeting the powerful charge straight on, angled his shield so that Rakan's momentum was deflected past. Then as Rakan tried to recover, Kalas unleashed the power in his own legs, driving sideways, pushing Rakan over the line.

'Damn it,' Rakan grimaced, as he recovered his balance, but his face wasn't angry; instead, he had a wry smile on his lips. 'Good thing I landed on my feet when I fell off the wall. Best of three?' he quipped.

Taran stepped forward. 'Better not. Next time you might land on your head!' and he laughed to take any sting from his words.

'Tell me,' Rakan nodded, smiling in the direction of Drizt, who was working with Maya alongside the other archers and crossbowmen. Is there any weapon skill you're not the best at?

Kalas looked across at the Eyre archers. 'There's no weapon I haven't mastered. But in archery, I have a strong feeling I wouldn't come close to mastering that man. I'm glad he's on our side, that's for sure.

'Now, enough of revelling in my weakness, time to join in training with the men.' Kalas instructed.

Taran nodded. 'Let's meet up after and see who has won the most bouts. I'm betting on me. You two are getting old, and won't have the stamina to see through the afternoon.'

'The ignorance of youth,' Kalas and Rakan both said at the same time, and laughed.

Then Kalas grew sombre. 'Let's just make sure the men understand that If they lose a bout, it means more than lost pride. It means they're dead.

'There's no best out of three in war.'

'Three days,' advised Astren, 'and the vanguard of Daleth's army will arrive.' The setting sun filled the chamber with its red glow adding a dramatic effect to this announcement.

Kalas looked thoughtful, resting his chin on his hand. 'Add to that another day for the main body of the army to catch up, for units to prepare. I estimate we can expect the assault to begin in earnest in four to five days.'

The room fell quiet at this announcement, and Taran looked around studying the reaction of those who sat in on the meeting.

Tristan and Astren appeared pale, and he wouldn't have been surprised if his look reflected theirs. His stomach churned at the realisation that soon death would be commonplace around them.

Rakan, Drizt, and Trom, on the other hand, seemed not to worry at all. Rakan sat there looking unperturbed, digging dirt from under his fingernails with a dagger. Drizt carried on drinking his habitual goblet of wine, and Trom being Trom, didn't seem to react much to anything and sat there like a statue.

Maya's face was etched with worry, so Taran squeezed her hand under the table around which they sat. He opened his thoughts to her, and they shared their feelings, finding courage in the other, and both felt stronger for it.

Taran found Yana's absence strange, but she hadn't been invited to the meetings at Kalas' instruction. She'd been part of their close group for a while, yet offered no tactical or military assistance, nor had a gift like Maya's that might help turn the tide of battle. She'd not taken the news of her exclusion well. Her argument with Kalas when he'd told her to focus on the role Tristan had assigned had echoed around the cold, stone corridors long into the night.

'You know why we're meeting,' Kalas spoke into the silence. 'I've been unable to solve the problem of Daleth's siege engines, and I want to know if anyone has any ideas?'

The silence returned.

Kalas shook his head in dismay. 'We still have a few days, may the gods inspire us.

'Even so, we still need to look ahead, beyond what happens here, for this battle is only the beginning of the war. However important, we know it cannot be won, so we need to prepare for the endgame and win that, whatever the cost.

'But how we do that when we can't communicate with the other potential players? The riders King Tristan sent will not reach the Eyre for another week, and the desert tribesmen for maybe a month. Once those riders arrive, we've no idea whether the request for help will be answered without condition or negotiation. Should the gods smile on us and help is sent, our new allies must join forces at a preordained position, to unite against Daleth; otherwise, they'll have no chance either.

A longer silence followed as everyone considered the dire scenario confronting them.

'I have the answer to one of the problems,' Maya spoke confidently.

The attention of everyone in the room focused on her.

'As you're aware, Astren has the gift of spirit travel and projection. So, why hasn't he reached out to those from whom we'd ask for help?'

Tristan looked vaguely annoyed. 'It's because he's never travelled to those lands.'

Maya nodded. 'Exactly. But I can travel anywhere, and Astren can too if I take him with me. We'll fly the spirit paths together, taking hours instead of months, and he can make personal representation for help this very night!'

An astonished silence met Maya's plan.

'Incredible,' whispered Tristan, his face full of wonder. 'Can you really do this?'

Maya nodded. 'I'm sure of it. I've yet to test the limits of my gift, but I took Astren into Laska's settlement when alone he wouldn't have been able to do so. I've travelled before to the lands from whence

Daleth came, so I see no reason that I cannot fly north, east, and south as well.'

Tristan's eyes shone. 'You're more valuable than all the gold in the world!'

Maya knew there was no higher praise to be had from a king of the Freestates, and bowed her head in acknowledgement.

Astren was smiling widely. 'This will work as long as I can convince the kings of these realms to send help.'

Trom dimmed the mood. 'If it doesn't, we'll all die for nothing. Even if it does, we still need to hold Daleth's army long enough for the plan to be worth a damn.'

Kalas nodded. 'What you say is true, but if Maya and Astren can overcome this problem, perhaps the other isn't insurmountable either. One thing at a time. Now, let's see what else we can come up with to defeat those damn siege engines!'

Daleth looked around at the sprawling encampment, waiting for his tent to be erected. He was a little tired, not that he'd ever show it, for he'd spent most of the day marching with different units of his army as they trekked east.

While he knew every one of his guards and Rangers by name, the majority of his army had never seen him. So, while he knew the power of fear and wielded that authority very well - admiration, comradeship, and even love could be just as powerful. Walking amongst his troops forged such bonds, so he told tales or jokes, making them feel a kinship.

Daleth wasn't blind to his own darkness, the pain and suffering his gift meted out on the land and those within it. But thanks to years of propaganda, everyone believed the Freestates was to blame, and these men would follow him into the nine hells to seek revenge.

He wondered absently if, without the amulet they wore, the men would see him in a different light. No, they'd follow him irrespective. He was a heroic figure, and when he walked amongst the camp, men held themselves straighter, standing proudly if he singled them out.

Occasionally of an evening, he'd challenge a soldier to a bout of practice swordplay, and men would gather to see him teach a lesson.

Despite them being childlike in their skill compared to him, he never shamed or mocked them. Instead, he praised their ability, made them feel pride, further strengthening the bond they shared.

As he turned toward his tent, he sighed in contentment. This was what made life exciting beyond measure, the adoration of his soldiers, the feeling of pursuing his destiny.

Destiny, yes. What was his destiny?

He paused, midstep. His life so far had been of conquest, first the islands of his birth, then the land borne to the west, and then the Ember kingdom. Now his conquest was taking him further eastward. Was he destined by the gods to rule the world, and just how big was it? What would he find beyond the peoples and lands he knew of?

He could scarcely believe it. The vanguard of the army was just three days' journey from arriving at the pass. It would be the beginning of the end for the Freestates, and the start of a new era for him.

The vanguard consisted of the engineers and their siege weapons, some of the larger ones already assembled with the smaller ballistae carried on wagons. They'd arrive first to position these weapons of destruction within range of the fortress' walls. Following shortly after that would be the heavy assault infantry, then the medium infantry.

The pass was relatively narrow, and the troops were organised to travel in order of engagement so that they could efficiently move into combat throughout the battle. Last up were the spearmen and cavalry who were irked by missing out on the fighting. Still, once the fortress fell, the lancers could indulge their bloodlust, chasing down any who fled and terrorising the countryside. The spearmen would be put to far better use later into the campaign on the open field of battle.

He was tempted to ride ahead, to catch up with the engineers and their heavy weapons on the morrow, but they were a dour lot, so he decided to stay where he was, at least for now.

In some regards, he was disappointed that there were only fifteen hundred or so defenders. What resistance could so few present against the might of his army?

His reverie was interrupted by a rider galloping into the camp. These scouts regularly reported on the condition of the roads ahead, and how many days away from the pass they were.

He beckoned the rider over to receive his report and then sat down amongst some nearby soldiers who were cooking their dinner over a fire. Their eyes shone with awe, and he reached into his tunic, pulling out a large hide sack of wine. He pulled the stopper free, drinking deeply before handing it to the man on his left.

'Drink, my friend, and pass it around. Just make sure there's some left for me at the end.' The mood relaxed as he leaned forward, looking into the pot, nodding in approval. 'Soon, we'll be dining from gold plates when we conquer the Freestates,' he laughed.

The soldiers cheered and listened intently as Daleth spun a tale of how the Freestates were responsible for the death of their lands, and how vengeance would soon be theirs.

Maya smiled, enjoying the warmth of Taran's arms around her, and tilted her head, looking deep into his blue eyes. They were on their bed, the sun soon to set, although this deep in the depths of the fortress it would be impossible to tell the time if it weren't for the timeglass and candles.

Taran couldn't help but smile back. 'You know,' he said, 'my heart misses a beat every time you smile at me like that.'

'Then maybe I should stop smiling to ensure your heart keeps beating,' she replied, pulling a frown.

They laughed softly, conscious of the others in their rooms nearby.

Maya let her thoughts wander as they lay there comfortably in silence, waiting for darkness to fall outside as the sun dropped below the horizon.

Following the revelation of her plan, the group had sat down, looking at various maps within the fortress that showed the known lands surrounding the Freestates. Now in her mind's-eye, Maya saw exactly where she needed to go. The swamps of the Eyre were to the north with the desert tribes far to the southeast. There had been other lands too, those of the Horselords to the south and other distant places, too far removed to be worth reaching out to.

Her role, while pivotal, was also narrow in scope, for beyond leading Astren to their destinations, she'd no part to play as he was the one able to project himself. Drizt and Trom had shared the names and whereabouts of their respective kingdom's leaders and how Astren should address them when the time came. The success of the mission would be determined by Astren's diplomatic skills. He had to convince the rulers to mobilise their armies and send them swiftly on their way to rally at Freeguard.

Her stomach was knotted with excitement. Over the last weeks, she'd travelled further and seen more of the world than ever before, and now she was going to use her gift to fly to places she hardly knew even existed.

Propping herself up on one elbow, she looked down at Taran. 'It's strange,' she said, 'I'm excited, but also a little sad.'

Taran's brow creased. 'Why?'

'Because I'm travelling to see new peoples and lands, and I won't be sharing it with you.' Maya frowned.

Taran was quiet for a moment. 'I feel the same,' he admitted. 'I'd love to share your journey, but instead, you'll be with another man. However, as long as it's only me who shares your heart, then I promise not to be too jealous.'

'I hadn't thought of that,' Maya mused, 'but I can assure you Astren isn't my type, even if he's often in my dreams.'

They both laughed comfortably at the play of words.

As the grains of sand fell through the timeglass, Taran leaned over to his side of the bed and picked up a small leaf, looking at it, before passing it to Maya. 'Don't be gone too long.'

Maya chewed on the sleep weed. 'You won't even know I'm gone. Now, hold me close and never let go,' she whispered drowsily. Her eyes began to close, and she felt Taran's arms strong around her.

Her eyes opened again, and she rose from the bed, looking down at Taran. She paused, trying to project her form with all her will, but then turned away, conceding defeated. She passed through the door into the passageway outside, to find Astren in spirit form awaiting her.

'Good evening,' he bid. 'We're going to travel further tonight than I've been in my whole life. I know the lands of the Witch-King in detail, but there are parts of the Freestates I've yet to journey to, let alone the lands of the Eyre and the desert tribes.'

Maya laughed. 'I was thinking much the same mere moments ago, and even though the importance of this mission should sober my thoughts, I'm still excited to start.'

Astren nodded. 'Maya, you have a gift that's simply breath-taking in its potential. Imagine what wonders there are still to be discovered in this world. Who knows, maybe you could fly to the moon!' and even though he said this flippantly, he stopped, shocked by his own words. 'Imagine if you could fly to the heavens and the homes of the gods. What might you see if you travelled there?' and his eyes took on a faraway look.

Maya cleared her throat, catching his attention. 'For now, let's keep focussed a little closer to home,' she said, and together they left the keep.

The horizon to the west glowed from the recently set sun as they flew into the sky.

'Where to first?' Maya asked.

'Let's head toward the desert,' suggested Astren. 'We go furthest to start, then work our way back.'

'Then try to keep up,' challenged Maya, and sped east, with Astren beside her.

Taran lay awake, the shadows on the ceiling capturing his attention. He loved the way Maya twitched a little as sleep took her, and the way her breathing settled into a soft rhythm.

He was also tired, yet tonight sleep eluded him, at least so far.

His thoughts were on Kalas' dire forecast that they couldn't win, that they could maybe hold for a week before being brushed aside. When they'd arrived at the fortress and had seen its size, it had instilled in him a sense of belief that they could hold this mighty place. Daleth's army would surely break upon these walls like a wave upon the rocks. But these walls wouldn't stand for long before the onslaught of the siege engines, however fierce the men who stood upon them.

So what future did they have to look forward to? Escaping here had seemed like a new beginning, yet now it seemed they'd eluded capture and death only to delay it for a few more weeks. Should they seek to run when the fortress was soon to fall, and if so would they get very far before being hunted down once again?

He remembered Yana offering them sleep weed once to ease the pain of their passing when death seemed imminent. Perhaps that would still be the best way?

Even as the idea came to mind, he angrily brushed it aside. The woman in his arms was everything he lived for, breathed for. If the best way to keep her safe was to get her away from here and stay behind to delay any advance, he'd die happy in the knowledge that she'd made it to safety.

Yet how to delay the advance? How could they defend against the longer reach of the enemy siege engines that gave Daleth's already superior forces a drastic advantage?

Maya had come up with the solution for reaching out to their potential allies, now he needed to find a way to solve their biggest problem. Yet the answer had eluded everyone so far, and he knew so little of warfare, even if he knew a lot about fighting.

Anxiety kept him awake, staring at the flickering shadows, his armour rack casting a moving form upon the wall, almost as if it were alive, moving, fighting …

Thoughts, plans and ideas jostled in his mind, then suddenly he smiled, and his anxiety drained away. He knew exactly what needed to be done. Maya's body felt warm against him, and the exhaustion of such a long day now took effect. 'You belong with me always,' he sighed, kissing Maya's mostly white hair that shone even in the darkness of the room, and with that, he fell asleep.

Kalas awoke before the gong and washed in some cold water by the guttering candlelight that flickered in his room.

His head, from the moment he awoke to when he fell asleep, was spinning with so many thoughts that at times he felt overwhelmed. Even though Taran, Rakan and the others helped; still, the success or failure of this defence rested on his shoulders.

There were so many issues and logistical problems to overcome, and he sat for a while trying to prioritise them, then pushed them from his thoughts.

None of them mattered a thing if they couldn't hold.

The enemy siege engines remained the most significant threat. They were far more powerful with a longer range than the fortress' catapults, so Daleth's army would standoff and bring the crumbling walls down while barely losing a man.

The morning gong sounded as he finished dressing, pulling on his boots. His stomach rumbled, encouraging him to get something to eat from the food hall. He hurried along the now-familiar dark corridors to help himself to a hasty breakfast. The hall was empty, apart from the small retinue of serving staff who made themselves scarce as the grumbling soldiers came in to help themselves. Kalas grabbed a final piece of cheese then headed up the flights of steps to Tristan's chambers. He knew the others would soon join him there, the exception being Yana. Despite the initial bonding over their shared heritage, she'd been ignoring him since her exclusion from the daily meetings.

The guards on the landing saluted him, standing back as he walked down the corridor towards the open door at the end. Tristan sat within the meeting chamber, eating.

He'd suggested to Tristan to eat downstairs with the soldiers, to inspire them by his presence, but everyone had their limitations. Tristan had scoffed at rubbing shoulders with the common men. It was becoming more apparent by the day that what initially looked like a king coming to save his people, was, in fact, a king trying to save his position and wealth.

He knocked briefly as he strode in, and Tristan looked up, nodding to a chair opposite. Kalas sat and helped himself to some watered wine from a jug on the table. He saw Tristan's brow crease slightly and wondered at how the man could be irked by his lord commander sharing the breakfast wine.

They sat in silence a while, and as the room brightened before the rising sun, Rakan, Drizt, and Trom joined them. Kalas used the time to give them a full report on his plans for the garrison that day, but he knew all of them were really waiting to hear from Astren and Maya.

Tristan's patience finally ran out, and he thumped his fist on the table. 'Where are they?' he demanded. 'To keep your king waiting is unforgivable. I'm sure in some realms this would be punishable by death!'

Kalas fixed Tristan with a cold stare. 'Fortunately, Daleth doesn't rule here quite yet, and we are far more forgiving. Am I right when I say that spirit travelling drains one's energy?'

Tristan's face reddened slightly. 'You're right,' he admitted. 'Astren has been known to sleep the whole of the following day when he travels far. Then again, maybe that's his way of just avoiding any other tasks I have in mind for him.'

They laughed a little, and the mood relaxed.

Rakan, at Kalas' request, talked about the different units they'd face in more detail.

Drizt took special note of the assault infantry when Rakan mentioned them. 'They have armour that can consistently turn aside our arrows?' he asked, sounding doubtful.

'Not entirely,' responded Rakan. 'But as many as seven out of ten will be deflected or not penetrate sufficiently to cause death. The armour they wear will be full plate, up to twice as thick on the front as normal. They're very slow, and mobility is their weakness, but they aren't expected to fight for long. They specialise in exploiting a breach or creating a space on the wall for others to follow. They're hard to stop. The funny thing though, is if they fall over, watching them trying to get back up can be quite laughable.'

Drizt looked thoughtful for a while. 'We need to craft arrowheads that can punch through, so we'll have to sacrifice range for weight. I'll give my men instructions to have heavy-tipped arrows forged at the smithy.'

He was about to say more, when Tristan, who was facing the doorway, looked up and smiled, although it didn't entirely spread to his eyes.

'Good morning,' Tristan bid, somewhat sarcastically, as Taran entered with Maya leaning heavily on his shoulder and Astren just behind them.

'Are you alright?' asked Rakan with concern, noting how pale Maya looked.

Tristan's Folly

'I'm fine,' Maya yawned, 'but I've never felt so tired in my life. After this, I'm heading straight back to sleep.'

They sat before Astren cleared his throat. 'To summarise, we have, thanks to Maya, been successful in securing some much-needed help.'

'Yes!' said Kalas, eyes shining.

'Don't celebrate too soon,' warned Astren. 'It isn't as much as we'd hoped. Firstly, the Eyre can only send five thousand archers, both men and women.'

'What!' stormed Tristan, slamming his hand down on the table, fixing Drizt with a glare as if he were personally responsible. 'A mere five thousand. Why the women? And why so few?' he demanded.

Drizt answered before Astren could respond. 'Because, King Tristan, we're not a warlike nation, and don't have a large standing army. We field just enough to ensure our western border with Daleth's kingdom is secure. So I can assure you, while the overall number might not be what you hoped for, it is almost everyone, and will leave the lands of the Eyre mostly unprotected. As to why the women … they're as skilled with a bow as the men. You've seen Maya's expertise first hand. Why would you doubt a woman's ability to fight?'

Tristan's glowering look dissipated a little, but even Kalas couldn't help but shake his head in disappointment at the number.

Astren continued. 'This force will take around five weeks to get to Freeguard, and will be placed under your command once there.'

Tristan nodded. 'So, tell me, what of the desert tribes?'

Astren's eyes showed his excitement. 'They're sending twenty-five thousand spearmen. All men,' he added, forestalling Tristan's next question. 'However, without Maya, there'd be none whatsoever.'

Tristan looked across at Maya and bowed his head. 'Why am I not surprised. Tell me what did you say or do to work this miracle.'

'You spoke of Sancen?' Trom rumbled.

Maya nodded. 'I couldn't speak directly to the king, but I listened as he refused to send any warriors. His argument was that Daleth was no more his enemy than the Freestates. I remembered Astren talking about how an agent of Daleth killed Trom's predecessor. So, I told Astren to say that desert blood had already been spilt by Daleth. Sadly, it transpired Sancen was King Ostrom's firstborn son.'

'Blood must be answered with blood,' rumbled Trom.

'So why didn't you think to mention this before?' snapped Tristan. 'If it weren't for Maya, we'd have had no help at all. Were you trying to sabotage their efforts?'

Trom leaned forward, his normally calm eyes taking on a harder look. 'I didn't mention it, because if King Ostrom believed you were in any way at fault, then my brothers would have come here to destroy the people of the Freestates instead of to help them. You, on the other hand, would have been captured and brought back to our king, so you could be buried alive near a fire ant colony. It would have taken you a week to die under his gaze, eaten alive, piece by tiny piece.'

Tristan paled as he digested the words.

Kalas interrupted by whistling softly. 'That's great news, but in total, we'll only have just over thirty thousand troops to face whatever forces of Daleth's are left when they break through.

'The biggest problem that remains unsolved are his siege engines. We need to bleed his army, reduce it to a size where there's a chance of defeating it on the battlefield. Yet those engines with their long-range will destroy this fortress with minimal losses to his forces. Thirty thousand men against one hundred thousand. There's only one way that battle will end.'

They sat there in silence for a while.

Taran had his arm around Maya, and her head was on his shoulder, eyes closed. He cleared his throat to draw everyone's attention to him. 'When I used to compete on the justice turf against a larger opponent with a longer reach, I learned the only way to fight is to narrow the distance, get close enough to strike. You have to increase the risk you take, but without it, you'll never land a blow and never have a chance of winning. This is what we should do.'

Tristan shook his head in disbelief. 'What does fighting with your hands have to do with getting pummelled to dust by Daleth's siege weapons?'

Rakan, Drizt, and Trom also looked nonplussed.

Kalas looked at Taran sharply and remembered the last time he'd faced the Witch-King fifty years ago. Terribly outnumbered, even worse than now, but with the finest daemon-possessed soldiers in the realm at his side. How all the strategy he'd learned was cast aside to make that final charge. That final beautiful charge that had almost worked.

'I chose wisely when I appointed you as commander,' Kalas said, smiling at Taran. 'Your plan is one of genius. You have solved our predicament when I couldn't even see the light for the fire burning in front of my eyes.

'The day after the morrow, we attack!'

Chapter V

The morning gong when it sounded, seemed subdued.

'We don't need to get up,' Taran complained, as Maya rolled out of bed, nimbly avoiding his attempt to pull her back.

Maya smiled over her shoulder as she began to wash. 'I have an idea for today. Now, quickly wash and get dressed.'

Taran moaned as he followed Maya's lead, and it wasn't long before they were in the food hall. Maya gathered breakfast, and Taran exchanged greetings with some soldiers until Maya came over ladened with food.

Taran looked quizzically at the amount, but Maya wrapped most of it up in a cloth, and they ate the rest, hard bread, cheese, and hams with some berries.

Just as they were finishing, Drizt and a dozen archers came from the passageway leading to the storerooms across the hall, arms full of dusty old arrows.

Drizt passed his load to one of his men, brushed himself off and sat down with them both. 'Those arrows are useless,' he coughed, 'but we can still salvage the arrowheads and some of the flights.' He lowered his voice conspiratorially. 'There's also several hundred bottles of fine wine in the storerooms that Tristan has laid claim to, but which I find helps wash the dust from my throat. He'd be furious if he knew I was helping myself.'

Drizt laughed and pulled a bottle of wine from the inside of his tunic, passing it to Maya. 'It looks like you'll need something to wash all that food down with, and now that you're in receipt of stolen goods, my secret is definitely safe,' he winked.

Maya leaned over to plant a kiss on Drizt's cheek. 'You're a scoundrel, but apparently a good friend; your secret's safe with us. Sadly, we can't stop to talk. Thanks to Taran here, this is our last day of rest, and we're going to enjoy it as much as we can.'

Maya stood, pulling Taran to his feet and Drizt waved them a cheerful goodbye as Maya led Taran out into the early morning sun and turned toward the rear gate.

Whilst the men of the garrison were not allowed out of the fortress at this time, Taran, with his rank of commander, could hardly be stopped.

Maya turned south, back along the route they'd travelled days earlier. They walked until the pass was out of sight, arms around the other's waist, strides perfectly matched, while the trees of the woods loomed ever larger before them.

Maya turned to Taran, a look of mischief in her eyes as she gave him a warm kiss on the mouth, gently biting his lip as she did so. 'Come, keep up with me if you can,' she challenged, then turned and ran nimbly toward the trees.

Taran followed, holding on to their food and wine. He was far less graceful and struggled to keep up as Maya weaved her way untouched past dangling vines and awkward branches. He marvelled for she truly was a creature of the forest, and his heart ached.

Fortunately, before too long, Maya stopped at a stream within the woods and turned around as Taran caught up.

'Here,' she stated.

'Here?' repeated Taran, gazing around.

'Yes, here,' she affirmed, taking his hand, holding it tight. 'Today is just for you and me,' and with that, she knelt.

The forest was already green, for it had been too far from Daleth's domain to succumb to his power, but as Maya let her gift flow and flow it became something beyond mortal imagination.

Around every tree, delicate vines grew and erupted in flowers of whites and reds, pinks and yellows. The forest floor right up to the edge of the stream became lush with grass, small blue flowers dotted everywhere. The trees stood taller, leaves flourishing, and the heady perfume of all the blooms filled the air with blossom gently falling like spring rain.

Maya stood. 'This is my gift to you.' she said, spreading her arms, turning slowly.

Taran looked around. 'I would never have believed someone could so captivate my soul. This is so beautiful,' he replied. 'Now, tell me, what makes your frown?'

Maya's brow was furrowed, and she took a deep breath. When she let it out, the words tumbled after. 'Despite all the danger and bloodshed, our time together has been like a dream. The more I've got to know you, the more I realised I wanted a future with you,' she murmured. 'I believed that taking a stand against Daleth would help keep that future safe, forever. But now I'm afraid.

'We decided to fight without knowing how unprepared the Freestates were. We now know the fortress will fall. So, if we stay, how can we survive? Do you think we should try and convince Tristan to make peace, open the gates, and I can offer to heal the land as Daleth drains it?'

Taran sighed. 'Daleth's hell-bent on war, on conquering, not just ruling. He's tried to have you killed ever since you escaped, so we cannot take that risk. Then there's Tristan. His culture disallows the giving of anything unless in exchange for something of similar value. He'd never give up his kingdom while there's blood left to be spilt in the veins of those who serve him.

'A wise and beautiful woman once said to me, *we must fight for what we love*. I would point out that woman was you. I genuinely believe we've no choice but to fight to keep each other safe, our friends safe, but also to keep this world safe.'

Maya smiled sadly, nodding in agreement. 'I'm sorry for letting my fears out.'

Taran shook his head. 'We share the same fears, but facing them together makes us stronger. I'm not sure what the days ahead will bring, but I wouldn't bet against us. Daleth will rue the day he tried to destroy what we have.'

'And what is it that we have?' asked Maya, a smile playing around her mouth.

Taran held her close and looked deep into her eyes. 'What we have is brighter than the sun, sought after more than immortality, rarer than a falling star and worth both living and dying for.

'What we have is true love.'

Rakan sat on his bed, several candles burning brightly. Across the coarse blankets were laid his weapons. In one hand he held his sword, and in the other, a sharpening stone, which he slowly brushed along the blade, honing it to perfection. This was a ritual for him that he'd followed over the years to relax when troubles burdened him, or he needed to sleep.

Not that he needed much sleep. Despite his rank, he'd often insisted on taking watch duty at night when he was in Daleth's army. Especially when they'd been training amongst the Eyre swampland. He hadn't trusted anyone but himself with his life, at least till now.

He'd fathered no children, had never wanted them, and he'd been so ugly that no woman would have borne them anyway. Yet now he was a father. Now he had Taran and Maya.

It was a warming thought to care about someone else, and to know that feeling was reciprocated. Until recently he'd cared for no one, and his biggest concern had been making a name for himself in Daleth's army. He'd been doing so well until his run-in with Snark had seen him cast out of the Nightstalkers.

Now, Snark was dead thanks to Taran, and he grinned as he realised there was still a way to become famous amongst Daleth's army. He just had to kill as many of his erstwhile comrades as possible before he was finally cut down. He was sure to face many who knew him, and couldn't wait to see the look of surprise in their eyes when they realised they'd been killed by none other than Rakan himself. They'd pay a high price for the slight he'd suffered.

He looked down at his hands, steady now, finished with their work, and his mind felt settled.

To keep his children safe, and to make that name for himself, required the same thing. He had to kill the enemy, kill them all until there were none left.

Standing, he buckled on his weapon belt. Tonight he'd make a start.

Taran looked to his left and right to see Kalas and Rakan step backwards over the battlements as the three of them were quietly lowered to the ground with ropes.

He felt his feet touch the ground, so cautiously moved a few steps into the near darkness, making room for those following and allowing his eyes to become accustomed to the night. Rakan and Kalas were beside him, not much more than shadows. The sky was dark, the stars mostly covered by clouds, and the gloom enfolded them like a blanket. As he waited, he heard, more than saw, the other garrison soldiers gathering. Faces were blackened with dust and oil, boots wrapped in rags, and they each carried just a sword and dagger. No one wore armour, minimising the noise they made so they could move with stealth, but also because it helped with the second phase of the plan.

Taran smiled grimly. Daleth had ordered his fortress dismantled so as not to hinder his army's passage. It was a sound strategy considering his forces were vastly superior and also the aggressor. Still, his tactic was going to cost him dearly this night. With the enemy wall and just about everything else cleared and dismantled, the three hundred strong raiding party had nothing between them and the opposing garrison except the long pass.

Drizt, Trom, and their men were irritated at being left behind. While they understood it was too risky to have the majority of the defenders outside of the fortress, they were impatient to draw blood. But, every man had to be pulled up the wall, and if a quick withdrawal were needed, there could be a catastrophe.

Taran wasn't sure if it was dread or excitement or both that had filled his veins the entire day, but the time to act had now arrived, and he felt a strange calmness descend upon him. Thanks to Astren, they knew Daleth's garrison were already in their tents, and there were just over four hundred of them with half a dozen sentries posted.

The pass was lit with a subtle silvery hue as the clouds parted to show a sliver of moon, and the final men to be lowered down came forward to advise everyone was present. Kalas gave the order, and they moved carefully along the pass, placing feet softly so as not to disturb or kick any loose scree.

Even so, as they moved forward, Taran's jaw clenched with every noise they made, and even his breath sounded too loud. Crossing this wide-open space made him feel vulnerable, and he knew that feeling would be shared by all the soldiers following close behind.

The slow pace was tortuous, but eventually, a flicker of torchlight up ahead marked the perimeter of the enemy camp. Taran felt Kalas' hand on his arm and stopped.

The dark form of Kalas leaned in close, pulling Taran and Rakan closer. 'Leave the sentries to me,' he whispered, and disappeared ahead into the darkness.

The order to halt was passed back through the ranks by touch, keeping sound to a minimum.

Taran was unable to follow Kalas' progress, and while it seemed forever, Kalas was back shortly. Taran could smell the blood on him.

'It's done,' Kalas whispered. 'Have the men make ready.'

Taran turned in the darkness as did Rakan, quietly moving along the front rank of waiting soldiers, and soon the soft whisper of swords being drawn could be heard like leaves rustled by the wind.

As Kalas led the way, the raiding party moved over the low remains of the perimeter wall, which had been so neatly taken down by the very men they intended to slaughter.

There they were. Fifty tents all neatly lined up in rows, in the cleared ground next to piles of rubble stacked against the sheer mountainside. The campfires were burning low, just as Astren had described.

The soldiers split up, six men surrounding each tent. Everyone turned to Kalas who stood by a fire, sword raised high above his head in one hand, a burning brand now in the other. He brought them both down, and the raiding party cut the ropes holding the tents upright. As they came down enfolding and entrapping their occupants within, muffled cries erupted which quickly turned to screams.

Taran felt nauseous as he thrust his sword into the writhing shapes at his feet. Everywhere, others were doing the same, and thankfully, an empty quietness slowly replaced the tortured screams. Four hundred lives had just been extinguished; all those hopes and dreams stolen away in a nightmare from which none would awake. A few of the soldiers vomited, and Taran couldn't blame them. Other than that, no sound was made. The orders had been strict, no voice raised, no conversation unless directed by an officer.

Then the next grizzly task began. Everyone knelt and cut open the blood-drenched tents for what they needed was to be found inside.

Taran found himself shaking, and was glad that despite the fires, it was too dark for anyone to see his hands. He'd always fought honourably and had thought that in the many battles to come, he'd stand proud afterwards if he prevailed. Yet this was a slaughter with no quarter offered, plain butchery.

Rakan came over, putting an arm around his shoulder. 'I might not have your gift, son, but I feel the same way you do. It feels wrong, but this is war, and there's no such thing as being on the side of the light, shining in your armour dealing clean, noble deaths. War is just filth; dirty, dark deeds all around. There can be no space in our hearts now for mercy or compassion. There'll be time for that should we win, but between now and then, this is as good as it gets. We killed four hundred with no loss of life to our own, just a few minor injuries. Until now, the men around us didn't believe they could win, but thanks to you and Kalas, they not only have hope, but they're beginning to believe, in you and him.'

Taran turned back to the task at hand, Rakan alongside him, gathering all the dark armour of the dead soldiers, then piling it in the middle of the square alongside where the tents had been pitched.

'Listen up,' called Taran, just loud enough to be heard. We've until dawn to dispose of these bodies. Keep the dead inside the tents, drag them to the side and cover them with rubble. Scatter dust to soak up the blood, and then find yourselves armour that fits, and make sure it's cleaned as well.'

Kalas came over to join them. 'That was dirty work, but it was well done,' he said. 'Now, we need to prepare for our next guests and ensure the men know what to do, because tomorrow, we face our enemy in the daylight!'

Maya sat beside Astren on the curtain wall overlooking the pass. She'd taken a small leaf of sleep weed earlier, so she could spirit travel and observe Taran as he'd crept toward the enemy camp. Now, having seen the slaughter, she felt sick to her stomach.

'Are we any better than they are when we murder hundreds in their sleep?' she asked of Astren.

Astren shrugged. 'I'm not sure I have the answer to that,' he replied sadly. 'Every one of those killed was a son, perhaps a father or husband, and their lives were as sacred as any in this world. So, on the one hand, this was a heinous deed. Yet on the other, those very same men would have happily tortured then slaughtered us were they able to. Unlike us though, they'd have felt pleasure at our screams, happiness in our agony, and empowered by our helplessness. Then, they'd have gone on to do the same or worse as they spread across the Freestates and beyond.'

Maya frowned. 'But they could have been captured. They weren't in any position to fight back.'

Astren sighed. 'I thought the same initially. But think about this. If those four hundred were kept alive, they'd need to be kept under constant guard for there's no gaol here. Could we afford to take fighting men from the walls for that? Then, if they rose up against us at the wrong time, they could destroy us from within. The risk of taking them in was simply too high.

'However we look at it, Maya, this night's deed, although dark, was I believe necessary. Yet I think you know this already. What really ails you is that Taran was the one who came up with the idea of striking first. Now, having watched him, you're worried that the darkness that's inside of us all, will grow and change him. Am I right?'

Maya lowered her eyes. 'I could see he had his doubts before and how he felt afterwards, and that lightens my heart a little, but he killed men in their sleep. How can he remain the same? How will his soul not be blackened?'

'Don't fret,' said Astren, squeezing her shoulder gently. 'First, from what you've told me, he's taken your lead in the past, choosing the way of peace when you crossed the giants' valley. Was that part of your story true?'

Maya nodded. 'It was. He sought to befriend them.'

Astren smiled. 'I believe you, although I still find it hard to imagine them as you described. If only I could actually see one. Secondly, if there's just one thing that will ensure Taran comes through this, it's the gift of what you share. He's so in love with you, Maya. With you by his side, he'll follow the path of light and will desire only to make you smile inside and out. He'll always strive to be the type of man you want him to be.'

Maya looked gratefully at Astren. 'Your words have made me feel a lot better. Thank you. You know, Taran said to me that what we have is true love - that it's something worth living for, but also dying for.'

Astren got up. 'You see, your Taran is a poet as well, and he'll do nothing to risk what you have. Be there for each other, and all will be well.'

As he walked away, to report to Tristan, he thought of Maya's words. *A love worth living for and dying for.* But then his smile faded, and he was glad Maya couldn't see, for that kind of love was also something worth killing and murdering for too.

Captain Malakar couldn't believe it.

Over forty days of dust, heat, rain, and mud, and finally, they'd made it to the fortress. The ruins were in sight, and this awful slog was soon to be over.

Even though he was an officer, he was on foot and had been the last two weeks. He didn't want to be closer to the lower ranks, but many of the oxen used to pull the siege engines had died on route. Now, every horse and man was helping to pull and push the engines and wagons.

He and his men had the honour of leading the army and had to arrive first, to position the catapults that had travelled all this way to destroy the Freestates fortress. He couldn't wait to see them smash those mighty walls. It would make all this pain worthwhile and then some.

They'd started off way before dawn to ensure they'd arrive before the sun reached its zenith, and as he looked up, he could see they were on schedule. 'Come on, boys. Let's get these in place before midday, and then we can spend the rest of the afternoon finishing off the wine,' he shouted, and this was met by an enthusiastic cheer.

He looked behind at the four siege engines being pulled by teams of men, oxen, and horses. Twenty additional men were assigned to each, adding their weight, pushing from the sides and behind. There were also eight wagons to transport pulleys and tackle as well as the smaller artillery pieces. They carried ballistae for firing long iron javelins that could outrange an archer. These could fire over the heads of Daleth's assault infantry with devastating accuracy, passing through a defender's armour as if it wasn't there. Beyond them, back in the distance, an hour's march behind were the heavy assault infantry carrying ironwood ladders.

He chuckled to himself because by the time his engines had been at work for a couple of days there'd be no need for ladders, and they'd have carried them all the way here for nothing. But he respected his king's thoroughness, and of course, there would be plenty more walled towns and cities to conquer.

All in all, he had two hundred and fifty engineers under his command. To a man, they couldn't wait to wreak havoc on the Freestates who were behind the unholy famine that had decimated their homeland.

He looked up at the remains of the Witch-King's fortress, nodding in satisfaction. The walls had been levelled, and the ground cleared to allow clear passage into the pass, where the huge artillery pieces would be positioned.

As they crawled slowly forward, he noted the coloured stakes in the ground marking out where units would be positioned so the order of battle could be observed. The rising sun was shining into his eyes, but he could vaguely see some of the garrison men waiting at the edge of the fortress' ruins.

'Typical, bloody, garrison soldiers,' he said, turning to a corporal puffing alongside him. 'You'd think they might come and help us this last bit of the way. But no, they're probably still wiping the sleep from their eyes.'

Yet even as he said it, lines of soldiers came jogging down the shallow incline, and his men roused a small cheer as they mingled amongst them, helping to push and pull the weapons of war to their destination.

Malakar tried to engage one in conversation, a sergeant from his armour, who was wearing a full-face helm. The man simply ignored him, pulling on the harness of one of the horses, lending it his strength.

If it hadn't been for the help the man offered, he would have taken this insult further, and perhaps he still would once the engines were in position.

It was unusually hot this early in the day, and Malakar was sweating profusely. He pulled a cloth from his belt and wiped away the sweat that was streaming down his face as they finally made it to the perimeter of the dismantled fortress. The siege engines' wheels began to turn freely now they were on levelled stone, and the mute sergeant stepped away toward a commander, who with fifty men, was waiting to one side.

The commander stepped forward, raising his hand, and Malakar did so as well, bringing the line to a stop behind him.

'Have your men line up the siege engines over there,' the commander pointed, 'and the wagons too.'

The commander's voice was muffled by his helm, and Malakar thought it not just unnecessary but rude for him not to remove it.

'My orders,' Malakar replied, assuming a voice of authority, 'are to position the siege engines and the ballistae in the pass beyond, not wherever you wish them to be. Those orders came directly from the Witch-King himself, so respectfully that is where I'll position them!'

The commander paused a moment. He nodded over Malakar's shoulder. 'What range do your siege engines and ballistae have?' he asked, his voice sounding metallic. 'To that boulder yonder or to the rocky outcrop even further away?'

Malakar looked back. 'Yes, the catapults will throw to the outcrop and the ballistae almost as far. Whatever the Freestates have, we can outrange them with these.' As he spoke, he noticed that the garrison men mixing in with his engineers were all wearing full-face combat helms too, and something started to feel very wrong. Why did they all have cloth wrapped boots, and what were those reddish-brown stains showing through the dust? Thoughts flashed through his mind as coldness gripped his heart. He had to warn his men quietly, for these soldiers were not who they seemed. As he considered his choice of action, the young sergeant turned to the commander.

'He knows,' the sergeant said, and as Malakar opened his mouth to shout a warning, the sergeant stepped forward, a dagger in his hand.

As Malakar collapsed to his knees, the dagger in his chest, he could hear his men start to scream. His last thoughts as blackness closed in were that he'd never get to see his beautiful engines at work.

Chapter VI

Daleth couldn't remember the last time he'd felt so full of anticipation and joy.

It wasn't just because he was walking amongst his assault troops in their heavy armour, exchanging ribald jests, or that the pass was just up ahead, signalling the end of this arduous journey. It also had nothing to do with the new life that trickled into his body as they moved closer to the Freestates.

It was because he was no longer bored.

These last fifty years he realised had been so utterly tedious. The initial invasion of the Ember Kingdom had been exhilarating, as had been the conquests of his youth. Yet once this land and its people had been subjugated, he'd had to wait two generations before he could further pursue his destiny.

He looked over at Alano who was riding alongside two hundred of his bodyguard and cursed, for it was him and his kin who'd forced him to wait all these years. No, he wouldn't let old memories overshadow this current feeling of joy, rather he'd learn from it.

Yes, while he looked forward to the slaughter of those who stood against him, maybe he could spare some as he had with Alano. Offer clemency to the strongest who survived. Give them the amulets from his own fallen so that they lusted for battle as much as his own men. Then his conquest could last for decades as he conquered the known and unknown world. Surely that was the purpose of his gift; to follow a destiny ordained by the gods themselves.

He looked to the sky, wondering if the gods resided amongst the stars, or on the highest mountain peaks as some suggested. There was not a cloud in sight as he pondered; it was clear blue and the sun warm, definitely a good omen.

He bid farewell to the men and made his way to his horse at the side of the column.

Alano's red eyes looked at him as he drew alongside and took the horse's bridle, ready to mount.

'You grow stronger, my king,' Alano said, in that brittle rasp of his.

Daleth nodded as he swung into the saddle, good humour flowing through him. 'Soon, Alano, you'll feast like never before, and both of us will feel new life run through our veins. This campaign has been long in the making, and you're one of the reasons I have an army to be feared that will go on to conquer the world. We'll not stop at the Freestates. This war will not stop until every kingdom known to man and the gods is under my control!'

The daemon's eyes flared, but he said nothing.

Daleth sighed at the loss of the man. The old Alano would have shared some pride about going to war with the fighting force he'd help forge.

'This is a day to remember,' he murmured, closing his eyes, feeling the warm caress of the sun on his face. Surprisingly, a low rumble of thunder sounded.

He opened his eyes, and shading them with his hand, looked up to witness four mammoth rocks reach the zenith of their flight before plunging down. He didn't have time to react before two pieces of masonry crashed just behind him, smashing into the assault troops, crushing scores of them, knocking others flying. Screams filled the air.

He turned back toward the ruins, to see the distant arms of his four siege engines being winched down, and hundreds of men swarming around them.

Alano's red eyes turned to him. 'To stay here is to die, we must charge,' he urged in a rasping growl.

Daleth recovered from his shock, and drawing his sword, whirled it around his head and pointed it at the distant enemy. 'Charge!' he screamed, and dug his heels into the flanks of his horse. His bodyguard followed, drawing their weapons as they leaned low.

The assault troops dropped the heavy ladders they were carrying, and ran, leaving the injured screaming as they lumbered after their king.

The wind whistled past Daleth's ears as his horse galloped at full speed toward the line of engines, and he realised that in front of the catapults were several of the ballistae. Even as he watched, they loosed their iron bolts. Fortunately, most flew high, but a dozen of his bodyguard were swept from their saddles, taking more horses down behind.

Daleth wasn't too worried. The distance was closing fast, and they were now inside the arc of the siege engines, one of which managed to loose its deadly cargo a second time. He didn't turn to watch the flight of the rock; instead, he fixed his gaze on the centre of the enemy line.

They had no spearmen to blunt the charge, and he saw them start to scatter, to turn and run. He laughed. This was a cavalryman's dream, to charge down a fleeing enemy.

But suddenly flames licked up around the engines and the whole western entrance to the ruins and the pass beyond were blocked by fire and billowing smoke.

Daleth and his bodyguard reined in their horses, fighting to keep them under control. 'The engines!' he roared, and his men leapt from horseback and ran forward with ropes and horse-blankets, beating at the oil-fed flames. They managed to isolate one siege engine at the end and two ballistae in front of it, pulling them clear even as several men succumbed to the heat to be consumed by the fire.

The other engines were beyond rescue, and Daleth cursed again and again as he watched them burn.

He dismounted as the assault troops finally caught up and turned to their commander. 'As soon as these fires die down, clear the remains of those engines and secure the pass so that we have no more uninvited guests. This will but delay their death by a few days, a week at most.

'They may have drawn first blood, and I salute them for that, but we will spill the last of theirs. That I swear!'

Yana sat deep in thought, the shadow of the first wall keeping her cool, enjoying the brief calm before the storm. She mulled over the last few days, reflecting that for the first time in her life, she had felt invisible, and hadn't enjoyed it one bit.

Back home she'd been the centre of attention, doted on by her grandfather, his retainers, and fawned upon by men who wanted her hand or just her body. She enjoyed privilege and had everything and anyone she wanted. But now, that had all changed.

Kalas first had the temerity to exclude her from the daily meetings even though she'd ruled Ember Town along with her grandfather. Then there was Taran. He was the first man she'd known since reaching maidenhood that not only resisted her charms but seemed to be utterly dismissive of them. She wasn't sure whether it was that, his smile, his broad shoulders, or the noises that came from his room when he and Maya coupled, that made her desire him the most. Now, she couldn't get him out of her head.

Her desire to have Taran to herself was becoming overwhelming. In fact, she no longer found herself caring for the gazes which the other men in the fortress sent her way, and began wondering if, for the first time in her life, she loved someone. She'd scoffed at the idea initially, telling herself not to be so stupid, but then it seemed to make sense and take hold.

Yet the warning words of Rakan and her uncle still hung heavy in her memory, so any pursuit of Taran would have to be subtle. She had to stay close and wait for an opportunity to present itself, and then let everything fall in to place naturally ... with a little help here and there. Taran would see her for what she was and would love her too in time, especially if Maya wasn't around to beguile him.

Tristan had instructed her to work with the healers who'd come from the capital. Initially, she'd seen this as beneath her but now recognised the potential in this appointment. It would show everyone her usefulness, compassion, and kindness, which were traits Taran seemed to admire. So since the healers had arrived, she'd worked with them, learning how to stitch and bind wounds, which salves to apply for cuts or blunt trauma, and which medicines would cause sleep, keep someone awake, or ease them into the next world without pain or suffering.

Despite greater proficiency in their craft, none of the healers had her confidence, for they were followers, not leaders, so she took charge, appointing herself over them.

Then, last night, three hundred soldiers had been lowered over the walls to raid the enemy. However successful they were this time, she would soon be needed like never before and would therefore be back in a position of influence within days of losing it.

Earlier, as the sun had risen, Yana had organised the healers, ordering them to the lee of the first wall to await the return of the raiding party. In addition, she'd organised the stretcher-bearers to bring buckets of water to help cleanse wounds or for refreshment.

Tristan, Drizt, Trom, and Maya, were all on the wall alongside the Eyre archers, who would if necessary provide the withdrawal with cover should it be contested.

Yana was shaken from her reverie by the sound of raised voices. She hurried up the steps to stand next to Maya, reaching out to gently hold her hand. She looked down the pass to see smoke billowing skyward in the distance.

It wasn't long before the raiding party became visible at the far end of the pass. They wore the dark armour of the enemy, jogging fast, but not in a panic. Behind them all, even at this distance, Yana spied Taran from the way he moved. Almost at the same moment, Maya's grip on her hand firmed.

'There's Taran,' Maya exclaimed, letting out a sigh of relief.

Yana feigned not to have seen him. 'Really, where is he?' she asked, and Maya excitedly pointed him out.

'See how Taran, Rakan, and Kalas were first over the wall, and now they'll be the last back. That's true leadership,' a nearby soldier commented to those around him.

Yana noticed Tristan glare at the man, having overheard his comments. From the way the king's eyes narrowed, she could tell he didn't like such praise being heaped on others.

The returning soldiers were hauled up over the battlements, and Yana directed those with minor injuries straight to the healers for treatment. She took two aside herself, applying salves and dressings from the satchel she now carried at her side.

Maya stepped forward to help with one who had a wound to his arm, but Yana quickly intervened and spoke softly in her ear. 'If help you must, use only bandages. Ensure you save your gift for those closest to you; otherwise, the youth you have left will soon fade. Now, leave the wounded to me and find that Taran of yours. Make the most of your time with him.'

Maya looked into Yana's eyes and squeezed her shoulder briefly in thanks, then went back to peering over the wall.

Yana turned to the soldier and began to treat his wound. While binding his arm, she looked around and noted that Tristan was staring at something, lost deep in thought. Following his gaze, her eyes opened wide, for, without question, Maya was the object of his interest. Yana quickly turned back to her work in case Tristan became aware of her eyes upon him.

Now, this was very interesting. It could be that the gaze was innocent, yet she remembered his earlier words of praise when Maya had sealed the tunnel; *that gift is beyond priceless*. This was definitely worth keeping an eye on.

She thought then of her warning to Maya against using her gift, caring words from a friend. Her father had taught her that the closer you got to someone and the more they came to trust you, then the less they would really see what you were up to.

She'd learned that lesson well.

Kalas sat stroking a large mountain cat on his lap, one of many that the resident soldiers had domesticated over the years to keep them company. These striped predators helped keep the fortress free of rodents who would otherwise ruin the stores. It purred as he scratched its chin, twisting happily at the attention.

The keep was so quiet after dark, yet not for much longer, for despite the victories of last night and earlier today, it was nothing more than a flea's bite to a horse.

Soon, these quiet hallways would ring with the cries of the wounded and dying, the entreaties of whom would wear down the morale of the remaining defenders. However, once the battle was joined, most able-bodied fighting men would sleep on or beneath the walls. Then the cries of the injured would echo unheard until such time as any survivors were forced into the keep for a final stand.

He was not afraid of death, that fear had long passed, and yet he was feeling afraid nonetheless. For despite his incredible skill with weapons, despite his recent return to youth, despite his new friends around him, he knew he was weak.

He stared into the mirror, looking at his reflection, peering deep into his own eyes, searching. His face while not handsome was strong, his shoulders wide, his arms corded muscle, yet his weakness wasn't physical.

'You see,' said a voice quietly in his mind, 'nobody can see us, no one will know. It will be our secret, just yours and mine. I'm here to serve you; you're the master now. I stand defeated and at your command.'

The fact that he hadn't sought Taran's help after the daemon had revealed itself again made him realise the truth. He wanted, no, needed the daemon to be part of him, to lend its strength, its fury, its senses, and what harm could there be in doing so. He'd felt elation when he believed it was gone, but then realised without it, there would never be a chance of fulfilling his oath.

It seemed that despite Taran having helped defeat it, what neither he nor Taran had known was that it hadn't been slain. Its life force was inseparable from his own. Instead, it had just been beaten and cowed, hiding away, waiting for a moment of need to quietly offer its help.

It had chosen the previous night to reveal itself as he'd crept along the pass, feeling blind, silently calling upon the gods to help him see in the darkness. Then in answer to his prayers, the gloom began to lift, and he'd been able to see the sentries with ease; their blood shining like fire as it ran through their veins.

'You cannot rely on the gods to help you,' the daemon had whispered in his mind, 'but I'll always answer your prayers.' He'd accepted the help without question or pause, feeling as if a long lost lover had stepped back into his life.

It was easy to justify. He wanted to fulfil his oath to slay Daleth, an oath he'd sworn not once but twice. It was a burning light that gave him purpose. Without it he was but another lost soul in this land of people with no honour or morals, save perhaps Maya and Taran.

He thought then of his niece Yana. While honour-bound to protect his blood kin, neither was there much goodness in her either. He saw someone who would manipulate anyone to reach her own ends, and he wondered what her goal now was. Did it remain as before, to steal Taran's heart away from Maya? He doubted she'd succeed, especially given there were only two days before Daleth, and his army, launched their attack and in all likeliness brushed them aside.

'Not if you let me help you,' soothed the quiet voice in the back of his mind. 'I will give you the strength to fulfil your oath. You and I will spill the blood of the enemy in the thousands, even more than on that glorious day when we last fought against Daleth. This time though we will prevail.'

Kalas nodded. 'You're at my command daemon. You'll do all and only what I ask for. If not, Taran will find a way to rid you from this plane of existence once and for all.'

The daemon whined submissively in his mind. 'I know your love of Taran, and I bear him no ill for his role in my defeat. Henceforth, I will help protect all of your friends while you achieve your dream. I ask for nothing but to serve.'

Kalas frowned. 'As long as you stay hidden from sight, then you can help me, daemon, but only if no one knows. Do you understand?'

Despite the hunger, his eyes stayed green as he peered at his reflection in the mirror, and he nodded in satisfaction. 'No one must know,' he repeated, as he carefully lifted the now sleeping cat. It opened its eyes to see why his fussing had stopped and didn't even have time to hiss before he bit through its neck and started to feast.

Taran stared down the pass, Maya's hand gripping his tightly. All along the wall, men stood in silence.

Two days had passed since the raid, with preparations continuing at a frenzied pace. Stores of food, water, spare weapons and arrows were strategically placed throughout the fortress. The killing ground between each wall had been cleared, and the deep fire trenches filled with oil-soaked wood. If a wall fell, the trench would be set ablaze, keeping any pursuers at bay. Not only would it give the defenders time to withdraw to the safety of the next wall, but would provide a much-needed respite while the fire still burned. It would also need to be filled before an enemy could successfully mount further attacks.

The mood of the defenders, almost jubilant after the recent victories was raised even higher when one hundred heavy crossbowmen from the southern border forts of Freemarch arrived.

Yet the buoyant mood was now being eroded by the sight of what filled the pass just beyond the range of the fortress' two working defensive catapults. There, in the centre of the pass stood a charred but apparently working siege engine. It towered above two ballista alongside it and the surrounding men. But it was the unbroken mass of soldiers that filled the pass from side to side with such menace that silenced everyone as they saw for the first time the magnitude of what they faced.

Taran was surprised by his own feelings as he looked upon the enemy. He'd expected to experience overwhelming nervousness or fear, yet as he stared at the massed ranks, he saw them as a threat to Maya. Consequently, he was full of controlled rage, burning with hatred, but kept these feelings firmly to himself, ashamed and shocked at their darkness

In contrast, the faces of the garrison defenders around him were ashen, so using his gift, he looked into their minds and felt shocked by the terror he discovered. Many were on the verge of running before the attack even began, and it would only take one or two, and then the others would follow in a flood.

He turned to seek Kalas' advice, but he was talking with Tristan, standing within the entrance of the gate tower.

Looking about he saw Trom in the courtyard below, leading prayers, his spearmen kneeling around him, heads bowed. Further back, Drizt sat below the second wall, laughing. The archers joked amongst themselves as if without a care in the world. Each had their different ways of dealing with fear, and Taran recognised that the garrison men needed a distraction.

He wasn't an orator yet he had to say something, he was after all a commander. So without further hesitation, he jumped up onto the battlements, standing high above the men.

He threw his arms wide as everyone turned toward him in surprise, and pulled a lopsided grin. He briefly looking down at Maya's upturned face, sharing his thoughts with her, asking for help.

'Men,' he cried, his voice powerful. 'We haven't known each other very long, but you know me well enough to understand the nature of the gift that I carry. You're aware that I could have used it to take all of your money playing knucklebones, but I didn't. I hope you realise by now that I can be trusted and that I'm always honest with you.

'As I stand here today, literally on the edge, death but one step behind me, I find courage in those of you standing beside me. When I look into your hearts, I see strength, resolve, and honour. But truth be told, many of us also feel doubt or fear. To deny that would be untrue to ourselves, to each other.

'Yet know this. As I look down the pass at our enemy, do you know what I read in their minds? I read the very same and more. They're scared, fearful, and now they look up at our high walls and see certain death awaiting them. They've already had to tread over the corpses of hundreds of their brothers, and know that we will give no ground, give no quarter!

'In my heart, I'm grateful to have you by my side, for I know that our desire to win is far greater than theirs. How do I know this? Because my truest gift isn't in my ability to read the thoughts of others. No, I share a gift more valuable than that with each and every one of you.'

He reached out his hand, and Maya took it, leaping nimbly to the battlements next to him.

'We are all gifted,' Maya continued, her voice clear, almost musical, 'gifted with the love of our wives, or lovers, children or mothers, fathers and friends. We don't fight here for ourselves, and I know it isn't all about the gold,' she joked, and many of the men laughed, 'nor is it about protecting the nation of the Freestates. It's about protecting those within it that we love, from those,' and she swept her arm across the pass, 'those who would kill, torture, maim, and worse if we allow them to sweep us aside.

'This is where we make our stand against the darkness, for we are the flame that holds back the night. Then, while we fight, we know that the allied armies of the desert tribes and the Eyre are gathering to ensure victory so that our children can enjoy the gift of children. Between us, we'll defeat this pestilence that would blight our lands for centuries to come. Together, we will kill the Witch-King!'

She raised her bow above her head, and the men lifted their swords and bows, spears and shields and roared.

Taran opened his mind, feeling the men's resolve burning brightly, and both he and Maya leapt down from the battlements. They walked into the gate tower with the adulation of the men loud behind them to find Kalas, Rakan, and Tristan waiting.

Kalas was grinning and came forward to embrace Taran and Maya. 'You both know the hearts of men,' he said. 'Truly, Taran, you earned your rank today if ever there was any doubt.'

Rakan echoed Kalas' words, before adding. 'You make me both proud.'

Tristan bowed to Maya. 'Your words stirred my blood; you have worth beyond measure.' He turned next to Taran. 'So, tell me. Those men in the pass, If they're scared of attacking, do you think they might retreat if we hold? Are they truly as frightened as you say?'

Taran thought for a moment. 'No,' he said. 'I lied through my teeth to stop our soldiers routing.

'They feel no fear whatsoever and cannot wait to slaughter us all.'

Chapter VII

'Well,' said Daleth, standing in the shadow of the siege engine, looking up at the ant-like figures on the distant walls, 'whoever they were, they seem to have given a pretty good speech. From the armour of the first, it was a senior officer, maybe the commander of the garrison.'

Alano next to him said nothing, and Daleth wasn't surprised, for he rarely spoke unless directly questioned. At times it was irritating, and at others, he appreciated the quiet company. However, several of his bodyguards responded, making jokes, and the mood was light and full of expectation.

Daleth could barely control his excitement and was impatient to unleash hell upon the defenders, and then the thought gave him an idea. With a denizen of the hells at his command, why not give them a taste before the main assault began.

'What do you think?' he asked, raising his voice so that his bodyguard turned toward him intently. 'Shall we start this day with some entertainment? How about like in the bard's tales, we offer our champion, Alano, for single combat against theirs. If they win, we go home, and if we win, they open the gates and let us through without us slaughtering them.'

Alano's red eyes flickered to him. 'We would not kill them all if I win?' he asked, disappointment thick in his hideous voice.

Daleth laughed heartily. 'Of course we would. I think it would be even more fun to kill them unexpectedly when they thought their lives were safe.' The men around laughed along with their king.

Alano's head bobbed in agreement. 'Truly, you have the soul of a devil.'

'You, and you, come with me,' Daleth commanded, nodding to two of his bodyguards. 'Alano, you wait here. We don't want to frighten them with those red eyes of yours just yet. I feel they might be a bit reluctant to accept my offer if they see you first.' His two chosen bodyguards carried large, full-length body shields as they strode down the pass toward the massive fortress, in case any defending archers decided to ignore the white flag of truce that rippled above them.

Despite having dreamed of this moment a thousand times, nothing could have quite prepared him for the reality of approaching those enormous walls. The majestic Forelorn mountains rose up either side, only adding to the grandeur of the place. Daleth had never felt insignificant in his life, yet for a moment he felt just that. As they approached, he noticed he was passing between some large markers that had been hammered into the rocky ground.

'We're in range of their archers,' one of his bodyguards said, and they drew closer, ready to protect their king with the shields should the need arise.

The rising sun was behind the fortress, and it was a little challenging to see. As they drew within earshot, Daleth could see the gate tunnel was blocked with something, although he couldn't be sure by what. Yet what piqued his interest the most was the state of the walls. They might have been huge, but many of the blocks appeared cracked and displaced, with the green stain of mould growing in the mortar. This wall was not as strong as it seemed from a distance, so the reports he'd received were accurate.

The one siege engine should be sufficient after all.

He stopped, stretching his wide shoulders, feeling the silence of the men looking down from above, and revelled in the moment. He spread his arms, raising his voice, knowing the walls of the pass would amplify it so that not just the defenders, but his men behind would hear his words.

'King Tristan,' he boomed. 'I hear you've come to stand against me when all we seek is safe passage through your lands to those beyond. Do we really need to kill you all when you could simply open your gates and welcome us as friends?'

He waited, letting his words sink in. While everyone would see through the lies, this was part of the game, and he enjoyed playing it.

From the tower closest to the gate, a figure wearing bejewelled armour came forth to stand behind the battlements at the centre of the wall. Daleth knew this had to be Tristan, for his finery shone like the sun. The Freestates king cut an unimpressive figure, and Daleth chuckled, waiting to hear his weak sounding response. He was therefore surprised when Tristan's voice rang out strong and deep.

'King Daleth. Welcome to the land of the Freestates,' Tristan replied. 'We're a hospitable people and would be happy to receive you on a state visit. Feel free to proceed personally as my guest to enjoy our hospitality, but you'll understand that this invite is only for a man of standing and wealth such as your good self. The rest of your men would need to wait here, or preferably go home.'

Daleth laughed coldly. 'I fear, King Tristan, that your offer shows the poverty which has fallen upon you in these times, and a poor king is not to be respected if my understanding of Freestates culture is clear. I believe your offer is nefarious and not to be trusted. So, I intend to continue through your lands along with my army whether they're invited or not. However, I'm willing to offer an alternative to the ill-feeling this might create.

'In days of old, champions would fight to the death to solve rival kingdom's problems, so death was visited upon one, not all. What say you to this. We, as kings, fight to the death, or if you're in ill health, our champions can fight to resolve this instead. If I or my champion wins, we enjoy free passage and simply pass through in peace. If you or your champion wins, my army will simply turn around and leave you to enjoy the luxury of your fortress unmolested.'

A long silence greeted his proposal, and he grew impatient waiting, and just when he was about to voice his displeasure, Tristan answered.

'Sadly, my skill is not in the use of arms, rather it is of the mind, yet I agree with your proposal that our champions will fight. Have yours come alone to where you now stand at midday, and our man will face him there. The gods choose the victor and decide the fate of nations.'

Daleth turned away, laughing to himself, his men behind him, shields raised, guarding their king's back.

This was going to be a good day.

'I wondered why you weren't on the wall all this time,' Drizt chuckled, 'and now it becomes clear. You were staying hidden just in case he recognised you. You were hoping he would issue a challenge.'

Kalas nodded. 'He doesn't know I'm here. Why would he? It's just a shame Tristan doesn't abdicate and pass his crown to me, so I can finish that undying filth once and for all.'

Tristan frowned, not rising to the joke. 'I'm not sure I appreciate the idea of abdication, although I accept your desire for revenge made you speak in haste. Still, I applaud you on your foresight. Do you think he will keep his word and turn his troops around if you defeat his champion?'

Maya laughed. 'Tell me, King Tristan, were Kalas to lose,' and she smiled disarmingly at Kalas as she said this, 'would you allow Daleth and his army to pass through uncontested?'

'No. What kind of fool do you take me for?' asked Tristan, still smarting from Kalas' suggestion.

'There's no insult intended. I'm simply pointing out that I believe both of you have no intention of keeping to this agreement.' Maya explained.

Tristan looked perplexed. 'So what's the damned point of having Kalas chop off some wretch's head when that still leaves the rest of his enormous army to fight?'

Trom was listening, and nudging Drizt with his elbow, winked, before asking loudly in wonderment. 'Is Kalas now the king?'

'No!' shouted Tristan. 'I'm king. Kalas is our champion!'

'Shame,' rumbled Trom, 'Kalas would make a good king, I think. He might even give us more pay. What do you think, Drizt?' he asked.

Tristan's face started to turn purple with rage when Rakan spoke up. 'On a serious note, why are you taking the risk when killing Daleth isn't the reward?'

'It's to give us another victory to give the men hope. Isn't that right uncle?' asked Yana. Everyone turned to see her standing in the tower entrance. 'Taran and Maya's speech was amazing,' she continued, 'and then we have our victories over their garrison and engineers. But you need to keep giving the men hope, for soon those small victories will be what they'll remember to keep their spirits up.'

Kalas nodded, moving to embrace Yana. 'You're right,' then he leant forward. 'I'm sorry we've had our differences these last days, niece of mine,' he said softly.

Yana rested her head briefly on Kalas' armoured chest. 'I needed to find my place in our new world, and you helped me see that.'

'Let's hope that Daleth's champion is happy to go along with our plan,' laughed Drizt. Then his voice turned serious. 'Rakan, do you have any idea who he'll send?'

Rakan took a few moments in thought before answering. 'I never met the king nor went to the capital. His finest men are the Rangers or his personal bodyguard, and we know Kalas can defeat even them with relative ease. Yet,' and he paused for a moment, 'there were rumours that Daleth and his finest trained with a creature from the nine hells, but I wouldn't give the story much credit.'

'I believed that giants were just from stories,' added Taran, 'but now I know they exist, and we have our own experience of daemons too.'

'It seems many tall tales have an element of truth about them, but we won't have a long wait to find out, for noon will soon be upon us,' rumbled Trom.

'I could help you, Kalas,' Taran suggested. 'I can link my mind and yours to that of their champion so you can read his every move.'

Yet Kalas shook his head. 'No, my friend,' he replied, resting his hand on Taran's shoulder in thanks. 'I'll fight whosoever stands against me and give them a fair fight in so much as there'll be one. I'll give them a clean death, and if for some reason I fail ...'

'I'll put an arrow through their champion's back,' finished Drizt, 'and then Taran will be promoted and become the youngest lord commander in the history of the world.'

They all turned as one of Drizt's archers came into the tower. He bowed briefly then turned to Kalas.

'There's movement amongst the enemy ranks, lord commander. It's time. Their champion comes forth.'

Kalas nodded. 'It is time,' he agreed, feeling elation surge through his veins before walking out into the sunlight, the roar of the fortress' soldiers washing over him.

Taran clamped his jaw to stop his teeth chattering. He was in a damp storeroom beneath the fortress, and if it were not for the torches burning brightly in their brackets on the walls, it would have been pitch dark for there were no lightwells here.

He was cold, and that was why he was shivering he told himself, or maybe it was the terrible slaughter that had raged throughout the day, the images of which kept flashing through his mind. However, it was more likely the anticipation of the task that awaited him this night.

Perhaps to delay what had to be done, he allowed his thoughts to wander back over the day's events, and still couldn't believe what had happened.

They'd followed Kalas out on to the wall to see a figure wearing a dark robe with a cowl concealing his head, stride forth from the enemy ranks. The warrior took his time as he approached, showing complete disregard to the archers above, turning his back to shrug off the robe to reveal dark armour and two swords sheathed at his waist.

He'd remembered feeling Kalas pause subtly in his preparations, perhaps even then knowing deep inside who his enemy might be.

Kalas had wrapped a rope around his arm and stepped into a loop, as Taran, Drizt, Trom, and several others between them had taken up the slack. 'Remember,' he'd said, flashing a smile to them, 'leave the rope down and don't forget to pull me up quickly once this is done,' and with that, he'd stepped back over the battlements and was lowered to the ground below.

The sound had been deafening as men shouted and horns blared, the noise reflected by the mountainsides, as Kalas stepped forward to meet his opponent. He'd shrugged off his own robe to reveal his shining, silver armour, in direct contrast to the darkness of his foe who turned around, aware of his presence.

What followed had been strange to see.

The dark armoured figure had removed his helm, casting it aside to reveal his face, his eyes glowing red, and Kalas had stumbled backwards as if he'd been struck.

The noise from the crowd had drowned out the words that passed between them, but it was evident for all to see that these two knew one another. Everyone, from Tristan to the lowliest garrison soldier quickly grew silent in anticipation.

Alano, as Taran now knew him to be called, had, after the initial brief exchange, drawn his swords and stalked toward Kalas who refused to draw his own. Kalas had raised his hands in a placating fashion, trying to reach out with his words.

Taran recalled Maya's nails digging into his arm as this red-eyed daemon had launched a ferocious attack on the unarmed Kalas, intent on cutting him down without mercy. As everyone gasped, watching in disbelief, Kalas had at the last possible moment rolled away from the flashing blades, yet however fast he'd moved, blood sprayed from a wound to his shoulder as one of the blades found their mark.

The roars from the enemy army had resumed again as their champion had pressed the attack.

Kalas had no option but to draw his swords then, favouring his left side. What unfolded before the opposing forces had again brought silence, but this time of disbelief.

Taran had fought and trained with Kalas, had seen him fight before and was in awe of his skill. Yet as he watched both men below him, he knew he'd never seen Kalas truly fight, until now. Unbelievably his skill was matched or even surpassed by his opponent.

The two fought back and forth across the dusty pass, leaving splashes of red, like paint on a canvas, as blood fell from them both. Their footwork left graceful sweeps as they spun and twirled, leaving a series of marks as if they wrote the story of their fight in symbols upon the very ground.

The sun had crawled across the sky, and still, the fight had continued. Thrust and parry, sweep and cut, leap and roll, and the sweet music of the blades as they rang against one another was in direct contrast to the death those instruments held.

Taran had no idea of how long they'd fought before a gradual shift in the balance of the fight became apparent. Maybe it had been the early wound to Kalas' shoulder, or simply that his daemon possessed foe was too strong, but Kalas began to defend more than attack. He deflected Alano's blades later and later, and suddenly the roar of the enemy encampment grew again as they crashed their swords against shields in support of their champion.

Kalas was forced backwards, and his footwork had started to flag, becoming more simplistic, his usual spins and twirls disappearing as he'd tried to conserve energy. Alano, on the other hand, had seemed to grow stronger, ignoring his wounds, pressing and pressing, driving Kalas right back to the walls of the fortress itself.

Kalas could barely lift his right arm now as the early injury and long fight seemed to have finally taken its heavy toll, and as everyone watched mesmerised, the final blows had been struck.

Alano had thrust with the sword in his right hand, and Kalas barely had time to parry it as Alano followed it in the same instant with an overhand strike with his other sword against Kalas' now useless right side.

The blow was going to cleave Kalas in half, armour or no, and yet suddenly Kalas' sword flashed up deflecting the blow, and in the next instant, Alano had crumpled to the floor. It took a moment for Taran to work out what had happened, and he doubted most of those watching had even seen it. Kalas' sword, had, in the instant after it parried the death blow, struck Alano across the temple with the crossguard, rendering him unconscious.

While both armies stood open-mouthed in shock, Kalas had quickly bent down, and with effort heaved the limp body of Alano up over his shoulder, and grabbed the rope which hung right next to him, stepping onto the loop.

Unbelievably it had been his plan all along to pretend his injury was worse than it was, to lure his old friend to this position whatever the risk. As Taran recovered from his shock, he and the others had grabbed the rope and furiously pulled both Kalas and Alano up from the ground far below.

As they were helped over the battlements, Kalas' face had been ghostly white from loss of blood, pain, and exhaustion. 'Don't kill him,' he'd pleaded before his eyes closed, his legs giving way.

Maya had run forward, and Taran didn't question for a moment as she used her gift on Kalas, healing his wounds, and then she also fell unconscious. Men ran forwards at Rakan's command to bind Alano and to carry them all back to the keep.

Taran turned to go with them, but Rakan had put out his hand, stopping him. 'Sorry, son,' he'd said, his voice low, the strength of his grip in direct contrast to the softness of his voice. 'You're commander of the fortress now. This battle is about to be joined, and we need you on the wall to lead the men.'

Taran had been about to angrily refuse when a sound like thunder bounced of the mountainsides. He'd turned to look along the pass to see the enemy advancing like a black wave, ladders tipped in fire rising above them as they sprinted toward the walls.

How they'd survived that first day, he had no idea.

Now, despite a day spent ending lives, he had to try to save a soul, except this one was likely already beyond redemption.

For staring back at him, were two red eyes, burning with hatred and flame from a realm of untold darkness. Secured by heavy chains to an iron ring embedded in the flagstone floor was the bloodied figure of Daleth's champion, Alano.

Taran closed his eyes and called upon his gift.

Daleth lay on his camp bed, staring at a lantern, fists clenched.

This should have been the best day in almost fifty years, as the first blood of the long-awaited conquest was spilt. Instead, despite the heady trickle of life drawn from nearby lands, the sense of elation he'd expected eluded him completely. But considering how this campaign had started, he wasn't surprised.

The enemy had taken first blood, slaughtering the small garrison then the engineers, and destroyed all but one siege engine. These were strategies he hadn't foreseen, and such personal lapses in judgement angered him immensely.

Then immediately after, there was the loss of Alano and the realisation that Kalas awaited on the other side of those damn walls before the battle even started.

He looked up, sending a silent prayer to the gods of luck. He'd been so close to putting himself forward to fight. What better way to show the men the leadership of a true king than to slay the Freestates champion? Thank the gods, he'd stuck to his decision to send the daemon. Ye gods, he could still feel the nausea from when the enemy champion had shed his robe to reveal that damned silver armour.

Nonetheless, it had been a spectacle he'd never forget, the display keeping him spellbound from the opening moment. Then as the fight progressed, he'd admired the skills of both warriors, safe in the knowledge that Alano had gained the upper hand. Right up to the final blow, when the ground under his feet shifted as Alano crumpled to the floor, played perfectly by that damned Kalas.

His haste in launching an attack on the fortress in anger had cost the lives of nearly three hundred of his assault infantry with many more injured before he'd signalled the withdrawal.

Yet his current angst wasn't for the three hundred lost today or the six hundred-odd men of the garrison and engineers, rather it was for just the one. Alano.

Alano had been taken alive, although for what purpose he couldn't be sure. Likely the reason Kalas hadn't struck a killing blow was that he hoped to regain the loyalty of his old sword brother.

It was time to decide if anything could be done or whether he should simply accept the loss. The latter was the best option, but Alano had been with him fifty years, and this gave him pause. While everyone else aged, withered, and died, Alano was also gifted with eternal youth and would serve by his side, always.

He suddenly remembered Alano's softly spoken words on their journey here. His curse had been in front of him his whole life. He ruled kingdoms, was surrounded by a hundred thousand troops, loyal to him, some even fanatically, and yet he travelled through life alone.

There was no love of his life, for they withered and die, nor children, for his seed was tainted. His only constant companion was Alano, who as a man had wanted to kill him and was now a daemon.

He sighed as he turned the wick on the lantern down. He'd give Tristan the opportunity to return Alano come the morning. Never since his coming of age had he asked for anything, instead, taking what he wanted if it wasn't given freely.

Yet ask he would, and he'd sow the seeds of division in the enemy ranks even as he bargained for his friend's life. Yet, if his only friend was a daemon, what did that say of him?

He thought back to his youth, something he hadn't done in nigh on eighty years, wondering how his parents had died. He'd never been back to see them after he'd left for his rite of passage. Had they died

Tristan's Folly

of hunger, old age or disease? No. It was likely they'd been killed by his bloodthirsty men while conscripting everyone to his cause and murdering those who didn't comply.

I'm so sorry I wasn't there at the end, he thought.

For the first time since the day he left home, his mother's kiss warm upon his face, he longed for her solace and tears ran down his cheeks.

As Maya awoke from the sleep that healing Kalas had induced, she found herself fully dressed on the bed, candles burning low, her body still gripped by exhaustion. Yet as her senses returned, all tiredness disappeared in a heartbeat at the realisation that she'd no idea what had followed the enemy champions defeat.

She leapt up in a panic, hurrying from her room to see Yana stumbling along the passage, blood on her arms and clothes, and ran to lend support. She was torn between staying to help or finding Taran, but Yana's obvious need kept her there.

Yana's room was a few doors away, so Maya helped her inside, guiding her to a chair in the corner. She then took a large bowl of water and cloth from a table and knelt down, cleaning the blood from her hands and face.

'Tell me what happened,' Maya pressed, trying to keep calm. 'Do you know where Taran is?'

Yana's face was tired, but she still pulled a smile. 'What you're really interested in is; whether Taran's safe. Well, he is. He was lightly injured as was almost everyone who defended the wall today, but I bound his wounds, and he's fine. However, we lost over seventy men today, and so many more are horribly injured.'

Yana shook as the horrors of the day appeared to momentarily overwhelm her.

Despite wanting to run from the room to find Taran, Maya stayed, waiting for Yana to settle. She gave her water as well as some dried food that was in the room.

'After you healed Kalas,' Yana continued, 'Daleth's army attacked. I'm not sure if they fully committed, but even so, they almost broke through. If it wasn't for Taran and Rakan rallying the men, I think they would have succeeded.

'Kalas returned earlier to relieve Taran, so I thought Taran would be here already. Now, go and find him,' Yana instructed. 'I'll be fine,' and with that, she began to strip off her bloodied clothes.

Maya rose to her feet and hurried from the room. She headed toward the keep entrance but had barely got underway when she turned a corner, coming face to face with Taran.

If Yana had been splashed in blood, then Taran had been doused in it. He was literally covered in gore, and Maya's hand went to her mouth. In stark contrast to his bloodied armour and face, his arms were wrapped in pristine white bandages, and Maya ran to hold him.

Taran raised his hands. 'Wait,' he said, as he backed away from Maya's advance. 'Let me clean up and get rid of this foulness first,' and they walked to their room in silence, Maya's anxious gaze upon him every step of the way.

Upon entering, Taran began to remove his armour.

Maya stayed his hand. 'Let me,' she instructed, and unbuckled the straps and cords that held it in place. Piece by piece, she hung it upon the armour rack in the corner of their room. Next, she took off his clothes, looking with concern at his body. While the bandages on his arms hid whatever wounds lay beneath, everywhere else was covered in a patchwork of bruises. His armour had deflected many blows, but they'd hurt him nonetheless. 'Lay down, so I can heal you,' she said, raising her hands.

Taran stepped away. 'No,' he said softly.

Maya's eyes shone. 'But you're hurt. Look!' and she nodded at the silvered mirror in the room.

Taran did as instructed, and indeed his body looked as bad as it felt, but he laughed it off. 'My princess. I thought you were attracted to more than just my body,' and he winked, but then became serious again. 'My injuries are light. These bandages just hide shallow cuts, and the bruises will fade given a few days. The cost of healing these is not worth you paying. Save your gift for when I need it.'

'Oh, and how am I supposed to know when that is when you're too proud to ask me?' Maya retorted, hands resting on her hips, eyebrows arched in exasperation.

Taran sighed. 'You'll know because I won't be in a position to ask for anything. Now, let me wash.'

Maya helped before she bade him sit and went to get clean water. On her return, she rinsed and dried his hair before laying out some clean clothing. As he dressed, she wiped the worst of the foulness from his armour.

Maya smiled as Taran got into bed. 'I know you need to rest, but tell me of your day and where you've been. Yana thought you'd have returned some time ago.'

Taran paused, thinking of the day, and how when he'd thought it couldn't get any worse, he'd had to look into the mind of a daemon. He shook his head. 'Would you mind if I don't? I just need to relax and sleep, and my tale would bring us nothing but nightmares.'

Maya measured the pain in Taran's voice. 'Of course. So, let me help you relax. Lay face down.' After Taran rolled onto his stomach, she knelt astride him and set to work massaging his back, her hands at times soft, then firm. Taran relaxed under her attention. Yet every time he twitched, edging into sleep, he awoke with a gasp.

After several times Maya leant forward. 'What keeps you awake when you're so exhausted?'

Taran moaned. 'I can't stop remembering,' he said. 'I lost count of those I killed and saw killed beside me. The screams and cries become so vivid as soon as I start to fall asleep. I want to dream of you, not that.'

Maya's hands continued their kneading as she considered his plight. Then she lay alongside him. 'I have an idea. Look into my mind. Share my thoughts as you try to sleep.'

Taran gazed at Maya as she stroked his hair, doing as he was told, and his breathing slowly settled, warmth flowing through him. Maya was thinking of her spirit journey with Astren. As he immersed himself in her memories, she flew over mountains and valleys, across forests and rivers, desert and dunes. As he relived her trip, he found himself at the forefront of her every thought. Each time she saw something new and beautiful, he felt her desire to share it with him, to create memories that would last them a lifetime. With such soul-warming thoughts in his head, he fell at last into a peaceful sleep.

Maya relaxed as Taran's breathing deepened, and he started snoring softly. She moved closer, wanting and needing his warm body against hers.

As her fingers caressed his back, she reached for her gift. Taran wouldn't be happy, but she loved him too much to allow him to suffer. As she took away his injuries, aches and pains, sleep overtook her as well.

Neither of them was aware when Yana opened the door to their room, looking at them both as they lay fast asleep in the gentle light of the candle and Maya's glow.

Yana stood there for a moment before closing the door and returning to her room, smiling. Her dreams were always good, she thought, for however much horror she saw, it would forever be eclipsed by one thing, one thought, one man. Taran.

Chapter VIII

'You'd better take that disapproving look off of your face when you talk to me, and remember exactly who it is you're talking to,' Tristan snapped.

Astren bowed his head quickly, cursing himself. 'I apologise,' Astren spluttered, trying to make amends. 'I thought saving the wounded would be more important than saving the wine stores.'

Tristan snorted dismissively. 'Our men won't fight with the strength born of desperation if they know they'll be taken from here the moment they get a flesh wound. Now, we have more important matters to attend to first.'

'We could only take half the wine …' Astren began to press.

'Are you not listening?' roared Tristan, his face turning red.

Astren kept his head lowered in deference.

'Good,' said Tristan, his voice calming slightly. 'Galain,' he called, and the sergeant of engineers came in. 'Pour us drinks and then leave,' Tristan ordered, and sat back in his chair, enjoying the moment.

'It's a good thing you've served me well of late, Astren. I swear you test my patience sometimes. Just don't think you're irreplaceable, remember your place and don't let this happen again. Now, back to the business at hand.

'I want a full report in the morning as to whether the Eyre and the desert tribes are ready to leave. Henceforth, ensure you communicate with their leaders every night, ensuring they make all haste. I also want you to ensure Freeguard is ready for my arrival, and the palace there is at my disposal.'

'Yes, my king,' Astren agreed.

'Now, to a more delicate matter,' advised Tristan. 'Amongst the wine and trinkets that I wish to take from this godforsaken place, I want you to use that sharp mind of yours to find a way to have one more item of value accompany me. This acquisition is to remain strictly between you and I, and if you don't succeed in this, be assured your place here at the fortress will be permanent.'

Astren's stomach flipped. He leaned forward, eager to understand what needed to be done.

Tristan's eyes gleamed. 'I want you to find a way to have the Lady Maya come with me when I leave.'

Astren couldn't believe his ears. Tristan had made it sound so matter of fact that for a moment he thought it was a joke, and he had to quickly swallow the laugh that wanted to burst forth. 'She won't come,' he replied, shock in his voice. 'There's no way she'll leave Taran. You've seen what those two have. Please tell me you aren't serious.'

Tristan's face went red, but then white as if all the blood had left his body. When he spoke, it was quietly and with a menace that made Astren shiver.

'Those who stay behind here will in all likelihood die.' Tristan said softly. 'I value wealth more than your life or any others, just like a true King of the Freestates should. Maya has worth beyond anything I've ever known, and I'll not risk her loss by leaving her here when I depart.'

Astren remembered what he'd thought about Taran's love for Maya. A love to live for, a love to die for, but one to murder and kill for. 'If Taran finds out what you're planning to do, he'll likely try to kill you,' Astren whispered, afraid of his own words.

'Then best he doesn't find out for your sake and mine. He'll likely meet his maker here anyway. Your task is to ensure she comes of her own volition, so no suspicion falls upon me. If you succeed, I swear by the gods of greed, you'll never want for another thing in your life. Find a way, and name your price! Now, leave me be. It's late, and I need to sleep, and you have errands to run.'

Astren left the chamber to find Galain hovering outside. He felt scorn for Galain, who was becoming a bootlicking sycophant, but then realised as he walked past, that he was hardly better. Damn it, he cursed to himself. Maya made him want to be a better man, a selfless man, but then he remembered Tristan's promise. He could name his price! He was a Freestates man, born and raised, and this was how the kingdom was built. All he had to do was find a way to make this happen, then all of his dreams would be answered. Time was a great healer, and both Taran and Maya were still young and would find others, should either survive.

Astren felt any disappointment and guilt slowly vanish as he walked down the steps. One day soon, he'd be truly wealthy, and the rich could afford to never feel guilt.

Kalas felt sadness grip his heart as he walked along the dark corridors toward where Alano was held captive. It was early, before dawn, and events of the day before played through his mind.

He'd awoken from the healing sleep Maya's gift had induced and rushed straight to the walls to find the enemy beaten back. Rakan and Taran were there amongst the soldiers, praising them, filling them with pride and hope to offset the horror.

Tristan hadn't been visible, and Kalas had felt disappointed that he'd sworn an oath to serve one who was falling short of his expectations of a king. Tristan's weakness of character was showing even more now that the battle had been joined.

He'd approached Taran, and requested help in saving his old friend. Without hesitation, Taran had agreed and returned with Kalas into the depths of the keep. Alano was chained in a cell, and Taran had gone in alone, only to return a short time later, pale-faced and shaking.

Taking Kalas' shoulder for support, Taran had swallowed hard. What he'd said had wrenched at Kalas' heart. Alano was beyond help, for there was no sign of the soul of his old friend. Taran had, by his shaken visage, conveyed the truth of those words without the need for further explanation.

Kalas hadn't been overly surprised, but he'd allowed his hopes to grow. When he'd faced his old friend below the walls, greeting him in wonder, pleading with him not to fight, the only answers he'd received were promises of death. What followed was an unrelenting attack to achieve that very goal.

The torch on the wall guttered, burning low, not that he was worried, for he could see perfectly well even in the pitch black.

He found himself standing in front of Alano's cell, opened the door without hesitation and walked through into the dimly lit room. Red eyes greeted him, and his heart felt torn with sadness. There sat his sword brother, Alano. His dearest friend, who'd filled the void left by his father and brother after they'd disowned him.

He wanted to release him from the chains, to find out what had happened those fifty years ago and since. To fight by his side and know the joy of true kinship once again.

Yet the daemon had won the battle for Alano's soul.

He stepped forward, untying the thick gag and stepped away, expecting the daemon to rage. However, it said nothing, simply observing him. Kalas shuddered, realising that he looked at a creature that he'd become himself, many times.

In the cell was an empty wooden crate. Kalas upended it and sat down. He stared at his old friend, waiting perhaps for the eyes to clear for a moment. 'You realise, daemon, that by holding Alano's soul captive, you guarantee your death. However, If you release him, let Alano regain control, then his life will be spared, and your existence will continue. Know I speak nothing but the truth.

'You were, no, still are my brother if not by blood then by oath. You were my closest friend for all those years. We could fight against Daleth together. Let's try to redeem our souls for the many heinous deeds we're both guilty of.'

Alano's head tilted to one side, and that rasping voice spoke. 'The Alano you knew is now but a memory. You talk of redemption; you speak of telling the truth. Yet you're beyond one and choose when to speak the other when it suits you.'

Kalas leaned forward, encouraged despite the words. 'My redemption will come when Daleth is dead, and yours could too.' 'This is my oath, and was yours once. What happened to that oath? Why did you serve him?'

The daemon smiled, yet it was twisted, horrible and split Alano's face into a caricature of what it should look like. 'The oath you speak of belonged to your old friend, and indeed he fought for fifty years to fulfil it. But I also made an oath, to Daleth, to fight and kill for him in return for my existence when we lay dying at his feet, not just once, but twice. A daemonic oath is utterly binding, which is more than can be said for a mortal's.

'So I stopped Alano from killing Daleth more times than I can remember. Now this form is entirely mine, I've no wish to give it back. Nor do I think the Alano you knew is in any fit state to take it.

'But you haven't answered my challenge about truth,' the daemon added.

'I spoke the truth about freeing you and fulfilling my oath to kill Daleth,' Kalas answered.

The daemon laughed. 'One truth does not make an honest man. The unspoken truth is that my brother resides within you, and I would not be surprised if all your friends believe he's still gone. Taran told me as much when he sat before me, trying to tell Alano he could be saved, just like you. Taran believed in what he said, yet despite this, I feel the presence of my kin within you.

'I felt it when we fought, and I feel it now. What would your friends do if they knew of your secret? Would they continue to trust you or cast you out, maybe even seek to kill you for fear that you might become like me?' The daemon laughed as Kalas' eyes narrowed. 'Fear not, even if I'm bound by oath to kill you, I'd have it by my hand and will not share your secret,' assured the daemon. 'You see before you a bloodthirsty creature, but as I look at you, I see a consummate reaper of souls who has taken more lives than I ever will.'

Kalas stood. 'You might wish to reconsider your position, daemon. Tristan will never allow Daleth or his forces to free you, nor can you escape. Your choices are simple; give up your hold on Alano, or find an early death by my hand!'

Frustrated, Kalas stalked from the room, bolting the door behind him.

As he walked down the corridor, it took all of his iron will to stop the tears. 'Why?' he asked his own daemon. 'Why would he rather die, than give up his hold, and why were you so quiet? I'd have thought you would be screaming for me to release him.'

The voice of the daemon was subdued. 'Like you, we're not oath breakers. My brother made a vow to serve, and it's not something he can break. He cannot give up control to Alano.'

'So, why are you ... sad?' Kalas questioned, wondering if he'd chosen the right question.

'I'm sad because I fear we have no choice but to kill him. When we do, we both lose a long lost brother. If we don't, he'll endeavour to kill us for the rest of his days,' the daemon answered quietly.

Kalas' heart, which had ached before, now felt like stone. 'After all these years, I find him, save him, and now I have to kill him.'

'Yes,' said the daemon. 'We are cursed, both you and I,' and there was no mockery in the play of words, for it was nothing but the truth.

Kalas picked up his pace; he was late to the wall.

Battle would shortly begin, and he felt cold inside, for he knew Alano's daemon had been right.

He was indeed a consummate reaper of souls.

'Should I kill him?' Drizt asked, as a rider came forward, a banner of truce rippling in the breeze.

Long shadows filled the pass as the sun rose, and the wall was manned in anticipation of an imminent assault. Yet the formations of enemy troops sat just out of range of the fortress' catapults, offering no threat. From their ranks, a rock of a man rode forth under the watchful eye of Daleth, who stood by the blackened siege engine in the middle of the pass.

'If it were Daleth coming forward, I'd wholeheartedly agree, but as it's only one of his minions, maybe we could hear what he has to say instead,' Taran replied.

'Mark my words,' Rakan interjected. 'Whatever he has to say, we won't want to hear it. If you don't want to kill him, then warn him off with an arrow past his ear, but better to keep him well away. Actually better to kill him.'

Taran turned to Tristan as Kalas was yet to be seen. 'What would you have us do?' he asked. 'Send him on his way, kill him, or let him approach?'

Tristan gazed at the rider. 'Our lord commander should be making that decision. He should be here, dammit.' Tristan drummed his fingertips on the battlement.

Taran waited patiently, watching as the rider came ever closer. The horse tossed its head, the smell of blood making it wary. The enemy bodies had been cleared to the side of the pass during the night, and except for the rocks throw by Galain's catapults, the rider's passage was unhindered.

'Gah, he's almost at the walls. Let him address us. What harm can it do?' Tristan decided.

Rakan shook his head in disgust at his advice being ignored but held his tongue as the rider pulled on his reins.

The messenger dipped his head to Tristan and removed his helm to be better heard. 'My name is Grisen,' he called. 'I am the head of Daleth's bodyguard, and my tongue speaks his will. Today our attack begins in earnest, and many of you will die, hundreds even. Maybe we'll be fortunate, and your defence will crumble this very day, and every one of you will be slaughtered.'

Even though Grisen looked at Tristan and Taran, every man on the walls heard the words and intent.

Rakan couldn't hold himself any longer. 'Or maybe we'll die of old age listening to a windbag like you,' he shouted down.

Grisen shielded his eyes against the rising sun with his hand, staring hard before answering. 'I see you for who you are, Rakan, the deserter. We all know your face and be sure you're marked, but I'm not here to talk to you, but to deliver a message to all the soldiers in your fortress.

'You need not die today, nor tomorrow,' he shouted, and turned, sweeping his arm back behind him. 'My king is willing to be magnanimous. He will allow you three days of rest, to bury your dead of yesterday, to allow you to live without fear of injury or death, and to have three more nights of dreaming of your wives and children.

'What does my king ask for in return for the hundreds of lives he is willing to spare these three days? My king asks for just one life, that of our captured champion. Furthermore, my king promises our champion will no longer participate in the assault in case you fear the consequences of him being unleashed upon you.'

'I told you not to let him speak,' growled Rakan, as the men along the walls looked across expectantly toward Tristan, hope bright in their eyes as the chance to avoid death was waved in front of them by the rider's voice.

'Dammit,' Tristan bemoaned, realising how clever Daleth had been with the choice of words his messenger had delivered. He turned to Taran. 'So, commander, what would you suggest? His offer sounds genuine, and we've nothing to lose and everything to gain. Each day we hold brings our allies closer. I say we accept his offer.'

Taran thought carefully. 'Alano is almost as deadly as Kalas. Yet playing for time is everything, so maybe we should consider it.'

'Maybe if he's willing to give us three days, perhaps he'll give us a week?' suggested Tristan.

Taran leaned over the edge, looking at the rider, reading into his thoughts and saw the deceit there. This man was gifted, of that, there was no doubt. His words carried the ring of truth, but as he looked into his thoughts, he saw the disguise. Somehow this man's gift was to be believed, to tell falsehoods and yet for them to sound genuine. He looked back at Tristan. 'His thoughts betray him. We could ask for up to a week, and the rider below would agree, yet the moment Alano is in their hands Daleth has no intention of honouring the agreement. The time for death is here. There's no escaping it any longer.'

'I don't believe it,' argued Tristan. 'I can tell he's speaking the truth.'

Taran leaned over the parapet. 'Tell me, Grisen. Will you give us till the day's end to give you our answer?'

Grisen looked up. 'Well, well,' he laughed. 'It seems that deserting to the Freestates has its benefits. From what, a corporal to a commander? It seems we overlooked your talent, or perhaps I should say gift? Either way, let me assure you, your face is also known. There will be no place you can hide either come the time. But in answer to your question, my king demands the answer now. So, what message would you have me give?'

'We should accept this exchange,' Tristan stated, authority strong in his voice.

Taran shook his head. 'Rakan had it right all along, let us be the ones to send Daleth a message.' He nodded to Drizt and leaned over the parapet again. 'Here's our message,' shouted Taran. As Grisen looked up, Drizt stepped forward and loosed an arrow that smashed through his teeth and out the back of his neck. Grisen's hands came up to claw feebly at the shaft before he fell from his horse, which ran away, leaving him kicking in the dust, his blood staining the ground.

Tristan looked horrified. His face paling with anger at his order being disobeyed.

Taran leapt onto the battlements before Tristan could say anything. Along the wall, men watched in shock as their hope of escaping death for the next three days soaked into the dust. 'Men,' he shouted. 'Daleth's messenger spoke falsely, there was to be no truce. Had we returned their champion, they planned to attack anyway. There's no truth out there,' and he gestured toward the enemy forces. 'They're deceit, they're darkness, and they're the stealers of dreams. But we are the candle, the flame, the star in the night sky and a beacon of hope.' He lifted his sword above his head, and it caught the light of the rising sun. 'We might not be the heroes of legend as we stand here today, but by the time this battle is over, we will be the heroes of legend tomorrow!'

The men all around raised their weapons in salute. 'Taran, Taran, Taran,' they chanted.

Tristan turned and stalked from the battlements, his face dour. Not only had Taran ignored his wish, but the men were beginning to idolise the young commander. Taran had a natural way with words that he felt threatened by.

He nodded to a small unit of soldiers chosen to serve as his bodyguard now Drizt and Trom were back commanding their countrymen. They followed closely as he walked toward the keep where there was a safer view of the battle and quick access to horses that were kept ready beyond the rear wall.

He grimaced. The men might worship Taran and even Kalas, and that was fine. They could all die together, thus giving him the time to make good his escape. He'd considered taking Kalas to command the alliance, but something was disconcerting about the man. Better Kalas die here trying to fulfil his vow. The arriving alliance forces would have competent commanders, especially the desert tribesmen.

He saw Maya as he neared the keep steps. It was rare to find her far from Taran's side, and she was hurrying down them with Yana. Here was the perfect opportunity to repay Taran for ignoring an order and the chokehold.

Tristan raised his hand, and they came to a halt. 'Good morning,' he bade, eyes warm, as he turned to Maya. 'I'd have you join me for breakfast, we have much to discuss.'

Maya began to protest, but Tristan held up his hand, and she stopped. 'Your king requests that you join him for breakfast,' Tristan stated firmly and walked up the steps.

'I'll tell Taran you'll join him soon,' he heard Yana say to Maya

Tristan glanced back to ensure Maya was following and saw Yana flash a broad smile. He thought she'd be upset at being excluded, but as he smiled back, there was a look in her eyes that made him wonder if the smile was for him or herself. She looked like a cat that had caught a mouse.

It's a good thing I'm leaving her here too, he thought, and felt a little better as his stomach rumbled and he walked into the shadow of the keep.

This would be an enjoyable breakfast.

Kalas looked over at the dead messenger and raised his eyebrow at Taran enquiringly.

Before Taran could answer, Drizt'z laugh forestalled anything Taran might have said. 'He talked too much. Taran asked me to shut him up, so I did.'

'So, I wonder why our guests aren't attacking?' Kalas mused, looking down the pass to see the mass of heavily armoured foe sitting around. Yet as he watched, the siege engine's throwing arm was being winched down, and he knew what was to come.

He pointed out the activity on the siege engine. 'We need to get three-quarters of our men sheltering behind the wall until we see where they target,' Kalas advised. 'If they're looking to create a breach, they'll aim for the same area, or if they want to cause casualties, we'll see the siege engine shifted after the first shot.'

As Kalas hurried off to the south of the wall shouting at his men, Rakan did the same with the centre.

Taran, before he even got to his section of the wall, projected his orders, and three of every four men began to run to the steps. Kalas' orders made sense. Minimise the losses, keep the men off the wall until needed. He heard a thump, then when something caught his eye, turned to see an enormous piece of masonry spinning end over end toward him. His heart almost stopped as it hit the wall below him, the shock of its impact knocking him off his feet. He lay there for a moment, stunned but grateful to be alive.

A soldier ran over, helping him up. 'No time to be lying down, sir,' the man said cheekily, before hurrying back to his post.

Taran looked along the pass to see the siege engine's arm being cranked down again. He didn't perceive any realignment and knew they'd hit this part of the wall again.

He turned, issuing orders, and the men either side moved thirty paces away from his position. Leaning over the parapet, it was obvious to see where the impact had landed for several of the wall's huge blocks were cracked, even if still whole. Quickly, Taran followed his men further along the wall, putting more distance between himself and the enemy's apparent target. Looking down into the courtyard, he spied Drizt. 'Keep your eyes skyward,' he shouted. 'If they aim higher, you and your archers should be able to reposition in time if you're vigilant.'

Not long after, a dull thump announced another huge rock lifting serenely into the sky, flying slowly at first before hurtling to strike the wall with a sound like thunder.

Even though Taran was now well away from the impact, still the shock travelled up through his legs, and he grabbed the battlements to steady himself.

He had no idea how long the wall would hold firm against such an onslaught, but he'd be happy if the enemy continued with this strategy. While the majority of the men took shelter, casualties would be kept at a minimum. It seemed everyone shared his opinion, for there was no sign of panic or concern amongst the defenders. If there'd been four engines, then it would have been different, but one, whilst dangerous, diminished the feeling of threat considerably.

His eyes followed the next rock as it flew, recognising with consternation that it was not toward the same target. As he watched, it crashed into one of the towers defending the gate, just above the height of the wall. For a moment, nothing much happened as debris flew in all directions, but then the tower seemed to sway before collapsing in a billowing cloud of dust.

Silence fell for a moment as if the very wind itself held its breath, but then the screams started.

The tower had held a dozen of the heavy crossbowmen who were so effective in killing the armoured assault troops, and Taran thought for a moment that the screams came from them. Yet, as the dust cloud slowly cleared, he saw the tower had collapsed inwards, down upon the men waiting in the lee of the wall for cover.

He saw movement in the piles of rubble and ran down the nearest steps calling for help. He turned to look for the healers to order them to assist, but they were already on the move, Yana leading them forward as other men gathered around. Taran felt nauseous. There was no good way to die in a battle, but at least dying with your sword in hand, facing an opponent, gave you a chance based on skill.

For the next few minutes, he heaved the rubble to one side, helping to pull bloodied, broken, screaming soldiers free. It was backbreaking work, and it was only when the pieces of rubble got too big to move, and the screams had stopped did Taran stand back, ordering the others to do the same.

As he took a brief respite, stretching his aching limbs, he saw Rakan and Kalas staring in consternation and opened his mind to them both. 'Do you think that was just luck, or were they aiming for the tower? Should we order the men out of the others until they launch a ground assault?'

It only took a few moments deliberation for Kalas and Rakan to both agree.

Taran ran tiredly back up the steps to the north end of the wall and looked at the top of the closest tower. A crossbowman leaned between the merlons, looking across at the devastation. Taran quickly projected the order for the man to gather his comrades and to get out as quickly as possible.

Even as he shared this thought, the thump of the siege engine sounded again, and he watched with horror as a large rock flew toward the tower he'd just ordered vacated.

In the courtyard, two dozen garrison soldiers sat almost directly below the tower, and he screamed with his mind for them to scatter.

Tristan's Folly

They leapt to their feet, grabbing their weapons, just as the rock impacted.

Come on, hurry, pleaded Taran in his mind, hoping to see the crossbowmen exit the tower. Tragically, before they could, its fate matched that of the first. It disintegrated as if made of sand.

Taran couldn't believe his eyes. Why were these lofty towers collapsing so quickly? Yet the answer was beneath his fingertips. The crumbling mortar and years of neglect had left the whole fortress in such a weakened state that the towers couldn't withstand a single impact.

The other towers were vacated, and throughout the morning the siege engine turned its attention on them. They didn't succumb straight away, but in time they fell. The enemy's triumphant roar wafted on the breeze at the uncontested destruction, growing stronger, eating away at the morale of the defenders. Once the last, proud tower crumbled, the siege engine ceased its pounding.

Taran saw Kalas waving. He reached out with his gift, opening his thoughts to him and Rakan again.

'They'll be coming soon,' Kalas shared. 'They tested the wall, which held firm, but now the towers are down they'll assault with their heavy infantry again. As soon as we see them prepare, get everyone ready to defend as quickly as you can.'

Taran broke the contact and looked down at the waiting men, rubbing his temples in an unsuccessful attempt to relieve his headache. Communicating in this fashion, especially over distance, required so much concentration, so now he simply yelled down at the soldiers reiterating Kalas' orders.

He spied Drizt with his archers holding station at the foot of the second wall and briefly shared Kalas' thoughts with him.

Drizt waved in response, and in moments the archers were running, crossing the small wooden bridges over the trench to join the garrison soldiers at the base of the wall.

Trom's men came forward too, standing back a little, held in reserve, ready to be called upon in groups of fifty. They'd left their spears at the foot of the second wall and instead bore short swords in addition to their long shields. As the battle continued, they'd rotate in, allowing the garrison soldiers to rest, or if a breach occurred and the enemy gained the wall, they'd step in much earlier.

A horn sounded, and Taran's head whipped around. The enemy infantry were readying themselves. Long, ironwood ladders swayed above them, and he called everyone except the spearmen up to the battlements. He knew without looking that Kalas and Rakan would be doing the same with their sections.

Drizt stood alongside him as the other Eyre archers took position between the merlons while the garrison soldiers stood behind.

Taran turned back to the base of the second wall, locating Galain and his engineers. 'Get ready,' he ordered, and Galain waved back.

Suddenly, there was a mighty roar like thunder which shook the pass as Daleth's heavy assault infantry surged forward. The tops of the ladders had large bulbs of firewood sap attached to them, and they burned fiercely, leaving trails of smoke in the air. The first attack had shown the defenders the effectiveness of this addition. The burning sap acted like glue, releasing an acrid smoke that made the defender's eyes stream. It also made pushing the ladders away extremely difficult due to the heat and adhesion.

Range markers that had been hammered into the pass had been broken down, but the rocks strewn across the pass from the previous day's defence still remained. Just as the enemy troops were about to reach them, Taran turned to Galain. 'Now!' he projected.

The next moment the two catapults shuddered as they launched their load over the defender's heads. They each threw half a dozen rocks about the size of a man's head. As these spread during flight, it was nigh on impossible for the attacking troops to avoid them as they moved in formation.

Taran couldn't help but wince as the stone projectiles hammered into the ranks of the enemy assault infantry, sweeping scores from their feet. Their heavy armour plate couldn't protect them from such devastating impacts, and even after the initial strike, more were knocked down until the rocks came to rest.

It took the catapults quite some time to be cranked back for another throw, but from hereon they would continue blindly without Taran's command until he ordered them to cease.

Now, as the enemy drew closer, the heavy crossbowmen and Drizt's archers joined the fray.

The crossbows' heavy bolts had the power to punch right through the shields and plate armour of the enemy, but without the security of the towers, they only managed two volleys before they had to retreat from the wall.

Drizt's archers, on the other hand, fired arrow after arrow in quick succession. Taran watched in awe as Drizt drew and loosed, drew and loosed; dropping back behind a merlon whilst selecting another arrow, before stepping out and releasing almost in the same motion.

As Taran peered carefully past his raised shield, he saw enemy soldier after soldier drop.

'The trick,' shouted Drizt above the roar of the noise, 'is to aim for the legs. They keep their shields high as they run and their armour is weaker there.'

Despite Drizt's success, his fellow archers were not doing quite so well.

'How is it that you never miss?' Taran yelled.

Drizt flashed a sly smile. 'Truth be told, you and Maya aren't the only gifted ones. But don't tell anyone!' A moment later, yet another enemy soldier dropped to the ground to be trampled by those behind.

The enemy were almost at the wall. Drizt, his archers, and the crossbowmen withdrew, running down the steps toward their positions behind the fire trench. The garrison soldiers raised their shields high as the enemy archers began to harass the defenders until their comrades reached the top of the ladders.

'Steady, men!' Taran shouted, also projecting his thoughts as his eyes passed over the soldiers either side of him. 'They'll be tired when they get to the top. Remember, aim for the hands, arms, or head, not the chest, their plate is too thick. They can't swing their maces if their arms or hands are off.'

With a swoosh, the tops of the ladders swung up, smacking against the wall. One of the soldiers next to Taran lowered his shield, leaning forward, to try and push the ladder away.

'No!' cried Taran, but it was too late. Three arrows hit the man, and while two bounced off his helm and breastplate, the final one took him in the eye, and he fell from the battlements, dead before he hit the ground below.

Another defender took his place, as Taran roared for every man to keep his shield high. The smoke from the burning sap was thick on the air. Taran kept one eye closed as did the other men so that at least one eye wouldn't be streaming when the enemy crested the parapet.

The enemy siege engine resumed its bombardment, shooting high. Fortunately, Drizt, Trom, and their men were far enough back to see the huge boulders coming and were well out of the way when they crashed to the ground.

The fortress' own catapults fired in response, and Taran was pleased to see the rocks crash down into a formation of enemy archers, decimating them.

The sap on the ladders burned out almost at the same time a grey metal helm loomed into view. Taran waited, and as the man looked up, he thrust, his sword passing through the slit in the man's visor, killing him instantly.

Like some mad music growing louder, all along the wall, the clash of steel on steel sounded and Taran briefly looked around, seeing the defence holding firm, the men resolute.

The heavy enemy made slow progress up the ladders and held their heavy shields and maces in one hand to keep the other free for climbing. When they reached the top of the ladder, they were at their most vulnerable as they climbed onto the embrasures which stood roughly the chest height of a grown man.

However, if they made it, they then assumed a height advantage and could deliver crushing blows with their maces. It was extremely dangerous and difficult to defend or strike against these armoured behemoths whilst they were between the merlons. Not dispatching them quickly also allowed the next enemy soldier to make the battlements uncontested.

As Taran's next foe reached the top of the ladder, he was unable to deliver a killing blow, and the enormous warrior was soon standing above him. Instead of fighting at such a disadvantage, he moved away, not only giving the soldier an uncontested leap to the wall but the defending archers an unobstructed shot. With a battle cry, the man jumped down, only to be hit by a crossbow bolt that punched right through his thick chest plate. As he staggered, Taran used the opening to shield-bash him over the rear of the wall.

As the soldier fell screaming to the rocky ground below, Taran stepped forward to sweep up the dead man's fallen mace. It was a terrible weapon, wide flanges around the heavy head. As the next assault troop reached the top of the ladder and began to haul himself up, Taran brought the mace down onto the man's armoured helm. Whereas before his sword had often glanced from the plate, the heavy blow crumpled the metal like a leaf. Blood gushed down the man's breastplate as he fell facedown, twitching. Taran leaned forward, shoving with all his might, and sent the body back over the edge to fall upon his comrades beneath.

Along the wall, the garrison swordsmen were dealing death feeling safer in the knowledge that a crossbowman or archer would directly assist if necessary. The tactic was working ruthlessly and efficiently, and whilst a garrison soldier would fall here and there, any gap was quickly filled by those waiting in reserve.

Taran dispatched a further five enemy soldiers without the need for an archers' assistance, but his arm was beginning to ache from wielding the heavy mace. He stepped back, beckoning for another soldier to take his place, pressing the gory weapon into the man's hand. He wanted to lead by example, yet knew he was crucial for coordinating the defence, and continually engaging in combat wasn't going to allow this. He ran down the steps, heading back to the fire trench, then looked around and gave the command to Trom and his men to rotate onto the wall.

The changeover began almost seamlessly, and some of the exhausted defenders began to disengage to find some respite.

Yana and her healers were on hand, and any injured went to her station near the gate tunnel. Stretcher-bearers were also running backwards and forward taking away those more seriously injured. Taran was disheartened to see an ever-growing line of dead garrison soldiers laid out in the lee of the second wall.

However, the curtain wall was holding, and as Taran looked along its length, he saw Kalas moving behind the defenders, ready to help the moment one was in trouble.

Rakan's central section was doing equally well, and Taran felt relieved, but then several of Trom's soldiers near the gate went down at once. The assault troops pushed outward along the wall, hitting the defending soldiers from the side, creating more space as others clambered over behind them.

'Rakan, to your right!' cried Taran is his mind, and Rakan spun around as the heavily armoured foe bore down on him.

'Drizt,' called Taran, 'focus your fire there,' he yelled, pointing, and sprinted toward the steps leading to the centre of the wall above the gate. He shouted at some resting and lightly injured men to follow him as he rushed up two at a time, watching even as he did, as the wall's defence began to crumble.

If they didn't repulse the enemy quickly, the wall would be lost. Glancing over his shoulder, he realised he was on his own. The men he'd called upon for help were backing away in fear toward the trench and the second wall, sensing impending doom.

He reached the battlements to find less than a dozen men frantically holding back the spreading tide of heavy assault troops.

With no reinforcements coming from below, they weren't going to be enough.

Chapter IX

Daleth smacked his mailed right fist into the palm of his left hand.

'Yes,' he cried, to no one in particular, 'we have them now, see how we gain the walls.' His mood which had been foul since the death of Grisen earlier in the day began to lift. The defenders were about to pay a high price for killing a man under the flag of truce.

Oh, but they were paying dearly now, and the defence of the first wall would soon crumble, and having tasted defeat, the enemy would not hold the second wall for long.

He wished he could be leading the assault, but while that damned Kalas was alive, the risk was too high. He was as confident in his ability as he was brave, but if he came up against Kalas, his dreams and long life would be over in an instant. He could see the man himself, in his silver armour, moving along the south side of the wall. None of the assault troops could find any purchase there whatsoever, falling from that section like heavy rain.

Yet a wall's defence was only as strong as its weakest point, and the centre of the wall above the gate was about to fall. The defenders were falling back as his men pushed outward, and every moment saw more attackers gain the walls. The sheer weight of numbers was starting to tell.

Daleth's eyes widened in glee as the long, mournful sound of a horn calling for a withdrawal was quickly matched by several others, louder and with urgency. Daleth punched the air, yet all of a sudden he stopped in shock, realising it was his own troops who were moving back, climbing from the walls, back down the ladders while those below pulled back along the pass.

'No, no, no!' he shouted, turning to the signaller next to him whose horn was nowhere near his mouth. The man looked back at Daleth and shrugged his shoulders, pale in the face. 'Sound the attack, man,' screamed Daleth, and the next moment the single note rose loud on the air. However, with all the other horns still sounding the withdrawal, it was lost in the noise, just one horn against many.

'What in the nine hells is happening?' screamed Daleth. 'We had them, we bloody had them!'

He looked on in disbelief as the enemy archers took to the walls again. They fired down into the retreating troops who fortunately had the discipline to back away, shields held high. Unfortunately, the damned catapults and their rocks knocked holes in the ranks of his men, shields or no.

'I want the fools who sounded the withdrawal brought to me. I want them here, and I want them here now!' shouted Daleth, his face red.

His usually unflappable bodyguard hurried off, pushing through the ranks of retreating troops as fast as they were able.

'Right,' said Daleth, turning to the crew of the siege engine who were but a few steps away. 'I want you to breach that damned wall,' he commanded. 'You stay here, and you don't stop even when it gets dark. Do you understand me?'

The men almost fell over themselves as they started to crank furiously on the windlass as Daleth gazed down the pass.

This day was a complete loss, but he would still find some enjoyment in it to mitigate his mood. Those fools who'd sounded the withdrawal would be screaming all night, and it would serve as a warning to others.

Failure or incompetence would all inevitably lead to death.

Maya was furious. She'd sat with Tristan the whole morning as he'd eaten food and watered wine that was brought to his chamber.

She felt conflicted. Her whole life she'd feared and respected the authority of the village seer and the laws of the Witch-King. She was used to serving, following orders. Recently though, having escaped, and experienced a taste of independence and a feeling of worth, she now battled with feelings of rebelling against authority.

She'd wanted to be on the wall with Taran, but Tristan had effectively ordered her to stay with him. Tristan was a king, her king, and had offered them sanctuary and a new country to call home. She felt strong, but not strong enough to defy his will, especially as he was trying to be civil and she'd sworn an oath to obey him.

He'd asked about her parents, the growth of her gift, and got her to retell the story of her journey with Taran and Rakan. He'd been very inquisitive, and Maya didn't feel that comfortable answering questions that at times seemed a little personal.

When the rumble of the first tower collapsing had sounded through the chamber, she'd leapt up, exclaiming in dismay at what she could see. Tristan had walked to the balcony and continued talking as he kept a wary eye on the destruction in the background as if it were nothing but a distraction.

Several times she'd tried to excuse herself, but each time Tristan simply ignored the request.

Now, he was talking of Freemantle and the joys of being a noble in the Freestates and how as a lady of the court, she could come to enjoy many privileges should they prevail.

She couldn't think of anything worse than being denied the beauty of a forest in Spring and being expected to wear dresses all day long in the middle of a city. Her jaw ached as she suppressed yet another yawn.

A knock on the door interrupted the one-sided conversation, and Maya looked up. Astren was ushered in bleary-eyed, and she leapt to embrace him. He smiled in surprise at the unexpected warmth and relief on her features, and all sleepiness seemed to fall away as he looked from her to Tristan.

'Astren,' Tristan exclaimed. 'As one close to me wants to leave, another arrives. How fortunate I am to have two such loyal subjects.' He turned to Maya. 'You may go. I look forward to our next meeting.'

Maya's feet barely touched the flagstone floor as she grabbed her bow from where she'd left it at the doorway and sprinted through the keep toward the entrance. Every soldier she passed nodded in respect, but she was in too much of hurry to afford them anything more than a sharp smile as she sped past.

Faster she ran, down the steps and into the courtyard, weaving amongst the soldiers, many of them covered in bloody bandages. She headed toward the curtain wall, aware of the ominous quiet that had replaced the cacophony of noise.

As she ran through the gateway of the second wall, she stopped, shocked by the scene before her. She'd not witnessed the direct aftermath of the first attack as she'd been recovering from the healing of Kalas, but had gathered from Taran how bad it had been.

Now she saw and felt it first hand.

For whatever reason, the fighting had ceased, but that didn't detract from the misery she beheld.

Where once proud towers had stood, there were now piles of rubble. The walls themselves were now streaked as if red paint had been poured over the battlements, yet she knew it wasn't paint.

Piles of dark, armoured bodies lay at the foot of the walls where they'd fallen, and as she watched she saw the Eyre archers moving amongst them, short swords ensuring the enemy were dead as they retrieved any usable arrows or bolts from the bodies.

There were also row upon row of dead soldiers laid out at the base of the second wall. Some white, some green and some brown, yet the blood was red irrespective. Gaping wounds glistened in the sun covered in swarms of flies feasting on the flesh.

A long queue of wounded soldiers waited patiently to be seen, and whilst Maya was desperate to see Taran, she was torn between the plight of the wounded and her own need.

She saw Yana working with the healers and went over to them. Yana looked up blankly as Maya approached but didn't say a word while concentrating on binding a man's leg.

Maya saw three healers pinning another soldier down who was screaming in pain. His face seemed to be hanging off on the left side as they tried to stitch it back on.

'Here, Maya,' Yana said, pushing a satchel full of bandages and salve into her hand. 'Sit with me,'

'Have you seen Taran?' asked Maya.

Yana shook her head as she wrapped a ragged cut on the back of another man's hand. 'I've been too busy.'

There was a loud thump, and men started shouting from atop the wall. As Maya looked up, she saw a distant boulder arching into the sky, heading for the north end of the wall.

The brutal noise it made on impact echoed loudly, and a cloud of mortar dust billowed, knocked loose to be swiftly dispersed by the breeze. If only the cries of the wounded could be so easily carried away.

As the sun moved across the sky, soldier after soldier passed in front of Maya and she lost herself in helping them. She wasn't trained, so she did what she could, applying healing salve, binding cuts, and directed those who needed more serious attention to the other healers.

The enemy siege engine thumped regularly, followed shortly after by the loud crack of impact. Maya soon found herself ignoring it as did everyone else as it became apparent the enemy was trying to make a breach.

From the corner of her eye, she spotted Taran high on the wall alongside Kalas and Rakan. Another soldier sat down in front of her, and she sighed. Today she'd have to be patient, and prioritise others' needs over her own.

So she turned to the man, one of the desert soldiers, gave him a warm smile, and began cleaning his wound. He moaned in pain. 'Tell me of your family and where you were brought up,' she asked, distracting him as she pulled a needle.

His face lit up as he talked of his wife and daughter, the love he felt shining through, banishing the pain he felt.

Maya felt like crying as she began to stitch, for she realised this man's family would probably never see him again. Yet she blinked away the tears and did the best she could.

If he could be strong, then so could she.

'I don't suppose you could tell Daleth's engineers, to turn their siege engine around and drop a rock on his head,' Rakan asked, winking at

Taran. Together with Kalas, they carefully inspected the damaged wall during the time it took the enemy to reload the siege engine.

They stayed low so as not to attract undue attention and out of respect for the danger posed by the enemy ballistae which so far had not been put to use, but which still stood in the pass.

Taran laughed. 'I could, yet I doubt they'd do so. Still, next time in the heat of battle, maybe I'll try for the fun of it.'

Kalas slapped him on the back. 'I might have already said it, but it's worth saying again. If it wasn't for your quick thinking, we'd have lost this wall, and I've a feeling we'd have been sorely pressed to have got many back to the second. It would've been a disaster. You've a cool head to have seen such a small opportunity, and your mind saved the day. I fear none of our skills with weapons would have sufficed.'

'It was a plan born of desperation and self-preservation,' admitted Taran. 'I'm just grateful some of their signallers were close enough to reach into their minds, and for them to be confused enough to sound the withdrawal. After that, it was just luck that others took up the call.'

'Don't belittle your actions,' responded Kalas. 'Your mind seized upon the idea, and you acted. Even If I'd been in your boots a hundred times, I doubt I would've seen that opportunity even once.'

'We've lost nearly two hundred of our men, either dead or unable to fight, yet I think we've killed about a thousand of their heavy infantry,' said Rakan, breaking into the conversation. 'Now, I have to raise the question. Is it even worth trying to hold the first wall anymore? The towers are down, and it's longer and lower than wall two. If we keep losing men like this, it'll be just the three of us left in less than a week.'

Taran kept quiet, ceding to Kalas.

'We hold it as otherwise we lose the catapults.' Kalas determined. 'We won't lose so many men tomorrow, and less the day after. Those without skill will die the quickest, and the best of us will live longer while we've the strength to do so.

'Today, when the wall almost fell, it was when Trom's men joined the defence. They're ferocious and skilled but are trained to fight in formation, behind shield and spear, not individually. We'll have them protect the archers and only bring them onto the walls when needed. They won't like it, nor will the other men, but that's how it will be.'

'I'm not sure how much more this wall can take,' Taran observed, as they moved away from the targeted area. 'Some of the blocks are shifting, and many have already cracked.'

'Hah, I'm glad it's your end of the wall then,' laughed Rakan, as they hastened their stride, watching as the siege engine launced another piece of masonry.

Kalas turned to them both. 'They won't be attacking again today,' he said. 'It's too late, but we'll have a noisy night ahead of us. They're determined to breach this wall.

'Taran, I want you to speak with the lightly wounded, raise their morale, and keep them busy. If they're in good spirits, those of sound body will have less to complain about.' Kalas winked behind Taran's back, having spied Maya down below.

'Rakan, you and I will talk with the men on the walls.' Kalas beckoned, turning away.

Taran made his way down the steps. Small groups of exhausted soldiers sat around, and he paused at each, using his gift to greet everyone by name. He praised them all, picking small parts of the battle from each of their minds, retelling them for everyone around to hear.

The tiredness lifted from the soldiers' eyes, to be replaced by pride as they realised that they were victors still. They'd faced the enemy and were still standing.

He approached the lines of wounded, their misery heart-wrenching to see. Using his gift, he took a subtler approach, addressing the men's fears, and realised that his power had evolved as it wasn't just his spoken words that calmed the men. He was now able to distract their minds away from the pain. He might not have Maya's gift to actually heal, but the effect was similar.

To the walking wounded, he gave tasks, forming them into small units. Not only did it make them feel useful, but it further took their thoughts away from the predicament they were in. Idle hands were dangerous, and soon everywhere, a sense of purpose returned.

He caught sight of Maya, sitting next to Yana and several other healers. They were splashed with crimson, as much, if not more than the injured they'd helped care for.

Maya's eyes shone as she spied Taran coming toward her and she leapt to her feet, rushing toward him, then stopped just short, looking at herself covered in blood, and then at Taran in his gory armour. She moved forward, going up on her tiptoes to plant a quick kiss on his lips.

'Do you have any injuries?' she asked, concern evident in her voice as she pulled his shoulder to turn him around.

'Hah,' he laughed, 'none that I'd be prepared to tell you about. For now, if I need help, I'll take an old fashioned bandage.'

'I keep telling her that,' piped up a voice, and Yana came forward to stand next to Maya. 'She needs to stay young, and using her gift unnecessarily won't help that at all. If you need bandaging again, just come to me. I'll look after you.'

Maya looked across at Yana, but saw only kindness in her face, and berated herself for allowing distrust to enter her thoughts. She knew Yana had been interested in Taran before they crossed the mountains. But here, Yana was only offering what she'd given to every other wounded man in the fortress.

Taran smiled. 'Be sure I will Yana. You've both done an incredible service today. I can only imagine you both fought as hard as if you were on the walls yourselves.'

Yana laughed. 'Indeed, I'm shattered, but Maya missed the worse of it, lucky her,' and without saying more, she moved away to talk with the other healers.

Taran looked across at Maya. 'What did she mean by that?' he asked, eyebrow raised.

Maya's face burned red. 'I only got here a short while ago,' she admitted. 'Tristan ordered me to join him for breakfast.'

Taran's eyes narrowed a little, then they relaxed. 'As long as you keep me company for dinner, I'll forgive you. Kalas believes the rest of the day will see a respite as they try to bring the wall down. So, how about we spend the rest of the day romantically?

'We'll start by helping the archers pull arrows from the bodies of the slain. Following that, we can check on the wounded again, ensuring their wounds are bound properly. Finally, as a special treat, we'll help move the dead, so we don't see their blank, accusing eyes every time we pass by.'

Maya shook her head, a smile playing at the corners of her mouth. 'Somehow, you find a way to bring light to the darkest of times.

Whatever we do, however frightening or tragic, it's time I cherish. For without experiencing the bad, how can we truly appreciate the good?'

She took his hand, and the two of them walked toward Drizt's men.

The archers greeted them warmly as they approached, for even in the light of the day, Maya shone at Taran's side. Amongst the many horrors of this siege, the two of them reminded everyone of what they fought to protect ... those they loved.

Yet amongst the warm faces, there was one that was cold. Yana scowled as she cut fresh linen into strips for new bandages, imagining herself at Taran's side with Maya out of the way.

One day, the chance would come, and it might come soon, she just had to be patient. There was now a powerful player confirmed in the game because Tristan was definitely more than just intrigued by Maya.

Yana just had to find a way to ally herself with the king, for there was none more powerful in this game of hearts.

Daleth swirled the wine around his mouth, the taste smooth and exquisite. He didn't often allow himself such extravagance, but sometimes while he strategized or ruminated, it stimulated his mind as much as his taste buds.

The assault troops had performed very well. Both times they'd been thrown into battle, success had been tantalisingly close. Not only were they well trained, but now they were becoming battle-hardened. He'd met with several survivors early, sharing their pain at the first wall being snatched from their grasp, listening intently to their reports on what they'd seen.

Daleth put his goblet to one side, rose from his chair and stepped out through the tent flaps.

He paused, feeling the anticipation of the many hundreds gathered around, waiting in silence at the justice that would shortly be carried out.

Before him knelt twelve signallers, hands bound behind their backs, faces pale, knowing that their lives hung by a thread. Directly behind them stood a dozen of the assault infantry who'd reached the top of the wall and then survived the withdrawal. They waited, holding their vicious maces, ready to carry out the death sentence on those who knelt before them.

Daleth found it fitting that the fools who'd sounded the withdrawal met their end at the hands of those whose victory they'd stolen.

'So,' said Daleth, and the kneeling men raised their heads. He looked the first one in the eye. 'Tell me, why did you sound the withdrawal? Who gave the order?'

The man shook his head, lowering it in shame. 'My king,' he replied. 'I've asked myself this a hundred times. I don't know, I really don't. I heard the order and sounded the withdrawal as instructed. I heard others sounding it too, so I didn't seek to confirm from whence the order came.'

Many of those kneeling repeated a similar story. The only signaller who hadn't sounded the withdrawal, and was currently absent, had been the one standing next to Daleth.

Were there traitors or sympathisers in the ranks who'd given these orders? Yet none of those before him said they could remember any specific man giving them instruction when he pressed them on it.

He needed signallers, but he also needed to set an example.

Daleth raised his voice so all those watching could hear his decision. 'The lives of many of our brothers were needlessly lost today when the first wall was within our grasp. The blame for this rests squarely on the shoulders of those kneeling before us. Such incompetence has no place in our army.' He nodded to the assault troops, meeting their eyes one at a time. 'You will kill half of those fools before you slowly. I want to hear their screams long into the night.

'Those of you who are spared, think again before you listen to words on the wind. You follow my signaller, no whispers, for his command is an extension of my voice.'

Daleth turned away, and the cries and entreaties of the condemned felt like music to his ears, and he felt energised by their terror. Their quick death would have fed him not at all, but this, this was akin to a feast to go with the wine.

A thump drew his attention. Tomorrow would be different. The siege engine's crew were hard at work, and he was sure the wall would be down by the morning.

Thinking of the gods made him wonder about Alano. Was he still alive, had he been turned somehow, or was he dead?

Daleth sighed. He knew the daemon wouldn't turn. It was loyal to its oath, and it was only ever the man who'd sought to kill him. If Alano wasn't dead already, he would be soon, and perhaps today's defeat had sealed his fate.

As the first screams of the signallers split the twilight air, he grinned.

The last signal they were sending was the cost of failure. He was sure the surrounding troops would hear their last message very clearly indeed.

Maya wrapped her arm around Taran's waist, and they leaned upon each other for support. However light Taran's earlier words had been, she'd found the rest of the day exhausting and horrific.

The piles of bodies at the base of the first wall had needed to be cleared away. Those from Daleth's army had their weapons stripped to replace those of the defenders that were notched and dulled. Any arrows and bolts were pulled free wherever possible, and the corpses were then carried up the steps, and tossed back over the wall from whence they'd come.

The defenders who'd been slain were afforded more respect. Whilst any weapons and armour were still removed, they were carefully laid at the base of the second wall, and the line of those dead had been long.

She'd worked ceaselessly by Taran's side, and neither she nor Taran had the strength or desire to talk while undertaking this gruesome task.

Beyond the walls, the enemy soldiers did much the same, but for them, it was more practical. They cleared the pass, stripping the bodies of the slain before piling the corpses against the mountainsides to ensure that subsequent attacks were unhindered.

Maya looked around. Torches had been lit along the walls as the sun began to disappear below the horizon. With everything that needed to be done attended to, by unspoken consensus, everyone began to gather before the line of the dead. Soil from beyond the pass had been brought in on hand carts by Trom's spearmen to cover the bodies, but it hadn't been enough. Now, it was as if the dead were attempting to rise again from their shallow graves.

Maya walked beside Taran as they moved amongst the mourners. Taran used his gift, speaking to the men softly, sometimes individually, sometimes in small groups, getting them to share the good memories. Maya watched as the abject sorrow on their faces was replaced with one of bittersweet remembrance.

'It seems my gift is evolving,' Taran spoke softly as they moved back, giving those praying some space. Not only did I influence the enemy horn blowers to sound the withdrawal, but I seem to be able to take away some of the sadness of these men. Although I fear it won't last long. The sight of the deceased will bring it back.'

Maya nodded. While the bodies lay partially in the open, the sun, heat, and flies would soon make bloated monstrosities of those who earlier that morning had spoken with their friends as they broke fast.

The flickering light of the torch flames reflected off faces lowered in silent prayer, most of which were streaked in tears, all of which showed sorrow. Trom and his men knelt, praying silently, even the Eyre archers were sombre.

Maya felt a tugging at the corners of her mind and flicked a glance at Taran, but it wasn't him. As she focussed inwards, her gift suddenly swelled, almost frightening in its intensity, taking on a life of its own, demanding to be released.

Everyone's heads were bowed, eyes closed in thought and prayer as her gift radiated with such force that it felt as if her body were expanding.

She felt Taran's hand tighten around her own, in surprise or support, she didn't know, but she continued to let her gift flow freely, trusting in its purity. Before her eyes, the scene transformed.

The dead soldiers had been laid on stony ground, at the base of the second wall, but despite this harsh environment, the soil of their makeshift graves spread upon them responded. Grass began to grow. It was long, lush, of a bright green so vibrant that it shone with new life even in the fading light. Blue flowers appeared, and then small saplings began to grow, roots pushing into the stony ground.

Within minutes, what had been a morbid, scene of despair had been utterly transformed. A beautiful shrine of nature now stood above the fallen, blossom from the young trees falling to create a soft blanket upon those now hidden beneath.

The flow of the gift and Maya's light diminished, and everyone began to notice what had been created.

A garrison soldier, tears running unchecked down his cheeks came to stand in front of Maya. 'Thank you,' he sobbed, and stood, his head bowed, silently, waiting.

Maya turned to look at Taran, a questioning look to her eyes.

Taran briefly searched the man's thoughts and several others as all the soldiers present began to line up behind this one silent soldier. 'They want your blessing,' he projected silently. 'Many here, see you as a goddess of life.'

'But I'm no such thing,' Maya contested, looking back and forth between Taran and the growing line of soldiers.

'I don't think that it matters to them,' Taran reassured her. 'You've helped their friends find peace in death, and now they need you to help find some peace in life, whilst it still remains.'

Maya reached out, laying her hand on the man's shoulder, and his eyes were bright with gratitude before he walked on, only for the next man to step forward.

'I feel like a fraud,' Maya thought, but Taran's hand squeezed hers firmly.

'No, my love,' he projected softly. 'You're a goddess of life for me too, for without you by my side, I'd no longer wish to live.'

Maya looked over and smiled. 'Then let us never be parted, for I feel the same,' she thought, and turned back to the next soldier who stood before her.

It was going to be a long night.

Chapter X

Kalas stood in the dimly lit corridor, waiting patiently outside of Alano's cell. The darkness wrapped around him like a blanket, and he found it comforting. He didn't question why, for surely that was how it had always been.

Taran was inside trying to work his gift upon Alano, to rid him of the daemon's control, acceding to Kalas' earlier request.

The door to the cell finally opened, and Kalas pushed himself away from the wall, recognising the failure etched on Taran's face.

'Is there any chance you'll succeed if you keep trying?' Kalas asked.

Taran shook his head slowly. 'Each time I try, I'm rebuffed with ever-increasing force. To glimpse the thoughts of that beast is to see and feel things that threaten sanity.

'While I believe your friend's soul is still alive, I've no doubt this daemon has no intention of letting it go, even at the cost of its own demise. It seems that its oath fully binds him, and even if it wanted to break it, which I doubt, it wouldn't be able to.'

Kalas' face was grim. 'I'll tell Tristan of our failure, and will follow his command. Alano will have to be put to the sword. I cannot tell you how deep, killing him will hurt me.' Kalas turned and walked away, head bowed, expecting Taran to follow.

Taran paused, pondering, standing in the dim corridor, then felt compelled to try a final time. He walked back into the cell to find those red eyes gazing at him, and he sat down, staring steadily back.

'Kalas would have you live,' said Taran. He spoke aloud, not trying to find his way through the daemon's thoughts as it was the daemon who had to make a choice.

'I know you've made clear your resolve, but soon, perhaps today or tomorrow, you'll be executed. If you don't agree to some kind of compromise, then Kalas has told me that without Alano's living body, you'll perish.'

The daemon, a smile creasing its lips, sat still and silent.

Taran got up to leave, and as he turned away, the daemon laughed. It was a disgusting noise, a gurgle, like someone drowning in their own blood. Taran looked back.

'Whilst I don't fear death like I once used to,' said Taran, 'I know at the end I would choose life if it were possible. So why is it you laugh when yours is soon to be extinguished?'

That twisted face leered and its voice dripped malice. 'Do you know that if you're gifted, then you're also cursed?'

Taran nodded tiredly. 'I've heard this before. Don't waste your time trying to unsettle me, this isn't about me, this is about you and your impending death.'

Alano's head twisted violently, from side to side. 'You know only the beginning of it, for if the gifted are cursed, would it not stand to reason, that the cursed are also gifted?

'So, let me tell you this, Taran thought-stealer. While you merged with my mind, I glimpsed your future.

'You think you should choose life because you have everything to lose? From what I've foreseen, you should seek a quick death on the battlefield instead. I swear on my blackened soul that if you live, you will die from the inside out!'

'Very insightful,' snarled Taran. 'I'll have forgotten your words by the time I help Kalas bury you.'

He left the cell, slamming the door shut. He was angry for the daemon had got the better of him again. Suddenly he shivered, and quickened his pace.

The sun would soon be up, and he wanted to be on the walls to meet it so that its warmth would banish the chill seeping through his veins.

Maya looked along the battlements as she sheltered behind a merlon.

The garrison soldiers fully manned the wall, kneeling down, waiting for the archers to start the day's killing.

Taran flashed her a smile, and she returned it, but he was sharing his thoughts, and there was no happiness in his mind, for there was none to be found. Not now.

Something strange caught her eye. It was as if the wall was covered in jumping insects. As she peered closer, she saw small grains of dust and stone dancing on the blocks. Thousands of feet pounding along the pass managed to disturb them, even at such a distance.

'Be safe, my love,' she heard in her mind, and then Taran stood, shining in his armour. He raised his sword, waving it above his head as he drew breath and then pointed it at the enemy horde. 'Archers, make ready!' he shouted, his voice strong, rising above the roar of the approaching.

Maya stood, and in one seamless motion, reached for her quiver, picked an arrow, nocked it to the string, and drew, aiming and ready to shoot. All along the wall, the other archers did the same. She knew Taran would be projecting his thoughts to Rakan and Kalas further down the wall so that the archers' first volley was coordinated. He might be second in command, but it was on his order that the day's slaughter would begin.

Drizt stood on the other side of Taran, a signal arrow ready, letting off a bright green flame.

Maya felt her insides quiver as she looked upon the horde of men streaming down the narrow pass. The first rank held body length shields, making them difficult targets, but the one behind carried the iron-wood ladders, resin burning, letting off trails of smoke. These would be the first target.

Maya didn't see or hear Taran give the order to Drizt, but the next moment his arrow flew arcing through the air. A memory of a shooting star Maya had once seen flash across the night sky in her youth sprang to mind, but now wasn't the time for nostalgia. She'd already picked her target and exhaled softly as she released the arrow, knowing even as she did that it would find its mark. The ladder bearer she'd tracked was heavily armoured, but her arrow was one of Drizt's new design, and its heavy head punched through the man's visor, killing him instantly.

Her second arrow was already mid-flight when she registered this. Unfortunately, this time it glanced off the rungs of the ladder in front of her intended target. Larger gaps appeared in the enemy ranks as the fortress catapults launched their rocks over the wall. Heavily armoured or not, whosoever those rocks hit, never rose again.

All along the enemy front ranks, men fell or stumbled. When a ladder bearer went down, the cohesion diminished as others struggled to raise the fallen ladder. Every time this happened, the archers took advantage. Yet the enemy was closing the distance, unstoppable like the tide, and Taran cried out the order for the archers to pull back. It was taken up along the wall, and after releasing a final arrow, Maya followed Drizt down the steps. She hoped to meet Taran's gaze, but he was too focused on the enemy and communicating with Rakan and Kalas.

Maya ran alongside Drizt, back toward the bridges over the fire trench.

'That was an incredible first shot,' Drizt said admiringly as they ran across, their boots thumping loudly on the wooden boards.

Maya shook her bow in acknowledgement, and they ran to Trom's men, who stood waiting, long shields ready to protect them. As soon as the attackers reached the tops of the ladders, the enemy archers would shoot arrows high over the walls, to try and kill the Eyre archers and catapult crews.

The catapults at either end of the wall thumped again, and Maya moved behind one of the desert spearmen who bowed his head briefly before she stood behind him. On the man's back, were several quivers full of arrows. Maya drew one, nocking it to the string and, along with the other archers, shot high over the wall, knowing that even without being aimed, the arrow would find a target.

She managed to loose half a dozen arrows when suddenly her shield-bearer and others shouted a warning. She knelt down as he stood over her, hearing several thuds as enemy arrows struck his shield.

'Clear!' he shouted.

Maya rose and released two more arrows, before ducking back into cover as the enemy archers increased their rate of fire. For a while she could do nothing as arrows fell around her like hail, rattling as they hit the ground, or thudding into the shields of the defenders.

She heard cries as several spearmen and archers fell when a piece of masonry thrown by the enemy siege engine shattered nearby. The shards of stone that hissed through the air on impact were as deadly as any arrow.

The sound of steel upon steel echoed from the walls as the enemy infantry made it to the battlements. Despite the risk, she and the other archers now continued to stand, trusting entirely to their shield bearers to block incoming arrows.

Maya kept her eyes on Taran, and the two men either side of him, holding an arrow drawn. Then as soon as an enemy scrambled onto the wall, she released smoothly, watching him get spun around, not just by her arrow, but by two others as well.

Draw and release, draw and release. She lost count of how many enemies toppled from the wall, but defenders were falling as well, and there weren't as many reserves to take their place.

'We must fall back,' shouted Drizt. 'Trom's men are needed to reinforce the defence.'

Maya's shield-bearer shrugged off the quivers he was carrying, and with an apologetic glance over his shoulder, ran forward in response to the commands of Trom, who was directing his men up the steps, to assist and relieve the tiring defenders.

Maya and the other archers withdrew, the blossom raining from the trees at the base of the second wall swirling around them. It was surreal, the beauty of nature at their back, and the hideousness of the butchery in front. She waited for her next target to present itself and released, watching her arrow glance off his helm. She had missed a kill, but the enemy arrows were also falling short of their new position. Unfortunately, being further back meant they were less effective, and the fighting on the battlements became more contested.

Trom's men reached the walls and replaced some of the exhausted garrison soldiers who rotated off, bloodied and gasping for breath.

Yana and her healers ran to and fro, treating those with minor wounds, while stretcher-bearers holding shields above their heads took the more seriously wounded through the gate tunnel back toward the keep. They returned with bloodied stretchers, carrying water to refresh those defenders who were managing to grab a short respite.

Maya pulled the last arrow from the quiver at her feet, shot, and missed her target, the arrow sailing over the wall. Now she only had ten left in the quiver on her back. She noticed that the other archers were picking their own shots far more carefully now that they were running out of arrows too.

Several bodies fell to the left of Taran in quick succession, and Maya saw dark armoured troops start to scramble over the parapet, pushing outward, trying to create more space for their brothers climbing up the ladders behind.

Maya could see things were about to go from bad to worse.

'Drizt,' she shouted, breaking into a sprint as she headed for the wooden bridge, pounding back across it. Arrows fell around her, but not as densely as before as the enemy archers' quivers also emptied, but they were still a deadly threat.

'Get closer to the wall. We'll be inside their arc,' shouted Drizt as he caught up with another fifty of his men following close behind.

Sure enough, the enemy arrows began to fall behind them as they ran closer, but not before several found their mark, and bodies littered the ground behind them.

Garrison soldiers were frantically pushing up the steps, responding to the threat, trying to add weight to the defence. However, the top of the wall was only wide enough for three armoured men, and they couldn't bring enough force to bear to clear it. However, the archers could now support them directly from below and helped turn the tide.

From this close below the wall, Maya, Drizt, and the other archers couldn't miss. The assault infantries heavy plate armour was designed to deflect attacks from in front or the side, but not beneath; so the arrows found their mark in the groin or armpit, punching through the light chainmail there instead.

The other Eyre archers emulated their tactic along the wall, rushing forward, and suddenly any enemy who reached the battlements were swept away before they could do much harm. But only while the archers had arrows.

Maya reached over her shoulder, and her hand came away empty, her supply now exhausted.

Once again, the defenders struggled without the additional support coming from below, and the bodies falling from the wall were of friend and foe alike.

'We need more arrows,' shouted Maya, and darted back into the open to pick up the spent shafts from the enemy. Most were broken from hitting the rocky ground, but some were still useable. Others followed her lead, and once again they bolstered the defence.

For how long this went on for Maya couldn't tell, but her shoulders ached, and her arms trembled from the repeated drawing of the bow. Just when she thought she couldn't take much more, the mournful sound of the enemy signal horns echoed on the air, and the enemy began to retreat, those who'd reached the walls, frantically pulling back.

The defenders were too exhausted to do much more than let them go. Enemy arrows rattled off the battlements, discouraging the Eyre archers from taking to the walls to harry the retreat.

Maya looked at Drizt and the other archers, surprised that they were doused in gore, then looked down at herself, seeing that she was splattered too.

She didn't know how long she and the others just stood there, staring, but then the cries of the wounded begun to seep into her numb mind. Men began stumbling down the steps, followed by Taran.

'Why did they stop?' she asked, wondering why her vision was dimming a little. 'Had they pushed for much longer, surely they would have broken through!'

A soldier ran by, holding a flaming torch, and started to light those on the walls, as others did the same.

Taran took off his helm, and his eyes looked hollow. 'It's because it's getting dark,' he said, voice hoarse.

Maya looked around incredulously. Everywhere men stumbled or simply sat on the ground in exhaustion.

Taran leaned in, resting his forehead on Maya's, closing his eyes for a moment. 'There is so much to do before we can rest,' he said quietly. 'Do you have the strength to help me?'

Maya lifted his chin with her hand, looking into his eyes, her own burning fiercely with love and determination. 'Always, my prince. We'll be there for one another until the end of days!'

Taran's eyes creased as he smiled, the brightness returning to them at Maya's words. He stood tall, pulling back his shoulders and took a deep breath. 'On your feet,' he bellowed at the nearby men, his voice echoing loudly. 'We owe it to those who died for us this day, to those who bled for us this day, to not rest until they're attended to!' He reached out with his gift, reinforcing the resolve of those around him and they responded, getting tiredly to their feet.

In the distance, a thump could be heard as the enemy siege engine resumed its onslaught of the wall, now that the attackers were well clear.

Rakan and Kalas came over and they all clasped forearms in greeting. Rakan passed around a full waterskin, and they drank deeply, unaware till then just how thirsty they were.

'These men deserve something more than just thinking about their dead friends, and dying on the morrow as they eat tonight,' Taran said, and the others nodded in agreement.

A smile began to form on Taran's lips as a thought came to mind.

Maya smiled too, for she knew that look. Taran, in the darkest of hours, had come up with some mischief.

Tristan sat looking out into the night sky, enjoying his dinner, washing it down with an exquisite bottle of wine. On his table stood a vase of flowers. He had no appreciation of such things normally, but these sought to remind him of Maya's gift. They'd been cut from the vines growing on the keep, so he looked upon them with favour.

It had been a worrying day overall, and his guard had kept horses saddled in case they needed to make a quick departure. Fortunately, the first wall had held, although, from this distance, it hadn't looked like the defence had fared well. Even now at regular intervals, a rolling boom like thunder would echo up to where he sat as that damned enemy siege engine kept up its destructive work.

Galain came over and respectfully whispered in his ear that Kalas was waiting impatiently outside.

The wine had put Tristan in a good mood, and he nodded his thanks. Galain was wasted here, he was a talented sculptor, and his respectful demeanour had brought him to Tristan's attention. Because of his worth, he now headed up the guard who would accompany him on the long road to Freeguard.

'Very well,' said Tristan, 'show him in,' and he took another sip of the wine. Elender might have betrayed him and siphoned off a small fortune in gold, but at least he'd had the good grace to spend it wisely on such divine wine.

Kalas entered, shining in his ever pristine armour, and Tristan felt his good mood evaporate. It didn't matter how respectfully the lord commander spoke, Tristan could always detect a hint of disapproval on his face. Still, he hadn't risen to become king through weakness, and he knew Kalas only had as much power as he gave him, so he took the initiative.

'Tell me of the day's events, in brief,' Tristan ordered, and leaned back in his chair without offering Kalas a seat or wine.

To Tristan's annoyance, Kalas just helped himself to a goblet, pulled up a chair and sat down. Tristan would in different times have exploded in rage at such lack of etiquette, but he knew the game Kalas was playing. Kalas was trying to rile him, and he would give the man no such satisfaction.

'Can I have some food brought for you?' Tristan asked, 'You don't look at your best, and the wine tastes better with a good meal.'

'Thank you, but no,' responded Kalas. 'I'll eat with the men later.'

Tristan raised his goblet in salute at Kalas' response. It was an insult of such subtlety that he couldn't help but admire it. At the same time, it helped reinforce his decision to leave Kalas behind rather than have him come to Freeguard. The lord commander had sealed his own fate. What was it with warriors, that they considered all those who weren't adept at violence as weak.

Tristan listened with interest to Kalas' report. The deaths of so many bothered him only insomuch as it meant the fortress was likely to fall faster. That meant there was less chance of the alliance forces of the Eyre, desert tribes and the Freestates having time to unite. Yet Kalas was adamant that the defender's losses would diminish as the weak were pruned from the strong.

What really took his attention, was when Kalas mentioned Maya's initiative in leading an action to repulse the enemy who'd found purchase on the wall.

'It's entirely possible we might have lost the first wall today without her initiative,' Kalas summarised at the end of his tale.

Tristan nodded, keeping his face impassive. Maya was truly a prize, and one he wouldn't risk leaving behind.

The sound of raucous laughter and the occasional song came up from below. Strangely, this annoyed Tristan, although he couldn't quite figure out why.

He took a sip of wine. 'Don't you think, Lord Commander, that the men should be getting some rest to ensure they're at their best for the morrow's battle? I would have thought that the necessity would be obvious!'

Kalas shook his head subtly. 'I think they need to enjoy the short life that still remains to them. Perhaps you could join me? We could go and mingle with them, get to know those who'd die for you. You could Inspire them with promises of how their families will be taken care of when they're gone!'

'You've given your report,' said Tristan, tired of the exchange. 'I think it's time you returned to the men. My men,' he emphasised.

The sound of chanting reached them, and Taran's name was repeated over and over.

'They could be chanting your name instead,' said Kalas, turning to leave, seeing the look of annoyance on Tristan's face.

'Oh, and why wouldn't they chant my name? I pay them gold and am their king. So tell me. Why are they chanting Taran's name when it seems that it was Maya who saved the situation today?'

'Ahhh,' said Kalas, it's because Taran discovered hundreds of crates of wine below the keep, and distributed it out amongst the men. I'm sure he didn't realise that you'd laid claim to them, and by the time Drizt told him, it was too late.'

Kalas turned back briefly, picking his goblet off the table, draining its contents in a single gulp. 'That's an amazing wine,' he said. 'It's just a shame there's so little left.'

Kalas saluted briefly before he strode off, leaving Tristan brooding.

Taran had no less than three times done something that would have seen him executed were it not for his usefulness. He now owed Taran a reckoning for the bruised neck, disobeying an order, and now the wine.

Soon he'd repay the debt in full.

The men might chant Taran's name now, but that hero-worship would end when Taran died defending this fortress. The young man would soon be forgotten, whereas he, the King of the Freestates, intended to live a long, long time.

Daleth hadn't slept at all.

He wasn't sure whether it was due to the siege engine shuddering in the distance with deadly rhythm or the strategies filling his thoughts, but he hadn't closed his eyes once.

In the early hours, he'd sent for a Ranger with a gift of concealment, ordering him to assess the wall under cover of darkness. The man had returned before dawn, excitedly reporting that it was on the verge of collapse.

To the surprise of many, upon receiving the news, he'd ordered the siege engine crew to stand down. It was as though the vision taking shape in his mind was placed there by the gods themselves.

Now, as the sky to the east shone with the promise of a beautiful day, he looked at the captains standing before him, sharing the plan. While it wouldn't change, he still asked for their opinion, not because he thought they could better it, but because this made them feel appreciated. It was small things like this that sealed their loyalty even further.

Unsurprisingly, all of them voiced their support.

'Today, my friends,' he said, rising, offering them each a goblet of watered wine from his own hand, 'today they will lose the first wall, and maybe even the fortress itself. Their time is running out. Now, prepare your men, we attack at noon.'

The men saluted, striding off, full of excitement, and Daleth returned to his tent, sitting down upon his bed.

Everyone's patience would be tested over the next few hours, but attacking too early would cause his archers' aim to be hindered by the rising sun in their eyes. They were pivotal to the plan's success, so the assault could wait just a little longer, to ensure their vision remained unaffected.

Give the enemy time to wonder what was happening. Likely their hopes would rise a little, thinking that no attack was coming, and then their hopes, like the wall, would come crashing down.

If the gods smiled on him today, maybe that damned Kalas would die in the fighting, then that way he could join the battle as well. Yes, there was a chance that everyone on that first wall would not see the sun set this night.

He reached for a goblet of wine and gazed into its red depths. His strong face was reflected back. The face of a warrior, the face of a king. The face of a man chosen by the gods.

Chapter XI

Maya awoke to find Taran gone from her side, and for a moment she felt sad that he hadn't thought to awaken her. But, it was his thoughtful nature that had let her sleep; that and the fact she wasn't always at her best when woken early.

She dressed quickly, her body a mass of aches, pulling on her gear and a chainmail shirt which Drizt had given her the night before, and secured a vambrace to her forearm. Tristan might have wanted her to help with the wounded, but she would continue to watch over Taran's back as he fought, and wild horses wouldn't be able to stop her.

She made her way quietly along the passageways, bow in hand, the faint noise of voices whispering as she passed an intersection that led to the barracks. The main hall was quiet when she entered, and she kept her head low, grabbing some food as she passed through, keeping an eye out for Tristan in case he tried to waylay her again.

Wild horses might not be able to stop her, but the king of these lands might very well try. However, either Tristan's mind was elsewhere, or she was overthinking the breakfast invite of two days ago. She left the keep unchallenged except for the nods and small bows the few soldiers she passed now gave her.

Maya ran through the open gates to the first wall to find Taran inspecting his section alongside Kalas and Drizt. Rakan was on the centre of the wall marshalling his men. Trom's spearmen were praying and Drizt's archers fooled around on some huge rocks the siege engine had thrown over the wall. She paused for a moment, wondering whether many of the defenders were sleeping in, for it seemed less crowded than usual. Then the realisation hit her. Those missing were indeed asleep, but would never rise again.

Maya walked over to Taran, and his eyes lit up as he saw her. She held out some bread, but as he stepped forward to take it, he instead swept her into his arms.

'Good morning,' he said, giving her a swift kiss before reluctantly letting her go. 'I'm sorry I left without waking you. You slept through the gong, so you obviously needed the rest. Come, tell me, what do you think of this?'

They walked along the base of Taran's section of the wall. The ground was covered in large piles of mortar dust and fragmented stone, yet the huge blocks that stood out from the wall were the main cause of concern.

Taran reached out to lay his hand on one, and it rocked beneath his touch. 'Kalas and I are wondering why they've ceased hitting the wall as this section is so close to collapse. In fact, when you look over the other side, it looks even worse, as half the blocks have crumbled to dust. But there are lots of men climbing over the siege engine in the distance, so Drizt thinks it's damaged. But the question is, what should we do now?'

Maya considered for a while, appreciating Taran seeking her advice. 'Surely the longer we hold the first wall, the better. They lose the most men when attacking across the open pass to our archers and catapults. Maybe we defend the first wall until Daleth's men repair the siege engine. The moment it looks like it's back in action, we move back to the second wall?'

They both turned as a laugh sounded behind them, to find Kalas listening to them both. 'I thought Taran was the mind reader. That's exactly what we'd decided was the best strategy. Conceding the first wall means losing our catapults. They're too big to get through the gates, and it would take days for Galain to disassemble them.

'So, we'll listen to our saviour of yesterday,' he said graciously. 'We hold the first wall for now but be well prepared to pull back.

'Taran, the decision on when we withdraw rests on your shoulders. Read the hearts and minds of our men. When they're close to breaking, or the siege engine reengages is when you'll pass the order.

'Yet to accurately judge the right moment, you can't be fighting on the wall. It was Maya who read and saved the situation yesterday while you were too pressed to do so. Your main worth isn't just in your sword arm, however much you wish to lead by example.'

'You're right,' Taran grimaced, acknowledging the truth of Kalas' words. 'I'll meet the initial attack, but step back before the fighting gets heavy.'

Kalas gripped their wrists. 'Time for me to find that rogue, Rakan. I've never seen anyone with such a capacity for drink,' he chuckled as he walked off.

Taran nodded and turned to hold Maya in his arms. 'Would you care to join me on the wall? We can watch the sunrise all alone but for the hundreds of soldiers around us.'

'Come, I know just the spot to get the best view,' Maya said, taking Taran's hand, to lead him up the steps. The soldiers standing watch on the wall gave them a little extra space, smiling to see the two of them together.

They ate hard bread and cheese washed down with water and then shared an apple Taran pulled from his pocket.

Maya sighed softly as she looked out into the pass.

'They're not showing signs of readying for an attack,' she observed. 'Maybe they'll let us enjoy some lunch as well.' She picked idly at some mortar between some of the stone blocks, pointing out how none were flush anymore with those adjoining them. 'This really doesn't look good. Just remember, if they repair that siege engine, you get off this wall and bring everyone with you, fast.'

The sun had risen by the time they finished eating, and Maya walked with Taran along the wall to greet Rakan, who embraced them both warmly.

'I've missed you both,' he said, with a somewhat shy look on his face. 'It's difficult to watch out for you both from afar. I long for the good old days of running and fighting by your side.'

'Now, don't get me wrong, these lads are not a bad bunch,' and he nodded to some of the soldiers who were listening in, and they smiled back, something akin to hero worship in their eyes. 'But, until they've killed a Ranger, they can't join our club. Can they?' and he laughed.

They all settled down for a while, and Rakan regaled the listening troops to outrageously embellished stories of the fights they'd been in on their flight from Daleth. 'Now,' he said, gesturing to Taran proudly, 'I trained him to be the best, and now he is better than me! All of you can be too if you just listen.' The men around all voiced their intent to make Rakan proud.

'However,' continued Rakan. 'I can't take credit for Maya's skill with a bow. Now, let me tell you about the time she … ' but he was interrupted as a horn sounded forlornly in the distance. As they turned to look over the battlements, movement could be seen as the enemy troops began to ready themselves.

Maya quickly strung her bow, and, with a quick wave goodbye, she and Taran hurried back to the north section of wall.

Taran ordered Drizt, his archers and the crossbowmen forward. Taran noticed the crossbowmen had daubed their cheeks with green face paint as a sign of appreciation and respect for being adopted into the Eyre ranks.

Drizt, as ever, had a smile on his face, but as he leaned against a merlon, the enormous block shifted, and he leapt back, watching it cautiously as it settled. 'That isn't good,' he cautioned. 'This part of the wall isn't stable at all,' yet whatever he was going to say next was drowned out by the roar of the enemy as the heavy assault infantry ran at the walls.

A few of the ladders from the previous day still remained in place as they'd proved so difficult to dislodge once the sap had hardened, and they carried yet more as well. There were new enemy troops in the pass now as the assault infantry numbers had been whittled down. These men were dressed in black uniforms and armour.

'They'll be Rakan's old outfit, the Nightstalkers,' judged Taran.

Drizt nodded. 'I think you're right,' he replied. 'By all accounts, they're a fearsome lot, especially if Rakan is anything to go by.'

Maya lifted her bow alongside Drizt, and Taran watched as she held it fully drawn without even a hint of effort. He shook his head in admiration. She was lean like a willow, and yet there was a strength about her too. All those years of hunting had made her as hard as stone, yet still soft in all the right places, he thought, with a smile.

As the enemy drew closer, Taran signalled, Bows thrummed, and arrows whistled through the air between the two forces, finding purchase in the enemy. Dozens crashed to the floor, yet, like a wave, they continued unchecked.

'Have they no fear?' shouted Maya, as the enemy simply ignored their casualties, and rushed toward the wall, trampling those who fell at their feet.

'Right,' said Drizt, 'time for us to leave,' and he grabbed Maya's arm and they ran down the steps.

Taran focussed on the enemy, keeping an eye on the siege engine, but as ladders crashed against stone, Taran glanced quickly over his shoulder.

Maya, Drizt, and his archers were crossing the bridges to the far side of the trench, where Trom's spearmen were ready to cover the retreat. They'd hold the narrow bridges after the withdrawing garrison soldiers crossed, delaying the enemy while the trench and bridges were set aflame. This would allow everyone to pass through the gates in the second wall, and for them to be sealed.

As the enemy climbed, Taran raised his shield, expecting the enemy archers to rake the walls as they usually did to keep the defenders' heads down. Luckily, the first volley of arrows flew high, and there were no casualties to the men around him.

Suddenly, the first armoured visor appeared before him, focussing his thoughts. He quickly hacked at the man's mailed hand as the warrior reached forward to steady himself. The soldier fell back, screaming as Taran's sword severed the chain links, biting deep into the flesh and bone.

As the next enemy soldier climbed up, an arrow smacked against the top of the man's helm. The moment his head snapped back, a second skewered his throat. Taran smiled grimly. He knew both Drizt and Maya were covering his section of the wall, and as a team, there would be none more deadly. Yet he couldn't stay here, not today, however much he wanted to inspire his section.

Another volley of arrows flew above him, and he beckoned to a waiting soldier who stepped forward to take his place. Taran moved quickly, running down the steps, heading toward the north section of wall closest to the mountainside. The enemy were not pressing the attack there, perhaps worried about the wall collapsing on them. He'd be able to monitor the defence relatively undisturbed while keeping an eye on the siege engine.

As he ran behind the wall, nearing the mountainside, something unusual caught his eye. The enemy arrows that had flown high lay on the rocky ground and Taran could see a strange haze around them. His stomach suddenly knotted in apprehension and then as the third volley of arrows flew over the wall above him, the enemy plan revealed itself.

The flame trench which had been newly covered in oil to protect their retreat began to burn.

He looked for Kalas and Rakan further along the wall. 'Retreat, fall back,' he screamed in their heads, conveying the urgency and sharing what he could see, and saw them react instantly. They ran along the walls shouting, pulling men with them as they went. No hesitation, for every moment lost, could be the difference between life and death.

Taran turned and started shouting at his men to fall back. 'Come on, quickly!' he cried, as the flames took hold. Men streamed down the steps, and whilst several were still fighting on the wall, he couldn't wait a moment more.

He turned with his men toward the narrow wooden bridge when suddenly the wall behind them exploded inward as the siege engine scored a decisive hit. Rubble and dust flew everywhere, and Taran was knocked from his feet by a piece of debris that glanced from his helm.

His ears were ringing as he staggered upright, turning to see some of his men pulling themselves to their feet. Others lay still, unmoving.

The closest wooden bridge over the trench was now on fire, and he could see Maya screaming, being held by Drizt as he staggered toward it. With a roar it suddenly collapsed, throwing half a dozen men upon its span, screaming into the fiery pit below.

Taran spun around, assessing the situation. The trench was on fire its whole length, and the other bridges were burning fiercely. They were too far away, and already impossible to cross. Fortunately, most of the defending soldiers had made it to safety, although at least fifty were still on the wrong side with him. He reached out with his mind, yelling desperately for them to form on him.

He turned, helping his wounded comrades to their feet, and as others joined them, they withdrew toward the wall of the mountain.

The heat from the flame trench was searing as they backed away and Taran could see dark armoured soldiers swarming the wall, all remaining resistance now crushed. He looked around, hoping for something, anything, but the only thing he could see was death.

Then through the clouds of dust, over the mounds of fallen masonry, the enemy infantry came, shields tightly locked. They saw Taran and the garrison soldiers he'd managed to gather around him, turned and advanced.

There was little time left, and Taran peered through the roaring fire. Maya was struggling on the other side, Drizt and Rakan holding her back from trying to run through the flames.

Tears ran down Taran's face, from the acrid smoke, but also from the sadness of it all. He wasn't afraid to die, but he was suddenly afraid of leaving Maya on her own.

'Look after her,' he projected to Rakan.

'I'll protect her with my life,' Rakan replied in his mind, before adding, 'I couldn't have asked for a better son.'

'Nor I, a father,' responded Taran, but then he broke the connection for there were but mere moments left.

He opened his mind to Maya, and her panic and desperation almost took him from his feet. 'Calm down,' he soothed. 'Listen to me, listen to me, we don't have much time,' and with his mind, he covered her anguish in a blanket of calm. 'I need you to know that I love you with all my heart, body and soul. I never thought I'd meet someone I wanted to marry, someone I wanted to have children with, but I found that someone in you. I'll love you for eternity, my princess, in this world and soon the next.'

He turned back to his men, opening his mind to them, using his gift to strengthen their resolve, to take away the fear that threatened to overwhelm them and send them to their knees.

'Come, my brothers,' he said, moving amongst them. 'Let us show the god of war our bravery and earn a place by his side for eternity!'

Taran raised his sword. 'With me!' he roared, and together they charged the enemy.

Tristan's Folly

Maya sat alone in her room, clutching a tear-soaked pillow.

At times throughout the evening, a succession of people had come to her side, holding her, yet she'd barely felt them at all. She had no recollection of the harsh words that had sent them on their way either.

The pillow still held Taran's scent, which brought her a little solace, but then made her ache for him all the more.

Taran's loss was her fault. She'd suggested they hold the wall and had left him there to die, not realising he was gone before it was too late. She'd been so focussed on her archery that she'd not seen the danger in front of her own eyes.

The flames had sprung up along the trench so quickly that she, Drizt, and the others had stumbled back from the terrific heat. Then the bridges were engulfed as some fool had soaked them with oil as well.

She'd not even had time to respond to Taran's final words, and now a thousand things flew around her head of what she would have said given the time. But there had been no time.

Taran had broken the connection with her before she'd had a chance to formulate any response. He'd gathered the men, walking amongst them briefly before positioning himself at the centre of the small line.

Along with Drizt, and his archers, she'd tried to help by shooting through the flames. However, the heat was so ferocious that the arrow flights disintegrated before they passed through, making them useless. Even with a clear view, it wouldn't have been enough.

Taran and his men had chosen to attack, and for a brief moment, the enemy fell back from their ferocious assault. Taran briefly broke the centre of their shield wall, but the enemy line was too long and started folding around the outside of the defenders. They were forced back, and the garrison soldiers began to fall.

It didn't matter that their desperation gave them a strength that allowed them to kill twice their number, there were hundreds more pressing in. One by one, they were cut down, screaming, until just Taran was left.

Maybe it was his skill that kept him alive or the embellished armour that made him stand out as the commander, but they left him till last.

The enemy stood in a semi-circle around Taran, and she could see him shouting at his foe, laughing at them, taunting, until five black-garbed warriors had stepped from amongst the massed ranks.

'They're Rangers,' Rakan had said next to her. One of them seemed to flow forward in an almost liquid fashion. Taran had flashed that silly smile of his just as the Ranger attacked and Maya had closed her eyes.

'By all the gods,' Rakan had exclaimed. She'd opened them again to see Taran standing over the dead body of the warrior although blood flowed from a wound in Taran's arm.

Another Ranger had stepped forward, more cautiously than his erstwhile brother, two swords weaving in front of him in a figure of eight. They flashed for Taran, and he'd swayed backwards, then spun sideways, so the man's momentum took him past. As the Ranger turned, swords flashing, Taran ducked, and his leg swept out, taking the man's feet from under him. Taran leapt, his foot pinning the man's left hand to the ground, parrying the other sword before hammering his blade through the man's mouth.

'I would never have believed it if I hadn't of seen it,' Rakan had whispered.

None of Taran's following jibes had brought any more warriors forward individually, they'd simply pushed forward on mass. The last Maya had seen was Taran falling under a flurry of blows, hidden behind the hundreds of men.

Maya had been half-dragged by Rakan as the remaining defenders moved back through the gateway, and the huge reinforced doors boomed shut behind them.

The ground had seemed to shift below Maya's feet then, and the next time she was aware of her surroundings she'd been in her room with Rakan by her side. They'd held one another for a while, faces stained by tears, grieving for the loss they'd suffered.

Now she was alone, terribly alone, and her heart felt as if it were broken in two. I would give everything to have you back, my prince, my own life included, she thought. As she lay on the bed, grief and exhaustion finally overwhelmed her, and she fell asleep.

In the room opposite, Yana wept too, crying softly, yet unable to share her grief with Maya lest it be seen for what it truly was. Like Maya, she would have given everything and done anything, but now it was too late for them both. Sleep came for her too, but for the first time, in a long time, it was full of nightmares.

The sun was setting, and torches were being lit as Tristan sat in his chamber along with Kalas, Rakan, Drizt, Trom, Yana and Astren.

Food was brought in, yet it lay mostly untouched other than by Tristan himself who ate voraciously. As he looked around, he noted that Rakan and Yana had reddened eyes. Kalas, Drizt, and Trom were, despite the losses of the day, less affected emotionally by the events.

'Tell me,' said Tristan simply, looking at Kalas.

Kalas looked back steadily. 'The enemy out-thought us, and we were lucky to escape with as few casualties as we did. We've now lost over half the garrison soldiers, one hundred and fifty spearmen and over one hundred and sixty bowmen. We have another one hundred seriously injured, no catapults, and on top of it all, we lost commander Taran.

'Before the battle was joined, we had fifteen hundred fighting men, and now we have approximately nine hundred. By comparison, I would estimate the enemy have lost over four thousand men. We are killing them at a rate of over five to one.

Tristan's face was white. 'Did I appoint the wrong Lord Commander then, that we have lost our first wall and so many troops within the first few days of battle? Was it was because our men were still drunk from last nights ill-conceived revelry? I thought you intended to hold this fortress long enough for our allies to have a chance. If this keeps up, it will be lost in less than a week!'

Kalas held his calm. 'We will hold. They'll need to spend the next couple of days demolishing the first wall. They cannot launch a mass attack through just the one breach they created, and they can't marshal their formations within range of our archers. Once they've done that, they'll need to fill in the fire trench. So two or three days for the wall, a day or two for the trench, and then we'll feel their fury once more.'

'How are the men taking the loss of the first wall?' probed Tristan.

'What about the loss of Taran?' snapped Rakan. 'Do we brush his loss under the carpet and just move on and talk about the damned wall?'

Tristan's face flushed an angry red to be addressed in such a fashion, and he was about to respond when Kalas held up his hand.

'Rakan, my friend,' Kalas intervened. 'His loss is felt keenly by many of us sitting here. However, I know none as much as you and definitely none more than Maya. However, lamenting his loss at this time won't help us. The time for sorrow will be when we win this war; otherwise, our souls will likely join his wherever it may be.'

'I doubt your dark soul, or mine, will end up anywhere near his,' growled Rakan, but he nodded, recognising the truth of Kalas' words and said no more.

Kalas watched Tristan, and seeing the king's anger had abated, continued into the silence. 'We must learn from this setback. We will dry the oil from the second fire trench with rock dust and soil, and only douse it again at the time of any withdrawal. The risk of doing it earlier is too great.

'We must use the next few days to rest and recover, but also to keep the men busy, sharp and focussed, not dwelling on the losses we've suffered. The lightly wounded will help, even if just to make bandages or learn how to apply them.

'Now Taran is gone I also have to advise that there's no hope of saving my old sword brother, Alano. Unless there's a reason any of you can think of to keep him alive, he'll die by my hand on the morrow.'

No one objected, and after more discussions, Tristan stood and raised his voice. 'I would consult with Astren in private. It's time for you all to leave until the morrow.'

Rakan stood immediately, but instead of walking to the door, he turned to one of Tristan's cabinets, opening one, and withdrew several bottles of wine. He brought them to the table despite Tristan's furious stare, opened them, then poured for everyone.

'Now,' Rakan said, raising his goblet, 'now it's time to remember a friend, a fine soldier, a kind soul, and my son.' His voice choked as he said the last word and he blinked furiously.

Kalas and the others stood, including a reluctant Tristan. 'To Taran,' they said, raising their goblets, and the drinking began.

Chapter XII

Daleth was ecstatic and sat with a dozen of his captains around a roaring fire. They were all noisy with laughter, drinking wine to celebrate the day's victory.

As far as the eye could see, other campfires were burning and despite the majority of his army not having been anywhere close to the battle, the story of this day's success had swept through the ranks, and the mood everywhere was buoyant. True, there were two more walls and a keep to destroy, but today had been the highlight of the campaign so far. His men had needed a victory, and this had come with a surprising reward.

He rose from his seat, laughing as he refused the invitations to stay and drink from men around other fires nearby as he moved back to his tent. His capacity for alcohol was as large as he was, but he wanted a clear mind for the day ahead. There were many things to be done that would need his attention.

The siege engine needed to reduce the first wall to rubble, and his men needed to fill the fire trench to enable them to safely cross over. He'd thought about using some of the many ironwood ladders, but he was thorough, and he'd rather lose men now filling the trench than have his attacks fail as his soldiers slipped on the rungs as they crossed.

He'd have the remnants of his heavy assault troops push the bodies of their erstwhile comrades and victims into the trench to help fill it once they'd been stripped of their armour, weapons and amulets. Such things were too valuable to waste, especially as the forges of the kingdom were cold and dead behind him. The satisfaction of his plan working outweighed the loss of two more of his Rangers. Maybe Alano hadn't trained them as well as he had thought, but he dismissed that idea the moment it came into his head. Alano was a perfectionist, and the Rangers were perfect.

Damn, why'd he go and think of Alano again? Was there a chance Alano was still alive, and if so, did he now have the means by which to secure his release?

He beckoned to the new captain of his bodyguard, Baylor, to follow him through the tent flap. He was a worthy successor to Grisen. If Grisen hadn't been killed by one of the filthy greenskins, Baylor was ruthless enough to have tried to kill Grisen sooner or later to have the honour to serve his king.

He sat and poured Baylor a goblet of wine, indicating for him to sit and drink. It was the small things like this that made his troops see him as a benevolent leader, and stopped them from seeing him as the life-stealer he truly was. People were so easy to manipulate. Throw them a few crumbs here and there, and they'd overlook that it was you that had starved them all their life.

He explained his plan. There were no downsides, but he wanted a second, calculating opinion, and Baylor was certainly the calculating sort and would be directly responsible for its execution.

'The only pitfall I see in your plan, my king, if you'll forgive me,' said Baylor, and Daleth nodded for him to go on. 'The only pitfall,' he repeated, 'is that it would seem to me that you favour this daemon spawn, and I don't understand why. He served a purpose, he trained your Rangers and your bodyguard including me, but he's a monster, and he is gone. Now you seek to negotiate for his return? it makes you look weak and almost dependent on him.'

Daleth thought for a moment. Why indeed? Maybe because he was a monster too.

'I'm glad you spoke your mind, Baylor,' said Daleth, rising to walk around the tent. 'Only a strong man, a fearless man would have said such a thing to me, and I appreciate your candour.'

As he walked behind Baylor, he swiftly reached around and drew his dagger across the man's throat. Baylor surged to his feet, clasping at the wound, but a moment later fell to his knees as his blood sprayed across the tent. One of the lanterns was covered, hissing as it cast a red glow throughout.

Tristan's Folly

'I do appreciate your candour,' Daleth said to Baylor, looking down into the man's fading eyes as he kicked him on to his back, 'but I'm anything but weak, and such a serious lack of judgement cannot go unanswered.

'Guards,' he called, and several more bodyguards ran in. They paused for a moment as they surveyed the scene, before two ran forward, to remove Baylor's body from the tent. The others started to clear the mess.

Daleth watched them closely. One rested a hand on his sword hilt, not as a threat, merely ready for action even if otherwise engaged.

'Krixen,' he said, and as the man looked up, Daleth pointed at him. 'You're now the captain of my bodyguard. I have a dangerous task for you, but I have a feeling, someone like you who's constantly on guard, will have a higher chance of surviving.'

'I live to serve, and I serve to live, my king,' replied Krixen.

Daleth nodded. 'Indeed, you do Krixen. Indeed, you do. Now, let us sit and drink, there's a lot to discuss.'

Tristan sat studying Astren, the large meeting table between them, enjoying his discomfort.

Loyal Astren, he thought, although of late he could tell the seer didn't entirely approve of his decisions. Whilst in itself that was fine as long as Astren carried out his duties, it made him wonder if any of the advisors back in Freemantle would do a better job.

He sighed. Some might be more astute, or loyal as long as they were paid, but none had Astren's gift. It was this alone that made the seer currently invaluable.

It was late into the evening, and Astren looked ready to fall asleep at any moment. After reluctantly drinking to Taran's demise, Tristan wasn't sure how much longer he could stay awake either, but he needed Astren focussed.

The loss of the first wall had shaken him, and he'd brought forward his plans to depart. He had Astren spirit travelling every night, visiting the alliance leaders whose troops were making good time. In contrast, some of the lords of the Freestates cities were frustratingly reluctant to leave their cities unguarded. They were keeping their garrisons to protect their belongings; the fools. Protecting wealth was laudable, but you couldn't spend that wealth when you were dead.

Nonetheless, he had Astren keep them aware of his heroic defence of the fortress.

It was all about ensuring that he maintained his position as king and exerted control at all times. In some regards, he was more powerful than ever before. He would soon be the overall commander of the alliance forces once they arrived, an army beyond anything the Freestates had ever fielded in its entire history. If he emerged victorious, he'd ensure those lords who'd refrained from sending help felt the full weight of his wrath.

For now, he accepted he wasn't a military genius, that was what commanders were for. He'd lean upon any expertise he could lay his hands on, and that was his strength; using those around him to the best of their ability for his own personal gain.

'What does my king require of me?' Astren hesitantly asked.

Tristan bristled a little at his choice of phrase, but then maybe he was just reading things into Astren's words that weren't there.

'What plan have you devised to ensure Maya departs with me?' demanded Tristan.

Astren shook his head. 'I cannot conceive any play of subtlety. My only thought is that with Taran's death, she has less reason to stay.'

'I came to that conclusion myself,' Tristan said, drumming his fingers on the tabletop. 'You disappoint me, Astren. I leave here in two days, and I want Maya with me. We need to make her understand that she'd recover better from her loss, the further away from the fighting she is.'

'She'll see through this, I'm sure,' said Astren. She just lost Taran today, and we shouldn't impose your desires upon her at this time.'

'What exactly do you mean by that?' snapped Tristan.

'You know what I mean,' Astren sighed. 'The others might not see it, but I certainly can. This isn't just about protecting her or the value she holds, which for a Freestates king is understandable. It's about your desire for her. I see it in your eyes and hear it in your words. She just lost the love of her life, and you're thinking of having her accompany you so that you can seduce her.'

'Silence,' roared Tristan. 'How dare you speak to me like that. I should have you executed! You forget your position once again! Let me make this clear. I'm not asking for your help, I'm ordering it. In fact, should I order Maya to come with me, I expect you to support that as well. It's not for you to question or judge your king, or my choice of consort.'

Tristan glowered at Astren who lowered his head in defeat.

An uncomfortable silence grew, but it was interrupted by a knock at the heavy door.

'Enter,' called Tristan, and the door opened to reveal Maya, flanked by two of Tristan's guards. She looked lost, her hair was dishevelled and hung limply across her face.

Tristan got to his feet, walking over to Maya whose eyes, he noted, were bloodshot red. 'Come,' he said, taking her unresisting hand and leading her to his chair. 'Sit. I'm so sorry to have intruded on your grief.' He pushed a goblet of wine into her hand. 'Drink. The wine will ease your pain a little.'

Maya didn't respond, she seemed to stare yet see nothing. Still, she brought the goblet to her lips and drained the wine in several gulps before Tristan took it from her hand.

Tristan sat next to Maya and stared meaningfully across at Astren. 'Astren and I have been talking. We've been so concerned, as have all your friends. In two days, I'll be leaving for Freeguard. I need to meet with our allies as they arrive and prepare the city for what's to come. Astren believes it would be better if you came with me. You'd have time to heal on the journey and can recover well away from the horrors of war. Isn't that right, Astren?'

Astren's heart was torn. He liked Maya, but wanted to be well away from the battle too, and knew Tristan would discard him if he didn't help. He thought again of the promise of riches and what his life could be like. He could do this.

'Maya,' Astren said, gently clasping her hands between his, looking into her vacant eyes. 'It will be safer for you if you came with us. We could really use your assistance too. Your gift could help our farmers and their crops so that we have enough provisions to feed the arriving armies. We need you, Maya. Will you come with us? Just nod, and I'll have a carriage prepared for you.'

Astren fell silent, awaiting Maya's response, and just when he was going to prompt her, she looked up.

Maya's voice was barely above a whisper as she replied. 'I understand you need my help, Astren, I really do. King Tristan, likewise, I appreciate your offer. But my answer is no. I'll stay. I've no wish to leave my friends that still live, or leave this place where the spirit of my Taran walks.'

Tristan nodded. 'I understand your reluctance Maya, believe me. Your wounds are fresh. But Taran's spirit doesn't reside in this place, it resides in your heart, and wherever you go, he'll be with you.'

Astren looked away, knowing he couldn't keep the distaste from his features at Tristan's cruel manipulation.

Maya was silent for a while before she let out a long sigh, her shoulders sagging, but then straightened up. 'My answer remains the same. I intend to stay, and when I fall, I'll find peace near to where Taran died and hopefully, his spirit waiting for me.'

Tristan shook his head. 'Maya, I don't wish to order you to come with me, I'd rather you came because you saw the right in it.'

Up until now, Astren had seen Maya walk in and sit down like the lost girl he'd once seen in his spirit travels. Now suddenly, at Tristan's last words, her eyes cleared and focussed, and this time her voice was as strong as steel.

She stood up, standing tall, looking down on Tristan, and her hand went to the dagger on her hip.

'I might well be a citizen of your Freestates,' she said coldly, 'but be assured if you ever seek to order me to leave this place at such a time as this ... Well, let's just say I wouldn't be going quietly.'

Maya stormed out of the room, and the door crashed with such fury that both Tristan and Astren winced.

Astren expected Tristan to explode, but instead, Tristan just shook his head. 'To have the loyalty and love of such a woman,' he said. 'She even looks my age now, don't you think?'

Astren laughed, but there was no humour in it. 'Trust me, Tristan, as your advisor, don't try to force that woman to do anything. Better to leave her here and hope she survives the fall and makes it back in her own time. Otherwise, your downfall might arrive a lot earlier at the hands of the one you seek to possess.'

Tristan nodded. 'You might be right, Astren, but the reward is worth the risk, and so will yours be, but only if you find a way to make this happen. Fail me in this, and you'll find yourself staying behind with the other expendables.

'Now, leave me. I've a lot to ponder, and I need to sleep. I expect to meet with you again in the morning.'

Astren rose and walked to the door. He had to find a way to coerce Maya into travelling with Tristan, so he could be rich beyond his dreams. He consoled himself with the thought that he'd be helping to save not just his life, but now, Maya's too ... he just had to find a way.

Kalas awoke, expecting to have a throbbing headache and yet he was wrong.

He looked to the timeglass and pushed himself out of bed. It was later than he'd intended to rise and he cursed at himself for drinking so much. But just like the others, he'd needed to find some distraction.

Yesterday he'd lost Taran to the hand of the enemy, and today he would lose Alano to his own. Yet he didn't have time to attend to that, at least not yet. He quickly dressed, donning his silver armour that shone, pristine, even though he'd hung it on the rack the night before dented and covered in gore.

'Truly, we are both cursed,' whispered the daemon in his head.

Kalas didn't reply as he hurried down the corridors, wondering at his current relationship with the daemon. It seemed to be compliant, never imposing, never demanding. It hadn't demanded blood in the last couple of days, and even this last comment was almost brotherly, sharing in the pain of the loss felt and that yet to come.

He wondered if his innermost thoughts were shared with it, but it didn't care to answer. He didn't hear the daemon's thoughts unless it directly addressed him, and this reassured him a little. He reached the main hall and saw some of the lightly injured night-watch eating having been replaced on the wall. Several of them idly kicked at rats scurrying beneath the tables.

The men nodded or raised hands as he passed through, and he took the time to stop and greet some despite his haste. He'd arranged to meet Drizt, Trom, and Rakan early on the wall. He wasn't worried about an attack; it would be days before the enemy were adequately prepared for the next phase of the assault. Even so, he was pleased to see archers positioned on the high wall, with many sleeping below.

Trom's men were praying as the first light of the sun touched the horizon, and he wondered for a moment if there was any point to it. He'd never known prayer to save a man's life even though many reached for its solace at the end.

Drizt whistled, interrupting his thoughts and beckoned from atop the wall. Kalas broke into a jog, hurrying up the steps to reach his side.

'We have a visitor,' Drizt advised, pointing.

Kalas looked, and there in the dim early light, atop the mound of rubble that marked the breach in the first wall stood one of Daleth's men. He had a flag of truce above his head, but perhaps knowing of his predecessor's fate, he had a large full-length shield and stood behind it at range, waiting to be seen and invited forward.

'Remember last time,' Rakan growled, walking over, his face etched with pain. 'I told everyone to kill Daleth's messenger before he started talking. Nobody listened, and then everyone regretted it. Listen to me now and put an arrow through this one before he opens his big mouth.'

Drizt started to select an arrow.

Kalas raised his hand. 'No. We hear what he has to say. However, this time I'll meet him personally rather than have him speak aloud and cast doubts in the minds of the men, in case that's Daleth's plan.'

Rakan still looked unconvinced. 'It might be a trap.'

'I don't believe so,' mused Kalas. 'The wall, even if we've lost it, will stop any surprise attack if he seeks to distract me, and the fire trench is deep enough to stop a rush from anyone hidden behind the wall.

'Drizt, ensure your archers are ready just in case there's something I've overlooked. We'll respect the flag of truce, because one day, it may be us underneath it.'

Kalas descended the steps and walked over to the spearmen who had finished their prayers. 'Trom,' he called, 'I'm going to meet an emissary of Daleths. May I borrow your shield to shelter beneath my friend, just in case a rain of arrows darkens the sky?'

Trom came across, handing it over. 'This has protected me my whole life. I've no doubt it will do the same for you. Do you want my spear too?'

Kalas bowed his head in gratitude. 'Thank you, but no. I've no intention of fighting this day if it is possible to avoid it, and I was always better with the sword than the spear. However, if you and your men can lend their strength to opening and closing the gate, then I would appreciate that.'

He turned to Rakan who had followed him down from the wall. 'I'm not expecting it, but if for whatever reason you're right and there's a trap, and I don't make it back; you'll take command. Now, let's get this over with,' and he strode toward the gates as the spearmen ran to obey Trom's order to open them.

The rattle of chains being pulled sounded from inside the gatehouse, and slowly the reinforced gates began to open outward, just enough to allow Kalas passage. As he stepped through, he heard them grinding shut behind him.

'Brother, can you sense any other presence here, or is it just the one messenger?' Kalas asked of his daemon kin.

He felt pressure in his head as though the daemon were physically straining to see, but it vanished almost immediately as the daemon responded. 'No, my brother, it seems it is just him and the two of us,' and it chuckled at its own joke.

Nonetheless, Kalas took his time, eyes searching as he traversed the open ground to the fire trench and the still smouldering ashes within. The other side of the trench was littered with the detritus of war. Rubble and spent arrows, broken weapons, and of course, bodies of friend and foe alike. Behind him, where Maya had worked her magic, the grass and saplings above the bodies of the slain seemed like a different world entirely.

Kalas stood waiting patiently, and Daleth's messenger cautiously came down from the mound of rubble, always behind his shield. Kalas wondered if there was a concealed weapon behind it.

He studied the way the man moved. The way his feet felt the ground before fully committing his weight and how he listened as much as he looked.

Kalas recognised him as a warrior born, yet felt little threat. He'd faced their best and found them wanting, and this one would be the same.

The man came to stand opposite, separated by the trench and bowed his head. His eyes roved, lingering briefly on the abandoned catapults, the trees and grass before assessing the archers high above on the wall.

'Fear not,' Kalas reassured him. 'I regret the death of your brother under the flag of truce, and I can assure you that it will be respected henceforth. You'll return whole to your king unless you break the truce yourself. I am the lord commander of this fortress and the Freestates forces. Now, deliver your message.'

The man visibly relaxed and lowered the shield a little.

'I am Krixen, and I speak for the Witch-King,' he said, his voice just loud enough for Kalas to hear, 'and I'm glad to be speaking with you, lord commander. My king, has an offer for your king, and believes it will be of interest to him, and potentially to you as well. Maybe it's too late, but nonetheless, here it is.'

The man spoke for but a few moments and Kalas stared hard at him, wishing he could verify the truth of the man's words, knowing that many of Daleth's closest were gifted.

'Wait here, and know safety whilst I convey this message to my king,' Kalas instructed. 'I'll return in due course with his answer.'

He backed away carefully as Krixen sat down upon the stony ground. The gates groaned open, and he found Rakan waiting anxiously as he entered.

Rakan looked closely at Kalas, noting the paleness of his face, eyes slightly dazed. 'Are you alright? What was the message?'

Kalas suddenly focussed. 'We need to find the king quickly. You need to come with me, for I'd have your counsel too,' Kalas urged. He dropped the shield and spear to the ground then ran off with Rakan behind, struggling to keep up.

Chapter XIII

Maya lay curled on her bed. She'd grown tired of the well-wishers coming in to see her, and was exhausted after a troubled night.

The meeting with Tristan had annoyed her immensely. Why couldn't she just be left in peace? A chair was now jammed up against the door to stop people coming in, and as she clutched a pillow, quiet tears fell again.

Taran was waiting for her alone, on the other side, and here she was, alone on this side. Her heart ached horribly, and she could barely draw breath through the pain. What was the point in carrying on?

Without Taran beside her, where was happiness to be found? She would never be able to see the beauty of a sunset ever again without her heart breaking for wanting to share it with him. Never would she see his warm smile, his blue eyes, feel his love burning like a flame. Not in this life. So why waste time when she could go join him now.

She looked over to the side of the bed where her dagger lay, blade shining softly in the candlelight. She'd picked it up many times throughout the night and put it back again, conflicted by what she should do, what Taran would want her to do.

'I'd do anything to have you back,' she sobbed quietly to herself, 'but you aren't coming back.'

Rolling up her sleeves, she looked at her wrists and the lifeblood pumping through them. As a hunter, she'd killed many creatures and now men too. So, what difference in taking her own life?

Taran had once said, *we have a love worth living for, but also worth dying for*. Now it made sense again but in a different way.

There was a banging on her door, but she ignored it.

Yes, if Taran was waiting on the other side, then it was definitely worth dying for.

She closed her eyes as her hand slid across the blanket, reaching for the dagger.

Again the banging, but soon it would fade away.

The leather-bound grip fitted snugly in her hand, and she knew the blade was so keen that she'd barely feel a thing. Enough animals had died to her hand to know they often slipped away without even knowing it was happening.

She let the cool edge of the blade linger against her wrist. Just one swift, firm pull across the veins was all it would take. She could lay here and dream of Taran's strong arms pulling her in close, his wide smile as he saw her again. Her heart would beat so hard when he looked into her eyes and told her that he loved her. They would have children in the next life, they could get married. Yes.

She took a deep breath, gripping the handle firmly.

Suddenly there was a crash, and as she opened her eyes in shock, Rakan almost flew across the room, striking the dagger painfully from her hand.

'No!' she screamed. 'I want to be with Taran. Leave me be, let me go!'

But Rakan was holding her tight, not letting her reach for the dagger again. He was saying something, but she couldn't even hear his words as her heart pounded so painfully in her chest and ears.

She struggled, but Rakan was too strong, and after a while, she gave up, exhausted, her sobs lessening.

Rakan spoke again. 'Look at me, lass,' he said, turning her chin so that she looked into his face which was wet with tears like her own. 'It's not time for you to die, not now, not yet. Not whilst our Taran still lives!'

'Taran is alive?' She said the words barely believing them. 'Don't lie to me, just to keep me alive one more day,' but Rakan's face was beaming, his tears were of joy, and he was pulling her to her feet, his excitement obvious.

'Quick,' he said, 'we have to go see Tristan. Kalas brought a message; Daleth wants to trade Taran for Alano.'

As they left the room, Yana, eyes red, looked around her door. 'What's happening?' she asked.

Maya grabbed her hand, pulling her along after them. 'Taran is alive,' she cried, and the next moment they were all running as fast as they could to Tristan's chambers.

Kalas had hurried toward the keep with Rakan and had made the mistake of sharing the news before they met Tristan. Once spoken, the words couldn't be taken back, and Rakan had left to tell Maya despite Kalas' protestations to the contrary.

Now he waited alone, standing on the balcony at the top of the keep, begrudging of every minute it took for Tristan, Rakan, and now Maya to attend. He tried to control his impatience as he looked west into the distance where Daleth's forces were rousing to begin the day.

The door to the chamber behind him banged open, and he turned to see Tristan enter the chamber, looking dour. The king poured himself some watered wine, and as Kalas came inside, ordered one of his guards to bring breakfast.

Tristan yawned, then look at Kalas. 'I hope you haven't roused me from sleep for something that could have waited. There's no sound of fighting, so I know it isn't an attack, nor would you be here if so. So, what brings you?'

Kalas took a seat, holding his dislike in check at Tristan's comment. 'I met a messenger, from Daleth,' he recounted, 'under a flag of truce. He told me Taran is alive, but barely. Daleth wishes to exchange him for Alano. He must conclude Maya is here and able to revive Taran, or it would be a worthless exchange.

'The messenger tells me it's unlikely Taran will see the day out, hence the urgency.' As he spoke, Kalas saw a strange look pass over Tristan's face, almost of relief perhaps, but he couldn't be sure.

Tristan shook his head. 'We know Daleth is a deceiver, Taran told us as much, and even if he hadn't, there's little reason to believe this tale.'

Kalas rubbed his chin as he chose his words. 'I saw Taran's body taken away, as did others; we thought as a trophy of some kind. I find it hard to believe he survived the many blows that were struck, and this may be just a ruse for Daleth to have his champion returned. However, I see no way such a trick could work if we control the exchange, so I think we should make a decision on the premise that Taran is alive.

Tristan leaned backwards in his chair, hands behind his head as he stared at the ceiling, deep in thought

Kalas sat, face impassive, although inside he was a man of action and was impatient for Tristan to make a decision or to at least start debating the situation. As he waited, there was a sound of hurrying footsteps, and Rakan, Maya, and Yana came into the room. A handful of Tristan's guards followed and shrugged apologetically at this rather hasty and unannounced entrance.

The guards turned to leave, but Tristan bade them stay.

'Is it true?' asked Maya breathlessly, 'that we're going to exchange Alano for Taran? When is this going to happen and how?' Her fingers clasped Rakan's arm as she talked, her eyes conveying her desperation.

Tristan ignored her, instead fixing his gaze upon Kalas. 'Kalas, you're without question the greatest warrior any of us have known. You're also lord commander of this fortress, answerable to me. So, tell us about Alano.'

Kalas shrugged. 'What's there to say that you don't already know. He was a warrior with skills beyond most mortal man when we served together, and since his possession by the daemon, he is nigh on without peer. The daemon has full control as you know, and will not relinquish its hold, or break its vow to serve Daleth, and that includes killing me or any of his enemies.'

'What would happen if he were to gain the walls, and you were not there to face him?' probed Tristan.

Kalas felt his heart sink at the direction of questioning. 'Without doubt, he could sweep a wall clear on his own, allowing Daleth's other soldiers to gain a foothold. No one could stop him but I, or perhaps a fortuitous bolt or arrow, but the daemon's senses would warn him of those threats. If he isn't killed instantly, he can heal himself in moments by draining the life from anyone around him.'

'Why are we discussing this? What are we waiting for?' exclaimed Maya. Rakan added his voice while Yana stood quietly behind them.

Tristan held up his hand. 'Silence!' he shouted. 'I've but one more question. Kalas, If you didn't know Taran at all and we stood here without Maya and Rakan demanding his release, what would you say? Would having Taran back balance with letting Alano go, whom you admit is death incarnate? Speak honestly now!'

A cold shiver went through Kalas, and he felt the eyes of everyone in the room like a weight upon his shoulders.

Tristan pressed again. 'Kalas, you swore an oath and are honour-bound to obey me. Again, I ask your advice. Would you exchange Taran for Alano? Is the reward greater than the risk?

Kalas slowly turned to look at Maya and Rakan, but couldn't meet their eyes. 'I'm sorry,' he said.

'You asked me for the truth,' Kalas responded, facing Tristan. 'The answer is … I don't believe so. The friend in me, the man who was saved by Taran, thinks we should make the exchange, but the lord commander in me, says no.'

Tristan rose as a shocked silence settled over the room. 'Then my decision is guided by the lord commander of this fortress.' Tristan stated firmly. 'There'll be no exchange, and Alano will be executed.'

'No,' screamed Maya, surging forward, grabbing Kalas. 'What have you done?'

'I won't let this happen,' shouted Rakan. 'I'll trade Alano for Taran myself!'

Fear and anger knotted Tristan's stomach. Even though he'd kept guards in the room, they'd be unable to save him if things turned violent. Yet he would win this fight. He knew a warrior's greatest weakness was honour, and he knew what Maya's weakness was too.

'Have you forgotten your oath so quickly? Tristan challenged. 'Does your word only hold true when it suits you to keep it? If Taran wasn't your son, you'd have made the same decision as Kalas!'

'But he *IS* my son,' Rakan shouted, yet his face was conflicted.

Tristan relaxed inside, growing more confident.

'He is, and a fine one!' Tristan placated, then turned to Maya. 'Would Taran exchange hundreds of lives for his own, knowing Alano would drain the life of innocents in days to come? Would he want you to pay that price?'

Maya's red eyes and lack of response were all the answer he needed.

'Kalas' decision stands.' Tristan stated. 'No exchange will take place, as every day the fortress holds is critical.'

Rakan's eyes were cold. 'My king,' he spat as he turned from the room, his arm about Maya's shoulders, pulling her with him down the corridor.

The guards shadowed them at a respectful distance.

Kalas followed, his head bowed, and even the daemon in his head was quiet. As he closed the door behind him, he never even noticed that Yana had stayed behind.

Tristan looked up to see Yana still standing there.

'Why are you still here? Leave!' he barked, pointing to the door, not bothering to look at her as he turned his attention back to his breakfast.

'Are you both foolish and blind?' asked Yana sharply.

Tristan spat out a mouthful of food. 'How dare you talk to me like that! 'Guards!' he called, and as they burst in, Yana backed away.

Yet her face was as hard as steel, and instead of fear, there was calm in her eyes as she locked Tristan's gaze with her own.

'I know what you want,' she said, 'and it's in your grasp. You're letting it slide away from you, and never again will you have this opportunity. If only you'd stop thinking with your stomach and listen to me. You have but a few moments to do two things or all is lost, forever.

'You want Maya …' Tristan began to object, but Yana pushed on. 'There's no point in denying it, so tell these guards to leave now so we can get you what you want!'

Tristan looked at the guards and waved them away, and as they moved toward the door, he called after them. 'Wait further down the hallway and make sure we aren't disturbed,' then indicated for Yana to continue.

'You played it well,' she said, 'by getting Kalas to make the decision to not go ahead with the trade. You removed a lot of the blame from yourself. But, you played the end game all wrong!'

'Assuming you're right, then how should I've played it?' asked Tristan. He leaned forward his eyes narrowing with interest. 'What should I have done?'

'I am right, so let's not play games,' said Yana firmly. 'You made the decision as you want Taran dead and out of the way. It was the obvious move, but not the clever one. Maya will kill herself if Taran dies. It appears Rakan actually stopped her from doing so when he brought the news to her. The next time she'll make sure no one can stop her. So let me tell you what you should do to stop that from happening, and get you what you want.

'Send your guards. Have one stop Kalas from passing your decision to the messenger, and thereafter killing Alano. Have him told that you're reconsidering, and for him to await further orders.'

'But why would I do that?' asked Tristan. 'If we go through with it, and Taran comes back, Maya will never be mine. Even my own lord commander says I shouldn't make the exchange!'

'Because,' said Yana, 'if the other guard brings Maya up here, you can demand anything from her as the price for saving Taran's life. I'm certain she'll do absolutely anything to save him from death, and I mean *anything*. You simply need to think of the price she has to pay, and she'll pay it. The key is to ensure the bargain you strike is unbreakable, so she has no room to escape.'

Tristan's eyes widened in surprise as he thought through Yana's proposition, understanding the power he now wielded.

'Guards,' he called loudly, and they bustled in. Tristan gave them their orders, and they sprinted down the corridor with all haste to deliver them.

'How can I reward you?' Tristan asked. 'You've not only seen what I value the most but given me the means to obtain it when my closest advisor was unable to do so. Do you want to join me to Freeguard, safe from the battle? Tell me, and it shall be yours, for you've played this game masterfully.'

Yana smiled. 'In time, I might well ask for a favour. Yet, my reward will come soon after you whisk Maya away to whatever future you decide for her. For now, I simply ask that my part in this remains strictly between you and I.'

Tristan snapped his fingers, laughing in appreciation. 'You'll be wasted here,' he said. 'You should come to Freeguard with me. You would do well playing the games of intrigue at the royal court.'

Yana nodded. 'All in good time, my king, but for now, I'll stay here with my prize. I'll stay here with Taran.'

Maya stood before Tristan, having been escorted back to the meeting chamber.

When she'd been approached by the guards, Rakan had come close to breaking some teeth. Fortunately, one of them advised that Tristan was willing to hear further from Maya should she wish to make a final plea. Thus Rakan had let her go as it was a condition she attended alone.

Now, as she looked at Tristan, with Astren sat at the end of the table and Galain observing, her feelings swung between desperation and hope. How had her hopes and dreams been dashed so quickly? She and Taran should have run, not come here to fight, but perhaps all was not lost.

'I'm sorry,' Tristan began, 'truly I am. I was led by Kalas and had he told me the exchange was worthwhile, I'd have gone ahead with it. We've stated the reasons not to make an exchange. Yet, I'm not without heart, and believe loyalty should be rewarded. So, I wanted to talk to you again. I've instructed Kalas to wait for my final decision before meeting with Daleth's messenger.

'Now, what should I do?'

'Make the exchange of course!' pleaded Maya.

'But for what reason?' Tristan asked intently.

'For what reason?' gasped Maya in astonishment. 'Because it's the right thing to do; because Taran is one of your commanders and his gift can help in the battles to come; because he's a good man, and because he's the love of my life. What else do you want me to say?'

'But I know all these things already,' Tristan shrugged, 'and I considered them before Kalas gave his verdict. You have told me nothing new. I was hoping for a reason to change my mind.'

'Astren, help me,' Maya implored. 'Tell Tristan to make the exchange.'

'He'll do no such thing,' stated Tristan firmly, and Astren stayed with his head down, writing furiously on a piece of parchment in front of him.

'Guards!' Tristan called.

'Wait, wait,' pleaded Maya, and Tristan waved the guards away as they entered. 'I need him to live; *we* need him to live. What will it take to get you to change your mind? Tell me!'

Tristan smiled. 'Ah,' he said, 'now we can make progress. This is the Freestates, and I'm its king. For me, it is all about what I can gain, and your question is well-phrased. It saves us time, and time is something Taran has fearfully little of. Let me ask you something. Are you a woman of your word? If you swore an oath, would you break it? If you signed a contract, would you honour it? Could you be trusted fully to keep to our bargain if we struck one? Because to break them with your king would be to have a sentence of death brought upon you, and upon the very man you seek to save!'

Maya nodded unperturbed. 'I've never broken a promise in my life.'

Tristan looked Maya firmly in the eye. 'Then, these are my conditions. This is what it will take for me to change my mind about having Taran exchanged for Alano, and for you to save his life, for he will surely need your gift to save him.

'You will come with me to Freeguard when I leave tomorrow. You will leave with me before Taran awakes to discover you gone. You will marry me once this war has been won, and thereafter you'll be crowned the Queen of the Freestates. You will tell no one of this discussion and our arrangement. That is the crux of it, but there will be more detail to follow. As I said before, should you break the terms, yours and Taran's life will immediately become forfeit.'

Maya couldn't believe what she was hearing, and she felt her legs start to give way. She sat down in shock, barely able to accept the implications of what Tristan was saying, but knowing that he meant every word.

'There must be some other way,' demanded Maya. 'I can serve you in any way you wish; travel the lands healing them, fight against

Daleth's armies. I could heal you should you ever become sick or wounded. Anything but what you've just asked for.'

Tristan leaned forward. 'This is not up for discussion, nor is there time for it. My terms are non-negotiable. If you wish to save Taran's life, then this is the only way, and soon even this way will be denied you. His life is ebbing away with every beat of his heart. If you don't decide now, the choice will be made for you, then you'll be responsible for his death because it's in your power to save him. Now swear to those terms or leave!'

Maya nodded, sobbing, her heart torn. 'I swear,' she said so quietly, that Tristan had to strain to hear her. Desperate thoughts flashed through her head. 'But, I have conditions of my own. First, you'll not attempt to lay with me until the night of our marriage. Second, we leave none of the wounded behind who can be saved.'

Tristan nodded, after all, the wine he'd intended to save had been drunk, thanks to Taran. 'Neither is unreasonable, for one is our custom when a king marries and the other common sense.

'Have you prepared the agreement for Maya?' Tristan asked.

Astren didn't say a word in reply. He slid the parchment he'd been writing on across the table, still refusing to lift his head to look at either Maya or Tristan.

Tristan read it briefly before nodding in satisfaction. 'Make your mark,' he said, turning the parchment around and holding a quill out to Maya.

In a daze she took it, and whilst she read the words, they barely registered, so she signed her name. There was no other choice.

'Galain, come forward,' Tristan ordered, and the sergeant approached. 'As you heard, we'll be leaving this place before first light, so have your men ready the wagons to assist in the transportation of the wounded. However, before you do so, have Lord Commander Kalas attend me. Please also ensure the Lady Maya waits discreetly in the study along the hall until she's summoned to heal Commander Taran.'

As Maya was led out, Tristan helped himself to a large goblet of wine and leaned back in his chair. Wine had never tasted so good. He glanced across at Asten, and his good mood began to evaporate. Astren's face was white, and tears ran down his face.

'Oh, for the sake of the gods, stop snivelling,' demanded Tristan. 'What's wrong with you?'

Astren's mouth opened and closed several times before he managed to form the words he'd obviously been trying to hold back. 'How could you do this? When did your heart wither and die to be replaced by such cruelty? You could have done this thing for nothing more than seeing the light of happiness shine in that girl's eyes, and for the generosity of the deed.'

'Generosity,' Tristan spat. 'How dare you insult me so? I should have your tongue removed. Have you forgotten what it is to be a noble of the Freestates? Wealth is everything!'

Astren wiped his red eyes. 'Then perhaps it's better for this world if our way of living dies with us. When you show the way forward by stealing that girl's life, to save Tarans, then you're no better than Daleth. You both take lives that don't belong to you.'

Tristan's face was cold. 'Astren, you're lucky you still have some residual worth to me. You failed in your task to find a way to have Maya accompany me, and now you again dare insolence! You are hereby stripped of your home, wealth, and belongings and will remain here when I leave tomorrow!'

'No!' cried Astren in horror, his hands raised beseechingly, realising what his outburst had cost him. 'I didn't mean what I said. Forgive me and take me with you, you need me!'

Tristan took a deep breath, still furious, considering his next move. 'You meant every word, so at least be man enough to own what you say, and the fate you've chosen.'

Astren knelt at Tristan's feet, grabbing his robes.

Tristan looked down, considering. 'You've but one final chance to redeem yourself. Serve me faithfully here, acting as my eyes and ears, and then maybe you'll have a place back at the court with your position and wealth reinstated.'

'I'll do it. I'll be the man you want me to be,' snivelled Astren as Tristan pointed toward the door, not even looking up.

As Astren left, Tristan leaned back in his chair. Sometimes things had a way of working themselves out. If he managed to hold on to his throne, he'd be the wealthiest Freestates king to have ever lived. Maya was invaluable, and she'd be bound to him by oath, by marriage, and by the life of the one she loved.

It didn't matter that she'd never loved him. Possession was what mattered, and none could deny her beauty even as she aged, so having her in his bed for a while would be quite pleasing. Of course, there were so many other younger girls he could call upon, but she might hold his favour for a while in this regard.

With some luck, Taran in his grief at Maya's disappearance would do something careless. He'd likely just get killed in battle and end his days here. Sometimes things just had a way of falling into place.

He smiled and finished his wine in a single gulp.

Kalas shook his head, unable to believe the turn of events, but inside there was a huge relief.

If all went well, Taran would be returned alive, and he wouldn't have to execute Alano. He'd tried to tell himself he wouldn't be killing his best friend, but he knew deep inside that twisted daemon, the soul of his friend still glimmered faintly. Better to kill him as they stood toe to toe in the sand, facing each other as men should. A warriors death.

Alano stood shackled next to him and was surprisingly silent, whereas, by contrast, the daemon in his own head gibbered away. It was as though having been denied the shedding of blood, it just wanted to complain.

'Silence, brother. Focus your senses, and see if any duplicity is planned,' warned Kalas in his mind. However, as he saw Krixen struggle over the rubble in the breach, the inert figure of Taran on a hand cart behind him, he realised this was unlikely.

The garrison engineers had worked swiftly through the remainder of the morning to fashion a small wooden bridge that they'd dropped across the trench. Kalas waited on the fortress side, unarmed as had been agreed.

He didn't need a weapon to kill Krixen, yet he'd every intention of keeping his oath that no blood would be shed under the flags of truce that fluttered above them. So while the walls were lined with Drizt's archers and the garrison soldiers, they had strict instructions not to attack. Not that any of them would risk jeopardising this exchange, for the mood of the defenders in such dire circumstances was as high as could be at the return of one who'd become dear to them.

Krixen approached slowly and stopped on the other side.

Kalas, through the eyes of his daemon brother, could see the blood pumping faintly through Taran's veins. Taran was as near death as could be, so Kalas didn't waste time and swiftly crossed the bridge.

Krixen reached for the hilt of his sword, that wasn't there, yet Kalas simply released the rope with which he'd led Alano. The chains binding Alano were incredibly thick and would require considerable time to cut through, a precaution Kalas felt was justified.

'I appreciate the honesty in which this exchange has been made,' Kalas said, as he took the handles of the cart. 'You're free to go without fear of death today. But, should I see you again, Krixen, that will no longer hold true.'

Kalas made haste, pulling the cart over the bridge. While doing so, he kept his gaze upon Krixen, who moved away, Alano alongside him.

Kalas quickly assessed Taran. The young man was in a terrible state. His armour had been removed, yet surprisingly, was in the cart. Because of this, his wounds were laid bare. There was blood bubbling from Taran's mouth, and a puncture wound in the chest which had likely deflated a lung. One arm was terribly twisted and broken, almost black, likely from the blunt blow of a mace. Additionally, his face and legs that hadn't been protected by armour were covered in cuts and gashes of various sizes.

All the wounds were covered in sticky salve, that stopped the flow of blood, but none of that would save him. Taran was beyond the help of mortal man, but not beyond the help of Maya.

The gate reopened, and Galain ran past to douse the wooden bridge in oil, setting it alight immediately he'd finished.

Maya stood waiting on the other side of the gate, and as he passed under the gatehouse, she ran forward with Rakan.

Kalas' instructions from Tristan had been strange but welcome. Taran was to be brought to the upper chambers alongside Maya for recovery. Kalas was surprised by this caring shift. He'd thought Tristan unworthy of his service, but perhaps there was something inside the king that was unselfish.

Kalas stood back as Maya knelt by the low cart, taking Taran's head in her hands. It was strange, for her face was a mixture of both joy and sadness. Her tears weren't the joyous ones he'd expected, but perhaps that was because Taran looked in such a terrible way. As he watched, her gift manifested itself, a glow surrounding her and then Taran.

Taran's wounds healed, and as they did the cart splintered and buckled, tossing Taran to the ground. Yet Maya's hands still held on to him, and her gift continued to flow.

The cart had been crafted from tower oak, and the timbers twisted, seeming to merge, as roots erupted from the long-dead timber and burrowed into the near-impenetrable rock beneath. The ground shifted, and Kalas stumbled in shock. Maya's gift had always been subtler than this, and then, at his feet, the very rock of the pass cracked and several nearby men lost their balance and fell.

The tree that suddenly erupted from the ground threw up chunks of rock and Kalas, overcoming his shock, ran forward, and Rakan did the same.

Kalas grabbed Taran's arm, lifting him onto his shoulder while Rakan picked up Maya, who'd slumped to the ground, eyes closed. She continued to glow even though she was now unconscious.

As they moved away, the ground buckled again, and they stumbled to their knees, fortunately out of danger. The tree grew taller and taller, reaching high above the wall, and still, it continued, until suddenly branches sprouted and a huge canopy of leaves erupted above them.

Maya's glow faded, and everyone stood open-mouthed at the towering tree amongst them. It dwarfed anything Kalas had ever seen, and these trees were renowned for their size. It was as tall as the keep itself, and its roots had thrown up mounds of broken rock between the walls as they twisted in and out of the ground like serpents.

'We need to take them to Tristan's chambers,' instructed Kalas, as he and Rakan carried Taran and Maya. With a procession of soldiers surrounding them, they hurried back to the keep.

As Rakan stared down at Maya in his arms, he noticed her hair was now pure white without a hint of black. He sighed sadly, for now when he looked at Taran and Maya, they looked such different ages. Would their love survive, he wondered?

Then his mood lifted again. He'd never seen a couple so happy, not that he'd had much experience. But their love was surely what love was supposed to be like, even if just in the bard's tales.

Theirs was a love for the ages, and happy at having reached this conclusion, he followed Kalas toward the keep.

Chapter XIV

Daleth looked down the pass expectantly, pleased with himself.

He'd concluded that Maya was at the keep with the other fugitives, and would be able to heal Taran as she'd done after the fight with Darkon and Lazard. He'd been proved right. Still, he'd been pleasantly surprised when Tristan had agreed to the trade.

Now he would soon have Alano back, and he was irreplaceable.

His choice of Krixen had proved sound, for he could see him leading the hooded figure of Alano in the distance as they climbed over the breach in the wall. Alano was shuffling and was probably chained. He would have done the same.

His smile of anticipation slowly faded from his face as his men began rising to their feet, pointing and calling out in surprise. He stared open-mouthed as into the sky pushed the largest tower-oak he'd ever seen. It rose to stand three times the height of the wall in the time it took him to draw no more than a dozen breaths. Then, as he watched, its canopy spread wide and green, fully half the width of the pass itself.

It was the most Incredible spectacle he'd ever witnessed. He knew Maya was able to heal the land, but this was a gift of such incredible power, beyond elemental in its strength.

He now regretted his decision to have her killed, for had he not passed down the order, she'd now be his captive. Then, this fortress would probably have fallen without Taran, Kalas, and Rakan joining the Freestates forces.

If there was ever a decision he could take back, that would be it.

To be able to harness such power even if he couldn't feed off the land she healed. The possibilities would be incredible. If she fell into his hands during this conquest, he wouldn't have her killed. Perhaps he didn't need to leave a wasteland behind him, perhaps he could use her after all.

But those thoughts were a distraction he could ill afford.

Once Alano and Krixen were safely out of the pass, the destruction of the wall would continue. It had to be reduced to rubble so that his men could advance over the remains without hindrance. He also had to think of his cavalry, who, once the fortress fell, would be let loose upon the lands beyond. They'd need smooth and swift passage through.

He passed an order to the crew of the siege engine, and they started readying their machine of war. He'd have men working shifts, ensuring it kept firing, bringing the wall down fully within two or three days. The trench beyond was another obstacle but could be filled with the rubble and dead. It would be overcome, like everything else.

He looked again at the tree. Amazing, he thought, truly amazing, and then walked toward his tent, calling for one of his guards. Alano was returning, perhaps a welcome home gift was in order.

Two other injured Freestates defenders had been captured along with Taran and kept alive while being tortured for entertainment. It was time to put them out of their agony. 'Bring me the two prisoners,' he ordered, 'and when Alano arrives and his chains are removed, have him brought to me too.'

It was always better to keep a dangerous pet well-fed.

'I'll be departing first thing in the morning before sunrise,' Tristan advised Kalas. 'The walking wounded will also leave at the same time, which means all the supply wagons and horses that have recently arrived will be coming with me. It will take two weeks for us to reach Freemantle, and then maybe a further three weeks to get to Freeguard. From there, I'll work with any other Freestates lords to ready ourselves for the arrival of our allies.

'We'll be working on readying provisions as well as recruiting the peasant levy as you suggested. The other nobles will be madly opposed to a commoner wielding anything other than a pitchfork or spade, but I'll make them listen.'

Kalas nodded. 'We'll hold for as long as possible before attempting a withdrawal. Fresh horses will be imperative if whosoever is left are to have any chance of outrunning Daleth's cavalry and making it to Freeguard. Ideally, we'll need five hundred horses. I don't expect that many to survive, but it'll give those who do spare mounts to keep ahead of Daleth's lancers. You need to ensure we get those horses, or there'll be no survivors.'

Tristan nodded. 'I place value in you, Kalas, that much you know, and what a Freestates king values, he's loath to lose,' he lied smoothly. 'Yet a withdrawal cannot be countenanced until such time as our allies arrive in Freeguard, so you must hold whatever the cost, for as long as it takes. I'll send those horses, but they're not to be used unless I give the order. To this end, Astren will be staying with you and will act as my eyes and voice.

'You swore an oath to obey me. Now, I know you have little respect for me …' Kalas started to object, but Tristan held up his hand and continued, 'but I need to know you'll keep your oath and fulfil this duty. There must be no retreat unless I countenance it. Do I have your word that you'll honour this?'

Kalas nodded. 'I'll honour my oath. We'll fight to the last or until our allies arrive at Freeguard, whichever comes soonest. However, I expect those horses here, ready to aid in our withdrawal should you order it.'

'I will do as you request,' Tristan said reassuringly. 'Just remember that the order to hold to the last applies to everyone here, with no exception.

'Now, to other simple matters. You'll have use of these chambers as from tomorrow. Commander Taran is already recovering in a room down the hallway, along with Maya.'

'I still don't understand what changed your mind. Why did you do that?' Kalas asked.

Tristan shook his head. 'That's not for me to explain to you, Kalas, so don't ask again. Just be grateful that Taran's alive and will fight at your side. This fortress now rests entirely in your hands and the future of the Freestates and all its people should you fail to hold it long enough. Prove to me that my trust in you is well-founded. Now, I've much to do in preparation for tomorrow's departure.

'You're dismissed.'

Kalas stood and left the room, and as he did so, the daemon's voice whispered in his mind. 'He has a soul almost as dark as ours, brother. He's not to be trusted, and a worthy king for us to serve, he is not.'

Kalas could only agree. Sometimes the daemon spoke wisely. It'd be no bad thing if, one day, the Freestates had a better ruler. It would need to be someone who wasn't afraid of battle, who didn't run away without shedding a drop of blood, who wasn't full of greed and avarice.

'What would you have done if you were king?' asked the daemon conversationally in his head, and Kalas found his thoughts full of visions of the Ember Kingdom reborn. They'd been golden years until Daleth had come and trampled it into the dust.

'Begone from my thoughts, daemon,' snarled Kalas, as he recognised the honeyed words and pictures were placed there, distracting him. 'My dream is to kill Daleth, not become king. So, stop trying to lure me with such.'

Yet as the daemon quietened down, Kalas began to wonder if it were not possible to have both.

Maya awoke during the early hours to a loud knocking on the door.

She found herself beside Taran, who was still in a healing sleep. She tried to wake him, but he was unresponsive and then she noticed a goblet by the bed. She picked it up and was not surprised to find it held an infusion of sleep weed. It seemed someone had made sure Taran would be sleeping for a long time yet.

It was better this way, she thought, for she'd not be able to hide the truth from him were he to wake, and she knew where that would lead. Taran would seek to kill Tristan and any guards who tried to stop him, and whilst that would be very satisfying … Maya caught herself from pursuing these thoughts; murder was something she could never countenance.

She'd bargained for Taran's life. Had she not done so, he'd be dead, and his corpse left to rot by now. She'd made a pact with a devil to secure his release, and now she would have to pay the price. To know Taran was alive and well was worth anything. That was why she'd done it; trading her heart, her happiness, her hand in marriage, for the chance for him to live.

She knew there was scant time left before the guards came to get her. They were going to depart before the majority of the keep's men roused. It wasn't just to get an early start, but to ensure Kalas, Rakan, and the others didn't see her leave and question why.

Her heart ached to spend these last moments wrapped around Taran's warm body, to close her eyes and wish that reality would disappear. Then, when she opened them, they'd both be far far away, but she knew what she had to do instead.

As they were in one of Tristan's well-appointed chambers, as well as the bed, and wardrobes, there were also desks. She opened the drawers and found parchment, ink and a quill. A sad smile flittered across her features when she realised that the very first message she would write to Taran would be to actually say goodbye.

She sat to write with a lantern's glow and the flames of the room's fire softly lighting the page.

The words didn't flow easily, for every few moments, she had to choke back tears. She told briefly of her all-consuming love, her desire and passion. She wrote of wanting to marry him, and only him, of having their children. That she wished they could look to the future together with wonder and expectation, for to be by his side was to know joy in its purest form.

She told him of Tristan's price, what she'd had to agree to do, to save his life. She explained that the price was something she'd pay again and again, for had he died when she'd had the chance to save him, her soul would have died with him. She asked him to consider what he'd have done to save her life were the roles reversed and asked for forgiveness for the unbearable hurt her choice would cause him.

Tears fell as she finished by asking Taran to do everything he could to save her should he survive the fall of the fortress, and this war be won. To seek her out and find a way to make their escape without resorting to murder. There was nothing Tristan wouldn't do to keep her in his avaricious grasp. They would need to take the greatest of care in their escape.

She carefully folded the parchment, and held it to her lips, then returned to the bed and knelt down beside it. She slipped the letter under the pillow, out of sight. Tristan would destroy it if found, and it might even put Taran's life in immediate danger. Voices and footsteps approached the door, and she leaned forward, kissing Taran's lips. 'This is goodbye, my prince. Come find me if you can. But If we cannot find a way to be together in this life, we must find each other in the next.' she whispered in his ear.

Her flowing white hair framed his face, and she stared long and hard, remembering his every feature, the curve of his lips, the strength of his jaw. She held his hand firmly, noting his youthful skin, and somehow this made their parting easier to bear. For she now looked nearer middle-aged and him still in the flush of youth. The cost of healing had been high, but it was something she would never regret.

The door to the chamber opened, and the guards stepped in quietly. They didn't say anything, first looking around in wonder, before bowing their heads deeply in respect as she rose and walked swiftly between them, her head held high and shoulders back.

No more would she allow her grief to show. She glanced behind a final time. To her surprise, the bed upon which Taran lay and the other furniture had been changed by her gift amidst her grief. The rose-wood from which it had been made was now living up to its name. Blooms hung heavy throughout. Yet whereas the roses should have been the brightest of red, they were instead the deepest black.

The door was closed behind her, and she turned to the guards.

'Lead,' she commanded, and they responded to the authority in her voice. Together they descended the winding steps and before long exited the keep to find Tristan waiting with his guards and all the wagons filled with wounded.

She walked amongst the injured men, many of whom were awake, giving them soft words of encouragement to be strong on the journey ahead. The guards showed her to a carriage, one opened its small door, but instead, she walked straight past and stepped up next to the man who sat holding the reins.

He looked shocked as she settled down next to him, and she looked across.

'What are you waiting for?' she said. 'My life in heaven is over for now, so lead me to whatever hell awaits.'

The man shook the reins, and the group began to move out. The horse's hooves were muffled, not out of sympathy to the majority of the soldiers who still slept, but to conceal their departure.

Tristan came to ride alongside, a look of satisfaction upon his face.

Maya closed her eyes so as not to see the fortress that had once held her hopes of salvation, and still held her one true love, slowly fall behind.

'God's help me!' Astren screamed, sitting up in bed, drenched in sweat. He wasn't sure whether he'd shouted aloud or in his dream, but no one came to investigate.

His heart hammered and tears ran down his cheeks as he tried to control his breathing, the feeling of terror and approaching death so fresh in his mind.

Ever since his meeting with Daleth, his dreams, when he finally slept had been peaceful. The absence of his recurring premonition had allowed him to start thinking of something other than the terrible fate that awaited him. Now though, the dream had come back even stronger than before, the horror of it overwhelming.

What had changed? The answer came quickly. Tristan was leaving, leaving him behind.

He looked to the timeglass. It was still very early morning, perhaps it wasn't too late.

He leapt out of bed, grabbed his rode, throwing it over his head before slipping on sandals. He dashed into the passageway, and ran, faster than he'd ever done before, his heart thudding in his ears as panic drove him onward.

He had to leave with Tristan and Maya; they'd understand if he told them.

One of his sandals caught on an uneven flagstone, and he tumbled to the floor, the strap breaking. He scrambled to his feet, and limped unevenly through the food hall, out onto the keep steps, words forming on his lips.

But there was no one to hear him.

His leaden footsteps took him slowly down into the courtyard, dimly lit by flickering torches, to the rear gates where some of Trom's spearmen stood guard.

As he approached, they crossed their spears in front of him.

'Now, where do you think you're going?' one of them asked, his voice deep, suiting the darkness of the night.

'Tristan?' was all Astren managed to gasp.

'He left quite some time ago,' offered the other guard.

As Astren went to push past, the guard put his huge palm against Astren's chest, shaking his head.

Astren felt his legs give way, and sobs wracked his body.

'Here now,' said one, crouching next to him. 'What ails you, man?' and he hauled Astren easily to his feet.

Astren couldn't find the words, and his only answer was the tears running down his face.

'Come,' said the guard, supporting Astren. 'Let's get you back to your room,' and he led Astren back into the keep.

It took a while, but Astren recovered his broken sandal while the guard spoke in a deep voice, soothingly talking of home.

'So, this is your room?' asked the guard as he opened the door, guiding Astren through. 'Why don't you get some more rest. Things won't seem so bad once the sun's up.'

Astren fell onto the bed, staring at the ceiling.

The guard looked around briefly, studying the portraits on the walls.

'These pictures would give me bad dreams. I'm glad you sleep here, not me,' the guard laughed softly, as he backed away and closed the door shut behind him.

Astren pulled a pillow to his chest, and brought his hand to his mouth, biting his knuckles hard to stop himself from screaming, and to stop himself from falling asleep.

He had to get out of here. He had to leave before the fortress fell.

Because if he didn't, his death by Daleth's hand seemed assured once again.

Yana stood outside the door to Taran's room, for once totally alone.

There were no guards, no Tristan, and more importantly, no Maya to contend with. She knew Taran would be asleep for a while longer; the infusion of sleep weed she'd been carefully administering would ensure that. The headache he'd awaken to wouldn't be pleasant, but it was for the best.

Nonetheless, she opened the door to his chamber carefully, her heart beating loudly as she slipped into the room, closing the door quietly behind her.

The heady smell of roses filled the chamber. She looked around the room in the glow of the fire at the change Maya's gift had wrought. Yana shook her head in disbelief. That such power should be so wasted on one who didn't know how to use it properly was an offence to the gods.

Her victory in this game of hearts was within her grasp, yet still, she had to tread warily. Kalas, Rakan, or others might rise early and find her here, and she couldn't be seen to be intimated in any way, or taking advantage of the situation. Yet this was too irresistible a moment to pass by.

Yana moved onto the bed next to Taran, scarcely breathing as she lay next to him, gazing at his profile and the rise and fall of his chest.

Just a few moments, she told herself, and carefully draped an arm across him, wriggling slowly closer. Just a brief embrace, then it would be time to keep her distance for as long as it took Taran to come to her. Grief and an empty heart could often drive a man to another woman's embrace for the solace it offered, and there were no others to compete with now.

She slipped her other arm slowly under his head, and as she did so, her hand brushed against something strange under the pillow.

Yana had made the bed herself, supervised Taran and even Maya as they were laid upon it, and there should be nothing but clean linen. Her curiosity was piqued, and she reached further under the pillow, putting aside this exquisite moment as her hands encountered a parchment sheet. She withdrew it and rose from the bed to sit down upon a chair covered in blooms and read the note Maya had written for Taran by the light of the fire.

Yana had only ever cried twice in her life; at the loss of her father, and then more recently as her brother died in her arms back at her grandfather's settlement. This letter brought tears flowing forth one more time.

As her eyes flickered across the parchment, and read the words of such poignant love and sorrow, she suddenly felt the most terrible guilt. She was so unused to this feeling that it took her a moment to recognise it for what it was. There was now no doubt in her mind that Maya held true love for Taran, sacrificing everything for his life; for her life with him was everything.

She wiped away her tears, looking across at Taran. She'd taken a woman from him who'd loved him to the moon, and would do everything to make things right.

What better way to do so, than to be the one to love him to the moon and back again? That way, he wouldn't feel the heartache for long. Taran would realise that despite him losing the one, there was now ... a better one.

Smiling in satisfaction, she curled the parchment into a ball and tossed it onto the fire. Had Taran found this, it would have changed everything. Without question, the gods must have led her hand to find this missive, and thus they not only approved of but guided her actions.

Yana almost skipped from the room, Taran would soon be hers, and nothing could stop her.

Taran cautiously opened his eyes to find himself in an unfamiliar room, devoid of pain save for a headache. He hadn't expected to awaken again unless to the nine hells. The last time he was conscious he'd been near death, staring into the eyes of Daleth, reading his mind. The king's thoughts were full of elation at the taking of the first wall, and his impatience to take revenge on ... Kalas?

Now, here he was with a headache, a bitter taste in his mouth, in a bed covered in heavy blooms.

He smiled as he realised that if his wounds were healed, and he lay in a room whose furniture had turned into rose bushes, then he'd been saved by Maya. He leapt out of bed, marvelling as he glanced over himself, noting the lack of any wound. Yet suddenly his happiness disappeared as he realised the effect bringing him back from near death would have had on Maya. This was a sobering thought. It didn't matter to him how she looked, but it mattered to her, and anything that brought her pain was nothing to be happy about.

Fresh clothes were laid over the end of the bed with his armour and weapons upon a rack. On a table was a platter of bread and honey, with watered wine in a jug, and his stomach growled in anticipation. He relieved himself into a chamber pot, and while he wanted to rush out and find Maya, he wolfed down the food, then dressed and donned his armour and weapons.

Looking out of a curtained window confirmed what he'd already surmised. He was on the top floor of the keep in one of the chambers Tristan kept for his personal use. It seemed his redemption also came with an elevation in status, and he chuckled at his joke.

He opened the door to his room and walked into the corridor. The sun was only just starting to rise, and the torches were still burning in their brackets on the walls. Something seemed strange, and he stopped, his hand going to the hilt of his sword. The guards that had been permanently stationed here were absent. He cautiously made his way toward the end of the hallway where the door to the meeting chamber stood ajar. He peered in to find it almost empty. The tables that had been covered in maps and charts were as bare as the cupboards that had previously held Tristan's wine.

He walked out to the balcony and was relieved to see soldiers on the walls below in the dim light. A short sigh of relief escaped his lips. He wasn't somehow alone, forgotten and left behind.

Then he gasped, registering for the first time the most enormous tree he'd ever seen standing behind the second wall, and shook his head in wonder.

It was time to find the others, so he turned and picked up his pace as he headed to the winding steps. Tristan, it seemed, had fled the nest; a little early perhaps, but that would explain how deserted these chambers were.

As he reached the ground floor to the eating hall, soldiers clamoured around him, slapping him on the back. He paused, enjoying the genuine warmth that flowed from them, then gently but insistently pushed through toward the corridors leading to his room. As he passed amongst them, he garnered that Tristan had left as suspected, along with many of the wounded and a number of soldiers acting as guards.

After he extracted himself from the crowd, he jogged through the dimly lit passageways, and turned a corner, almost bumping into Rakan. Rakan wore the biggest smile and tears glistened in his eyes as they both embraced.

'You're a sight to ease my heart,' said Rakan. 'I honestly thought you were lost to us for good. I never want to go through that again, and if I found it bad, then that was nothing to what Maya went through. So where did you leave her, is she still sleeping?'

Taran looked confused, so Rakan continued. 'We put you both in Tristan's chambers yesterday, and she's not in your old room, the door is open.'

'Tristan has left?' Taran said, half querying.

Rakan nodded. 'All yesterday afternoon we were readying the injured who were well enough to travel. Tristan always planned on leaving after the first wall fell, but none of us thought it would be that quickly. He departed in the early hours, and even Kalas thought it best that the fewer men who saw their king leave them behind, the better.

'Well,' interrupted Taran, 'if Maya isn't in our old room or in the upstairs chambers, she must be with the healers or something. Let's go find Kalas, he'll be on the wall I assume, and we'll see Maya when we see her.'

Rakan could see that despite the nonchalance in his voice, his son was slightly hurt, so he put his arm around Taran's shoulders in support. To feel someone's absence keenly was to be without complacence. Of late, since the removal of his amulet, Rakan had become reacquainted with many emotions and was as happy as could be at Taran's return. Strangely though, the grief he'd felt when Taran seemed lost was deeper than the high that followed his return. Perhaps not feeling at all could sometimes be better.

The two of them walked through the keep, passing soldiers who greeted them with respect and warmth, then out into the growing morning light.

Taran was keen to find Maya, but as they walked down the keep steps, Kalas was exercising in the courtyard, encouraging many of the soldiers who'd risen early to follow suit.

'We probably have five days' respite before we feel the force of the enemy again,' called Kalas, as he came toward then. 'We can all use this time to practice and in some cases, improve.' As he said this, he tossed both Taran and Rakan a practice weapon. 'How about you two face off against one another while I watch for a moment.'

Taran hefted the heavy wooden blade and began circling Rakan, unconsciously reading his movements, the subtle shift of his shoulder as Rakan launched his attack.

It was as if time slowed when Taran fought with his fists, and now swordplay was becoming the same. Rakan began to execute a short stabbing thrust as an opening move, but Taran was already sliding forward. Taran swiftly moving to the outside of the thrust, spinning past as the flat of his blade thudded into Rakan's stomach.

Rakan stumbled back, eyes wide open, more in shock than pain.

Kalas clapped. 'Where did you learn that move?' he asked.

Taran shrugged. 'I think I saw you use it to defeat one of Trom's men when we first arrived,' he answered.

Kalas laughed. 'Try me,' he said, and raised his sword, saluting Taran. Kalas led with the same move, and Taran responded as he had with Rakan. He spun, his blade flashing out, only to find it deflected before Kalas tripped him. He rolled smoothly when he fell, but as he gained his feet, Kalas' blade tapped his neck.

'Again!' Kalas demanded.

This time Taran read the parry and trip, nimbly jumping over Kalas' leg, spinning in the air, aiming a cut for the back of Kalas' neck, but Kalas changed his tactic and defeated him.

Each time Taran learned the move immediately, and the dance extended longer and longer until finally, Kalas called a halt. A crowd of men were watching, and there was a hushed silence as the two combatants moved apart.

'That, was amazing,' said Rakan, coming forward with a flask of water for his two sweating friends.

'It's more amazing than you realise,' said Kalas. 'Taran, here, learned over fifty consecutive moves and carried them out flawlessly after only having been shown the error of his ways once. His gift is evolving, and it would seem he's absorbing the skills of those around him.

'When I first met him, I would have killed him in a heartbeat, yet now he would give me pause, even if the outcome were the same. Who knows how high his skills will rise if he lives long enough and doesn't find himself on the wrong side of a fire trench again.'

Taran warmed under the praise and was shocked at himself. He knew his gift had grown of late, allowing him to influence hearts and minds, but now this. He'd almost had the measure of Kalas at times toward the end, such was the way he read his moves. The thing was, Kalas seemed to have an almost infinite number to call upon.

They moved to stand in the lee of the third wall, watching as the other soldiers resumed training when Rakan cleared his throat. 'I have to ask,' he said. 'Physically, it seems you're in fine health thanks to Maya, 'but tell me, how are you otherwise. Did they torture you?' Worry creased his brow.

'Daleth wanted to,' Taran replied, 'but his soldiers had done such a good job at cutting me into pieces, there was no point.' Taran shuddered as he recalled the pain. 'I'd rather forget everything that happened from the moment the wall fell until I awoke this morning. Yet, one interesting thing I remember was a thought in Daleth's mind. He was impatient to take revenge against, well, I'm not sure, but the image looked like Kalas, I think.'

Kalas looked amused. 'You think? It seems I must try harder if you and he are unsure.'

They all laughed, but the moment of levity was interrupted as again Taran wondered to the whereabouts of Maya. 'I need to find Maya,' he said.

Kalas nodded. 'Afterward, it's important we meet. We also need to round up Drizt and Trom, perhaps even Yana. So, go and get Maya first, as we need to prepare for the onslaught to come.'

'The problem is, Taran here has lost Maya,' said Rakan, but he didn't laugh, for he saw the concern in Taran's eyes. 'She wasn't with him when he awoke, and we haven't seen her today, which is quite unusual.'

They looked around and saw Yana talking to some of the healers in the shadow of the wall.

'Yana,' Rakan called, and she looked over, waving. 'Have you seen Maya?'

Yana shook her head. 'I've not seen her since yesterday,' she called, before turning back to her group.

'This is strange,' said Taran, worry creeping into his voice. 'Can we meet in a turn of the hourglass to give me a chance to find where she's hiding?' He laughed, but the look in his eyes betrayed concern as he walked toward the keep, asking men he passed if they'd seen her.

Rakan shook his head as he and Kalas watched Taran walk away. 'That young man was born into the wrong world at the wrong time. He and Maya deserve more than this considering what they have between them. Maybe we should allow him an extra hour to take into account how they'll be feeling when they find each other,' he winked at Kalas.

Kalas chuckled. 'If that's the case, let's make it two,' and he shouted the change in plan to Taran who waved in acknowledgement.

'Right, let me see if I can teach an old man like you some new skills,' Kalas challenged, raising his sword in salute.

'Old,' spluttered Rakan. 'I do believe I'm younger than you! Oh, hold on, Drizt wants a word,' he said, pointing behind Kalas.

Kalas turned around. 'Where?' he asked, then turned back to find Rakan's wooden sword at his throat.

'You might be better than me, but I'm craftier,' grinned Rakan.

I'll be sure never to forget that again,' acknowledged Kalas. 'Now, let me show you the true meaning of swordcraft!' and their practice began.

Chapter XV

Daleth sat contemplating, his chin on his hands as he looked at the sun rising over the fortress and the colossal tree that rose above it.

He'd always considered himself gifted beyond all others yet as he stared at the tree rising high into the sky, he felt a doubt, of sorts. Surely nothing could eclipse his power of longevity, but the sight before him was awe-inspiring, and he couldn't remember the last time anything had ever given him such pause.

Movement caught his eye; the crews surrounding the siege engine were moving it further down the pass. Now the enemy had lost the first wall, he didn't need to worry about them manning the catapults behind. It had become quickly apparent that they'd only had two working. With those abandoned, his own crews could act with impunity, and being closer would ensure no shot would miss.

With good fortune, it would be but a day or two before the main wall was brought low. The filling of the trench would be contested by the enemy archers, but a shield wall would keep the majority of his men safe.

He glanced at Alano sitting alongside him. It was good to have him back, yet perhaps he'd hoped more for the return of his general as opposed to the daemon alone.

He was also wondering whether the exchange was as one-sided as he first believed. Alano had just told him of Taran's extraordinary gift. To be able to see into the thoughts of men, guess their moves, know their intentions. It helped explain the death of the Rangers by Taran's hand.

The Rangers were a bloodthirsty bunch, and they'd wanted to be thrown into the assault to claim some honour, but this part of the conquest was not for them. The fortress was like a slaughterhouse, and even they'd be vulnerable climbing a ladder or cresting a wall.

Fortunately, their disappointment at being held back had been assuaged by a mission that would suit their exceptional skills. The discovery that Taran, Rakan, and Maya were at the fortress had given rise to a strategic opportunity that they'd seek to exploit whilst tying up a loose end. They'd left earlier that morning.

The siege engine thumped, and Daleth, distracted, turned, watching in satisfaction as a huge piece of masonry flew through the air to strike the wall near where it had collapsed. More crumbled to the ground. Yes, a day or two at most indeed.

He looked again at Alano.

'Why is it that despite surrounding myself with those gifted in the ways of killing, I feel that Maya and Taran between them are gifted beyond them all?'

Alano shook his head, a look of twisted indifference on his features. 'Only you can judge the worth of those who follow you, my king.'

Alano rose and stalked away. The blindness of man, the daemon thought … *surrounded by those gifted in the ways of killing*. If only Daleth wasn't so blinded by conquest and revenge, perhaps he might see he hadn't necessarily surrounded himself with the gifted; he'd surrounded himself with the cursed.

Taran gripped the sleepy man by his shoulders. He'd spoken to every man awake but then realised that perhaps he should be talking to those who now slept, who'd been awake during the night hours. They might have seen something that the others hadn't.

At the back of his mind, Taran felt a suspicion growing along with the nausea in his stomach, and as the soldier's bleary-eyes cleared, Taran released his hold.

'Relax, Bynor,' said Taran, using the man's name, stepping back now the man had sat up. 'I'm sorry to wake you, and don't worry, the walls aren't being overrun or anything serious. I just need to ask you a question. Were you on duty when King Tristan left in the early hours of this morning?'

The man nodded. 'Yes, commander. 'I saw the whole thing. Some of us were helping get the last supplies settled on the wagons because it was taking too long and the king was impatient to leave.'

Taran smiled his thanks. 'That was a job well done. Was the Lady Maya with the group when they left?'

Brindle nodded. 'Yes. She arrived just as they were about to depart.'

Taran felt like a knife was twisting in his stomach as he tried to formulate the next question but then decided not to ask one. Usually, he only used his gift in a time of need, because looking into people's minds wasn't always pleasant, but he had to see for himself. It would be easy now the memories were at the forefront of Bynor's thoughts.

'Thank you, Bynor,' said Taran, as he used his gift. First, he coerced the soldier to sleep, which took but a moment for the man was exhausted, and then looked into the man's thoughts.

He saw Maya from Bynor's perspective as he'd been helping to load supplies, so it was just glimpses of her as she walked amongst the wagons. From what he saw, her face was composed, almost devoid of emotion other than compassion at the suffering she witnessed. The final glimpses were of her climbing onto a carriage to sit beside the driver and then Tristan riding alongside on his horse looking pleased.

After that, she was no longer in the man's thoughts. Taran walked from the room, almost blindly, slowly making his way through the keep, his head spinning.

Maya was gone, really gone, left with the wounded, left with, and Taran could hardly bring himself to think it ... left with Tristan. He couldn't understand it and sat down on the steps leading to the upper floors. He leaned back against the cold wall that matched the sudden coldness in his heart, not knowing what to do.

He'd wandered aimlessly before he'd met Maya, looking for something missing without knowing what it was, until one day he'd found it in those brown eyes, frizzy hair, graceful movement and musical voice. From the moment he'd started to really know Maya, his life had begun to take on a purpose and meaning. Now in her absence, he suddenly felt lost, unsure of what his purpose was any longer.

Should he pursue her? Yet how would he even find her in this unknown land and what would happen if he did?

It wasn't the fact she'd left. He was strangely glad that she was putting a safe distance between her and the fighting. It was because she'd left without saying goodbye. She hadn't looked happy in Bynor's thoughts, but she'd gone without telling him why.

He hadn't seen this coming, not even a hint. As he sat there, heart beating with trepidation, tears welled then coursed down his cheeks. His emotions swayed between heart-stopping sadness and confusion.

He didn't know how long he'd sat there, but slowly he became aware of Rakan next to him.

'Tell me,' said Rakan, and put his arm around Taran's shoulder, and was surprised when Taran's body shook with silent sobs.

'She left this morning, with the wounded, with Tristan,' Taran struggled to say. 'I thought what we had was enough to conquer everything … but it seems a peasant boy cannot compete with a king.'

'Don't say that, son,' said Rakan, although he was shocked by Taran's revelation. He searched for the right words. 'You're jumping to conclusions without knowing all the facts. I'm sure there's more to this than we know. You two had something the like of which nobody had ever seen. The kind of love you find once in a lifetime. Just because she left doesn't mean that isn't still the case and to think she left to be with Tristan is not something I would believe for a moment.'

Taran nodded his head, a glimmer of reason returning as he calmed. 'Perhaps you're right. Maybe I'm jumping to the wrong conclusion. But, she left; no goodbyes, nothing.' He stood, his face showing the inner conflict. 'Why didn't she leave a letter or tell you or Kalas?'

Rakan was perplexed. 'I really don't know, but I suggest you think on this; she's safe away from here, and she'll have a good explanation when you meet her again.'

Taran smiled, but there was something sinister to it. 'I hope you're right. Because if ever we deal with Daleth, and I find Maya's disappearance was Tristan's doing, then I'm going to make him pay, be sure of that.' He stood, stony-faced, and walked up the steps.

Rakan followed behind. For Tristan's sake, the king had better not have done anything stupid, for there'd been something frightening in Taran's eyes there for a moment. It was the look of someone who'd just lost everything and was teetering on the edge, about to replace the emptiness with just one thing that Rakan knew only too well.

The fires of revenge.

Maya sat atop the carriage that Tristan or perhaps Astren had organised. It didn't matter who, all Maya knew was that it took her away from her hopes and dreams toward despair. To think, the fortress was the most dangerous place in the land, and yet it was where she most wanted to be.

It had passed midday some time before, and the pace set was relentless. The driver of the carriage shared that they were heading toward Freemantle where they'd stop, before moving on to Freeguard.

As they rode, she kept her face composed. Inside she might be feeling despair, but on the outside, her visage was strong. All around rode soldiers that Tristan had seconded as his bodyguard, and as she looked at them, she suddenly felt more a prisoner on the way to her execution than when she'd first been captured. True, she wasn't in chains, and these were Freestates men, but her freedom had been stripped away, and this time Taran wasn't amongst her jailors.

The pain of Taran's absence was both physical and emotional. It was as if her heart had been ripped from her chest. Almost as bad was not knowing what was happening at the fortress. Taran would have awoken some time ago to find her absent. How was he, what he was doing, and what he was thinking?

Had he found her letter, had he understood her choices and was he grieving as she was? Of course, he was grieving, she thought, but that made her feel worse. To know she'd caused him pain and wasn't there to ease it in the next breath added guilt to the list of negative emotions that beset her. She thought then of his planning to rescue her, and even if that day were far away, she felt a little better.

Needing a distraction, she hopped down from the carriage, and as the guards turned toward her in consternation, she jumped into the back of a wagon carrying the wounded. The men within looked up in surprise as she leapt in, and she greeted them with a smile that she didn't feel inside. They were in a terrible state, being bounced around, already in pain from their injuries, only for it to be made worse by the relentless jolting they endured.

'Here,' she said, 'let me take a look at you,' and took hold of a healers satchel that was in the corner. She began to assess the bindings of the men. Some bandages needed replacing where blood and pus had soaked through. Yet despite the pain it must have caused to peel them away, they all suffered in silence, grateful for her care. Where necessary, she applied small amounts of sticky, fragrant salve to reduce inflammation or pain and to help fight infection.

Throughout the day, she moved between the fifteen wagons, doing all she could for the injured. Each carried four men, and when the wagons halted for the day in a roadside clearing, she was exhausted. The injured were incredibly grateful, but she didn't stop there. As fires were lit for the night, she organised Tristan's guard to help; organising them to cook, then share out food and water to the wounded.

Tristan tried to intervene, saying they should secure the camp and organise his food first, but her withering look silenced him as she moved amongst the wounded a final time, checking they'd all been attended to.

Some of those with lesser injuries managed to stretch their legs, grateful for the respite from the day's journey, for these were not the most seriously wounded who'd end their days at the fortress. These men would hopefully recover in time, given proper care, and Maya was determined to help them one and all to achieve just that. They bowed as she moved amongst them and she nodded back, accepting their respect, and enjoyed how much it annoyed Tristan that they gave this to her so willingly, yet not him.

After she saw to the wounded, she helped herself to a bowl of hot meat with vegetables and moved away, watching the sunset to the west. Taran would have loved the orange and red hues that splashed the clouds. The thought spoiled it for her, and she spooned the stew into her mouth, remembering how Taran had smuggled her food when she was imprisoned. It had been simple, dry, wrapped in leaves and yet it had tasted divine, maybe because she'd been ravenous, or perhaps as it had come from his hand.

She wanted to feel strong, yet the wound of separation was so fresh. She still found it hard to believe that they'd found each other, only to be separated, not by the enemy, but by a supposed ally.

As she sat in thought, she was shaken from her reverie by Tristan coming to stand before her. 'Come eat with me,' he said and begun to turn away.

Maya caught his eye. 'No,' she said simply.

Tristan's face, which hadn't looked too happy before, twisted into a scowl. 'You'll do as you're ordered,' he growled.

Maya didn't flinch. 'We made a bargain,' she said calmly, even if she didn't feel it, 'for me to leave with you, to even be your wife in time, but liking you was not part of the bargain. I can assure you, that any feelings of gratitude or warmth for taking us in when we sought refuge, disappeared the moment you manipulated me into this situation.

'This might be how things are done in the Freestates. You might trade people like you trade goods and judge your wealth by owning me and others, but you'll never own my heart or my love. So, let's not even pretend, shall we?'

Tristan stood looking at her, and his face calmed. 'On top of your gift, you're strong-willed, and not someone to be trifled with. But I know your weakness. I didn't become King of the Freestates by chance, nor by kindness and least of all by generosity. You have a choice; come and sit with me, or we leave a wagon of the injured behind when we depart in the morning. They'll die, and it will be your choice.' With those words hanging in the air, he moved away, sitting down on a fallen tree near the fire.

Maya stared after him, aghast. She knew, without doubt, this wasn't a bluff. With a heavy heart, she stood, and with slow steps walked across and sat down on a rock opposite Tristan.

'That's better,' he said. 'See how good you are at saving lives. Now, let's pass the time by helping you to understand what's expected of the Queen of the Freestates.'

Maya looked to the west, but the sun had set, and the sky was dark. There were no stars, there was no light. Just like my life, Maya thought, as she spooned the now tasteless food into her mouth.

She looked at Tristan, feeling a rage grow inside her. How easy it would be to reach for her gift, and to have the tree he sat upon root itself within his body, for it to tear him apart from the inside. Her fists clenched, nails digging into her palm as Tristan started to talk. She'd consciously accepted the bargain he'd offered, and however vile Tristan was, she couldn't become a murderer. Yet, perhaps a small splinter …

Tristan yelped loudly, and jumped from the log, rubbing furiously at his backside.

Maya felt a rush of guilty satisfaction as Tristan hobbled off, calling for Galain. It might still be a dark night bereft of Taran's company, but at least it was now a peaceful one.

Two days had passed since Maya's disappearance, and as Kalas looked around the meeting chamber at the top of the keep, the mood was subdued.

Taran's was distant, and his visage was dark, eyes staring into nothingness. Kalas wanted to try and snap him out of it, to tell him now was not the time for grieving, but intuitively he knew this would not help. In matters of the heart, the mind held little sway, and it could push Taran into who knew what foolish action.

Rakan was somewhat distracted, a father worried about his son.

Drizt and Sancen had also been affected by Maya's departure. In fact, there wasn't a person in the whole damned keep whose spirits hadn't sunk to the bottom of the abyss, except perhaps for Yana whose face remained neutral.

Maya, it seemed, had been pivotal to the morale of the entire garrison, from the common soldier who viewed her as some goddess of life, all the way up to Taran to whom she was the goddess of love.

But it wasn't this that Kalas was worried about, even if Maya's disappearance was proving a catastrophe.

The first wall which he'd thought would take up to three days to demolish had come down in two, and the enemy were already making progress in clearing paths through the rubble.

Daleth now had his ballistae and archers keeping everyone on the wall pinned down. The Eyre archers were now unable to disrupt the work without great risk, so Kalas had ordered them to step down, unwilling to risk further losses.

'Things are not looking good,' he began. 'We'll have less respite than I hoped for, and Daleth will soon turn his siege engine on the second wall. We all know it's in a weakened a state like the first, so I don't think it'll take much longer than a few days to be breached.

'That damned siege engine is going to bring our resistance to an end sooner than I feared and I don't think there's a damned thing we can do about it. But, I want your thoughts on the situation.'

Drizt looked around at the stony faces and spoke for the room. 'I hate to say it, but I think you're right. We could attempt a sortie to burn the damned thing, but Daleth's troops protect it day and night. We'd be overwhelmed and slaughtered.'

'We should have just burned them the moment we captured them,' said Rakan, 'but hindsight is a useless skill. At the time, I was just as happy to turn them against Daleth's army. Who'd have thought these walls would come tumbling down so quickly?'

Trom nodded in agreement. 'We needed those early victories, and there was no mistake in the choices we made. Without them, the morale of the men wouldn't have held so long. The problem is since that time we've suffered nothing but setbacks, and those are becoming a distant memory. Added to this, Maya leaving has brought the men's morale to near breaking point.'

Trom looked at Kalas' frowning face, shaking slowly, but carried on regardless. 'I know it's a painful subject, and I'm sorry to raise the point. Whilst no one feels her absence like Taran here, even my men who pray to the gods of the sand saw in her something ethereal and holy. She gave us faith, she gave us hope, she created light from the dark.' Trom reached out as he said this, gripping Taran's shoulder. 'We share in your loss brother, and may you both drink the sweet water in the oasis of love again one day.'

Taran nodded in thanks but didn't say a word as he stood, walking quickly from the room.

Drizt shook his head. 'Only those dearest can hurt us the deepest. Taran looked in less pain when he was brought back to us half dead.'

Rakan nodded. 'There are only two things I know of that can take away my son's pain in the short term; one is to get Maya back, and the other is death.'

'He'll heal in time,' suggested Kalas, 'but that's something none of us will have unless we come up with a solution to Daleth's siege engine. We've come back to our original problem. Is there anything we can do?'

Rakan, Drizt, and Trom shook their heads in response, while Yana seemed deep in thought and didn't seem to be too focussed on the question. Kalas hadn't expected an idea from her, but at this stage, he'd take ideas from anyone.

After a few moments of silence, Kalas continued. 'Well then, we use today and tomorrow to continue honing the men. Those who are still standing are better than those who've fallen before. We'll bleed Daleth as long as the remaining walls protect us, and hope they last longer than the first.'

Kalas turned to Yana. 'Go see Astren. Tristan left him behind so we could continue to communicate, but I haven't seen him in days as he's been spirit travelling so much. Make sure he knows to attend our meetings both morning and evening from hereon. He's now the only way we can reach Tristan and know the position of our allies.'

Yana stood up. 'I'll go see him now,' she said. 'If he has anything interesting to say, I'll come to find you.'

As she left the room, her mind turned back to what Rakan had said. The only things that could take away Taran's pain were Maya or death. Yet an idea was forming in her mind, and the more she thought about it, the more she liked it.

She now knew of a third option and was sure it would work, but it was all about timing. If she timed it perfectly, there was a chance she'd end up with Taran far sooner than she'd envisaged.

She hummed a tune as she descended the steps, and despite the coolness of the keep, she felt all warm inside, everything was coming together.

From behind a merlon, Taran carefully observed the enemy troops as they toiled in the distance over the remains of the first wall.

A long line of soldiers with heavy shields protected those who'd been chosen to clear paths through the rubble. Just beyond them, ranks of enemy archers and the two ballistae were ready to engage.

As he watched, four wide avenues were being slowly cleared through the piles of rubble as oxen and horses pulled the large blocks of stone to one side while men with enormous metal hammers pulverised the smaller rocks. The workload was huge, but Daleth had thousands of men working in shifts, and whereas Taran thought it would take forever, the progress they made was surprisingly fast as fresh men were rotated in.

In the distance, the siege engine that would be their doom had been brought closer, and Taran wondered why they were waiting before they attempted to bring down the second wall. Maybe Daleth hoped to replicate the last breach that saw so many of the defenders caught and trapped, himself included.

He thought about that moment once again, and pain hit him like a physical blow when he recalled that had been the last time he'd spoken with Maya. He was glad he'd told her his innermost feelings, but also felt slightly foolish. He'd have done anything for her, absolutely anything for their love, and yet she'd left him. Why? He cursed himself, annoyed at his weakness, remembering Rakan's words. He shouldn't doubt Maya, something else was afoot, and until he knew exactly what had happened, he'd be grateful she was safe from harm.

Nonetheless, despite logic replacing his wayward thoughts, he was glad his helm concealed the torment etched on his face from the other men on the wall. He could almost feel their pity for him even if he didn't read their minds, and the anger this evoked in him helped push back much of the pain.

His mood was grim as he stood there, so much darkness festering inside that he barely recognised himself. He'd always been carefree, happy, living life on the road or so he thought. But then he'd met Maya and realised that had all been a lie. Despite knowing many women, he'd never experienced love and never looked beyond the day ahead. Then, with Maya in his life, he'd dreamed of the future in a thousand colours, knowing what he wanted his life to be, feeling a purpose for the first time.

Now, confusion was being replaced with a burning desire to strike out, inflict pain, and visit his grief a hundredfold on the enemy. Yet, what if Tristan had stolen Maya away, and what would he do if Maya was complicit as well?

The thought jolted him. What was he thinking? She was the love of his life, and he was so foolish to doubt her feelings, and he needed something irrefutable to remind him of them.

He spun, walking down the steps, brushing past Rakan as if his father wasn't there. Through the open gates of the third wall he passed, but instead of turning toward the keep, he crossed the courtyard toward the final gateway leading to the Freestates beyond.

Trom's men were on guard, more to ensure no garrison men deserted than any fear of an enemy attack. As Taran walked purposely toward them, they moved aside.

All he could think of was to lose himself in the forest, find the oasis Maya had created for him, and maybe there find some solace, anything to counter the darkness that threatened to swallow him.

He strode along the pass, his pace swift and determined and turned south to retrace the steps they'd taken but mere days before and stopped in his tracks. For the first time since Maya had left, for the briefest of moments, surprise completely removed his grief as a shadow caused him to look up.

Whilst his future still looked dismal, perhaps for everyone else, it might have changed for the better, for three giants stood before him.

The leader who he recognised as the Elder of the giant folk knelt before him and touched its forehead to the floor. The other two did likewise in a surprising sign of fealty.

Taran felt his heart sink, and looked longingly toward the distant forest for a moment, knowing there was no escaping his duty now. Also, the only way to communicate with these giants was to open his mind to them, and this was the last thing he wanted to do.

He sighed and sat down on the grass as they did the same, their massive clubs across their laps.

Taran opened his mind and was surprised to find that his gift responded a little slower than usual. He welcomed them, and as the sun passed its zenith told them of what had befallen since they'd last met. He told them everything except for Maya's departure. Yet it seemed there would be no escaping the subject.

'Where is your mate?' asked the Elder. 'Your thoughts are tinged with sadness, nay even darkness and are much-changed from when we last talked. You should seek her company to take away your pain. We often talked amongst ourselves, discussing the love you two shared that made you shine on the inside and her on the out.'

Taran fought back the tears as he tried to control his emotions. 'She is no longer with us. She journeyed east three days ago, and we remain to hold the fortress for as long as we can.'

Fortunately, none of the giants questioned this further, perhaps because they could feel his torment, or just that they accepted what he said at face value. Whatever the reason, he was grateful.

'We should hasten to the keep,' Taran suggested in his mind, 'although I think it prudent that you wait outside until I have a chance to prepare the men for your arrival. I fear if they see you approaching from the rear of the fortress, they'll leap over the walls and pray for mercy from Daleth himself.'

The giant's amusement at his comment cheered him a little.

'Come,' Taran said, rising, 'let's go.'

As they strode, the Elder posed a question. 'What were you doing when we came across you?'

Taran looked back over his shoulder for a moment, pondering.

'I was trying to find a gift that someone had given me once,' he answered somewhat evasively.

'Did you find it?' asked the Elder.

'No,' Taran replied. 'I fear it might be lost to me forever.'

Daleth walked around the campfires, leaving the comfort of his tent to mix with the common soldiers and the not so common.

His bodyguard shadowed him, although not once did he ever think he'd need them unless on the field of battle. Yet, whilst Kalas was alive, he kept them close, and it wasn't just his bodyguard that shadowed him. Occasionally he'd see red eyes blinking briefly before they disappeared. Alano kept watch like a ferocious dog would over its master, and Daleth felt reassured he'd done the right thing by making the trade once again.

The last four days had seen wide pathways cleared through the rubble of the first wall and the fire trench filled in. He was grateful that the Eyre archers hadn't contested the latter. They'd just watched, keeping low, denying his archers or the ballistae a clear shot.

The siege engine remained in position in the centre and tomorrow would see it resume its rain of death and destruction on the defenders. A keen-eyed crewmember had spotted a split in the wood, and instead of pounding the second wall during this time, its throwing arm had required bracing with sap and rope.

Once the fortress was conquered, there'd be a plentiful supply of timber to build more. The wood in the kingdom behind him was useless, mostly diseased, dying, and rotten, virtually unusable except for firewood.

He walked amongst the Nightstalkers, sitting down to share their wine and food as he fed them stories of glory and slaughter from his youth. These men were almost as tough as the Rangers, yet sadly they weren't gifted and thus never achieved such heights of excellence. Nor had they received Alano's training which was why the Rangers' skills were nigh on unmatchable. Unmatchable it seems unless by Kalas, or now Taran, who'd killed two single-handily before his capture.

Daleth looked toward the fortress. It was hard to distinguish, and for a moment he wondered why, but then he realised that no torches were brightening its walls. Maybe they were conserving the oil for the second fire trench. They certainly didn't have enough soldiers for a night sortie, yet it niggled at him. He beckoned to Krixen, who moved smoothly through the gathered soldiers to be at his side.

'My king.' Krixen bowed his head subtly in deference.

Daleth turned to him. 'You've a nose for danger, in fact almost a gift for sniffing it out. The fortress' torches are unlit this evening. Do you think we should be concerned?'

Krixen thought but for a moment. 'We should double the guard although they obviously don't have enough men to challenge us on open ground, be it day or night, so I doubt we have much to …'

But he never finished his sentence, for an arrow erupted from his mouth in a bloody spray having smashed through the back of his skull, and suddenly screams filled the air.

Horns sounded the alarm, and Daleth grabbed a shield that had been stacked nearby as a rain of arrows fell.

'Damn those bloody Eyre archers,' he laughed, as arrows fell from the sky. 'Stay calm,' he called out, as shields were raised all around. 'This is nothing but a small bite from a fly.'

Surprisingly the screams intensified. Daleth cautiously looked from under his shield, across the camp lit by hundreds of roaring fires to see three gigantic figures crash into view. They wielded clubs the size of tree trunks, and dozens of men were flung aside with every swing, thrown through the air like ragdolls as the giants charged up the pass.

Daleth's bodyguard converged all around him, and Alano ran past, his sword drawn, heading toward the nearest giant figure as the soldiers fell back before this colossal onslaught.

Too late, Daleth realised the giant's intentions. One of them surged forward into a formation of men, taking dozens of cuts, yet even as the monster fell to its knees, it brought the club crashing down onto the siege engine, smashing it to kindling. A strange sound came from its throat as it succumbed to the flurry of blows and his men swarmed over it like ants on a corpse.

The two surviving giants began a mostly uncontested, but hasty withdrawal. To be within reach of those huge clubs was to risk certain death, yet as Daleth watched, Alano sprinted and slid to a halt in front of one. The giant's stride barely paused as it contemptuously swept its weapon to knock the daemon aside. At the last possible instant, Alano rolled under the swing, between the giant's legs, and his sword flashed, hamstringing the giant in a single blow.

The giant's leg folded and again that same strange cry filled the night sky as it swung again, but the fight was already over. Alano avoided with ease the same blow that had crushed dozens of others and leapt, driving his sword through the giant's eye, into its brain.

The other giant turned and ran, with Alano and a dozen other men sprinting after. They were about to fall upon it, for the beast was hindered by numerous wounds when the rain of arrows focussed on the small group. Alano threw himself to the ground, pulling a dead body atop of him, while the others without shields fell pierced, unable to find cover.

The remaining giant made its escape and captains began organising the soldiers to help with their fallen comrades and to be ready for a further raid, yet none came.

How had they managed to make an alliance with the giants, and were there any more? Daleth doubted it, for they'd have used them in this attack, wreaking far more devastation than they already had. The giants' strength wouldn't be in fighting behind the fortress walls, and a surprise attack like this could only be successful once. No, there had only been three giants, and now there was but one. Yet, the following days would show the truth of his deduction.

Daleth spent a while talking to some of the injured men, assessing the damage. He expected maybe two hundred or so were dead at the hands of the giants, and a further hundred at the hands of the Eyre archers firing blindly into the dark sky. Many more bore wounds, but thankfully most were non-fatal. With his army so vast, the number of men lost was inconsequential compared to the siege engine's destruction and losing it made his blood boil.

Daleth stormed back toward his tent surrounded by bodyguards. He was furious, for all hope of seeing the enemy walls crumble swiftly had disappeared at his own lack of foresight to predict a night assault.

As he approached his tent, his humour returned a little to see so many of the men nearby still asleep. The noise of the fighting had been enough to awaken the dead, yet these soldiers had slept through it. Then suddenly Alano was by his side, eyes glowing fiercely with bare steel in hand.

'Attend your king, and be on your guard,' Alano rasped, and the bodyguard closed in, shields raised as they came to a standstill.

'What's this about?' demanded Daleth, irritated.

Alano's face showed that twisted smile. 'My brother was here looking for you, and perhaps he still is!'

'How do you know?' asked Daleth, as a cold fist gripped his heart.

'Those men are not sleeping,' responded Alano, 'they're all dead. I see no life running through their veins, and I can smell their blood from here.'

Daleth drew his sword, anger replacing the brief fear that had gripped him. 'Come,' he commanded, and his men gathered around. Two of his men pulled back the tent flaps, then recoiled for a moment before pushing inside, and Daleth followed.

Alano stepped ahead of him, looking around, and turned back. 'I believe he's left, but I like what he's done. This looks like home,' he rasped, and then laughed such an ugly, evil laugh that many of the soldiers flinched to hear it.

Daleth's eyes opened wide. Some of the men who'd been guarding his tent had been killed and brought inside. In a horrific act of butchery, they'd been dismembered, and their entrails used to adorn the tent poles. Heads, piled upon his bed, stared back, eyes wide in terror even in death, while their torsos sat on the chairs or were propped against his desk. It was as grisly a sight as Daleth had ever seen.

'He'll keep coming, until one day he finds you,' Daleth heard, as Alano walked outside. Daleth could only look on as his men started removing the bodies.

Surrounded by a whole army, and still, he'd never felt more vulnerable.

Kalas was coming.

Chapter XVI

It had been a long night, and maybe for that reason, everyone in the chamber was in a quiet mood, thought Rakan, as the morning sun poured in through the stone arches leading to the eastern balcony.

Whilst he and Taran had stayed on the walls, Drizt, his archers, the three giants and Kalas had disappeared into the night. Taran was furious at not being picked to go, but Rakan had known it was the right decision. Taran was struggling to remain level headed at the moment and would likely have got himself killed, and perhaps others with a thoughtless, rash action.

The sortie had been a success, although not a complete one.

Kalas had dressed in armour taken from the corpse of an enemy officer in a desperate bid to find and assassinate Daleth whilst chaos had descended as the giants attacked the siege engine. He'd found Daleth's tent having followed Astren's directions, but the Witch-King hadn't been there. Kalas had miraculously returned without a scratch, but this part of the mission had failed.

Drizt's archers had also returned unscathed despite having inflicted many casualties upon the enemy.

Success had come with the destruction of the siege engine, yet at the very same time, this incredible achievement seemed to have come at too high a price. Of the three giants who'd come to their aid, two now lay dead, and the third, the elder, was sorely injured. Had they just lost two men, they'd have considered it an amazing success, but the loss of the two giants seemed almost too significant a loss to measure.

How was it that the lives of two of these creatures seemed worth more than the lives of two men ... yet that was how it felt.

Rakan looked around the room. Kalas was seated, silent for the moment. Drizt and Trom whispered although the desert man found it hard to keep his booming voice low at all. Yana sat with them too. She was becoming more important by the day, having organised the healers into a cohesive group, and kept many men from the grip of death. Rakan begrudgingly acknowledged that she was a good asset to the defence, and when their eyes met, he nodded at her and saw the surprise briefly in her eyes as she nodded back.

They now waited on Taran and Astren. Taran had been erratic since Maya's departure. Rakan knew he was hardly sleeping, seemingly plagued by nightmares that sometimes made him call out in his sleep.

As they waited, eating bread and honey with some watered wine, a guard came running in, breathless. He didn't bother with any formalities, merely calling out to Kalas. 'We need you, Lord Commander, we need your help now.'

Everyone sprang to their feet and chased after the guard who clattered down the first flight of steps to the next landing, and then as everyone followed him, he pointed down the corridor.

This floor was never used, for its passageways only led to arrow slits around the keep's circumference. As they looked through an archway, they saw Taran holding a dagger against the throat of Astren who knelt on the floor, crying in fear.

'Taran,' cried Rakan, running forward. 'What in the name of the gods are you doing? What's wrong?'

'He knows what happened with Maya,' shouted Taran, eyes wide with anger, 'and he's not telling me!'

Rakan slowed, holding his hands out. 'Look at me, son. You don't need to use your dagger to find out, you're not thinking straight. Use your gift if you have to. There was never any need to use force.'

'I can't,' whispered Taran. 'I'm too tired, and I can't concentrate enough. Astren avoided me when he saw me. I could see there was something in his eyes, and for a moment, I could read it in his thoughts. He knew Maya was leaving with Tristan. Now I need to know why!'

He pushed the dagger, and the blade drew blood. Astren started crying.

'Taran, that's enough.' Kalas commanded. 'He's as much a pawn in this game as we all are. Did you put a dagger to the neck of the soldier who first told you of Maya? Would you hold it to mine or Rakan's if either of us knew something?'

The anger in Taran's eyes flared a final time, then his shoulders sagged, and the dagger dropped to the floor with a clang. Rakan went forward, kneeling down beside Taran, picking up the weapon. 'Come with me, let's take a walk. You need some fresh air to clear your thoughts.'

Taran allowed Rakan to pull him back along the corridor, leaving Astren curled up on the floor.

As they did so, Yana leant in. 'Taran's not wrong,' she whispered. 'Astren has been acting strangely of late,' and then she moved down the corridor to help Astren to his feet, behaving as if all was well.

'You see,' Taran said to Rakan, as they began to descend the keep's steps, 'even Yana has noticed it.'

'Taran,' said Rakan soothingly. 'Your anger and grief are not only stifling your gift, but, and these words come from a loving father, it's also clouding your judgement. Astren, even if he isn't a close friend, doesn't deserve to be threatened because he followed the orders of his king, our king. People are dying all around us every day. Last night, two giants gave their lives so what, we might hold this chunk of rock another week or two longer. They lost their lives, whereas you have yours still. Maya is safe, just hold on to that thought for now, and only that thought.'

Taran looked into Rakan's eyes, his anger fading. 'I know, father, I know,' he said sadly, 'truly I do. But it's as if Maya took all the goodness in me when she left. I may as well be dead the way I feel. I know it was wrong to hurt Astren like that, but I needed to know why so badly.'

Rakan took Taran by the shoulders, looking into his eyes, fixing him with his gaze. 'I know I can't help take your pain away, but I can tell you the first place you should direct it, and that is toward Daleth and his army outside of our gates. First and foremost, he's tried to have us killed more times than I can remember. So if revenge is what you seek, if dealing pain and death are what you want, then let us get it right. Let's first visit it upon the Witch-King himself. After we've dealt with him, and if after we discover that Tristan has done something heinous, we go find him and settle matters. What do you say?'

Taran, calmer now, looked into his father's eyes, seeing suspicion raised there too.

'Let's kill them,' he said. 'Let's kill them all!'

Kalas stared at Astren's shaking form, cowering in front of him.

Long shadows reached across the chamber, courtesy of the now setting sun, and Kalas poured some more wine, offering the brimming goblet. Astren took it, spilling much of the liquid down his robe before he brought the goblet to his lips, draining the contents.

Yet despite the soothing alcohol, and Astren's confrontation with Taran having been earlier in the day, Kalas could tell the seer was a nervous, guilty wreck. However, he'd at least dutifully turned up to take the daily report for Tristan, but he wasn't ready to discuss that quite yet.

'Did you know about Maya?' probed Kalas, but Astren just shook his head, eyes widening in panic. 'You're Tristan's closest advisor. I can't believe for a moment you weren't aware of arrangements for Maya's departure.'

Kalas leaned forward. 'Look at me,' he demanded, and had to repeat himself several times before Astren finally managed to return his gaze. 'I don't believe you, not for a moment. Even if Taran hadn't glimpsed it, a good liar, you're not. Do not lie to me!'

'You remind me of my father,' murmured Astren, the wine giving him a little courage.

'What did you say?' growled Kalas dangerously, eyes staring intently.

Any false bravado Astren had gained, drained away like the wine he'd drunk, yet Kalas' eyes lost focus, no longer boring into his, rather they became distant, before suddenly intensifying again.

'Taran, upon his return, said that Daleth had thoughts of revenge against someone that looked like me. Your words now make me wonder if perhaps he saw an image of my father. Yet it doesn't make sense. Laska is so old, and no one made the connection between us until I told them, despite our names.

Astren, relieved he was no longer being pressed about his involvement in Maya's disappearance, grasped upon this unexpected line of conversation. 'Perhaps the last time Daleth saw your father, was when he was younger during the fall of the Ember Kingdom, and that is the last image he had to call upon?' he suggested, his voice quiet.

Kalas snapped his fingers, his eyes wide. 'That would explain it. Daleth now knows we all made it here through the valley of the giants. Maybe he seeks to not only destroy my father out of revenge for assisting our escape but intends to use the valley to outflank us in case we somehow hold. Damn him. There are nigh on a thousand innocent people in the town, and if my guess is right, they'll be slaughtered, each and every one.

'You will make the spirit journey to Ember Town and scout the route to see if an attack is on its way and forewarn my father if that's the case. If not, then do not bother him. He'll not be happy to receive any message from me, irrespective of the reason.'

Astren nodded enthusiastically, keen to please Kalas, his mind full of thoughts. 'But if an attack is on its way, even if I warn them, where would they go?' he asked. 'If they leave the lands Maya healed, they will still die, as they won't be able to outrun Daleth's troops.'

Kalas drummed his fingers on the tabletop. 'There's no other option, they'll have to seek sanctuary in the valley and pray to the gods that the giants don't slaughter them. We were accepted, thanks to Taran and Maya, but who knows whether a thousand people entering the valley might push the giants to violence again. But what we do know is the Rangers will slaughter them without hesitation.'

Astren sighed. 'If they stay, they die. If they enter the valley, they will likely die there too. But I'll do as you ask. At least they can choose their fate.'

Kalas scowled. 'Ensure that you do. Afterwards, make your report to Tristan, but you'll keep what happened with Taran to yourself. Tell him only that with the siege engine destroyed we might hold for another two weeks. I expect you here in the morning, to let me know of what transpired with Laska. Best make it before first light and do your very best to avoid Taran at all times, and for that matter, Rakan too.'

Astren stood up, turning to leave.

'Oh, one more thing,' called Kalas.

Astren turned back, and for the briefest of moments, the light of the setting sun caused Kalas' eyes to glow the strangest of colours.

'Don't ever lie to me again,' warned Kalas. 'It would not end well for you!'

Yana finished cleaning herself up, washing the last of the blood from her hair. She looked at herself in the mirror, and despite the tiredness around the eyes, she smiled. Her whole life she'd been privileged, her grandfather spoiled her, and she'd never worked, tilled the fields, or tended the livestock like everyone else. Instead, her every whim was met, and she'd never wanted for anything.

Yet here she was, working from dawn to dusk, elbow-deep in blood and she'd never been happier, never felt more alive. The healers respected her, bowing to her leadership skills. The soldiers knew that one day they'd likely need her, so went out of their way to be gracious and charming. She held the lives of everyone who came in screaming and crying from terrible wounds in her hands, and it was within her power to snuff it out, or sometimes to extend it.

Several times she'd played with the herbs and medicines, changing the doses to see what effect it might have. She marvelled as some of the injured who should have survived, slipped away, never even knowing that death had crept up upon them.

Here, she had power over almost all men ... but not the one she wanted the most. Soon though, Taran would fall to her skills. Without Maya, his injuries were now tended by her, and in time Taran would find her healing hands elsewhere upon his body.

She saw a flush rise to her face in the mirror and laughed to herself. Pulling her clothes straight, she left her room and walked the short distance down the passageway to knock on Astren's door.

Astren's run-in with Taran had scared her. Astren, being Tristan's closest advisor, might know of her involvement in Maya's disappearance. Should Taran glean that information once his gift returned, then everything she was working toward would be lost.

In her sleeve, she'd concealed a small dark weed leaf. It was tasteless, and it was probably better if Astren didn't awaken from his spirit travel this night. It could be easily explained, he'd been exhausted and likely imbibed too much sleep weed.

There was no response, so she knocked again.

'Asten, it's me, Yana,' she said softly.

Footsteps approached the door, and it was pulled open a crack, and Yana pushed through, past the surprised Astren, who hurriedly shut the door behind her.

Yana looked around, peering at the fading pictures. They looked unpleasant. 'I wanted to see how you are,' she murmured, turning to Astren before wandering around his room. She idly touched things, making her way to the bedside table where a goblet stood.

She sat down on the bed, Astren's wide eyes following her, flummoxed by her presence. Picking up the goblet, she held it to her mouth. 'You don't mind if I have a sip of your water?' she asked, licking her lips slowly.

'No, no,' Astren stammered, 'it's infused with sleep weed. You mustn't drink it.'

Yana stood up, turning her back on Astren as she put the goblet back on the table, dropping the dark weed leaf into the goblet, before swirling around in a cascade of hair.

She knew Astren wasn't too trusting of her, but her charms were working on him, and his eyes were wide as she flashed him a dazzling smile. 'Tell me,' she asked, probing gently for information. 'How did you get Maya to leave with Tristan?'

A frightened look began to appear in Astren's eyes, and Yana was relieved, for had Astren known it was her idea, then he'd have used that knowledge now. More importantly, it also meant Tristan had kept his side of the bargain and could be trusted, to a point. She didn't need to kill Astren now, but as dissatisfaction washed over her, she decided to anyway. Something akin to arousal flooded through her, making her body tingle.

'Fear not,' she whispered softly, taking his hand and guiding him to the bed, then sat next to him. 'It's alright. If you're not comfortable answering, I understand. Just make sure you stay out of Taran's way until his anger calms, and keep on the good side of my uncle, and you'll be fine.'

Yana reached out, taking the goblet, and passed it to Astren, holding his gaze with her own. 'Dream of me when you sleep,' she said huskily, then stood, leaving Astren open-mouthed as she walked toward the door.

'Shall I give Laska your regards?' stammered Astren.

Yana stopped, the words confusing her as she turned around to see Astren raising the goblet to his lips. *Give Laska her regards?*

She almost flew across the room, striking the goblet from Astren's hand, hitting him hard across the face while doing so, the contents of the goblet spraying everywhere.

Astren fell backwards, scrambling to the corner of the room, where he huddled, his knees pulled up to his chest, tears pouring from his eyes.

'I don't understand,' he cried. 'What have I done wrong? I promised Kalas I'd warn Laska if an attack was coming, there's no need for more threats!'

'Calm down, calm down,' soothed Yana, but it was just as much for herself that she said this, for her heart was thumping so rapidly. Would her action have brought about the death of her beloved grandfather?

She moved slowly around the room, picking up the goblet, rinsing it, then refilled it from a water jug, before returning to where Astren cowered.

'I'm sorry,' Yana said, her smile disarming, and she saw Astren relax a little. 'I made a terrible mistake,' she continued. 'You see, I was going to kill you, even though I don't need to, well, not unless you mention this. Yet it seems you still have your uses, so ensure you deliver your message. I'll be waiting with my uncle in the morning to hear your report, so best put some sleep weed in your water and get on your way. Don't you think?'

She pressed the goblet into his shaking hands and gently lifted his chin, her eyes as cold as the grave.

'Dream of me,' she said again. Her accompanying laugh was cruel as she turned, leaving the room, closing the door behind her.

Astren sat shivering, looking at the closed door. Yana's beauty was breathtaking, but she was evil incarnate in human form, and her uncle was little better. The paintings on the wall caught his eye. He cried a little then, for he felt as if he were nothing, surrounded by the power of kings and daemons.

Laska stood on the steps of his hall, looking out at the town around him. It was a warm night, yet it was late and likely he and the town guards were the only ones up, with everyone else asleep. Lanterns flickered here and there, casting evil shadows that threatened to come alive and leap out as if a daemon to snare the unwary.

A daemon like Kalas, his son. No, not his son. He had no sons left. Kalas had spurned the family and then been cursed by the gods. But if Kalas was cursed, what did that make an old relic like him? An ancient lord from a long-dead realm who'd lost two sons, a grandchild, and now Yana as well.

Laska gasped, pain gripping his chest, and he steadied himself against a wooden post. He should have died before he could see his children and grandchildren die. Now, he was going to witness the death of everyone else he cared for because Daleth's Rangers were coming and there'd be no stopping them.

He closed his eyes, waiting for the pain to subside. It took longer each time, and maybe next time or the time after, the pain wouldn't go away, and it would engulf him.

Death at the hands of the Rangers, or at those of the giants? He couldn't decide which scared him the most, but they were equally as deadly. Damn Astren, for bringing the news of their arrival, for scaring him half to death with his ghostly appearance. Damn Daleth, for coming to steal away any hope of the townsfolk enjoying the utopia that surrounded them.

The air he breathed in was fragrant, sweet with the smell of flowers in bloom, healthy grass and trees. It was a taste of paradise of which he'd never seen the like. Perhaps it would be easier to die in paradise, but there was more to it than that.

The pain in his chest hurt, but then allowing Daleth to enjoy being the direct author of his death, and those around him, would hurt much more. It also seemed there was every chance that the Rangers would subsequently seek to force a route across the valley to flank the defence of Tristan's Folly. Anything that stymied the Witch-King's ambitions was too irresistible to pass by.

He smiled bitterly as he looked into the darkness, his mind made up.

The Rangers would arrive in about ten days. It gave little time to convince the people of Ember Town to leave their lifelong homes for a chance at life in the valley and to prepare for the exodus. It was a place that only a handful of guards had seen, and most thought of it as a fairy tale to scare the few children who'd survived the death of their mothers. They'd only be able to bring what they could carry in their hands and on their backs.

Flashbacks of the slaughter the giants had wreaked upon his father and men, and then subsequently Daleth's soldiers those fifty years ago, invaded his thoughts, making him doubt his decision.

But then he remembered Maya, working her magic, and the mighty giants kneeling at her feet.

'Please,' he gasped, turning his face to the night sky, tears coursing down his cheeks. 'I know I've never offered you anything but my scorn until now, but I ask this of you. Allow my people to live, just name your price!' He stared up, waiting, hoping for an answer, a sign, but there was nothing.

He turned, slowly trudging back into the hall, his heart full of sorrow.

Tomorrow he would tell his people. The beginning of the end was approaching.

Kalas awoke in a sweat. He lay in a sumptuous bed, having taken over one of the rooms vacated by Tristan. It was before dawn, but that didn't matter, his vision was fine even in the dark.

His sleep had been plagued by gruesome images of feasting on helpless victims, and they were getting worse. He knew it was the daemon's dreams interrupting his rest, but as long as they just stayed as dreams that was all that mattered.

Thoughts of his father entered his mind. For whatever reason, despite the many years, the pain they brought never diminished, and it was his biggest regret that the two of them had never reconciled. He'd won so many battles in his life, but winning back the love of his father was beyond him. Even forewarning Laska would likely have served to reinforce his father's decision to disown him, for his father would blame him for invoking Daleth's fury.

He sighed. Astren had done as he'd asked, and the terrified, almost pleading look in the seer's eyes had convinced him that Astren had completed his task as ordered. Yana who'd unexpectedly brought some food to break fast with, also agreed that Astren told the truth. Nigh on two hundred Rangers were on their way to Ember Town, and it was more than possible that such elite soldiers would be able to decimate the giants and force a route through the valley, falling upon Tristan's Folly from behind. Not that he was sure the fortress could hold out for so long for that to be a problem, but that was no good reason to ignore it.

It was strangely hot and uncomfortable, and Kalas threw off the blanket, sitting up, and stopped in confusion as he looked down upon himself. He was fully clothed. He'd been exhausted last night as with every night, head spinning with logistics and concerns, but he was sure he hadn't fallen into bed without undressing.

Shrugging it off, he stood, enjoying the feeling of strength in his limbs. It didn't matter how hard he fought, how late he stayed up, the strength of youth flowed through him, and he faced every day with a vigour that inspired those around him.

Padding across the chamber, he stopped before a mirror, and looked in, then peered closer. What was that caked around his mouth? Food from the night before perhaps. He lifted some water in his hands from the washbowl and scrubbed it away before donning his armour and weapons then strode from the room, heading down the steps to the food hall.

It was unsurprisingly quiet when he arrived. The night watch was yet to come in, and it was a little early for the majority of men to awaken. The food was from last night, and he realised he wasn't hungry at all; the sight of rats leaping from a table the likely cause for the departure of his appetite.

One of the healers entered, stifling a yawn, and Kalas raised a hand in greeting. The healers were the unsung heroes, and Kalas knew that however brave he might believe himself to be, he wouldn't have been able to stomach their role.

'It was so good of you to visit last night,' the healer called.

Kalas waved over his shoulder as he strode toward the keep entrance. She must have mistaken him for someone else.

His eyes opened wide as he walked down the keep steps. Even though Maya was gone, the effect of her gift still remained. While the grass on the courtyard floor had been worn away by the traipse of a thousand footsteps, the outside of the keep was still ablaze with colour, the vines flourishing, finding purchase amongst the crumbling mortar.

The soldiers didn't care that Tristan had left, and he laughed to himself as he walked toward the second wall, for neither did he. Maya, however, had made where they lived a place of beauty. No, he corrected himself, it was because she'd made where they would die one.

The night's watch stood upon the wall, and after ascending the steps, he greeted them, remembering most of their names like any good commander would. He spent time talking to them quietly, making sure that they knew he'd be at their side each and every day.

A cool breeze blew, thankfully taking away the smell of the dead, to be replaced by the scent of the blooms by the keep. He looked over the wall to where Maya had created the shrine to the early fallen and sighed. Soon it would be trampled and destroyed as if it had never existed.

He gazed down the dark pass, eyes piercing through the darkness. He didn't feel hate as such toward the enemy. Even his oath to kill Daleth wasn't built on such emotion, although some might argue the desire for revenge required hate. It didn't. There was little difference between him and them, all trained to kill, to destroy instead of training to save life or create. He could have chosen to stay with his father and his brother, living a simple life, but no, he'd chosen to become a warrior, a slayer of men without peer.

'You could be so much more,' whispered the daemon's voice in his mind. 'You're destined to be so much more. The future holds opportunities that you can shape to your will. If you would see the end to war, to slaughter, you could be a benign king, ruling with fairness and equality. If you chose to rule the world, by conquest, that is also within your grasp. Or, you could rule by popular demand, following the will of your people. You would need only ask them how to lead, and they would adore you for it.'

Kalas mulled over the daemon's words. They were honeyed as usual, yet not demanding, offering choice.

He turned to the man next to him, a soldier in his thirties, who stood quietly, conscious of the lord commander next to him and wanting to seem diligent in his duty.

'It's Yolan, isn't it?' asked Kalas, and the soldier smiled.

'Almost, my lord,' responded the man, an appreciative smile on his face. 'It's Yolar.'

Kalas nodded. 'I won't get it wrong again, Yolar. Tell me, given a choice right now, if you could change what you are, where you stand, what would you choose? What do you think your friends would choose?'

Yolar chuckled, then straightened his face. 'I'm sorry, it wasn't that your question was funny, but last night the lads and I were quietly chatting about exactly that. All of us when we heard about the invasion, well,' and Yolar looked to his feet, embarrassed before raising his head once more, 'we all wanted to run away and only stayed because of the gold we were promised. But now, all that gold wouldn't make us leave, not for a minute. I don't know how to put this to you. Maybe you'll understand. I've never felt so alive as of now,' the man gushed. 'The sun rising, the smell of those flowers the Lady Maya brought to life. It's like I'm seeing, tasting, and smelling things for the first time. Then there's the fighting. I know I'm good at it now, really good, and when I kill someone, it's as if I have the power of a god. I'm sorry, commander. What do you think?' Yolar fell silent, embarrassment etched on his face at having shared too much.

'You see,' whispered the daemon in Kalas' head. 'If you ruled these men, giving them what they wanted, they would want nothing to change, other than for you to lead them into battle for the rest of their lives, as their king.'

Kalas turned his attention once more to Yolar, and he gripped his shoulder, looking into the man's eyes. 'What do I think?' Kalas repeated, and then broke into a smile, eyes shining.

'I think you and I should be gods forever!'

Chapter XVII

A horn sounded, and in response, no further armoured figures crested the battlements.

Taran risked a glance over the edge to see the enemy withdrawing. 'You can stand down!' he shouted to the soldiers around him, and they gratefully collapsed where they stood, in the blood and gore that drenched the battlements. Everyone was exhausted, as Yana and the healers hurried forward to pass out food and water.

It had been three days since the two giants had given their lives, and since then, Taran had immersed himself in the killing. With every blow he landed, every life he took, he thought of Daleth and sometimes Tristan, and took pleasure in visualising their deaths before him.

There were only ten stretcher-bearers left, and they were as exhausted as anyone. They came up to the walls, shaking those who sat there, unsure at times who was dead or simply too exhausted to respond. Often the living were even more doused in blood than the fallen.

The second wall was shorter than the first as the pass narrowed and despite now only being around seven hundred strong, this still allowed the defenders to man the battlements in rotation. Trom's spearmen who'd initially been held back, now rotated in with the rest. They had either become quickly proficient in swordsmanship or were dead.

The Elder giant still suffered from his injuries, yet several times had come to the fight when the enemy gained a foothold, turning the tide for the defenders. Unfortunately, the wounds it had sustained in the night-time sortie were yet to fully heal, and it rested near the keep, recovering its strength, yet ready to help when called upon.

Taran turned to look up as Rakan and Drizt came along the wall. Half of Drizt's archers fought from the towers of the second wall now that the enemy siege engine was destroyed. They helped the defence more from ever from this vantage point, fully aware that if the wall fell, they'd be trapped with no chance of escape.

The other half fought from behind the wall, sending over clouds of arrows, or helping to pick off attackers as they reached the battlements. They were down to no more than two hundred archers from the original five. Daleth's archers had taken a heavy toll as well as the ballistae.

Taran reckoned Trom's men numbered roughly the same and the swordsmen of the garrison maybe three hundred.

'What happened to your hand?' Rakan pointed as Drizt sat next to Taran, noting with consternation some dripping blood.

Drizt looked down. 'I've been an archer my whole life, and not since I first drew a bow as a child, have my fingers bled. I don't know how long my men can keep this up. They are all in a similar state or worse and we're almost out of arrows. Soon we'll draw steel and stand by your side.'

Taran's smile was cold. 'It's better to see the pain in the eyes of your enemy when you kill them, the despair as they realise their life is over. You'll find dealing death with your sword far more enjoyable.'

Drizt flicked a glance at Rakan, who subtly shook his head. Taran had turned from a happy young man into what Rakan had once been, a remorseless killer. Occasionally Rakan saw glimpses of the old Taran in quiet moments. His face sometimes softening as his thoughts drifted away during lulls in the battle.

Horns sounded.

'Ye gods, so soon,' moaned Rakan slowly getting to his feet, but staying low. 'I'll keep you lads company here for a little while if you don't mind. Kalas said he'll keep an eye on my section.'

Drizt, always nimble, was on his feet quickly. 'They're wearing us down with fresh men all the time,' he said. 'They know we can't hold much longer if we can't sleep or rest properly. Once we're out of arrows, they might even start with night attacks.'

The soldiers remained hunkered down as Drizt, and his archers started dealing death from afar. Medium infantry were attacking, and whilst they had shields, they were not full length and nor was their armour plate, and almost every arrow found its mark.

Drizt was truly gifted, Taran noted in admiration. The Eyre captain would crouch below the parapet, then move along, rise up and draw in one motion, loose an arrow, then drop back down in a heartbeat. He never showed himself for more than the briefest moment before moving along the wall and repeating it once again. It was a prudent move, for the enemy archers never had a moment to sight on him, and he dealt death with impunity.

Drizt laughed as another of his arrows found its mark. It wasn't that he enjoyed taking life, but it was the ultimate test of his skill. He was gifted of course, and perhaps it was an unfair advantage. Yet, to find a target, recognise its speed, draw and loose, knowing the arrow would find its victim was wondrous even after all these years. His bleeding fingers didn't bother him, he was simply lost in the joy of his skill. Five men had fallen to his arrows so far, all clean deaths. There would be time for one more before he withdrew to the safety of the courtyard below.

Some of his men were falling from the wall. The enemy archers were sharp today, or perhaps more likely his men were just getting tired and slow, but not him. Selecting an arrow, feeling the smooth straightness of the shaft, he noted one of the feathers was slightly twisted, and his mind calculated he'd have to aim a handspan higher to compensate.

He stood drawing the bow, marking his target, released in the same instant and saw that damned daemon Alano with the red eyes standing behind a shieldman, holding a bow, looking directly at him. He knelt back down, turning to wink at Taran and Rakan who both looked aghast.

Dizziness suddenly washed over him, and he fell back against the wall as Taran and Rakan rushed to his side. He could scarcely believe it, a green feathered arrow protruded from his chest. He hadn't even felt it. That damned daemon must have loosed before he even stood, for he hadn't seen it coming.

'He got me with one of my own damn arrows.' Drizt tried to laugh at the irony but coughed up blood instead.

'Lie still,' said Taran, then began shouting for a healer.

Drizt reached out his bloodied hand. 'It's too late, that was a fine shot. I couldn't have done it better! He read exactly where I was going to be. How did he do that?' His voice faded at the end, and his eyes started to close. But they struggled open a final time.

'Take my dagger,' he whispered to Taran, fumbling with the leather arm guard that held his poisoned blade,' something to remember me by. Bury me, bury me in the forest if you can,' and with that, he let out a final rattling breath.

Taran let out such a loud cry of grief that even above the roar of the advancing enemy, men looked over to see him cradling Drizt in his arms. The Eyre archers, seeing their leader dead, called out to one another in their own tongue and instead of retreating from the walls loosed arrow after arrow in a berserk rage. Such was the ferocity of their barrage that Alano and the other enemy archers had no choice but to retreat out of range.

Soon the Eyre archers had exhausted the arrows in their quivers. With their bows now useless, they cast them aside, drawing short swords to battle the enemy soldiers who'd reached the top of the wall. Then the slaughter began all over again.

Taran was overwhelmed by grief and bloodlust. His gift which had been much harder to call upon of late came back with a vengeance and he slew like a god of death.

Further along the wall, Kalas killed with wild abandon as well, the daemon in his head exulting in the bloodletting, urging him, helping him, driving him into a frenzy.

Rakan stayed near Taran, killing with cold efficiency, keeping an eye on his son, ready to step in should he need help, but he needn't have worried. Taran was for a while as untouchable as Kalas. He focussed on the men coming up the ladders. These were Nightstalkers, and Rakan was enjoying himself immensely as well.

'Filak, is that you?' he cried, driving his sword between the man's teeth, enjoying the look of amazement as the man recognised him at the moment of death. 'Dragan, you always were a slow bastard,' he cried, lopping off a man's hand as he tried to pull himself onto the wall. 'Watch out, it's a long way down,' he laughed evilly, as the man fell screaming.

He looked to his right to see Taran lift a fully armoured man above his head. The man's body was limp, which wasn't surprising because he had no head. It was an amazing feat of strength, and Rakan's eyes opened in wonder.

'This is what awaits you all,' shouted Taran, throwing the corpse over the battlements, and he focussed his gift and let it out in a blast with a shout of such rage at the approaching soldiers in the field, that their charge faltered.

Horns began to blow, and the next minute the enemy were withdrawing without having gained a foothold.

'I'll kill you all!' screamed Taran, at their retreating faces. 'I'll kill every one of you. Do you hear me? I'll kill you all!' He kept on screaming in grief and anger, the men around staring.

Rakan moved swiftly to put his arms around Taran. 'Come with me, son,' Rakan said softly in Taran's ear, his voice somehow reaching through Taran's rage, causing him to quieten. 'They won't be coming back today, you can be sure of that. Now, we need to do something else.'

'What do we need to do that's more important than killing those bastards?' snarled Taran.

Rakan didn't allow Taran's anger to faze him. 'We need to bury a friend,' he said quietly.

All the anger seemed to leave Taran in an instant, and his shoulders dropped. 'A friend,' Taran repeated. Yes, Drizt had been a friend. 'I know exactly the place,' he said.

Together with the remaining Eyre archers, they gathered the body and carried Drizt to his final resting place.

Maya looked ahead, and despite her constant feelings of anger and pain, for the first time in ten days, just for a moment, she felt something different; awe.

'Many people feel the way you do when they first see it,' offered Tristan, riding next to her, seeing her reaction.

Maya didn't answer. The soldiers and wagons continued past as she paused to admire the sight, for there below on the plain, lay the city of Freemantle.

From a distance, it looked like it could be the centre of the known world, for trade roads led off into the distance like spokes on a wheel. The whole city shone in the midday sun, for it was made of white stone, but what really caught the eye was the palace in the middle, for its roof shone as if on fire.

The roads heading east were busy with wagons as the wealthiest folk fled the city, forewarned of the imminent fall of the fortress and the slaughter that would be visited upon them if they stayed.

'Whether they be rich or poor, they'll all be welcomed in Freeguard. We'll leave no one behind who wishes to be saved, for I care for all of my people,' said Tristan.

Maya looked across. 'You care for the rich because of the wealth they bring, and as for the poor, you need their strong arms to wield swords and spears, or they'd likely be left behind to rot. Do not seek to impress me with your false compassion.'

She dug her heels into the flanks of her horse and held on tight as it cantered forward. Before this journey began, she'd never ridden a horse before, and yet she was learning fast, and her backside and thighs no longer hurt like they had at the start. She was pleased to note that Tristan still sat uncomfortably; it had by all accounts been a large splinter.

The journey had been tough, both physically and mentally, she reflected, as she followed behind the wagons.

Physically, learning to ride had been a challenge, and looking after the wounded had also taken a lot of energy as she tried to keep them as comfortable as possible. Many suffered terribly, but whenever she came to tend them, they all made an effort to hide their pain. She could have easily run alongside the wagon train, but learning to ride had been a welcome distraction, keeping her mind occupied.

Mentally it was draining, constantly projecting nothing but a strong face, despite feeling brokenhearted. Additionally, she was struggling to spirit travel at night, however hard she now tried.

Upon leaving the fortress, she'd initially found some solace knowing that she could look upon Taran any evening she chose. She'd initially determined not to, knowing it would bring too much pain before she was ready to suppress it. However, by the third night, she'd felt strong enough to try and had flown directly to the fortress, yet it hadn't been easy or fast.

Three giants had rested in the pass beyond the walls, and her spirit had lifted a little, making her travel easier, so she'd flown into the keep, to the chamber where last she'd left Taran. When she'd entered, it had been empty, the roses creating a scene like a funeral. Next, she'd journeyed into the depths of the keep to their old room. That was where she'd found him, curled up on the bed asleep, holding a pillow tightly to his chest, something he'd never done before.

She sat down next to him, reaching out to stroke his hair, but it passed through him without feeling, leaving her crying invisible tears. Even worse was that while she watched, Taran called out in despair and awoke from a nightmare, sitting up in the dim light.

For a moment she'd felt elation, that somehow he might see her. But from his wide, empty eyes, tears had run unchecked down his cheeks, and he stifled sobs as he lay back clutching the pillow once more.

Her heart had almost broken, and the upsurge of grief seemed to trigger a strange force. It had pulled on her spirit irresistibly, and she'd barely had time to register the journey as she'd swiftly returned over the many leagues to where she lay.

The moment her spirit and body had joined, she'd awoken to find her own cheeks wet. The despair she'd felt then had nigh on overwhelmed her, and it had taken a long, long time before sleep came for her again.

Frustratingly, she'd been unable to spirit travel again since that night, unable to fly in the spirit realm as her sorrow weighed her down.

Bringing her focus back to the present, she cantered past the wagons. The injured soldiers waved to her, and she returned the gesture. They were good men for the most part, and they appreciated how much she'd done for them during the journey.

Later, as they entered the city, Maya's eyes opened wide in wonder. The trade roads leading in were lined with the wealthiest merchants' houses, their façades columned and intricately carved. They were positioned here, she learned, so they could be the first to take advantage of goods coming in and out.

Opulence was everywhere. She thought back to her village where the small market area in the centre was the filthiest, messiest part because everyone used it so often. Yet here, no expense had been spared, and it was exactly the opposite.

Even the blocks of stone that made up the roadway were a creamy white, and these wide avenues led straight to the royal palace which lay in the centre some way distant. Statues and carvings graced the pavements, and Maya dismounted, leading her horse by the reins as she inspected the art in admiration.

'If you appreciate the beauty of these works, then you've a lot more to look forward to. These are but the works of our lower artisans. Wait until you see what the palace holds. Much of it is already being moved east, but the larger pieces will need to be left behind. I doubt even Daleth will seek to destroy such masterful works,' said Tristan.

Maya looked over her shoulder at him. 'It's incredible that the human hand can create such things, and they are marvellous. But I'd rather live in the wilderness and see the beauty of nature's embrace anytime.'

She went to turn away, but Tristan spoke.

'Wait! If that's the beauty you desire to see, when you're queen, you'll have the power to create what you will, acquire what you will.

'I know you think my greed makes me less of a man, less of a king, but in this realm, people have sought to accrue wealth above all other things. I'm what everyone aspires to be; the wealthiest man alive.'

Maya looked at him, shaking her head. 'You still don't understand,' she said. 'You might have everything you say and are as rich as the gods, but the value of one's life shouldn't be measured by how much gold is in your pocket. It should be measured by how much love you have in your heart. I was wealthier than you could ever be, and now I stand before you poorer than a beggar with no food. You took that wealth from me, and no gold, no finery, no status will ever replace it.'

Maya mounted her horse again. 'I now see this place for what it is,' she said grimly. 'This is a city built on the exploitation of others, and now to me, it's ugly,' and she spurred her horse toward the palace.

Tristan stared after her, gathering his thoughts, then turned to Galain. 'We'll be staying no more than two days to ensure the most valuable items are saved. Requisition wagons from the poor quarter if we need extra. Likewise, many of the injured in the wagons can now walk, thanks to Lady Maya's care. It seems she's already helping me to retain my wealth.'

'Do you want me to organise for the five hundred horses to be sent back to the fortress?' asked Galain.

Tristan paused in thought, having inconveniently been reminded about Kalas' demand. It would be so much tidier if all his troubles disappeared when the fortress fell. He'd be happy to see the back of them all, except Astren.

Astren was useful even if he sometimes spoke out of turn. He'd definitely learned his lesson well and had been reporting judiciously every night. He'd make sure Astren was saved.

He turned to Galain. 'Tell me, as my captain and advisor. What are your thoughts on this matter?'

'If we send that many back,' responded Galain, 'we'll be short of horses to pull the treasure wagons. Surely saving your wealth and the future wealth of the Freestates is your duty as opposed to trying to save all the men in the fortress, most of whom will soon likely die.'

Tristan paused for a moment. 'You're right to remind me of my priorities. It's likely there won't be many men left to ride them when they arrive. Organise for ten men to leave with a hundred horses today.

'I also want riders to travel far and wide calling upon the peasantry to come to Freeguard. We need to make sure the people are aware of the invasion and answer my call to arms.'

'My king, if I might be so bold,' offered Galain. 'I think most will be too scared to answer that call. They care for nothing but the dirt they farm, and coin, not for the greatness of your reign. We should offer coin, maybe even land. Of course, they won't get it, but more will come if they see a potential gain, as otherwise, they'll think that all we offer them is certain death.'

'That's it,' said Tristan, his face lighting up. 'We don't tell the peasantry of the coming war. Instead, we tell them of my betrothal, and that all who attend the coming celebration will be gifted with a gold coin, food, and drink. We'll hold it in four weeks, so everyone will rush to ensure they get there. Then once they arrive, we press-gang them into service.'

Galain bowed low. 'Truly, that's the most devious plan I've ever heard. That'll have them swarming like bees around honey.'

'In that case,' said Tristan, 'let's make all haste to reach Freeguard with all the wealth we can bring with us.'

He dug his heels into the horse's flanks and followed Maya toward the palace. He couldn't wait to see her face when he shared the good news.

Daleth leaned back in his camp bed and carefully placed his empty goblet on the table, already feeling the drowsiness of sleep weed induced slumber overtaking him.

It had been a long time since he'd felt the need to travel the spirit paths. Everything he wanted was right in front of him to be seen with the naked eye, and everything behind him was in the past, dead and dying. Not forgetting spirit travelling was unnecessarily tiring.

Yet however thrilling it was to watch the siege, he wanted a little distraction, and the closer the fortress came to falling, the more useful his Rangers would become, if only they could get into position soon enough.

When Rakan and Taran had first been identified upon the walls, it became apparent that the only way they could have got there was through the valley of the giants.

He'd always intended to revisit Ember town in his own time to deliver justice upon Laska and the fugitives, but now it seemed the old man had somehow outfoxed him. If Laska had managed to get the fugitives safely through the valley of the giants, then the Rangers who were almost there should have few problems.

In the distant past, he'd toyed with the idea of using force to cross the valley, but memories of the giants slaughtering his men with ease had stayed his hand. Yet he hadn't the elite and gifted Rangers back then, trained by Alano, and now it might be they wouldn't even need to force their way across.

Even as he considered this, he fell asleep, and the next moment opened his eyes, rising in spirit form. Unhurriedly, he willed himself upwards, examining the defences of the fortress before him. It was frustrating that beyond the second wall, it was mostly obscured. It would have been enjoyable to spy on the meetings of the defenders, to know of their plans, but he hadn't the skill to force the fog, and he cursed his limitations.

Turning back along the pass, he drifted over his army's encampment, pleased with the discipline although he expected nothing less.

His army stretched out like a black stain into the plain beyond, dotted with the orange glow of campfires burning everywhere. As only a small proportion of the army could be brought to engage the fortress, the remainder were tasked with chopping down the dying, rotting, forest trees for kindling, and spent their days, axe in hand, or sharpening their formation and weapon skills.

He looked at the sky above, wondering at the stars, the eyes of the gods. He willed himself higher, but as ever, could fly little further than the clouds and drifted down, disappointed but not surprised. The gods may well favour him, but he wasn't one of them, yet.

It was an amazing feeling to fly above the land, and he couldn't wait to travel the lands beyond Tristan's Folly, to be able to soar above its verdant pastures.

There was no need to rush, although taking longer would mean he'd feel more drained on the morrow. He flew lower, drifting just above the tops of the trees. There was little sign of life, and he was grateful to travel this way, for many areas were turning into diseased swampland, and the smell would have been foul.

In the distance, he could see the glow of numerous campfires and moved toward them. As he drew closer, he descended to the forest floor, his astral feet not disturbing a leaf as he took his time, walking around the camp at a distance. It was the camp of his Rangers, and there was no need for stealth in his current form, yet he wanted to check their readiness. Despite having absolute faith in them, he would never be complacent.

Almost a full hour later, he walked toward the middle of the camp. Upon a log sat the astral form of Nivek, waiting patiently for his king as arranged.

Nivek rose and bowed, fervour glowing from his eyes as he looked up.

Daleth smiled, reaching out to grip Nivek's forearm in greeting. It wasn't as though he liked Nivek, he found himself unable to bond in any way with those who served him, but he appreciated the man's utter loyalty, skill, and devotion to his trade.

'I found all ten,' said Daleth with a mock disapproving smile.

'Then you only found half of them,' Nivek spoke with pride. 'Let me guess, you forgot to look up.'

'In the trees, really?' said Daleth in admiration. 'Those sentries deserve an extra measure of ale when you return.'

For the next half an hour, Daleth spoke to Nivek of the siege, knowing that to engage him in such a way only served to strengthen the bond of servitude.

'So,' Daleth advised in conclusion, 'their defence is now crumbling even if they are admirably resilient. I want you to hurry and position yourself behind the citadel to kill any defenders that attempt to withdraw.'

'Look,' interrupted Nivek, suddenly rising to his feet, pointing into the night sky, his gift of far-sight as keen as ever.

Daleth stared, then against the stars saw a figure moving swiftly northward, close to the mountains.

'Shall we pursue and kill him?' asked Nivek, rising off the ground, hand on his astral sword hilt.

Daleth thought for a moment, then shook his head. 'No, but how interesting that Tristan's little spy has come this way. There's nothing for him to see here, and the only thing south is Ember Town. Daleth thumped his fist into his palm. 'How many days before you get there?' demanded Daleth.

'Four days at the outside,' replied Nivek.

'No. Now you will make it in two,' said Daleth, his eyes piercing as he gazed at Nivek. 'Somehow our plan has been discovered.' An image of Taran flashed into his mind, and he cursed. 'I think I know how too. So, that means Laska is forewarned.'

'He cannot stand against us, even if he knows. If he seeks to run he will die, maybe a day or two later, but he and all of his people will die,' assured Nivek.

'Then make it so,' demanded Daleth, staring into the sky where Astren had disappeared. 'I don't want you to leave anyone alive. Men, women, children, animals, they all die. Not a trace is to be left of that town that isn't a charred wreck or corpse. Report to me before you cross the valley. Whilst Laska and his people won't even give you a moments pause, the giants are not to be underestimated.'

As Nivek bowed, Daleth rose into the air, heading back towards the pass and Tristan's Folly.

Strangely he was able to fly faster and higher than ever before.

He opened his arms to the sky. The gods had favoured him again.

Laska looked down from his vantage point, leaning heavily upon a gnarled wooden staff, water running down his face from the incessant rain.

He waited near the end of the treacherous mountain path that snaked back and forth up the mountainside. A path that both led them away from death and towards it. His chest was tight from the ascent, and he willed his heart to beat slowly, afraid that the next bout of pain would bring him to his knees.

It had been a terrible last few days. His people had not wanted to listen at first and had been in denial over what was coming. For the first time in their lives, they'd known happiness, with full stomachs from fresh food and fruit. Animals, drawn by the verdant lands that surrounded the town had arrived in abundance, providing fresh game for the hunters, and a bright future lay ahead of them all.

Of the almost one thousand souls of Ember Town, seven hundred had decided to leave, including the few parents with children. The youngest were five years old, for no baby or mother had survived childbirth in recent years.

The others wanted to take their chances, not believing that Daleth would be interested in them, and had also seen an opportunity to take

Tristan's Folly

over some of the better houses and the great hall. They'd not live to enjoy them.

Before dawn, Laska and his few guards had marked the route with torches encouraging an early start, but it was going slowly. People knew the Rangers wouldn't arrive for another couple of days and were reluctant to leave the warmth of their homes.

The first of his people started to pass by, and Laska took the time to encourage them all. It was dry inside the mountains, he assured them. Several of his men had gone ahead to light torches along the tunnels that led to an enormous cavern. There, the exiles could gather before making the remainder of the journey.

As the people passed, his guards checked what everyone carried. In the town below, another group of guards were doing the same before anyone made the ascent. Men and women wore a pack on their backs, full of dried food and fruits, and in their hands, they carried tools; shovels, hoes, saws and hammers. Others would bring sacks of rope and twine, nails and leather. The children were also ladened and carried small cages with chickens or piglets inside.

It wasn't as if he thought they'd have a chance to use any of them, for the giants would likely slaughter them all out of hand. Yet he'd reassured his people that all would be well. The giants were now friendly due to the magic of the Lady Maya who'd healed their valley. If only he believed his own lie. But if the gods somehow smiled, then his people would be ready.

The looks on the faces of the people that passed were despondent. They were soaking wet, they'd left almost everything behind, and were heading into the unknown, all on his word.

He grimaced. Damn the Witch-King, damn Astren, and damn Kalas, his cursed son.

There he went again, recognising him as his son. As he thought of Kalas, his heart started to beat irregularly, causing a spasm that made him cry out a little in pain. He gripped his staff, trying to stay on his feet, and managed to forcel a smile as the next small family trudged wearily by, fugitives in the dark.

For hours he stood, leading by example, standing in the rain, sheer force of will keeping him there, bestowing smiles on those who passed by. How many had entered the mines he didn't know, so he turned to his captain of arms, Nestor. 'How many?' he croaked.

'Three hundred, my lord,' replied the crossbowman, a huge man whose weapon was covered in hide and strapped across his back.

The sound of banging reached his ears, and he nodded to himself. Two guards were already weakening the tunnel supports before everyone was through. The passages had held firm for almost seventy years and would need to be brought down behind them. Oil had been used to soak the old timbers, and the tunnel roof and walls weakened.

A gust of wind caused all the torches on the paths to gutter. Half had already succumbed to the rain, but the pitch managed to keep most alight nonetheless.

A sodden, young guard approached, helping a fragile old woman. He carried a leather flask and held it out to Laska.

Warmth emanated from it as he took it and Laska grunted his thanks. He unstoppered it, smelling the spices that infused the warm wine, and drank deeply, feeling the chill in his bones recede. It wasn't a cold morning: it was the cold of being ancient, at being one step from the grave.

More people went past, and Laska breathed a sigh of relief, as these were the two families with children. Before Maya's arrival, the youngest of the settlement had been so thin and weak. Yet, a few weeks of experiencing good food, clear water and air untainted by the spores of rotting wood had seen a dramatic change in the young faces of the two boys who accompanied their parents. Despite being a horrible morning, they shone with youthful vigour and mischief.

He had to admit to himself, that whilst he'd cursed Maya, Taran, and Rakan for the death of his grandson during his grief, they'd saved the lives of the whole town. His decision to help them had been the right one.

Laska looked to Nestor. 'Four hundred and forty-five,' the man offered without needing to be asked. Laska shook his head, noticing the sky becoming lighter to the east. Had he really been standing here so long? His aching legs and sore back told him the truth.

'Go hurry the rest,' Laska ordered the young guard with the flask, 'tell them we seal the tunnel at noon,' and the man ran dutifully down the path, past the flickering torches and the trudging figures. A short while later, Laska looked over the rocks bordering the edge of the path. He could see the young soldier pushing past a group of cloaked villagers walking up the mountainside several turns lower down.

Laska turned away, then felt a chill pass through him. He looked back over the edge and spied the group. They wore threadbare cloaks, so what had aroused his suspicion? Then he realised. Where others struggled up the mountain, these flowed like spirits over the ground, and there were five of them. Rangers!

They were here days earlier than Astren had foretold, damn him.

His heart spasmed, and he moaned as tears came to his eyes. The captain turned to him, and Laska beckoned him over. 'We must move to the cave entrance, quickly,' Laska ordered, urgency in his voice.

Nestor took one look at the fear in Laska's eyes and started pulling him up the path, almost lifting him off his feet, shouting at the other nearby guards to follow.

The feeling of fear that gripped Laska was infectious and spread to those they passed, and the next moment everyone was pushing and pulling, trying to reach the tunnel entrance up ahead.

Suddenly, distant on the wind, screams rang out, and flames began to soar from the town below. It was raining hard, but despite this, soon half of the town was going up in flames.

Panic spread across the mountainside, and chaos ensued as people thrust forward, frantic to reach safety. Only the huge captain at his side kept Laska on his feet as he moved with as much haste as his frail legs would carry him. As they reached the tunnel entrance, Laska pulled himself clear of the captain's grasp and stood back from the flood of villagers running by.

'We need to fire the timbers, the enemy is upon us!' Laska shouted at his wide-eyed men. 'Now,' he commanded.

'But there are people still coming up the mountainside,' replied a young soldier, disbelief in his eyes, 'my father hasn't got here yet. We need to wait!'

'My family are out there too,' said another and his comment was echoed by two more.

Laska didn't hesitate and grabbed a lantern from the wall. Yet to his disbelief, the soldier who'd argued with him, tore it from his grasp, extinguishing it while screaming obscenities

The captain, Nestor, came to his aid, pulling the soldier off. As the others remained frozen at this terrible turn of events, panicking villagers continued to run past them.

Daylight cast its gaze over the path leading to the cave, and the glitter of steel caught the group's eye, as around the nearest bend five men came, swords in hand. Heartlessly, they struck out indiscriminately with their weapons, slaughtering everyone before them as they surged toward the entrance. Heart-wrenching screams sounded as those ahead tried to escape the death behind.

'For the love of the gods,' cried Laska, 'fire the timbers, or we all die!'

Nestor, who'd been trying to restrain the young soldier without using too much force, pushed him roughly to the ground. He forced across the stream of fleeing people and grabbed another lantern from the other side of the passageway. Taking two steps forward, he drew his arm back and cast the lantern with all his might at the passage wall to the side of the entrance. Oil spewed everywhere as it shattered, and between one breath and the next, flames whooshed upward.

Screams of agony replaced those of panic and fear as several villagers pushing into the cave got caught up by the splashing oil, their clothes bursting into flame. They stumbled forward a few more steps before collapsing to the floor, writhing in agony as others turned back to help.

The captain grabbed another lantern, even as people continued to run blindly through the flames, severe burns preferable to the swords of the Rangers outside, and cast this against the other side.

'No,' cried the young soldier, whose father was still outside. He rose to his feet and drew his dagger, lunging forward. Before Laska could shout a warning, it was hilt deep in Nestor's side.

Roaring in agony, Nestor spun, lashing out with his fist, spinning the young soldier to the floor. He staggered a little then sank to his knees, pulling the dagger from his side, then plunged it through the eye of the man beneath him.

The flames were ferocious, greedily consuming the oil-soaked timbers, and were rapidly advancing down the tunnel toward Laska and the remaining guards.

Laska wheezed with every breath, the smoke thick, his chest tight and painful as he went to help the captain who was struggling to his feet. Blood frothed, falling from the captain's chin as he stood and shook off Laska's hand.

'My family are already in the caverns,' the captain groaned through gritted teeth. 'Make sure they stay safe, don't let me have died for nothing,' and so saying, he picked up a sledgehammer from against the rock wall and moved toward the flames.

Laska watched in horror as the captain's hair caught on fire, but the man ignored it, standing in the passageway, swinging the hammer to hit the tunnel roof again and again. Laska knew if the tunnel didn't come down, once the fire died, the Rangers would follow and so did the captain.

Laska slowly backed away, watching as the captain's clothes blackened and smoked, and yet still the man swung the hammer, even as his flesh began to melt. His screams now followed Laska who stumbled backwards.

A deep rumble caused the ground to vibrate. Laska grabbed a wooden support as the tunnel shifted beneath his feet, and then the rumble became a roar. The tunnel roof collapsed, dust billowed, and for a while, Laska could do nothing until the shaking of the mountain stilled.

He pulled a torch from a bracket and moved cautiously forward. The rockfall had completely blocked the tunnel, burying the captain, putting an end to his torment. They were at least thirty paces from the entrance, and there was no way the Rangers could hope to clear a passageway to follow.

Laska's legs were weak, and his eyes streamed with tears from the smoke, leaving dusty tracks down his face. He sobbed and wheezed as he turned, stumbling along the passageway, eyes peering through the dust. Two guards came to help him.

He didn't know how long it took before they came to the large cavern to find everyone there. Some clapped and exclaimed in delight as they saw him, seeing him as their saviour, others wept or cried in pain from burns. Some muttered darkly, blaming him for what had happened.

As he stood looking around, he'd never felt less like a lord. The desire to simply sit amongst them, and pretend he was someone else was nigh on overwhelming, but he couldn't, not yet.

He sucked in a breath, which ended in a gasp as his heart seemed to stop for a moment, then found the strength to raise his voice. 'We have a long walk ahead of us to reach the sanctuary of the valley. Let us grieve those who are lost when we have the time to do so, but that time is not now.' He slowly made his way through the crowd, amongst those who touched his robes, reverence shining In their eyes, to those who turned away in disgust.

Laska sighed. They'd escaped one certain death only to head straight toward another, but he needed to keep up the lie a little longer. He needed to give his people hope.

The sound of children's laughter made his head turn sharply, and he couldn't help but smile, albeit tinged with sadness as did many others around. The two boys who'd arrived safely saw this as nothing but a big adventure and ran around happily, oblivious to how close to disaster they'd been.

'See that the injured are cared for,' Laska ordered, turning to one of the guards. 'I want us to leave within the hour so we can reach the valley by this evening. Now, I need to rest.'

Laska moved to some rocks, and lowered himself down carefully, his heartbeat fluttering like a bird.

The two boys ran past him, wooden swords flashing as they laughed and whooped.

The cavern blurred as tears ran down his cheeks and he turned his face away, worried they might see it. He wasn't scared, he wasn't frightened, these were tears of sadness.

He'd had two sons once.

'Forgive me, Kalas,' he whispered, and closed his eyes.

Chapter XVIII

Astren scurried through the corridors toward his room.

He moved furtively, looking over his shoulder every so often, and then jumped as a cry of pain sounded from a room that was used to hold the seriously wounded. Healers swept by, scowling as though his health was an affront when so many were dying nearby. They looked like denizens of the underworld, for they were splashed with blood and the flickering torches added to the nightmarish scene.

The healers had recently moved all the injured men inside. For the last two days, torrential rain had fallen. On the one hand, it brought a merciful halt to the fighting, but on the other made the already miserable lives of the wounded unbearable as they lay unable to move in the deluge.

Not that the heat had been better. A plague of flies feasted upon the wounded and the hundreds of corpses that the defenders were too tired to do anything about.

Sadly, the injured were simply exchanging one torture for another. The fortress was now overrun with rats that took any opportunity to feast on a dying man's flesh, and the panicked screams of their victims as they did so, were horrible to hear.

What had happened to all the domestic mountain cats who'd prowled the corridors of the keep? Astren had no idea, but now there were none to be seen, whereas before they'd kept the rats to a frightened handful.

The rodents were such a problem that several lightly injured men had been pulled from the walls to stop the rats from spoiling the food stores. Yet it seemed that battle would soon be lost as well.

Those soldiers strong and fit enough to fight only returned to the keep to eat. Otherwise, they slept at their posts, in the lee of the walls, or under the Tower Oak. They preferred the wrath of the elements to the piteous sounds of their dying comrades.

Astren felt so alone. He didn't fit in with the gruff fighting men, and the sight of open wounds nauseated him, so he was shunned by the healers; thus, he rarely left his room.

In the early morning, he would break fast and visit Kalas, reporting on Laska, Tristan and the progress of the Eyre and desert folk. The evenings would see the visit repeated. Kalas, in turn, would pass on details of the day's losses, and an estimate of how long they could hold, for Tristan. Otherwise, apart from visiting the food hall or the latrines, he'd keep to himself.

His visits to Kalas always left him feeling uneasy for there were times when he sensed a terrible darkness in the man.

The fury in Kalas' eyes when he'd relayed the fate of Ember town had left him fearing for his life. How was he to know that the Rangers would half their journey time to fall upon Laska's settlement early? Why couldn't Kalas appreciate that half the townspeople and Laska were likely still alive as opposed to being furious about those who'd died? The Rangers were returning northward, evidencing the fact that the route to the valley was closed. His mission had been a success!

Then there was Yana. How could someone who looked so beautiful be so devoid of goodness? Her hand had been on her dagger the whole time he'd given his report, her eyes promising pain.

Finally, what might Taran do if he ever found out the truth about Maya's disappearance? At least Taran's anger seemed to have abated, and whilst he wasn't friendly, he made a point of being courteous in any meetings they both took part in.

He didn't know who scared him the most, but it was probably Yana.

He sighed, but it almost came as a sob.

Kalas, Yana, and Taran all left him shaking when he saw them.

He relaxed as he went deeper into the mountain toward his room. Quietness descended, and he embraced the tranquillity. In the past, Taran, Maya and the others slept close by, but not one of them used their rooms anymore.

Kalas stayed in Tristan's old chambers. Taran now slept on the wall and hadn't returned to his room in a while. Rakan, well, he was never far from Taran and Yana fell asleep in the rooms that held the wounded. So this part of the keep was his alone.

As he walked along the corridor, the dusty smell changed to one of sickly cloying sweetness, that had, over the last week grown stronger.

He paused outside the closed wooden door to what had been Kalas' room and gently sniffed. Sure enough, the odour was coming from within. He went to open it but was surprised to find a padlock upon the door where none had been before. This was very strange.

There'd been enough death of late for him to recognise the smell of rotting flesh. It was likely a dead rat, or two.

He walked further along the corridor, entered his room and sat upon the bed. The pictures on the walls stared at him, taunting. 'You won't see me die here,' he laughed nervously at them. 'Even if Daleth doesn't intend to keep his word, Tristan has sent horses. I'll escape from you, one way or another!' Yet even as he said the words, a chill ran down his spine.

He lay down. What time was it? Still morning, and he was so, so tired. He'd sleep for a little while and regain his strength. It would be a long day of self-confinement here before his evening meeting with Kalas. Then, when the sun set later, he'd visit Tristan, and on his way back, he'd check on Kalas' room if he had time. Yes, that smell was so bad, he'd make time.

He closed his eyes and fell asleep almost as soon as his head hit the pillow.

Anger rose inside as Daleth listened to Nivek's report, and he did his best to keep his feelings hidden in his thoughts.

'I'm sorry, my king,' Nivek concluded. 'It would take months to clear the tunnels assuming they didn't collapse, so having hunted down and killed any who hid or ran, we're now returning to rejoin you.'

Daleth took what pleasure he could from Nivek's recounting of events. The Ranger had performed his duties to perfection, and the failure of his mission did not lay with him. The visions of the slaughter he and his fellow Rangers had meted out upon the whole town was exquisite to behold.

The race up the mountainside had Daleth's heart pumping in his chest, and he'd sensed Nivek's despair match his own, when the flames had blocked the tunnel entrance.

'You did well,' Daleth consoled Nivek. 'Credit to the old man, I didn't believe Laska would have the stones to do what he did, leaving half his people to die. Fear not, there's no dishonour here. You and your fellow Rangers will have a myriad of opportunities in the future to redeem yourselves.'

In his mind's eye, Daleth felt Nivek's appreciation at his choice of words, and he broke their connection. Whilst failure would never be something Daleth could accept, sometimes the hands of the gods interfered.

Like now, he thought, as he looked at the water flowing past his feet. His tent remained standing, the sides rolled high, and whilst it kept the rain from drenching him completely, his boots and feet had rarely been dry these last two days. The sky offered no respite, remaining heavy and dark with clouds.

He stood, then reached out to grab his chair as it started to be swept away by the current. Never had he thought this assault would last beyond two weeks, for in his dreams he'd seen the defenders swept away like the chair.

Ducking under the raised side of the tent, he walked out into the downpour, looking up as the rain beat down, standing tall under its onslaught. He raised his arms, spreading them wide, and smiled as Alano appeared, red eyes glowing, yet looking as dejected as the tens of thousands around them.

'I think I'd take the fires of the hells over this rain any day of the year!' Daleth exclaimed, and looked closer at Alano. 'From the look of you, I think you would too!'

Alano's eyes flared red, casting a light upon the ground.

'Be careful what you ask for,' rasped the daemon, 'you might not find the heat to your liking!'

Daleth waited, expecting Alano to say more, but the daemon just turned and disappeared into the downpour. Daleth grinned, water coursing down his face as he thought of the desert spearmen that fought within the fortress, for they must be suffering more than anyone.

They'd never see their homelands again, nor feel the heat of the desert sun, but he would. He'd enslave their entire nation one day, and then he'd never have to stand in the rain with his boots full of water again.

He ducked under the tent and growled. His chair had washed away, and worse than that, a table had overturned, spilling its bounty of warmed wine. He closed his eyes, calming himself. What were a few days of delay when he had a thousand years of conquest to look forward to?

The thought warmed him more than the wine ever would have.

Rakan sat looking up at the sky and opened his mouth, letting the rainwater quench his thirst.

It was hard to keep his eyes open, the rain was coming down so hard, and yet his spirits were high as was everyone's on the wall. It was far too early for the late autumn rains, and yet the season felt like it was upon them already. The sky was dark, the clouds low, heavy and full, and it had not stopped for nigh on four solid days.

The enormous amount of water rushing down the mountainsides, into the pass, had created a river heading westward. Daleth had halted all attacks, and his ballistae were covered in leather hides to protect them from the rain.

It was a godsend, for the men of the fortress had been on the point of complete exhaustion, and now had time to rest and regain their strength.

The healers had come around earlier, handing out fragrant herbs to everyone. Combined with the deluge, they'd helped provide the means by which the defenders could wash away the gore that they previously hadn't the strength to remove. It was a light-hearted moment for them all. The men had stripped and cleansed, the walls swiftly covered in lather, and Rakan had watched as Taran smiled, thinking of better times as he'd washed close by.

Rakan had felt his heart lift to see his son begin to mend.

The death of Drizt, while heart-breaking for them all had been the catalyst for the healing process to begin, opening Taran's eyes once again to the value of life. They'd buried their friend in an oasis of such stunning beauty that it had taken Rakan's breath away. Taran had explained how Maya had created it for him. No doubt it had reminded Taran of how strong their love had been, and how fortunate he was that she was still alive and safe while their friend was dead.

Now when Taran talked about Maya, it was with the belief that one day he'd find her again and everything would be as before, for how could love that had created such a place of beauty ever fade?

The five days following Drizt's burial had seen so many others die. The defenders had been worn down and with just over four hundred remaining, had been brought to the brink. Just when it seemed they would be overwhelmed, the gods themselves had intervened.

The rain had started the very evening that Kalas was going to concede the second wall, and ever since it had helped wash the fortress clear of blood, and cleansed the wounds they'd all suffered. Yet the most important healing it had done was to their souls.

Men were laughing again, and Taran's gift, which had deserted him for a while, returned. Taran was a favourite of the defenders, a popular commander who lifted their spirits everywhere he walked, talking with them, as much for his sake as theirs.

It wasn't just the men Taran now mingled with, but the remaining giant who'd almost fully recovered from its wounds. Fortunately, they hadn't been too severe even if they'd been numerous.

The Elder giant looked so sorrowful, Rakan thought, as it sat cross-legged, dwarfing Taran in the courtyard below. They sat under the Tower Oak that Maya had brought forth, along with many of the men who decided that enough rain was enough.

Rakan stood, looking out along the almost empty pass. Daleth's army had withdrawn to the plains beyond, and he laughed a little to himself as he saw the knee-deep river of water that would have swept away tents and put out fires. If only it had been colder, almost all the attackers might have died from exposure, but sadly the weather was too mild.

On the horizon, he could see a hint of light, where the clouds were distinctly thinning. Damn. It seemed the rain might soon come to an end. Still, even if it stopped now, it would be another two days before the last came down the mountains.

He'd better tell Kalas.

The idea of going into the keep soured his mood a little. It was easy to forget the suffering of the seriously injured when they were out of sight and couldn't be heard, but once inside, there was no escaping it.

It wasn't that any of the injured were his direct friends. He was only close to Taran and Maya, and maybe Kalas and Yana a little. They'd come so far together and ever since his amulet had been removed, he couldn't help but care. For the first time ever, he felt guilty that he was fit and well, while so many counted the hours until they died, and die they would. If they didn't succumb to either their current wounds or infection, they would perish shortly after the last wall fell to the swords of the enemy that had put them there in the first place.

An overdose of sleep weed would surely be the best way for them to go, but until there was no other option, the healers were doing the best they could.

'Right, lads,' said Rakan, as he walked toward the steps. 'If our guests come up the pass in boats, let me know, otherwise enjoy the rest while it lasts, for the sky's getting lighter, and the rain will stop soon.'

He felt a chill in his bones. The rain might be stopping, but soon after, that's when the storm would really hit, and it wouldn't stop this time until they were washed away in waves of blood.

Laska sat at the cave entrance, looking down upon the verdant valley before him. His remaining guards kept the hundreds of people waiting impatiently further behind him, but they couldn't hold them for much longer.

They'd made the journey by days end as planned, and yet when Laska had reached the entrance, he'd called a halt and told everyone to be prepared to wait. His people initially accepted his order and had not grumbled, simply obeying, but now, after keeping them waiting for a further full day, their patience was nearing its end.

They were almost out of torches, which meant soon, those in the tunnels would be in pitch black, and also, people were having to relieve themselves near where they waited, so the stench within the tunnels was unbearable.

If he didn't give the order to enter the valley soon, they would walk over his body, orders or no.

Yet still, he hesitated.

As he sat there, images of times past continued to flood his memory. His father's terrible death and his own anguish swept over him, pushing aside the recent experience of the giant's kneeling at Maya's feet to one side. Maya was responsible for saving their land, but Laska's father had been responsible for bringing death to it.

Shouts echoed down the tunnel, the frustration and fear of his people making themselves known.

Why couldn't he find the courage? There was no sign of the giants, yet he knew they were there, watching him as he searched for them.

Sweat ran down his brow, the pain from his heart thudding erratically, taking all his strength away.

'We can't hold them back much longer, my lord,' one of his guards advised, looking at Laska with concern.

Laska levered himself to his feet. 'Then tell them its time to see what awaits,' he advised, and stumbled out into the open air.

Slowly he made his way down the hillside, his old feet shuffling, his eyes surveying the beauty of the landscape around him. This valley had always been lush, and yet now it was awash with vibrant colours. His hands brushed over flowers, disturbing hundreds of butterflies that danced in the air all around.

He was halfway down the hillside now, and he looked behind to see his people spreading out from the cave, reticent to follow him down, fearful of the stories they'd been told throughout their lives. Yet their eyes were wide with wonder at what lay before them, and they pointed everywhere. If Ember Town had been a piece of paradise, then this was where it had been carved from.

Yet suddenly, the cheer and optimism died down as Laska watched, and the cries of excitement, turned to that of fear as people started jostling back toward the cave.

Laska knew, before he even turned around, what he would face.

Tristan's Folly

He shuffled about and there striding toward him was a giant, a club resting upon its shoulder.

The ground shook as it closed the distance in but a few strides. It stopped before him, its face impassive, and Laska didn't even have the strength to draw the sword from his side. His breath came in rasps, and he suddenly realised that where he stood was where his father had fallen, torn from his life.

He could barely focus. A loud painful banging filled his ears, and with shock, he realised it was his heart, frantically beating its last.

He saw the giant's hand grasp the club handle firmly and then from behind him, he heard screams of panic. No giants had gone past him, so it couldn't be them. Had the Rangers somehow made it through? But as he turned back, he saw the reason. Down the hill, running, screaming, laughing with joy, chasing the clouds of butterflies came the two boys.

They ran with wild abandon, free from the confines of the caves and their parent's remonstrations, and they ran as fast as their little legs could carry them.

Past Laska they flew, straight between the giant's feet, and around and around they ran, waving their little wooden swords.

The giant bent down, reaching out a huge hand, but they didn't try to evade. Instead, knowing no fear, they jumped into its palm, then climbed swiftly from his grasp, running up his arm to sit upon the giant's shoulders.

Laska sank to his knees, the drumming in his ears getting slower and slower. The giant put aside its club, and a smile broke its craggy features in two. Warbling erupted from its mouth and through darkening eyes, Laska saw dozens of giants come forth, bearing baskets ladened with food which they left on the hillside before backing away.

Tears fell down Laska's face, but now, for the first time he could remember, they were tears of joy.

His heart gave a final, almighty beat as he looked to the sky. The gods had granted him his wish, and he gladly paid their price. Even as darkness overtook him for the last time, it seemed strangely tinged with light.

The sound of horses and men arriving had brought Taran to his feet. It was almost time for the evening meeting, and his presence would be required shortly. He walked out from under the Tower oak's canopy, feeling the heat of the setting sun lash him across the side of his face.

The sun had reappeared with a vengeance the day before. The humidity was now fierce, but the flow of water from the mountainside was still forceful. It would be another two days before Daleth could think to bring the full might of his forces against the dwindling number of defenders once again.

He glanced over his shoulder, looking back at the Elder, and shared a final thought of gratitude. The giant leaned back against the Tower oak and closed its eyes. Its injuries on the outside might have fully healed, but those on the inside still caused it pain.

He passed gratefully into the shade of the gate tunnel, enjoying the cool air before stepping into the courtyard in front of the keep. Trom's men were busy around the rear gate, leading horses back out into the pass, keeping the area clear and ensuring the mounts were fed and secured.

He shook his head in self-reflection as he walked toward the steps. Over the last week, the turmoil in his head had gradually lessened, and his belief that Maya hadn't abandoned him had helped to mend his heart. Now, because of this, it seemed his gift had returned as strong as before.

Upon opening his mind to the Elder after the mission to destroy the siege engine, he'd discovered sorrow that far exceeded his own. It transpired that the loss of the other two giants was a tragedy that went far beyond their obvious strategic value. The two dead giants were the Elder's sons, who, having failed in their efforts to persuade him to stay in the valley, accompanied their father, only to die before his eyes. The magnitude of such a loss put Taran's into stark perspective.

Since then, he'd spent as much time as possible with the Elder. Somehow, they'd helped the other find solace, sharing memories of brighter times. He came to see how he'd overreacted to Maya's departure, pushing away those who'd sought to reassure him.

He had everything to be grateful for. All of his pain was based purely on the delusion that Maya's love had somehow perished. Next to the tangible loss of the Elder's two sons, his was nothing, and he now felt humbled. Maya might be gone, but she was safe and alive, which was what he would have wished for.

That realisation, combined with Drizt's death and the sight of the oasis Maya had created, had helped Taran recover from the darkest place he'd ever been; a pit of despair in his own mind.

The Elder also reinforced his decision to stay and fight, by sharing stories of tyrant kings long-forgotten, pointing out that this time it was different. Daleth's gift of eternal youth was at the cost of all around him, and this world would eventually die unless he was stopped. The only way to protect Maya, wherever she was, was to defeat Daleth, first and foremost.

Shouting reached Taran, and recognising Rakan's voice, he looked up. His father was berating some soldiers by the keep steps who hadn't protected their weapons with oiled rags from the storm. Taran couldn't help but laugh at the looks on their faces, but more so at their thoughts. It seemed they were more terrified of Rakan than Daleth's army on the other side of the walls, and well they might be.

Rakan turned as Taran approached, eyes smiling warmly.

Taran responded in kind, recognising the relief in his father's eyes.

'Old habits die hard,' Rakan laughed. 'Anyway, I've just seen Kalas. He warned tonight's meeting might be longer than usual as we'll be joined by one of the riders who brought in the horses. We'll have a lot to talk about now the rains have stopped, so, I'm going to get myself some food before it starts. Care to join me?'

'I'm not hungry,' Taran replied, and when he saw a look of consternation flick across Rakan's face, he added. 'No, really. I'll grab something after. My talks with the Elder make me realise how lucky I am and I want to spend a little time helping others like he's helped me.'

Rakan's face cleared of worry, and as they entered the keep, he stayed in the food hall, whereas Taran made his way deeper, toward the corridors where the injured were being housed.

Taran kicked several rats from beneath his feet, and as he looked around, saw they were darting everywhere. They'd have to be dealt with, or disease would soon be rife, and he made a mental note to have fifty men come in here later to kill as many as they could.

The sounds when he stepped into the corridor were soul-wrenching for they were of utter hopelessness. Whether it was screams or moans, they all held that terrible dirge. Death was coming, and for some, it couldn't come soon enough, and for others, they were trying to fight it until their last breath.

With his gift returned, he walked into the first room, then backed away quickly, choking back vomit. The room had no living inside, rather it was full of various limbs that had been removed and were piled up against the walls. There'd been a writhing mound of rats feasting on them, and Taran knew this was only compounding the problem.

Where the cats had gone that had been so prolific was beyond him.

He walked to the next room and tentatively stepped inside. There, on bunks, were the first of the injured. Again the smell was indescribable, but this time he kept his face straight as several of the bed-bound soldiers turned toward him.

There was a mix of hope and hopelessness all at once in their gaze as if through some miracle, he might be able to save them from this torment, bring them back to health. He couldn't do the latter, only Maya had that gift and, she was gone, but if his gift let him, he could perhaps do the former.

He walked amongst them, speaking softly, reaching for his gift, and it answered. Most of the time, he didn't even know what he said, and knew, for the most part, they couldn't hear. Irrespective, he reached into their minds, guiding their terrified thoughts to happier times, happier places.

As he left the room a short while later, the sound of misery had ceased. The men now slept, exhausted, and their faces were peaceful even if tinged with death.

His head pounded, but he forced himself from one room of injured to the next. Many of the healers he met initially looked upon him with something approaching hostility, as he was of the kind who inflicted such ills on others. However, by the time he left, their eyes were filled with tears of gratitude.

By the fifth room, his head felt like it would split apart, and he could barely walk. As he staggered in, Yana came hurrying over, taking him by the hand, leading him to a chair from which she swept some blood-soaked bandages.

'Tell me, what ails you?' she demanded, looking into his eyes in consternation.

'My vision is blurring, and there's pressure in my temples. I've been helping the injured find release from their pain, but I experience theirs every time I enter their minds, and it's crippling me,' Taran explained.

'Just sit here, I'll be right back,' Yana commanded, and disappeared out of the room.

In what was likely but a few moments, but which seemed forever, Yana returned holding a goblet. 'Drink this,' she instructed.

Taran did as he was told, quaffing it in desperation, and fortunately, the pain began to ease.

He opened his eyes in amazement. 'Thank you,' he said, grasping Yana's hand in gratitude. 'I know I've nothing to complain about compared to these souls, but my head felt like it would split in two.'

Yana said nothing, leaving her hand in his.

Taran stood up, letting go, not noticing the look of disappointment that flashed across Yana's features and moved to sit down next to a young lad who had barely seen sixteen summers.

'Tell me of your truest love?' he asked, and as the young man briefly thought back through the pain, Taran captured the image and fixed the memory in place. Taran's eyes were misted as he stood up, for the image was that of the lad's mother, for he'd never known another woman's love in his short years.

He went around the room, reminding each of the wounded of happier times, leaving them peaceful as death approached. As he stood at the doorway to the room, it was now quiet. He looked over to the young man, but Yana was pulling a sheet over his face.

Taran strode out, tears falling, for in some ways reminding the men of their own loved ones, to bring them happiness in their fading moments, again brought his own loss to the surface once again.

Yana came into the corridor, but he turned away, not wanting to share his grief. She called to him about the meeting, but he ignored her.

Instead, he continued going from room to room, helping not just the injured but the healers as well. They suffered terribly from exhaustion and the trauma of having to deal with such horrific injuries day after day. As he left the final room, he bumped into a bewildered-looking healer he'd not encountered before.

She stopped and looked at Taran and gave him a brief but perfunctory smile as she looked up and down the corridor. 'I've lost two patients,' she said.

'Then if you've only lost two, you're skilled beyond most healers,' responded Taran with a bow, and walked past, hurrying toward the long-overdue meeting with Kalas and the others.

'No,' she said after him, 'they haven't died, they've just disappeared.'

Taran didn't hear the words, for his thoughts had turned toward Maya. She still loved him, he just had to hold on, survive this carnage, and then find her. They were meant to be together, and their reunion would be something the bards would sing about. Nothing and nobody would be able to stop this from happening.

He almost skipped up the flights of stone stairs to the upper floor. He was a little late for the meeting and hurried into the chamber. Kalas, Rakan, Trom and Astren were talking with a man Taran didn't recognise, but who wore the garb of a Freestates soldier. Yana was also there, observing but not participating.

Torches were being lit by several guards who sketched brief salutes as they left the chamber, continuing with their evening task.

The soldier who'd been responsible for the horses' delivery, glanced briefly over his shoulder as Taran walked in and dipped his head in acknowledgement before turning back to Kalas. 'So in summary, lord commander, the king has only sent one hundred horses and no more will be forthcoming.'

Kalas thumped his fist hard against the table. 'Damn him,' he shouted, 'and damn you, Astren, as well. You must've known this but decided not to tell me. This isn't something you simply overlook.'

Astren quailed before Kalas' anger, backing away.

Rakan's face was dark. 'How will we decide who lives or dies?' he demanded. 'I suppose one of those horses is supposed to be for you?'

Astren couldn't speak, but he managed to nod.

'I thought you were somehow different!' Kalas hissed. He turned away with a look of distaste on his face and returned his attention to the soldier who looked uncomfortable at what was being said. 'Will you stay and fight with us, soldier?' Kalas asked. 'I know the others who accompanied you have already left, but every sword arm will help.'

The man shook his head. 'I fear I cannot. We were all given further orders to scour this side of the kingdom and direct the peasantry to Freeguard.'

'Thank the gods,' said Taran, 'at least Tristan is trying to round up men to bolster the alliance army, but he'd have done far better to help save those who are already trained.'

The soldier looked perplexed for a moment before he shook his head. 'I don't know anything about that, my lord,' he said, noting Taran's armour and recognising him for either nobility, a soldier of rank, or indeed both. 'The king is inviting every citizen to Freeguard and offering a reward to those who attend his betrothal celebrations.'

'So, who is his betrothed?' Taran asked, aware of the sudden silence in the room as everyone awaited the man answer.

'He is to marry the Lady Maya,' the soldier replied.

Taran didn't hear the soldier's screams, for he wasn't aware of grabbing him, nor hitting him over and over. He didn't hear Rakan and Kalas shouting his name, nor feel them and Trom trying to pull him off.

But suddenly everything went dark, and he was falling and falling into a black abyss.

Chapter XIX

'I shall have to report this,' said Astren. 'Murder, let alone of a king's emissary is punishable by death.'

'You'll do no such thing,' Kalas retorted, his eyes brooding. 'Taran didn't mean to kill him. Sadly, with perhaps the exception of you, we have all done similar or worse, and I also hold Tristan partly responsible too!'

'I don't answer to you,' blustered Astren, but his words lacked strength, and inside he was as frightened as he'd ever been. The soldier Taran had struck lay dead, cold on the floor. Taran was on the floor too, unconscious, first from Kalas' blow with the hilt of his dagger, but now from sleep weed which Yana had administered.

All the poor soldier had done was tell of Tristan's forthcoming marriage to Maya. Astren tried one more time, his voice barely above a whisper. 'My duty is to tell the king.'

'Let me make this perfectly clear for you,' explained Rakan, leaning forward, his voice also a whisper, but whereas Astren's was quiet through fear, Rakan's was quiet with menace. 'Ask yourself this. Were my son to be sentenced to death, what do you think I would do to the man that was responsible?'

'I'm wondering to myself,' mused Kalas, 'whether I've any use for a man who holds back on vital information, such as the arrival of one hundred horses instead of five hundred. What else have you failed to mention to me, Astren? Are we even on the same side? I'm beginning to wonder.'

As the two men glared at him, Astren whimpered and scurried from the room.

Tristan's Folly

'Now I question whether he knew of the trap set for us by Tristan when we first arrived,' Yana muttered, as she knelt by Taran's side. 'He denied it of course, but now I no longer believe it.'

Kalas nodded slowly, looking thoughtful. 'It matters not what we think. Tristan is our king for better or worse and Astren his voice. I swore an oath of fealty, and that is not something I take lightly. So, let us hope for Taran's sake that Astren says nothing.'

'Why?' asked Rakan. 'Because you don't want to kill Taran if ordered to do so?'

'No!' Kalas responded firmly. 'It's because I've no wish to be an oath breaker, which defying that order would make me. Now, enough of this. I doubt Astren will ignore either of our warnings, at least whilst we are here, and Tristan is far away.

'Trom, take Taran down the hall and put him in the chamber he recovered in last time, then hurry back. Yana, you'll stay with Taran and keep him asleep for two days. I'm not sure that in itself will be enough, but I'm hoping maybe with forced rest he'll awake free from the darkness that overwhelmed him on hearing the news.'

As Trom disappeared with Taran over his shoulder, Rakan and Kalas looked at the soldier's body on the ground. 'Leave it to me. Trom and I will deal with it later,' offered Rakan.

'So be it,' agreed Kalas, as Trom returned. 'We must now focus on the matters at hand. The rain is abating, in two days Daleth will relaunch his assault. We know his tactics; he'll simply wear us down with nonstop attacks. Had it not been for the rain we would have already been overrun. A new problem we face is that the fire trench is now completely useless. There's nowhere for the water to drain, the bridge timbers are saturated, and I won't risk soaking them in oil in case Daleth manages to ignite them like last time. So when we pull back from the second wall when it inevitably falls, there'll be little respite.'

'We need to decide who gets the horses,' Trom rumbled.

Kalas nodded. 'I've been giving it some thought. Yana and her healers will all go. It's easy to take a life, anyone can do that, but not many can save them. They all get a place. The wounded will be given the choice of ending their own pain, there'll be no saving them.'

'I agree about the healers,' Rakan approved. 'So that leaves only ninety mounts. Well, the gods will help us, for who knows how many men will be left to ride them when we the times comes.'

Kalas was quiet for a moment, contemplating. 'I swore to Tristan that we'd fight to the last unless he gave us permission to pull back. Every day that can be squeezed from Daleth gives our allies more time to gather …'

'But let's not forget,' interrupted Rakan, 'that there's no way to holdout in the keep as we can't block the entrance without Maya. If we withdraw there, we'd only gain hours, and no one would survive. I came to terms with dying a long time ago, but I don't think throwing it away in a pointless last stand is what I had in mind.'

'Tristan, has shown he has no honour,' added Trom in his deep voice. 'I agree with Rakan. A few hours isn't worth the life of those who remain at the end.'

Kalas drummed his fingers on the table. 'This doesn't sit well with me, but nor did Tristan spiriting away Maya either or sending so few horses. I'll think about this further, but I'm inclined to agree. There'll be no strategic advantage to be gained from an extra hour or two that warrants the death of those who fought so hard.'

Gloom descended upon the chamber as the sun finally set, and the flickering torches did little to offset the chill.

Rakan rose tiredly, feeling his age. 'It's time to ensure the men are fed, and we need to address those damn rats. Soon there'll be more of them than there are men in Daleth's army, and if they reach our stores, we'll all die with empty stomachs.'

'Then how about we share them with Daleth and his men,' laughed Trom, with a rumble like thunder. 'Instead of killing them, we smoke them out, drive them through the gates, down the pass. The amount of food Daleth must have to feed his army will be vast, just imagine if the rats got hold of some of that.'

Kalas' eyes lit up. 'There hasn't been much to make me smile of late, Trom, and this certainly won't turn the tide of battle, but everything helps. It will give the men something to do, help our injured and healers and cause Daleth no small inconvenience if we're lucky. Trom, have your men take the first shift, Rakan you organise the garrison soldiers and archers for the second. Have men work their way down from the second floor and up from the fortress depths at the same time. Let's be generous with these gifts to our friends.'

Trom and Rakan departed, leaving Kalas alone, watching the sun slowly disappear over the horizon, his thoughts dark and brooding on a pressing issue.

What to do about their own resident rat?

What to do about Astren?

Astren hurried back toward his chamber.

He was furious, but also scared. Had his good intentions of trying to help everyone amounted to nothing simply because of serving his king? Surely that is what they were all supposed to do?

True, he didn't like Tristan much either; in fact, he'd hated his manipulation of Maya on the one hand, but on the other, admired how he always got what he wanted. Tristan epitomised what being a king of the Freestates was about.

Kalas, Rakan, and Taran … everyone in this damn fortress treated him as if he was nothing. He had a villa, with servants and a life of luxury awaiting him; if only Tristan forgave him. Yet all they saw was weakness because he hadn't killed men with a sword or his bare hands.

Perhaps he'd show Rakan and Kalas his strength, and ignore their warnings. He'd tell Tristan about the emissaries murder, and the ecstatic king would reinstate his loyal servant, Astren in gratitude.

He felt stronger, more self-assured as he descended the steps. He'd ask Tristan's permission to take a horse and ride from this place immediately.

He walked through the food hall, ignored by the men therein, toward the corridors leading to his room and steeled himself for the sounds of torment that would strip his soul with their despair. Yet as he walked past the first few doors, there was no sound whatsoever.

Had they all been given sleep weed, he wondered, to speed them on their way already? Shocked that the healers would kill them all so soon, he pushed into a room, trying not to breathe through his nose for the smell of dying remained even in the absence of the sound.

He walked around the bunks to see the injured sleeping, all with peaceful looks on their faces despite suffering from horrific injuries.

A healer rose from her chair, placing a finger to her lips to warn him to silence as she took his hand, turning him around and leading him back out through the doorway.

'What happened?' he asked in wonder.

The woman's tired eyes looked into his. 'The young commander, Taran, is what happened. He has somehow taken all their pain away, all their sorrow, and because of him, they're at peace. Some might even survive because of his intervention. I never thought a man of war could save lives rather than take them, but just like the lady Maya, he has a gift for healing.'

'How many did he help?' asked Astren, already knowing the answer.

'All of them,' replied the healer. 'All of them. May the gods favour him!'

Astren bowed as he backed away, continuing on, looking briefly into the rooms as he passed to see the same in each one.

As he neared his chamber, he passed Kalas' room again. The smell was sickening, and he laughed as he hoped there were a dozen dead rats on Kalas' bed, just in case the lord commander felt the need to sleep here again.

He'd take a look on his return from reporting to Tristan. Even if the thought of rats in Kalas' bed brought him some comfort, the smell truly didn't.

As he entered his room, he lit new candles and lay upon the bed. The sun had set, and he'd get this over and done with as quickly as possible.

He chewed on some sleep weed as he was impatient for his spirit travel to begin. Tristan had left the capital over a week before and was now on his way to Freeguard. Even so, the route was familiar, and Astren flew fast and straight, not taking his time to enjoy the freedom and sights the journey often afforded him.

Freemantle was eerily quiet as he flew over it, yet around the city, lights flickered as those citizens who'd decided to stay behind scoured the empty homes for riches.

He didn't pause, but kept on, pushing east to find the bright lights of Tristan's camp a third of the way to Freeguard. As he flew closer, there, on a large, rocky outcrop was Maya in spirit form, her face a picture of sadness. Astren decided to leave her to her sorrow, but she saw him, lighting up with such a glow that Astren had no choice but to go to her.

'Astren,' Maya cried, as he flew to her side. She embraced him warmly, despite the pain showing in her ethereal eyes. 'I cannot tell you how good it is to see you.' Maya clasped his hand. 'Dally with me a while before you see Tristan. I know you're here to report to him, but seeing you has lifted my spirits so much, and they've never needed lifting as much as they do tonight.'

Astren was torn, but he sat down beside her, and her light and warmth drove away his own dark feelings, and he remembered just how special she was to him. He'd been partly responsible for her pain, and yet she forgave him without ever having blamed him in the first place.

'I'm finding it so difficult to fly the spirit paths,' Maya said with sadness. 'I've only managed to see Taran once, and his suffering broke my heart.'

Before Astren could answer, Maya, lowered her voice even if no one could see them or overhear them. 'I can trust you, can't I?' and she went on without pause. 'I know I shouldn't have, but I left Taran a note under his pillow explaining everything about Tristan leaving me no choice. Did he tell anyone of it? Has he said anything? Does he understand my actions, and is he planning to come for me?'

Astren was shocked at Maya's confession, and he felt his anger rise as he thought of his mistreatment at Taran's hands. He thought to share the pain, the suffering, and the terrible darkness that had engulfed Taran ... but as he looked at the shining hope in her eyes, the love there so bright, his anger evaporated.

He took her hand, thinking quickly, knowing that if she was unable to spirit travel, then she wouldn't find out the truth. 'My child. Taran found your note, and though he suffers, your note brought him solace. He talks of finding you again all the time, and amongst all the darkness we're enduring, he's a beacon of light, just like when you were by his side.' Then as he said the words, Astren considered his conversation with the healer and recounted to Maya what Taran had done for the wounded.

Maya pulled Astren close. 'Thank you, Astren. I'm so glad you're our friend.'

Astren put his arm around her shoulders. 'Fear not,' he said, 'love such as yours is a flame that can never be extinguished. Now, I have to go. I need to report to Tristan. You know how angry he gets if he's kept waiting.'

'Visit me tomorrow night if you can, and the night after,' implored Maya, as Astren moved away. 'Save me from the boredom of my imprisonment, and please, tell Taran, tell him ...'

'I know,' smiled Astren, turning to look back. 'Don't worry, Maya. I know what you want me to tell him. I'll act as a go-between until you can make the journey again once more.'

With that, Astren moved across the encampment until he came across Tristan, surrounded by minor nobles and soldiers in his spacious tent. He felt guilty at his duplicity, but was excited to tell Tristan about Taran, to be back in favour again and would save this to last.

He projected himself just outside of their circle so as not to startle them.

Tristan turned to him. 'Report,' Tristan barked, and Astren began sharing all he could think of, starting with the rain and then the casualty numbers.

After a while, Tristan waved his hand dismissively. 'What's wrong with you? I'm not interested in how many men die, or what the weather is like! All I want to know is if that damned fortress you made me waste so much money on is still standing, and for how much longer, so I know whether it will give our allies the time to reach us.'

Astren stood there, open-mouthed. It was always about money, not people's lives. Tristan wouldn't care for the murder of the lost emissary, only for the power it gave him over Taran were he to know. Maya's recent words echoed in his head; *I'm so glad you're our friend.* Perhaps it was time he placed friendship above wealth and station.

'Apologies, my king,' bowed Astren. 'Forgive my lapse of judgement. I can see now what's important and what isn't. The citadel will hold for another week, beyond that it's hard to say,' and he faded away before Tristan gave him permission to do so, feeling a little satisfaction as the king's face turned red with annoyance.

Astren flew back to the citadel as fast as he could, anger making him swift, but this time his annoyance was aimed at himself.

As he arrived, only the night watch on the walls were awake. It was past midnight now, and everything was quiet. He worked his way through the keep, the corridors empty, and the torches burning low. He was about to enter his room when he remembered the smell and turned around.

He'd make amends with Kalas, Rakan, and Taran; find a way to rebuild their trust in him and friendship. Tell Taran everything. They'd understood what had motivated him to make such poor choices.

He passed through the door, yes, these were good men here, they would understand ... but this train of thought stopped abruptly, for as he focussed on the room, he felt a chill pass through him like never before.

It was so dark, but in spirit form, he could see well enough nonetheless. He looked down and there at his feet piled against the walls were human and mountain cat corpses. Yet these bodies weren't just dead, they were shrunken as if drained from the inside. His astral heart was pumping furiously as he noticed movement on the bed, and he moved closer to see an injured soldier in the arms of ... No. He couldn't believe it. It was Kalas!

As Astren stared, frozen in shock and revulsion, Kalas bit into the dying man's neck, and drank noisily with relish until he cast the shrivelled husk aside.

Kalas' head slowly lifted, eyes glowing red, and a smile slowly split the bloodied face. A smile so twisted in evil, that Astren would have barely recognised him.

'Hello, little rat,' Kalas rasped, with a voice from the depths of hell itself.

Astren fled.

He flew to his room, but even as he tried to join with his body, he was unable to awaken it. He'd taken too much sleep weed, and his body refused to respond so soon after digesting it.

'Gods, help me!' he cried, as still in spirit form, he saw the door to his room open and Kalas stalk in. A low, evil laugh echoed around the chamber, and as Astren looked around, his dream flashed to mind. The long-dead kings, the torturous death, but not by the hand of Daleth or his minions, but instead by the hand of Kalas!

'Please,' he sobbed, dropping to his knees, 'I'm your friend. I warned your father. Have mercy, by all the gods, have mercy!'

Kalas, the daemon simply pushed the door shut.

'I'm interested to see whether you'll feel the physical pain your body is about to suffer as I feed upon it,' that horrible voice mused.

Astren screamed, and Kalas, the daemon, began to feast.

Daleth gazed west at the sky and saw sunshine break through the clouds.

It had been a week of autumn rain in the midst of summer, and he no longer felt blessed by the gods as he had done of late.

He'd had to move most of his forces back onto the plains, only keeping a small number forward to keep an eye on the fortress. All the tents had been dismantled as the flood water rushed by. Cold food, with no fires, and no shelter during this downpour had been punishing. Everyone was in a foul mood, and fights had broken out frequently.

He was impatient to start the assault again, to focus his men's anger and impatience on the enemy. Still, even now, the torrent ran around his calves, and no soldier could fight efficiently with their boots filled.

Another unpleasant side-effect of the downpour was the hundreds of bodies being washed into the camp.

His men were not bothered by their dead comrades; the type of men they were and the amulets they wore saw to that. Yet still, it caused more work, for Daleth could ill afford to let disease set in, so they'd had to be dealt with too. There never seemed to be a time when something or someone wasn't calling for his attention or creating work.

The torrent was cold, but Daleth ignored it, setting a strong example for the men around, enduring with them. Bodies continued to float by, dislodged from the piles his men had made against the side of the mountains to ensure the route of attack was clear. Something heavy bumped into his leg, and he ignored it until suddenly it moved. He gazed down to see a large brown rat hanging onto his leather trousers just in time to see it about to bite him.

Daleth swiftly grabbed the creature behind the neck, crushing it in his fist and cast it away, only for another to cling on to him, then another and another.

All around, men flailed at the rodents that were carried along in the current having been swept from the mountains. No, he thought, looking into the distance, they were from the damned fortress! Considering the amount that were floating or swimming past, this wasn't just a coincidence. They'd set these vermin against him on purpose.

Rats were no one's friend, for they carried disease and ate through everything, and then it hit him. They were releasing these rats to try and spoil his army's supplies.

He shook his fist at the fortress in the distance.

They'd have to spend another two days now, drying out, and then at least another day ensuring they'd eliminated the flood of vermin and ensured their stores were free of contamination.

Damn them. They were a far better adversary than he'd ever anticipated, and now nature itself had turned against him. He looked at the huge tree standing over the fortress. They were likely all dry and warming themselves over fires, but it wouldn't take long to burn it all down.

His forces had come so close to victory before the rains came. Now the defenders couldn't have more than maybe a quarter of their original forces left whilst he still had over ninety thousand men. Yet nigh on eight thousand were dead when he'd expected to lose no more than two thousand, and this battle was still not over.

Daleth grimaced. He could respect the fight the defenders had put up, but it was always just delaying the inevitable. Once the attack resumed, there'd be relentless assaults, day and night until the fortress was his, and the first battle in his conquest of the Freestates was won.

Yana sat watching over Taran. It was almost time.

Two days had passed since Trom had brought Taran here, and despite the nigh on irresistible desire to have him moved to her room, to hold him in her arms, she hadn't allowed her judgement to be clouded.

Instead, she'd spent time around the fortress, talking to the lightly wounded and eating alongside the other healers. The pause in hostilities could have allowed her to stay by Taran's side, especially as the suffering of the seriously injured in the lower levels had been alleviated. Still, she'd kept her distance.

Yana looked about, satisfied that the roses had been cleared, and the chamber returned to its original state. The door to the chamber she left ajar so that Rakan, Kalas, or even Trom could see in as they often walked past.

The strange thing was, now it was time to let Taran wake, she was as nervous as she'd ever been in her life.

During those years living in Ember Town, she'd broken many hearts. One, a young sergeant of the guard who'd become infatuated with her, had taken his own life when she'd cast him aside for one of his friends. Men could do the strangest of things when their hearts were broken, so she was wary, yet at the same time prepared.

Taran moaned softly, and his eyelids fluttered as he started to come around. Yana had plenty of water and platters of food, for he'd be hungry when he awoke as she'd only been able to spoon thin broth into his mouth while he slept.

Yana had cleaned and buffed her leather clothing, knowing how well it showed off her physique, and the laces she'd left open on her shirt served to draw attention there very well indeed.

Taran's eye's snapped open, and he looked around the room, disorientated.

'What happened?' he moaned huskily, for his throat was dry, and he reached out to take the goblet Yana offered.

Yana didn't smile but simply kept her face impassive as she responded. 'You killed a man with your bare hands who'd done nothing but bring bad news. Kalas had to knock you out with a blow to the back of your head.'

Tristan's Folly

Taran groaned as his hands quested carefully over his scalp, finding the tender lump there, and then the groans intensified as his memory flooded back. 'Maya's getting married to Tristan,' he whispered.

'That's why you chose to commit murder,' said Yana. 'and now we're all worried as to what you'll do next.'

Taran had his eyes closed, but tears seeped from under the lids. 'Please go. Leave me. I've no wish to share my grief with anyone,' and he lay down, turning his face to the pillow.

All Yana wanted to do was take him in her arms, but that time wasn't yet. She took a deep breath. It was now or never.

'You're heartbroken,' she said harshly. 'You can barely breathe, and it's as if your heart could stop at any moment. Pain like you've never known fills every fibre of your being.

'You're already thinking, why is life worth living, if there are no colours to see, no laughter to hear, no love to feel or taste? The dreams you laid at Maya's feet, have been trodden on and kicked aside as if they didn't exist. Your life which had purpose and meaning now has no value whatsoever. You long for the release of death, for you know deep inside, that nothing will ever match what you had, nor will even come close.

'So, what's the point in going on, in fighting, when it's easier to die, for that's the only thing that will bring you peace.'

Yana drew her dagger, it's razored edge glinting in the fading light and lay it on the table next to the bed, and gently spun it.

'Nobody, including myself, can do anything to heal your pain. The only person who could is now marrying a king of wealth and power; for despite Maya's honeyed words and gentle touch, you're beneath her. She'll spend every night from hereon in the bed and arms of another man. Every night you live, this will be a dagger to your heart, adding to the thousands thrust there before.

'But maybe the one dagger on the table there holds the answer.'

Taran's eyes were red, and tears flooded so hard down his face that Yana could barely continue … but she did.

'So, I say to you, kill yourself now. Let Tristan take what was yours, let him have what was yours, do nothing, say nothing, just fade away.'

Taran's hand slowly reached for the dagger, halting its spin before picking it up, staring at his reflection in the polished blade.

'What do you think, Taran, broken-heart? What do you think when you look at yourself? Surely the only option is to slash those wrists, your throat?

'But what if there's another way? A way where the pain goes away immediately and forever. A way, which in time would allow you to exact revenge on a king, and on anyone else who wronged you.'

Taran's eyes were bloodshot red as he looked at her, a terrible danger shining within, a burning anger at being so brutally hurt by her words. Yet Yana's heartbeat quickened, for the despair had disappeared entirely.

'To fight the enemy, sometimes you have to be the enemy,' she whispered, stepping closer, pulling from behind her back something Taran had seen before.

'Here is the answer to all your troubles, and the key to finding your revenge,' she said, moving around to stand beside him. 'Allow me to take your pain away, and all you desire will be there for the taking.'

In answer, Taran said nothing, but he pushed back the blankets, stood, and leaned his head forward.

Yana allowed herself a smile of triumph as she fastened one of Daleth's amulets, taken from a corpse, around Taran's neck. She held her breath, for she'd gambled everything on this … this one moment. Would it work as had been described? Would it take away all the feeling, or would he kill himself irrespective, or even her? His body which had been slumped, devoid of strength, began to straighten even as she watched.

Taran's eyes cleared, becoming hard. He stretched his arms, feeling the strength in his limbs. 'To take away my pain, and all I desire will be mine,' he said.

Yana, felt her insides melt as Taran reached out slowly, taking her head in his hands, and as he leaned forward, she closed her eyes, lips parting, sighing in anticipation.

Instead, she felt Taran's lips brush her forehead, and her eyes snapped open as he pulled back.

'Just because this deadens the pain, hardens the soul, and increases the basest desires, it doesn't mean that I've lost my memory. I know what you want Yana, but I gave away my heart a long time ago, and now, thanks to this amulet, it feels dead. You're not what I desire. The death of a king is!'

Taran opened the door, ushering her out.

For a moment, Yana felt anger, but then it dropped away, and she smiled over her shoulder. 'The best things in life are worth waiting for and fighting for, and I'm willing to do both, Taran, heart-stealer.

'Just you wait and see. You'll be mine one day. Just you wait and see.'

Chapter XX

Today, Daleth would relaunch his assault, thought Kalas, yet for the first time in weeks, he found himself unable to think clearly on the day ahead.

Before him sat Taran, Rakan, Trom, and Yana. It seemed strange without Drizt, nor had they chosen a replacement, for there were too few archers left to warrant a leader, so they fell under Rakan's command.

Taran seemed different, but Kalas couldn't understand why. He wore his armour as usual, embellished and bright, but despite that, he couldn't have appeared darker. Taran had shown many emotions of late, sadness, confusion, anger and then blind fury, but now there was a cold hardness to his face, indifference within his eyes.

Something had changed in him as if his broken heart had been replaced by one of stone.

Rakan sat close beside him, a loving father who only saw what he wanted to see in his son, and there was a look of relief on Rakan's face that Taran seemed strong once again.

Trom as ever sat patiently, quietly, but Yana … there was something different there too, almost a look of satisfaction. She glanced surreptitiously at Taran, hoping no one would catch her looking.

Kalas tried to focus as everyone's eyes followed him, pacing back and forth as he pulled his thoughts together.

'We know what to expect,' he began, 'for we saw Daleth's strategy before the rains struck and this remains his best option. His forces will attack, there'll be no pause, no respite and this fortress will fall. Only the gods know how quickly.

'We'll contest the second wall only until they're close to making a foothold, then whatever archers we have left will cover our withdrawal to the third.

'Yana. This is when you'll ensure that your healers leave. You'll also give the severely wounded the choice to take their own lives, or make the decision for them if they're not in a position to do so.

'Once on the third wall, we won't be spread so thin, and we'll make Daleth pay dearly to take it. However, much like wall two, when we can no longer hold, we'll pull back, but this time use lantern oil to buy us some time.

'When it falls, I'll give no order to fight to the last man, despite Tristan's insistence. No one knows outside of this room anyway.

'Those who are left must take horses and find their way to Freeguard. Daleth will let loose his cavalry shortly after the fall, so many won't make it. Because of this, when that time comes, it will be every man for himself.

'Rakan, Taran, and Trom, you need to ensure you escape, for I fear even if Tristan doesn't deserve them, he'll need your skills.

'Hopefully, he'll have raised a large peasant levy to join the alliance forces, and together, with a lot of luck, and your leadership, it will be enough to defeat Daleth's weakened horde.'

'It will take more than luck, it will take the intervention of the gods,' said Rakan. 'Daleth's trained forces will outnumber Tristan's alliance by almost three to one. However large the peasant levy, it will never be enough.'

'You're likely right,' Kalas admitted, 'but we swore an oath to serve. Amongst friends, I can honestly say Tristan is not the king I would have hoped, but one thing we know to be true. If Daleth wins, he will be far worse. His reign will last until these lands, and countless others lay dead, and that will make the sacrifice of all those who died here worthless.

'Trom, Rakan, Yana, please leave, attend to your duties. Taran, I'd have a word.'

As the others filed out, Taran turned to Kalas. 'You need not worry for me,' Taran said sincerely. 'I'm ready to do what needs to be done, and the only ones to die at my hand will be my enemies.'

Kalas nodded. 'I know Taran, I know. But it's not you that I'm worried about.'

'Then, who?' asked Taran.

Kalas couldn't look in Taran's eyes, for suddenly he felt ashamed, so he kept them lowered. 'It's me, Taran. It's me. I've done terrible things, terrible things.'

Taran's laugh echoed around the chamber. 'Then you're in good company. Let's do terrible things together and bring fear to our enemies.'

'You don't understand,' explained Kalas. 'My daemon has returned. You defeated him, but he was never slain, for his life is indelibly linked to mine. For a while, I felt that I was in control, and there was no harm, but I realise now those were his thoughts, not mine. Now, during the day, I am who I've always been, but during the night, I've been wandering the keep, and death has walked with me.'

Taran leaned forward. 'So what have you done?'

Kalas' hands were clasped, white-knuckled, as his eyes finally met Taran's. 'The daemon feeds, and I can only watch in the background as he does so. I've fed on our own, the seriously wounded who would have died anyway, but last night …' He drew a deep breath, drawing strength, then carried on. 'Last night I killed Astren, for he discovered what I was doing and the daemon acted out of self-preservation in case he told Tristan or the others.'

Taran looked grim, but stood, reaching out and gripped Kalas' forearm. 'Your secret will stay safe with me, my friend. Use your daemon, for the strength he gives, for the life he bestows upon you. Use him to help slay our enemies, all of them. This battle will soon be over, but the war will continue on. To defeat this evil we face, I fear we must become evil ourselves. The good will not prevail in such a fight.'

Kalas sighed, his face showing gratitude at Taran's readiness to forgive, but he shook his head, looking Taran firmly in the eye.

'I thought for so long that my oath to kill Daleth justified the means. Ever since the daemon awoke within me, I've been killing not just the guilty, but the innocent as well in my misguided quest to fulfil that oath. Now, thoughts of not just death, but kingship fill my mind. What would happen if I kill Daleth at a later date only to take the throne myself such as I am, replacing one monster with another?

'Then, of course, who might the daemon decide to kill next? What if I'm wounded in the interim, or he feels threatened? Will I kill Yana, Rakan, or you ... draining your life to extend mine? This is a risk you cannot take, and I cannot bear the guilt any longer.'

'What is it you want me to do?' asked Taran. 'Are you asking me to kill you here and now and have the blood of a friend on my hands?'

'No!' Kalas replied. 'I've decided to die here, attempting to fulfil my oath. There'll be no retreating for me when the fortress falls, and not only do I need your help, but I want you to understand what to do next. When I fall, you'll become lord commander. That rank will carry with you if you survive and you must carry on this fight to save the land but also to save yourself.'

As Kalas said this, he pointed to a scroll on the table. 'That confirms my order to abandon the fortress when wall three falls, and that my rank passes to you upon my death.'

Taran swept up the scroll, tucking it into his shirt. 'Initially, I'd thought to die here too, but now my thoughts are of taking my revenge on Tristan instead. So yes, I intend to save myself and return to Freeguard even if just to ensure that happens.'

Kalas gripped Taran's shoulders, looking at him with concern. 'That is not what I meant, Taran. You need to save your heart, and more importantly, your soul before it's too late. Once I would have said something like that in jest, but I carry a daemon within me, so now I've little doubt that my soul will forever be in torment when I die. You're a good man, and even without your gift, I would've thought so. Yet when you're with Maya, you're something beyond that ... you're extraordinary. When people looked at you two together, you could see in their eyes that they wanted to be like you, to love like you. That's your truest gift, not the reading or influencing of minds, but to make people want to be better versions of themselves.

'You two bring out the best of what is in each other and all those around you, and you should be fighting to reclaim that, not to avenge it. For in revenge there'll be no reconciliation I can assure you, at least one that isn't so drenched in blood as to be a mockery of what it should stand for.'

Taran stood quietly for a moment, reflecting on Kalas' words. 'I appreciate what you said was as a friend, but I tell you this. My heart no longer cares for what you describe. It's a distant memory, and I'm glad it is, for it can hurt me no more, and I'll never put myself in a position whereby I feel such pain again.'

'Oh, Taran,' Kalas exclaimed. 'You might think yourself the stronger for this decision, but sometimes embracing our pain takes more courage than pushing it away. Yet I'll not seek to preach any further, for who am I to advise. I've made more mistakes than anyone I know.

'I honestly don't think this war can be won, for even if we kill Daleth, likely one of his commanders will take control. We need a bigger army, and there are not enough friends for the Freestates to call upon. All I know is if revenge is truly what you seek, then you must first defeat Daleth. If you attempt it the other way around and kill Tristan beforehand, you'll never succeed in your quest to kill both, for the alliance will fall apart before a sword is swung.'

Taran nodded thoughtfully. 'What you say makes sense, but how about you kill Daleth for me instead, and save us all a bit of time and trouble!'

Kalas' fist clenched, and his eyes shone brightly. 'I should have died alongside my true king all those years ago. You should have seen it, Taran, even if we were possessed. Less than a thousand knights against one hundred times our number. It was glorious. We slew them in the tens of thousands.'

They both embraced.

'Let's go be heroes,' said Kalas laughing. 'Two mighty heroes. One with the power to read and alter minds, and the other the greatest swordsman of his time.'

Taran shook his head, a wry smile upon his face. 'Two mighty heroes, one with no heart and one with no soul. Hardly what the bards sing about.

'Both gifted and cursed we are,' he added, remembering the Elder's words of long before. 'Both gifted and cursed.'

Maya sat astride her horse, a beautiful white gelding presented to her by Tristan in one of his obvious attempts to buy her forgiveness or affection. She'd initially thought to turn it down, simply to spurn his crude effort, but had after consideration, accepted it.

Despite only riding it since leaving Freemantle, the creature had bonded to her, perhaps sensing a kindred spirit that longed to run free, to escape to the wilderness. Its large eyes seemed soft, belying its considerable strength. It had a regalness about it, tall and proud, yet without arrogance, and when she'd first approached, it had lowered its head slightly as if in homage.

She leaned forward, ruffling its mane, and it whickered softly, appreciating the fussing, and she suddenly laughed to herself even as her heart felt some pain. She knew why she liked the creature, for it reminded her of Taran.

They'd left Freemantle after several days, all the while messengers brought in a flow of information and left again with instructions. Riders were sent out, their task to rally the people to come to Freeguard, and she hoped for their sakes they came. To stay in their homes, their farms, meant facing a grim death at the hands of Daleth's army when it broke through the fortress.

When Astren had visited her those days past, she'd felt her soul lighten, and yet since then, he hadn't kept his promise to come and see her. It seemed he no longer visited Tristan either, for she'd heard Tristan cursing his name over the absence of reports and not knowing what was occurring at the fortress.

It was unlikely Tristan's Folly had fallen, for the last news had been that they expected to hold out at least another week, but now she was worried. A hundred possibilities kept swirling through her mind about why Astren might not have been able to come.

It seemed the more she hurt, the more she worried, and the further she got from Taran, the harder her gift was to reach. She could enter the spirit world, but flying seemed impossible. Even healing the land was proving to be difficult, much like when she was younger.

Suddenly thoughts of losing both her father and Taran threatened to overwhelm her, and she leaned forward in the saddle, wrapping her arms around the horse's long neck. It stayed still, supporting her through this brief moment of weakness.

They travelled eastward, and their pace was fast, for the injured had continued on ahead as Tristan saw to the rescue of his wealth. They travelled with a sizeable number of new soldiers now, who having only recently taken the uniform of the king's guard, were looked upon with disdain by the older ones.

Tristan rode up alongside, and Maya hoped her eyes weren't red as she turned toward him, without a hint of warmth on her face.

'Come on,' said Tristan, 'if you can show affection to a horse, at least you could meet me with a smile.'

Maya was tempted to feign throwing up but instead looked blankly back.

Tristan sighed. 'It seems simple pleasantries are currently out of the question. So on to business. We have a problem. Astren hasn't reported in the last two days, and I'm blind to what's going on with the Eyre, the Desert tribes or at the fortress unless you're able to use your gift to help. I know you won't do this for me, even if as your king and betrothed I ordered it, but in doing so voluntarily, you'll be helping to save the lives of many. Who knows, maybe you'll see Taran on your journey.'

Maya considered his request then nodded. 'I will try. But be warned, I've been unable to spirit travel of late. It would seem, my king, that breaking my heart has broken my gift and likely diminished my worth. Perhaps it would be better to let me fly free so I can better serve you once again.'

Tristan looked at her long and hard. 'You still have worth, even if it's simply as a rallying call for the peasantry to come and witness our marriage. Fear not, you still have your uses. Try tonight,' he ordered, as he turned the head of his horse and cantered off to the head of the line.

Maya's horse neighed softly, shaking its mane. 'I know,' she said, 'I know. I've no wish to do anything for that man, but to see Taran again, I'll try for as long as it takes.'

The day passed slowly, and Maya was impatient for nightfall, yet she made the most of the journey. The countryside was a patchwork of fields, some given to crops or grazing, and yet many areas were still wild and untamed. She drank in the beauty of the landscape, the rolling hills and the different shades of green against a blue sky with fluffy clouds.

Yet how much better would it have been had Taran been here? He'd have found shapes in those clouds, pointed out a flower, or exclaimed in wonder at the birdsong. The world seemed more alive in his presence, embellished by his many stories. It wasn't that she hadn't heard most of them, for by now there were few left unspoken, it was the comfort of his voice, the way he talked with his hands which he said was something he'd picked up from her.

This time, thinking of Taran didn't hurt so much, and in fact, her heart felt happier than it had in some time.

Galain, who captained the guard, eventually called a halt to the days travel. She'd wondered why Tristan had chosen him at first, but his skill in wood crafting and engineering meant Tristan's tent went up quickly, the fires were lit without a problem, and of course, he had a rare skill in sculpting that played to Tristan's vanity perfectly.

Maya's tent was put up next to Tristan's, but as ever she shunned it. She was a hunter, so the outdoors held no fear for her, and she loved being under the open sky. When she was young, she would often fall asleep outside in the backyard of her hut, staring at the stars, wondering if, as her father had told her, they were the eyes of the gods.

She first unsaddled, then rubbed her horse down, finding comfort in the routine. She'd noted many of Tristan's men didn't bother so had talked to the ones who did. They'd told her how it bonded a horse to you, kept its coat healthy and stopped the saddle from irritating if debris was on the coat.

Every time she paused, the horse would turn its head and give her a gentle nudge. 'You love your fussing, just like Taran did,' she said, offering an apple as a bribe to leave her alone. She tied its reins to a branch and then sat down to eat her own dinner.

She didn't finish everything and wrapped the leftover smoked meat in leaves for leaner times if they arose. Not that she'd ever see lean times again while riding with the king.

With her stomach full and her horse cared for, she prepared her place to sleep, taking time to gather grass and ferns, before laying down and pulling a blanket over her. The night time weather was mild, and as she lay looking at the stars, she fell asleep. She dreamed of when she'd bathed with Taran for the first time, and the happiness of the memory served as the catalyst to free her spirit. This time it felt as light as a feather when finally, she drifted free of her physical being.

She was impatient to see Taran but thought to save the best to last, so she flew east, travelling over the kingdom until she passed the city of Freeguard with its walls. She then turned toward the southeast, watching as the green grasses started to thin until finally, she flew over a vast stretch of desert. It wasn't long before she came across a large marching army, the warriors moving in square formations in the near darkness. She estimated the first to number almost a thousand men strong, and indeed there were twenty-five squares. The desert tribes were honouring their promise, and they were closer than expected, perhaps only between two and three weeks away.

She then retraced her path to Freeguard before heading north-west toward the kingdom of the Eyre. Sure enough, their army was also well on its way, but she found them resting, laughter and good cheer abounding as the men and women gathered around their campfires. She smiled to herself, for she could see that just like Drizt, these folk whilst skilled in the art of killing, had hearts that managed to stay bright even in the dark.

Finally, she turned southwest to take her toward the fortress. She travelled fast and high, in time seeing thousands of lights twinkling like fireflies.

She flew down swiftly to see the enemy forces stretching into the distance, large fires lining the pass to help Daleth's army attack in what would otherwise be darkness. Every fifth soldier bore a burning torch to light their way as they waited their turn to climb the ladders, to deal death, yet, they were falling like heavy rain from atop the wall.

She remembered Kalas saying that only the best of the fighting men would have survived this long and surely this was true. With relentless practice, they were only improving as long as they drew breath and avoided injury.

She floated above the wall to see Kalas fighting like a whirlwind. He had his own stretch of wall to himself, and anyone who crested near him found themselves in death's embrace in moments.

Further along, the other soldiers killed with ruthless efficiency, short swords stabbing out from behind shields. Trom and his men were back to using spears, standing behind the swordsmen, impaling the rising men and thrusting them from the top of the ladders before many had a chance to even gain a foothold.

The sounds were horrifying, the screams of both the dying and the living as they vented their desperate anger on the other.

She saw Rakan with a few green-clad archers standing back from the wall, ready to direct their aim when required. The Elder giant was there as well, ready to pluck men from the walls with its huge hands or crush them with its club. She could only imagine the other two must have fallen, for where else would they be at this time?

Then she spied Taran, and her heart soared in one moment and then plummeted back down in the next. He was fighting like she'd never seen before and he looked almost as deadly as Kalas. Ass she watched, Taran gutted his next opponent, twisting the sword in the man's belly, holding him upright before pushing him off the wall. He killed his next opponent quickly, and despite having a moment's respite, used it to hack off the man's head. Maya watched in disbelief as he threw it high into the air laughing. The men around followed his lead, not just killing, but enjoying it, revelling in the slaughter.

What was becoming of Taran? She could barely recognise his face as he slew with a frenzied passion.

Suddenly Daleth's men forced onto the centre of the wall, and Rakan and his few archers couldn't bring them down quickly enough as they spread like a stain. The giant stepped forward to sweep them away, but suddenly stumbled back, a huge iron dart from one of the ballistae piercing its shoulder.

The next moment, cries to pull back shouted from every defender's lips, and like a flash flood, Kalas, Taran, and everyone else ran down the steps and raced back across the bridges over the fire trench. The giant stumbled back and climbed with difficulty over the wall for it was too big to fit through the gate and collapsed in the courtyard, trying in vain to pull the iron shaft out.

Those who were wounded or not fast enough were cut down, and Maya estimated there were now no more than three hundred men left as they ran through the gates and slammed them closed behind them.

Kalas, Taran, Rakan, and Trom were bellowing at the men, and suddenly Kalas seemed to stare straight at her, then he bowed his head slightly, and for a moment she swore his eyes shone red.

She flew backwards, but he turned his attention to getting the men to the walls. The final one was much shorter and a little higher, and as the men ran to the top, they were able to catch their breath, for the enemy troops were taking their time, opening the gate to the second wall, allowing troops to gather with more ladders.

Maya was finding it harder to watch, the slaughter was so horrific. She looked for Taran again to find him sitting with his back against the battlements. Yana leant over him, tending to a wound on his arm, eyes shining with warmth despite the horror around her.

A pang of sadness, mixed with jealousy brought astral tears to Maya's eyes. In response, she felt a pull on her spirit-form to return to her body, and it quickly became too irresistible to fight.

She took a final glance at Taran while Yana tended to a soldier next to him.

Why did her last glance of Taran, have to have Yana in the picture, she thought, as she was drawn swiftly back to her body.

She awoke instantly upon her return, her heart hammering from what she'd witnessed, and despite the hour, walked to Tristan's tent. As she approached, the guard pulled back the flap allowing her to walk straight in.

Tristan met her with a broad smile. 'Have you come to share my bed?' he asked with good humour, raising an eyebrow.

'I've come to share news,' she replied coldly. 'The desert king's forces will arrive within three weeks, the Eyre in less than one. But the fortress, that will fall in less than two days, of that I'm sure.'

Tristan's face turned white at this last piece of news.

'It seems, my king, that Daleth will be looking to join our betrothal celebrations soon,' she said sarcastically, and hastened from the tent, her heart pounding before Tristan had time to say anything more.

She took her time, wandering around the camp before returning to her horse, trying to control her breathing and eventually lay down on her makeshift bed, pulling a blanket over her.

Taran, she thought. *Be safe, my love.* But he was so far, and she felt so so alone, and sleep took forever to find her.

Taran didn't know how he could still lift his weapons, he was so tired, and except for Kalas, every defender felt the same. Two full days and nights of fighting had brought every man to breaking point, yet again and again, they'd managed to push back the horde. Each attack took a terrible toll, and the ground on both sides of the wall was littered with mounds of corpses, both friend and foe alike.

There'd been minor breaks in the fighting, just enough to rotate a few men off to get light injuries attended to, but now they couldn't last any longer. There were perhaps eighty men left. They'd been the best, but now it didn't matter. They weren't enough, and they'd given their all.

There was currently a welcome pause in the fighting, and the reason for this could be seen approaching. Daleth, surrounded by his bodyguard, pushed through the massed ranks of his troops, getting close enough to witness the final assault.

Kalas came over to Taran and Rakan. 'It's almost time,' he shouted, straining to be heard above the cries of the mortally wounded around them.

'Are you sure you still want to do this?' asked Rakan, who was now aware of Kalas' intent.

Kalas nodded in return. 'You know the reason why,' and for a moment, his eyes glowed before he managed to take control again. 'The daemon is trying to wrest my will away from. Come this night I fear I'll be as much a daemon as Alano. My thirst for blood is becoming insatiable, and it won't matter from which side it's drawn.'

Taran looked around. The defenders could barely stand, and the Elder giant was suffering horrifically with such a terrible wound to its shoulder. It sat barely moving, its large eyes locked on Taran.

'They know this next push will take the wall, so if we don't organise ourselves now, no one will escape alive,' advised Kalas, looking to the sky. It was mid-morning, and the rising sun bathed everything in its glow, but it only served to highlight the bright, red blood that was splashed everywhere the eye turned.

Kalas turned to Taran. 'I know you've been struggling to use your gift, but if ever there was a time, it's now. Let's start getting the men mounted and see if your giant friend can help us one last time.'

'Trom,' called Kalas, and the big man ambled over. He always seemed to move and talk slowly, yet when it came to fighting his reflexes were like lighting. 'Get your men, it's time to leave. Get them mounted, the rest will follow in a moment.'

Trom looked at each of them before extending his hand, gripping them one by one. 'No, my friends,' he rumbled. 'Most men of the desert cannot ride, and we never run. We live or die on the field of battle. Never in our history has any of my kind fled. What better way and place to die than facing the Witch-King's horde? We'll hold the final gateway,' he said, 'and give you time to make your escape.'

Taran looked at Trom thinking to dissuade him, but the man's face was set, so he simply nodded and ran down the steps, his legs shaking from fatigue. He turned back to the men on the walls and focussed. His gift felt so clumsy to use now, yet he still managed to find it. 'Get ready to withdraw,' he called into their minds.

Each man reached down by their feet, picking up the clay flasks that had been placed there. Taran gave them a few moments as some flasks had been buried beneath fallen comrades, but then the men were ready. He heard the roar of the enemy once again and knew they were making their final assault.

'NOW,' he projected, and the flasks were smashed against the top of the wall before the men turned and made haste down the steps. They all hobbled, for none had escaped injury, but the will to live drove them at a pace they might not otherwise have managed toward the horses beyond the rear gate. Once there they'd immediately mount and head east.

The top of the wall was empty except for the piles of dead, and Taran waited, with Kalas, Rakan and two archers. As they looked up, enemy troops suddenly crested the wall.

The Eyre archers didn't need an order, and the next instant, their fire arrows thunked into the oil-soaked bodies, and the top of the wall became an inferno. The attacking soldiers screamed, beating futilely at the flames as they were engulfed, and the smell of charred flesh mixed with that of the dark black smoke.

'Help me,' Kalas instructed Rakan, as he stripped off his silver armour and exchanged it for the dark armour of a Nightstalker who lay dead at the base of the wall. 'Now, you wear mine,' he instructed

Rakan. 'I know you've always wanted it,' he said with a laugh, clapping him on the shoulder.

Rakan sighed. 'I will remember you, my friend. You're the best I've ever seen,' and he quickly discarded his battered set for Kalas' pristine, silver armour.

Trom, and his remaining men, about forty of them, were briefly gathered in prayer by the rear gateway. They knelt, touching their heads to the floor, their ironwood spears and shields beside them, preparing themselves for death. The two archers went to join them.

Taran approached the Elder giant who struggled painfully to its feet. 'You should have left,' thought Taran, 'when you had the chance.'

The giant shook its shaggy head. 'My children died here,' it replied, 'and thus, I will too. The blessing of children is both a gift and a curse, young Taran, for to see them die before you do, is the cruellest of things. Do you understand your own curse now?' thought the giant sadly, and Taran nodded.

'Sometimes,' thought the giant, holding Taran's gaze with his large brown eyes, 'it's not unknown to be gifted more than once!' and with that, it bent down gathering up its club. 'If you ever need sanctuary from the lands of men or even your own thoughts, remember you can always find it in our valley.' With a final resigned smile, it ran unsteadily to the wall and climbed over into the midst of the thousands of waiting troops. It was ablaze with oil, and it's strange warbling erupted like birdsong even though it must have been in agony.

Above the roar of the flames, Taran could hear screams as it slew, swinging its club, but before long it fell, disappearing from view, and he knew it was dead.

Rakan came over, resplendent in Kalas' armour. 'Come, son, time to mount, everyone has left except Trom and his die-hards. Those archers are staying too.' He pulled Taran hastily to the gateway in the rear wall, to where Yana waited with three saddled horses for each of them. Taran swung himself up into the saddle of one as Rakan also mounted.

Behind them, the spearmen of the desert closed ranks, forming a line six men thick and eight wide across the open gateway. The two Eyre archers stood to the side, short swords in hand.

Trom turned and raising his shield hit his ironwood spear against it three times in salute, his men following suit. 'Come visit us in the oasis of our forefathers,' Trom bellowed. 'Let us tell them together one day of how well we died!' His eyes locked with Taran's before turning away. 'Shield wall!' Trom shouted, as his men turned their backs on Taran and Rakan. The desert men stood motionless, shields raised, spears extended, watching as the flames slowly died down.

'We should go,' cried Yana, tears in her eyes. She knew of her uncles plan to try and kill Daleth and that even if he succeeded, he would die whilst undertaking the deed. 'We need to get a headstart if we're to stand a chance of escape,' she continued.

As she spoke, the flames atop the wall dwindled, and almost immediately after, black-clad shapes appeared on the wall. Thick smoke still billowed from the corpses, and the smell was awful. When Daleth's men saw the thin line of men waiting at the rear curtain wall, they called down over their shoulders, and a dozen descended into the courtyard to open the gates so their comrades might enter.

Instead of attacking immediately, warriors continued to push through the now open gates until the rear courtyard was filled with at least a thousand of the enemy. All the time they said nothing, standing silent, waiting.

Then through the gateway, head and shoulders above even the tallest, Daleth himself appeared. He was surrounded by his bodyguard, their eyes scanning everywhere, lingering on both Taran and Rakan.

'He's a huge bastard, isn't he!' growled Rakan from within his helm, and Taran could only agree.

Daleth stared at Rakan in his silver armour as he slowly climbed the steps until he stood above the gate tower amongst the corpses of defenders and attackers alike. There, the Witch-King drew his sword, slowly lifting it to point at Trom and his men, Rakan, Taran, and Yana.

'He really thinks you're Kalas,' said Taran, appreciating this part of Kalas' plan, as Rakan drew his sword, returning the gesture.

'Time for us to ride like the wind?' suggested Rakan.

Taran looked around for Kalas but couldn't see him, so he reached out a hand. 'Not yet, father,' he said. 'There'll be a time for running shortly, but this is still a time for dying, and I still have a part to play.'

Daleth breathed deeply. The heady smells of charred flesh, spilt blood, death and horror made him feel light-headed, and the moans of the terribly wounded, brought him to a state of near euphoria. At last, victory was his, and the whole of the Freestates would soon follow.

He had climbed the steps to the wall above the gate, revelling in the way his troops shrugged off their tiredness to stand straighter as he looked down upon them.

There was no sign of Tristan, and he'd have been most surprised had that not been the case. He hoped he hadn't decided to flee the kingdom but was instead gathering another force to face him, for that would only make the conquest of the Freestates even more enjoyable, and that would only be the start of it.

He knew Tristan could never muster enough men to defeat his army, and whilst he knew some of the Freestates cities were walled, it would make no difference, they'd fall swiftly.

He had lost nigh on ten thousand men to fifteen hundred, and couldn't help but admire the defenders who'd cost him so much time and resource to overcome them. Now the last of them stood awaiting death bravely and with resolve. The losses he'd suffered here at the fortress he saw as an important lesson, and he'd learn from it as any good commander would.

Regretfully, but not unsurprisingly, that damned Kalas was still alive, sitting astride a horse alongside Taran in his embellished armour. For a moment he hoped they'd fight and fall alongside their comrades, but the fact they were mounted with horses to spare meant they would flee to fight another day; unless his cavalry ran them to ground first.

He drew his sword, pointing it toward Kalas, Taran and the other men in salute. They deserved recognition for their achievement.

It was time for the glorious and bloody ending to begin. He was well-positioned to look upon the desert spearmen's last stand and was about to issue the order for the final assault, when, out of the corner of his eye something unusual caught his attention.

Turning in surprise, for a moment, he couldn't fathom what was happening, for clouds of smoke still lingered. Yet, as he watched closely, along the wall moved one of his Nightstalkers, and those before him fell like a silent wave breaking upon the shore.

Daleth felt a cold shiver run down his spine.

He turned quickly back toward the man on the horse, noting for the first time, black hair, not fair, spilling from the base of the silver helm. It wasn't Kalas in that armour, it was someone else!

'Kalas is on the wall,' he cried, pointing his sword toward the oncoming daemon. His bodyguard looked confused, unsure what he meant as they saw the approaching Nightstalker, but the next moment hell broke loose.

Men, who'd been unaware of death approaching them, began to draw their weapons. For many, it was too late, and for those that managed to, it mattered little anyway.

He watched open-mouthed as Kalas spun and twisted toward him, his swords a blur, flinging men aside like dolls in a mist of blood.

'Kalas is coming,' Daleth heard, and then it was only his bodyguard between him and death.

Kalas started cutting through his finest men. They fell, one after another, yet it wasn't without cost. For as Kalas drew closer, Daleth could see blood flowing from cuts to both Kalas' arms and legs and his helm had been dashed away.

Daleth hefted his sword and drew a heavy dirk, opening his arms wide, roaring his own challenge.

Suddenly, Kalas staggered, as an arrow took him in the side and he dropped to one knee.

Daleth's remaining bodyguard surged forward, and for a moment, his view was obstructed by the sheer number of men on the narrow wall between him and the daemon.

Yet, they too fell away, to leave Kalas bloodied, standing before him. A dagger was buried hilt deep in his shoulder, while the broken shaft of the arrow jutted out from his side. Sweat and blood ran profusely down his face, while bright red rivulets covered his arms and legs. Kalas swayed, barely standing with wounds that would have killed a normal man.

All of Daleth's men in the courtyard just stood staring. Unbelievably, none ran up the steps to his aid, seemingly transfixed by this spectacle. It was just him and Kalas, but the daemon was on his last legs.

Daleth roared and stepped forward to bring his huge sword crashing down in a chopping blow. Just as it was about to land, Kalas spun on his left heel, his sword flashing out. Daleth stumbled back, pain erupting from his stomach, so acute that he could barely hold his weapons. Yet, he pushed it aside and attacked again. But even in his wounded state Kalas deflected Daleth's blade with contempt, and as Daleth overbalanced, it bit into the stone wall, jarring it from his hand. Before Daleth could recover, Kalas' blades bit first into one thigh, and then the other, and Daleth crashed to his knees in front of Kalas, who loomed large in front of him.

'You can't! You can't kill me!' spluttered Daleth in shocked disbelief. 'I'm gifted by the gods, I'm destined to rule forever!'

Kalas lifted his blade, and Daleth could do nothing but stare in defiance as it flashed down.

Kalas had hidden in plain sight, playing dead upon a mound of corpses, covered by the thick smoke and blood as the enemy had clambered over the top of the wall to find it uncontested.

Fortunately, those following had decided to enter through the gate when it was opened, so there were only twenty men between him and Daleth with his bodyguard, and on such a narrow wall he would face them one on one all the way to the Witch-King himself.

This was the best and only chance he'd get to fulfil his oath, and he sent a silent prayer to the gods that Taran was able to help.

He'd moaned audibly, pushing himself to his feet and the nearest soldier had turned toward him startled, but then relaxed as he saw the armour, offering his hand to help.

Pulling the soldier close, he'd driven his dagger up under the man's chinstrap into the brain before dragging it clear and letting the body fall from the battlement. Swiftly, he'd fought his way along the wall, and now he stood above Daleth, the daemon in his mind crowing at the slaughter, at his victory.

He brought his sword crashing down, for he knew he had little time left. Taran had managed to use his gift to keep the enemy in the courtyard in check, but not entirely, and the arrow had pierced his lung. He could feel it filling with blood, and the dagger had likely severed an artery. Of course, he could heal himself should he drain the life of one of the many here, but not this time, he thought, it's time for me to die.

Yet just as he exulted in finally fulfilling his oath, his sword was deflected at the last possible moment, and all of a sudden he was being pushed back by Alano's frenzied counterattack.

Kalas was already terribly injured, and within moments, he was bleeding from a dozen more cuts. Death was coming swiftly for him, for in this state he couldn't defeat Alano. He even saw the death blow coming. Alano had always telegraphed the spinning thrust slightly and as he twisted, Kalas, instead of futilely trying to avoid the blow, stepped forward, closing the distance.

The pain of the blade punching through his body and out his back was excruciating. As Alano stood, eyes shining, their faces barely inches apart, Kalas thrust his dagger under Alano's unarmoured armpit into the heart.

They stood there for a moment, locked in a strange embrace before they both collapsed to the floor. Just like the last time death was almost upon him, the daemon in Kalas' head fled to hiding in the back of his mind, and likewise, Alano's eyes cleared, and Kalas lay there looking into the face of his old and dearest friend.

Alano coughed blood and reached out to grip Kalas' shoulder. 'Forgive me, my brother,' he croaked, his imploring eyes full of tears. 'I wasn't strong enough. Please forgive me.'

Kalas tried to smile through the pain. 'There's nothing to forgive, my brother,' he gasped, but Alano had already died.

He looked at Alano's dead face. Finally his friend looked at peace. The sun was shining and he absently wondering why it gave no warmth. His vision began to darken, and he was sure he could hear the distant screams of tormented souls ready to welcome him to the nine hells.

Then, from the encroaching darkness, a blinding light appeared. Kalas feebly lifted a hand to shade his eyes, and someone grabbed his wrist. With his last drop of strength, he focused on the light and therein stood his father; young again, and strong as an ox.

'I may have deserted you in life, my son' his father's voice boomed, 'but in death, I'll not make the same mistake. Come with me!'

Tears flowed briefly from Kalas' eyes before they closed a final time. The last knight of the Ember Kingdom was dead.

Yana's cry of sorrow suddenly split the air, and the scene that had stayed frozen thanks to Taran's gift, suddenly came back to life again.

Daleth was on his knees, blood pooling around him, but he still had the strength to raise his arm and point. 'Kill them all,' he croaked, and then with more strength, 'KILL THEM ALL!'

As men now rushed to the Witch-King's side, a thousand warriors surged forward at Trom and his men.

'We need to go, NOW!' shouted Rakan, and he reached to grab the bridle of Taran's mount. He turned the heads of their horses and spurred them eastward as the sounds of battle cries split the air behind them.

They rode at a furious gallop for a while before they reached a small rise, then turned back, shadowing their eyes to see in the distance that Trom and his men still fought in the narrow confines of the gateway.

'Kalas almost got him,' said Rakan, shaking his head in wonder. 'That damned Alano. If it wasn't for him, this would have been over. Even so, I reckon Daleth's going to take a while to recover from those injuries. Kalas might not have killed him, but without doubt, the pain that tall bastard is going to endure will make him wish that Kalas had.'

Yana's sobs made them turn. Her eyes implored Taran to console her, but he turned his stony eyes away, and it was left to Rakan to put his arm around her shoulder.

'We'll never see his like again,' Rakan said to Yana softly. 'Be glad that he found you and knew you, and you, him. Now, we need to move. I've a feeling Daleth's cavalry might not be raising the chase quite so soon, but that doesn't mean we need to tempt fate.'

Taran stood in his stirrups looking back a final time.

'Let's not waste their sacrifice,' he said. 'We need to give our illustrious king the news about the fall of his fortress and the return of his new, faithful, lord commander. Kalas has given us something we didn't have before. Time. We now have time to prepare for the final battle, for I doubt we'll be seeing Daleth on the field this side of winter.'

'Whether it's this side of winter or the next, we'll still not be able to beat his army,' suggested Rakan. 'We just don't have the numbers.'

'I've some thoughts in that regard, but whether we win or lose the fight against Daleth, I swear I'll put Tristan in his grave,' said Taran, face grim. 'Are you with me?' he asked, turning to Rakan and Yana.

'I'll always be there for you, son, you know that,' said Rakan, reaching out to grasp Taran's arm. 'If that's what you want, we'll gut him together.'

Yana nodded. 'You know I'll follow you wherever you go, Taran heart-stealer,' she said, wiping her eyes.

With a final look back they dug their heels into the flanks of their horses and headed east.

THE END OF BOOK TWO

M&M
♥

If you enjoyed this book, the next book in the trilogy;
The End of Dreams
will be coming soon as an e-book and in paperback